# HEART IN TWO

## Book Two

# YVONNE MAPHOSA

ISBN: 978-0-7961-5057-8

Editor: Philani A. Nyoni
Proofreader: Busisekile Khumalo
Cover: Kumbirai Muchirahondo

Printed in South Africa by Creda Communications

Available on Amazon.

Goodreads: Yvonne Maphosa
Twitter: @Yvonne_Maphosa
Instagram: @Yvonne_Jacquie
Facebook: Tales by Yvonne Maphosa
TikTok: @Yvonne_Maphosa

*For the girl I was in Mambale. The one who dreamt big and loved fiercely. Who ran barefoot to school in winter and wrote her name on the ground under the moonlight. This one is for you.*
*We did it, kiddo.*

# Heart in Two

# *PROLOGUE*

I step off the bus and a blast of heat smacks me in the face. I feel like going back inside to brace myself for the intensity outside. The air is so heavy, I'm suffocating and breathing heat into my lungs. It's going to take a while for me to get used to this weather.

I wait for my suitcase with the other passengers, breathing through slightly parted lips. I feel like my heart is sitting on my lungs. I cradle the bag Don gave me, holding on to it so tight as if I'm holding on to him. It's like being stuck in a nightmare and failing to wake up no matter how hard you try.

I finally get my suitcase and suddenly don't have enough hands to juggle all my luggage.

"Taxi?" a man calls, already handling my suitcase.

"Yes, please."

He overcharges me but I'm too weak to negotiate. I exhale in short breaths and slowly take in hot air. I might as well be in hell, both in my head and in the physical.

I'm glad the driver doesn't try to hold a conversation with me as we glide over the familiar road. I check my phone and there are still no new messages. I text Don that I arrived safely and barely stop myself from texting Chelsea. I don't know what to say to her.

The driver looks at me pitifully as I sniff back tears when I hand him the money.

*"Kuzolunga."* He says, *everything will be alright,* when he hands me my suitcase. If only he knew the half of it.

I nod anyway and tell him to keep the change; my way of thanking him for not prying into my thoughts and for the kind words.

I haven't been home in a long time and this is not how I imagined my return. I push the gate in but it stubbornly resists, dug into the ground. *Yeses!* I lift it up, rousing a thin cloud of dust that irritates my nose. The gate squeaks noisily when I finally push it open. It's held together by so many wires, it might as well be made of them.

I wrestle with my bags and finally manage to get all of them into the yard. An instant pang of guilt washes over me. While I was throwing R80000 parties, my grandmother was living in a house with a roof that's almost falling in. I had forgotten how bad the situation was back here. The paint around the house has all peeled off, leaving behind a grimy residue that no amount of bleach can scrub off. The once-white walls have turned a horrid mouldy black at the bottom, probably from water logging. I feel terrible just looking at it.

I struggle with my suitcase and my bags until I make it to the door that opens into the kitchen. Its wood is splintered so badly, it's almost falling off its hinges. It stopped closing completely sometime when I was in high school. At first, it would soak up moisture and swell up during the rains but close in dry weather, until one day it stopped fitting into its frame altogether. Couldn't my mother have used some of the money I sent her to at least buy a door?

I step into the kitchen and I feel out of place. It's completely dilapidated! It's nothing like Don's big kitchen with the granite countertop and white cupboards, or the old but decent kitchen in the apartment I shared with Chelsea. One of the cupboards is missing its door and one of the windows is covered with plastic and tape. What exactly did they do with the money I sent?

As I stand next to the stove, frustrated by its state, memories come flooding back. I remember being greeted by the aroma of my grandmother's cooking after school. She had a way of turning even the most basic meal into a culinary masterpiece. Life was simple then. I had big dreams. I was going to make it out there and renovate this house. I was going to make so much money that both my mother and grandmother would never have to work again.

I failed.

High school was beautiful. Back then, the last thing I wanted was for anyone to visit me here. I was too ashamed to have people seeing where I lived. At school, I had successfully sold the image of a rich girl who had it all. I had the proper English and the accent, thanks to the family my grandmother worked for before the country *went to the dogs;* and moved to Australia. I pretended I was still staying in a house just like the one my grandmother's former bosses had. Even my best friend at the time had never set foot inside our home. It worked though: I got the hottest guy in school and had people eating out of the palm of my hand. I was so popular, no one even cared how average my academic performance was. Thinking back, it was a little sad, but it was the only way I knew how to survive in a world that judged you based on the size of your parents' bank account. Between being authentic and popular in high school, I don't regret my choice. And somehow, secrets, lies and living above my means followed me to adulthood.

I hear footsteps approaching and I snap out of it.

"Sisi," I greet my mother as she walks into the kitchen.

"Lotus! What are you doing here?"

I try to rein in my emotions but I fail dismally. I let out a choked cry and sniff back the tears.

"And then?"

I wish she could give me a hug and not ask me anything right now.

"Chelsea told me that you lost your mind. I thought she was joking!"

"Sisi, please..."

"No, my baby, no! You can't tell me that you left everything behind because a man told you to. With all the men in the world, Lotus, you chose to throw away everything for a good-for-nothing low-life? Didn't I tell you that he would spit you out like chewing gum when he was done with you? I told you, but you thought you knew better! Look at you now."

I look at her and my heart breaks all over again. I have never needed her like I do now.

I leave my suitcase in the kitchen and carry my small bags to the bedroom. I hope she doesn't follow me or else someone will catch hands. I walk into familiarity, except now that I have experienced better, it feels like I stepped into the hub of poverty. This room is in desperate need of a make-over. A ceiling would be a great start. The walls need painting, the broken wardrobe needs to be tossed out, the suitcases messily stacked on top of each other need to be burnt and the floor needs to be tiled. We might as well set everything on fire and start over.

I move some of the suitcases aside and shove the bag with the money, gun and drugs in the one at the bottom. It's not the best hiding place but it will do for now.

I throw myself on the bed and scream into a pillow. I'm never going to hear the end of me coming back home!

After a moment, I compose myself as best I can. I take a deep breath, wipe away the tears and chant my mantra in my head.

*'I'm strong. I'm beautiful. I'm sexy. I'm the prize. Positive vibes only.'*

I don't believe the words as I say them, so I abandon the mental chanting and reach for my phone. The messages I sent to Don earlier still haven't been delivered. I try to call him and his phone goes straight to voicemail. *Aaarrrggghhh!*

I lie back on the bed hoping to miraculously fall asleep.

"Lotus!" I'm jolted from my thoughts by my grandmother's voice.

My heart leaps into my throat and I scramble to compose myself as I sit up and try to act normal.

"Mama."

My mother is standing by the door, her arms crossed over her chest, chewing gum with an attitude. I wonder if she already told Mama about my situation or if I still have a chance to cook up a believable lie. My grandmother has always been Mama, and my mother has always been Sisi.

"My child." My grandmother envelops me in her arms. "Why didn't you tell us you were coming?"

"It was all last minute, Mama, I'm sorry."

She looks at me with concern and I fight to keep the tears at bay.

"What's wrong? Your face is swollen and your eyes are red. What happened? Did someone hurt you?"

I shake my head vigorously. "I lost my job, that's all. I thought I'd come home and regroup."

"Oh, my sweet girl. Come here." She pats the space between us and I move closer to her.

My mother rolls her eyes before walking away.

I fold myself and rest my head on my grandmother's lap.

"It's alright. It's not the end of the world. Everything will be fine. You're home now."

It's as if she pressed a button because the tears pour out. She coos to me the way she used to when I was younger and tells me that everything will work itself out.

\* \* \* \* \*

I must have fallen asleep because I wake up alone in bed, covered with a small blanket.

"You're awake," my grandmother says, entering the room. "I boiled some water for you to bath. Go and wash while I finish making your food."

"Thank you, Mama." I push myself up to a sitting position.

My body hurts in places it shouldn't. That bus seat really did a number on me.

I had forgotten how difficult bathing from a dish is. The first thing I'm getting done in this house is a shower, then I'm going to throw away everything in that spare room and turn it into my bedroom. I don't see sharing a room with my mother working well.

I feel better after changing into clean clothes. When I'm done fixing myself up, I join my grandmother in the kitchen. I even manage a genuine smile when I taste the samp and stew she made for lunch. It's comforting and familiar. It reminds me of simpler times.

My mother is barely talking to me, and when she does, she's making sarcastic comments or asking questions she knows I can't answer in front of my grandmother. I don't understand her passive-aggressive behaviour. Why is she mad at me?

The rest of the day passes in a blur, alternating between being doted on by my grandmother and checking my phone for any sign of communication from Don or Chelsea. I will even appreciate a smoke signal at this point.

My phone chimes and I open WhatsApp excitedly. Finally!

*'Hey baby. How are you? You've been quiet. Please talk to me.'*

Oh, *mann*, Dalubuhle Mthethwa. Not today!

I ask to be excused around 4 pm so I can take a nap.

I'm exhausted but I'm too distressed to fall asleep. I send another message to Don and take a deep sigh while mentally chanting, '*I'm strong. I'm beautiful. I'm sexy. I'm the prize. Positive vibes only.*'

\* \* \* \* \*

My grandmother storms into the room, her face twisted in what I think is anger.

"Why did you lie to me?"

"Ma..."

"What is this about you leaving Cape Town for no reason and running here? Why, Lotus?" she shouts, her voice rising with each word.

"Mama..." I start but she cuts me off with an angry eye.

"You said you lost your job knowing very well that you quit! Then you abandoned the flat you shared with Chelsea and left her stranded alone! What's going on, Lotus? Are you on drugs?"

"It's not like that."

"Then what is it like? Huh? What is it? Tell me the truth!" Her hands go on her hips.

I look down and swallow.

"I'm sure all this has something to do with a boy. You threw your life away for what, Lotus? Tell me the truth!" she yells.

I bite my lip and keep looking down.

She shouts at me some more, her words breaking my heart, and my tears spill uncontrollably. I can't tell her the truth. What would I even say?

"I had high hopes for you. I wanted you to get out of this place. But look at you now. You turned out just like your mother! You know what, *mntanam*, do whatever you want. I'm washing my hands," she says with a finality in her voice.

That stung! I turned out like the one person I tried so hard not to be like. Maybe these things are hereditary after all.

I lie back on the bed and look at the roof, listening to my heart struggling to beat.

\* \* \* \* \*

When my mother comes to bed, I can't bring myself to look at her.

"Have you spoken to Madonna?" She eventually breaks the silence.

It feels like a lifetime ago when we had that disaster of a dinner with Don and she insisted on calling him Madonna.

"No. My messages to him are not delivering and his phone has been off. I don't know what's going on."

"He'll call, don't worry."

I appreciate her concern but she broke me in ways she can't fathom. She had no right!

"Why did you tell Mama?" My voice comes out thinner than intended.

"I didn't."

"Then how did she know?"

She looks down at her phone and types something.

"Sisi, if you didn't tell Mama, then how did she know?"

She sighs and looks at me like I'm annoying her. "Chelsea."

"Chelsea?"

"She called to check if you arrived safely. She then asked to talk to Mama and she assumed you told her everything, so she let it out that you quit your job and moved out of the apartment."

"Wow."

"She's worried about you. We all are. You have to go back to Cape Town. Chelsea said you can move back in. I can try and talk to John to give you your job back."

"A one-night stand with my boss and suddenly you can tell him what to do? It must be nice."

I see pain flash across her face and I turn away and pull the blanket up to my head. My mind is stuck on Chelsea deliberately ratting me out. She knows that I would never want my grandmother to see me in the light she painted me in. And she called my mother but didn't bother to call me? Just wow!

I open WhatsApp and start typing a message to Don.

"Hey!" My mother yanks the blanket back before I can finish.

"What?"

"You will not talk to me like that! You hear me?"

10

Delayed reaction? I don't have time for her.

"I'm talking to you!"

"Sisi, what do you want from me? You have your precious Chelsea. Why are you bothered about me?"

"Watch your mouth!"

"Or what?"

"I will slap you if you think I'm your friend! You threw your life away for a guy who changed his number as soon as you got onto the bus and now you're taking your stress out on me!"

It will be better if I remain quiet because if I speak, I will be called disrespectful.

"What you did was very stupid! You're going to regret it for the rest of your life. That man is done with you! Of all the men out there, you picked one right out of the gutter. A gangster, Lotus?"

"You're one to talk. You got knocked up by a gangster who didn't even love you. You dropped out of school and left everything in Cape Town because of a man. So, no, Sisi, you don't get to lecture me about gangsters when you have a whole child with one." I say it like the child in question is not me.

The slap catches me by surprise. I feel numb, then I see stars, then I go deaf for a moment. Before I can reorient myself, she grabs my phone and hurls it against the wall.

"What the hell are you doing?" I get up, my hands still on my jaw.

She walks to my broken phone and stomps it, crushing it under her foot. She reaches down, pulls out the sim card, and before I can stop her, she chews it. I know she's dramatic but I did not expect her to go to such extremes. She knows my phone is my life!

"Why are you doing this?" I get on my knees, trying to salvage what's left of my phone. "What the hell is wrong with you?"

"What's going on here?" my grandmother's voice cuts through the noise. "Have you lost your mind?"

"Look what she did to my phone!"

"Lotus beat me up!"

"That's not true!"

"Hey, hey, hey! I don't want to hear it! Stop it, both of you!"

"But Mama..."

"Enough! Lotus, out! You, clean up this mess and behave like an adult for once!"

I sit on the couch with my phone, sobbing silently. The screen is shattered into sharp shards. It's completely ruined. I don't understand

how everything escalated so quickly.
I hate her!

# *ONE*

Every other morning, I find myself sitting on the verandah, lost in memories. I scold myself for being stupid, then remember to be kind to myself, right before screaming into the void of my mind. I can't shake the memory of that final moment at the bus stop in Bellville. I can almost see Don standing in front of me, his eyes ever so hypnotising, saying *'I love you, Lotus'* for the very first time. Those words are carved into the depths of my soul and I repeat them in my head an unhealthy number of times. I replay the moment, smiling to myself, until tears are steadily flowing down my face. I let out a stifled cry when I remember him saying something goofy before planting a kiss on my lips.

*'It's only temporary. I'll come for you when all this is over,'* he promised. *'We'll be fine, my skat.'*

I thought he would come for me in a week, maybe two, and call me every day, but it's been two months with no word from him. His voice, the morning I left Cape Town, echoes in my head. *'I'll miss your snoring the most.'* I miss him so much, it's driving me insane.

I should probably accept that the love of my life was trash, like the rest of them. That my mother was right when she said he would sell me dreams, then run me out of the city when done with me. But how can I when every corner of my mind is filled with thoughts of him? Everything reminds me of him. I can't even do something as basic as make a cup of coffee without a memory of him crossing my mind.

I have tried to reach out, but all my messages remain with one tick and calls don't go through. Each attempt chips away at my heart, leaving me feeling emptier than ever. Even though it's clear that he has forgotten all about me, I still cling to the hope that maybe, just maybe, he'll reach out. That somehow, against all odds, he will come for me like he promised. That his word means so much to him that he will have no option but to fulfil it. But the delusion is wearing off. It's been two months of radio silence.

Life is playing out without me and I don't even have a front row seat to at least watch. Don, Chelsea, Caleb, Fierce, and even Hilton - they were my world, and without them, I'm lost. It's like everyone forgot about me the moment I left.

I had to get a new phone. For reasons I didn't understand, they said they couldn't do a sim swap, so I had to get a new number. I knew Don's number off my head but his phone did not go through then and hasn't since.

I have sent Chelsea hundreds of messages on Instagram but I've been ignored every time. She reads my messages but never responds, no matter how long my paragraphs get. She did me wrong, so please don't ask me why I'm the one trying this hard.

I tried reaching out to Fierce on Facebook. We were supposed to go to Thailand. She promised! I guess, just like the rest of them, the promise meant nothing. But she hasn't posted anything in over three months, so I can't exactly say she ignored me. The only thing that kept me going when I sat on that bus on my way home were thoughts of infinity pools, cocktails, bikinis and floating baskets. But now I'm depressed, stressed and tired of being shouted at. I hate it here.

Chelsea may not be talking to me, but at least she left me with Dalu. Remember how she told him that gangsters were forcing me to leave Cape Town? I was the perfect victim, and Dalu wanted to be a superhero as always and save the damsel in distress. He emailed me and we exchanged numbers. I guess he meant it when he said, *'I don't know what happened between you and the guy, but it's okay... I forgive you. You don't even have to tell me about it. Let's start over.'*

So yeah, we started over, or rather, we picked up where we left off. I don't have anyone to chat with on WhatsApp so I chat with him quite a lot, if once a day can be considered a lot. He's too endearing, which is a turn off, but I'm currently in no position to be picky, so I respond with emojis, type short messages and avoid his phone calls as much as I can. Oh, he didn't mean the part where he said '*You don't even have to tell me about it'.* He asked me to explain everything so we could start on a clean slate, and I promised to do so in person. The truth is I don't want to explain myself to him, or to anyone for that matter.

"I'm going to the shops. Do you want to come?" my grandmother says through the window, pulling me out of my thoughts.

"No, thanks." I keep my voice steady to not betray my emotions.

"Are you alright?"

"I'm okay, Mama, thank you. Please bring me NikNaks."

"Alright. Don't sit there for too long. The sun causes headaches! If you fall sick, I'm not taking you to the clinic. You raise my BP enough as it is."

My grandmother blames me for her BP. I pointed out that everyone on earth has blood pressure, so she should use the word 'high' before BP. I meant it as a joke but she quickly reminded me how I got an education, failed to use it in my field and was now trying to use it on her. It was said in such a harsh tone that it hurts even remembering it. At least she's talking to me like I'm a person now. The first month back was hell. She was convinced that I had gone mad. 'Possessed' is the word she used. After the big smack down with my mother, she sat me down and demanded to know why I had abruptly left Cape Town and 'abandoned' Chelsea. I gave every excuse I could think of, each worse than the last, until she just let me be. I guess she accepted that I was just like my mother, poor at decision-making.

"Lotus!" My grandmother appears around the corner, startling me. "Are you crying again?" she says, her tone more accusatory than concerned.

"I'm not." I quickly dry my face and straighten my shoulders.

"Enough of this!" She thrusts my shoes into my hands. "Put these on. We're going to the shops."

I know better than to argue, so I put my shoes on and follow her out of the gate. I hate being outside because people don't know how to mind their business. They talk about me without doing much to hide it.

I walk behind her, not ready to catch up yet in case she says something mean. Her mood-swings are unpredictable.

I don't know why she dresses like an old lady. She has no business wearing that heavy skirt over a dress, and wearing that *doek* in this weather must be a crime. It's as if she's hiding her figure, concealing the curves that undoubtedly turned heads in her younger days. I think she hates her body because she believes it's what tempted my grandfather, the racist farmer who abused her for years and left her battered and broken. If my mother hadn't told me, I would have never known. My grandmother never talks about her past but she wears the scars too vividly. It's like her life experiences are etched into the lines of her face, and along the way, she somehow forgot what it's like to be truly happy.

"Lolo, how are you?" she says when I catch up with her.

"I'm fine, Mama."

She stops and looks at me. "I mean how are you? How are you doing?" Her brow furrows as she studies my face. "You're crying every day and your eyes are always red. What exactly happened in Cape Town, *sana lwam*?"

"Nothing, Mama. I'll be fine, I promise."

I can't tell her that I fell in love with the type of guy she warned me about, then he asked me to drop everything and leave Cape Town, then ghosted me.

She reaches for my hand and I cling on to hers, afraid she will let go if I don't hold on tightly. It's not often that she shows me this much warmth. Usually, she shouts at me and expresses her disappointment in many words.

"Lolo, my girl. I don't know what happened in Cape Town, and I have a feeling you'll never tell me the truth." She looks at me pitifully, her grip tightening slightly. "Even though I'm disappointed in you, I'm still your grandmother. I want you to be happy."

Tears well in my eyes but I manage to hold them back. I wish she hadn't done this on the street.

"Now, enough with the self-pity. It's been two months! It's time to pick yourself up, dust yourself off, and start living again. You're young; you can't give up on life now."

I needed to hear that. "Thank you, Mama."

"Now, cheer up." She pats me on the back.

"Yes, Mam..."

"You won't believe what the ladies are planning!" She derails before I can return the love, and the moment is lost.

She starts talking about how the ladies in her *stokvel* want to misuse their funds by going on an unnecessary vacation. I don't point out that it's their money and that there is nothing unnecessary about taking a break. I laugh hard as she exaggerates everything. For the first time in a long time, I feel like everything is going to be alright.

We finally make it to the *spaza* shop, a makeshift structure made of maroon-painted panels with a small cut-out window. The shop owner greets us enthusiastically and hands my grandmother the airtime and NikNaks she asked for. He rings up the items, chatting us up the whole time and talking about the weather as if we can't feel the heat for ourselves. He's behaving today because I'm not alone. Usually, he gets overly familiar and makes remarks I don't appreciate. Underneath that fake smile there's trash.

We walk back home slowly, my grandmother still complaining about how irresponsible her friends are.

Now that I feel reconnected to her, I muster the courage to ask something I have been meaning to for over a month now.

"Can we go to town on Wednesday?"

"To do what?" She eyes me suspiciously.

"I want to spend the day with you and buy some things for the house."

"Where are you getting all this money that you have been spending? Did you rob a bank? Is that why you came back home? Are you a fugitive?"

Oh, the drama!

"I told you it's my severance package. I just want to spend it on you."

"Well then, Wednesday we're going to town. It will be like when you were still my little girl."

I can't wait!

I'm glad she doesn't know that there is no way Dr. Dirk would have given me any money after the way I dropped the ball at work. It's a miracle he didn't fire me when I started skipping work without much explanation. I would go AWOL for days on end, then pop up and pretend nothing ever happened. Looking back, he was a good boss and he showed me a lot of grace. I can't believe I miss work! I guess it's true that you never miss the water till the well runs dry.

My spirits are lifted and I'm bursting with ideas of what we will get up to in town. I'm going to settle all her outstanding accounts, pay a year's worth of our municipal rates, buy a lot of groceries and take her shopping. She needs a new wardrobe and a few bags. I don't remember her buying anything new for herself when I was growing up. Her entire life was about making sure my mother and I were fine. Looking back, I don't know how she managed to keep a roof over our heads all those years.

"Is that the man who will be renovating my home?" Her eyes light up with excitement as she points at a bakkie that has seen better days.

"It must be."

A man in a blue Conti suit steps out of the bakkie when we reach our gate. He takes off his hat and politely greets us.

"Welcome. Come on in. Let's have some tea," my grandmother says after pleasantries have been exchanged.

I'm really home. In Cape Town, business is business, there is no time for sharing tea.

I top up the sugar in the canister as I wait for the water to boil. The contractor came highly recommended by the owner of the house he renovated on the other street. His calloused hands hint at years of hard work, but nothing else about him says 'construction', if you know what I mean.

My grandmother's hands are fluttering with excitement as she gestures animatedly and her eyes are glowing with enthusiasm. It makes me happy to see her like this. There is a youthful energy about her today. When I was younger, she always looked tired. She always had something on her mind and used church as an escape and prayer as a crutch. Life wasn't very kind to her. She worked seven days a week as a live-in maid, scrubbing floors, doing laundry, cooking and giving the children of her bosses the comfort she couldn't give us. I was too young to notice how broken she really was. I just enjoyed the food that came from the main house and the hand-me-downs they gave me. Having lived in the township before moving into that big servant's quarters with my grandmother, I was in paradise! When the family left for Australia, we found ourselves back in the township.

So, seeing her laughing like this is making me emotional. I think she needed these renovations to feel alive again.

I steep the tea to perfection and plate the *vetkoeks* my grandmother made last night. No one makes *amagwinya* like her! I make my way to the dining room with a dish in one hand, a jug in the other and a towel draped on my arm. I wash their hands, then return to the kitchen for the teapot and tray.

"Are you not joining us?"

"I'm not hungry, I just want NikNaks."

I have been eating a lot of NikNaks lately. I sit on the couch and crunch away while chatting to my mother. My mother and I are good now. That violent rage of hers brought us closer together. After we got over the *'I should have aborted you'* and the *'Like you did all the pregnancies after me?'* we kissed and made up.

I eventually told her everything so she could understand why I left my job, my best friend, my man and the life I knew behind to come here. I had to leave Cape Town. I wanted the General out of the way so badly, I didn't think things through. Don tried to make me see reason but I wouldn't listen. After the General was shot, I found out he was my father. I confronted Don about it in front of Hilton and Caleb, and that didn't end well. As if that wasn't enough, against my better judgement, I called the General while he was in the hospital and told him I was his daughter. He never acknowledged it or called me back. He just coughed uncontrollably and then I saw on the news that he was dead. Don then asked me to leave town. A gang war had been brewing for a while, with rival gangs fighting for turf. There were also internal conflicts within the packs of the Wolves. Some of the Wolves were upset that Don had given away a taxi route and other benefits to Reptile's gang. He sacrificed a lot for me, so when he asked me to leave Cape Town, I knew I had to. He couldn't fight in the war and protect me at the same time.

Saying it all out loud made it sound worse, and as I expected, she judged me harshly. But then she let it go and became a mother to me for once. I found it easy to forgive her because she didn't rat me out to my grandmother.

"Lolo, clear the table and join us outside," my grandmother says.

I get off the couch and do as instructed. When I'm done, I go to the bedroom and count R10 000 from the bag I carefully hid. I place the notes in a plastic bag, the way taxi drivers in Cape Town did when paying Don & Co.

My grandmother is overflowing with ideas, some impractical and others too over-the-top, and the contractor is politely engaging her. He won't be doing much today; it's just a few formalities and solidifying the discussions we have been having over the phone.

"Thank you for taking this on. It means a lot to us," I announce my presence.

He nods, his eyes crinkling at the corners as he smiles. "No problem at all, Miss. We'll have this place looking brand new in no time." He sounds confident and reassuring, and my grandmother is excited, so I'm happy.

I hand him the plastic bag with the deposit and he doesn't bother counting the money. I guess I look as trustworthy as I am.

"I'll make sure this place is the envy of the neighbourhood." He looks at my grandmother and she laughs heartily, then threatens not to pay him if he doesn't fulfil that promise.

The work will be slow since some of the material has to be imported, but patience is a virtue and good things take time. My grandmother walks the man out and I go back into the house.

My phone pings and I sigh after reading the message. What to do, what to do? I lie on the couch, tapping the back of my phone with two fingers, trying to talk myself out of it. I need to think with my head, not my heart.

*'It's time to pick yourself up, dust yourself off, and start living again. You're young, Lolo. You can't give up on life now.'*

I finally give in to my grandmother's wise words. I open the message and reply, *'I'll come on Friday. Get the tickets'.* It's probably a bad idea but I have to start somewhere, right?

I end up on Instagram, scrolling through strangers' profiles, feeling like my life sucks. I'm tempted to post something to convince the masses that I'm having the time of my life, but my loyalty to Don has me in a chokehold. I promised to stay off social media. The sacrifices I continue making for that guy!

I switch accounts to the one I created for my mother so I can post something in the Stories. I have to handle her Instagram because we all know her love for shorthand is very interesting. I gave her some money to start a catering business. It's going slow but I have faith that it will pick up, and hopefully she will start making enough to quit her job at the supermarket. It hurts me every time I see her nursing a migraine. That job stresses her so much yet pays her so little.

Speaking of which, I need to get her a new phone on Wednesday because the one she has now is broken in too many places. Also, as a businesswoman, she needs a good phone for communication and quality pictures for her social media pages.

"What a lovely man. I've no doubt he'll do a wonderful job," my grandmother says, joining me on the couch.

"I think so too. I can't wait for them to start." I shift so she sits more comfortably.

"I can't wait to host the ladies from church when the renovations are done." She smiles dreamily. "You know, you should come with me to church tomorrow," she says as if the thought just occurred to her.

"Okay."

"Okay?"

"Yes! What time?"

She studies me for a moment, her eyes narrowing slightly. "Alright then, 10 am we should be there."

"It's a date."

She keeps looking at me funny. I always refuse to go with her to church meetings during the week. The only time church walls see me is on Sundays.

"By the way, I've been meaning to talk to you about something. I'm going to Johannesburg on Friday morning. I have a job interview."

"Really? That's wonderful, my girl! We should pray that you get the job. It will be good for you." She lightens up and a pang of guilt tugs at my conscience.

# *TWO*

**M**y grandmother wakes me up very early to prepare for my trip to Johannesburg. She's in high spirits as she irons my blouse and makes me breakfast. It's too early to eat, but I force the porridge down because of the love that went into making it.

Before I leave, we get on our knees and she prays for me to get the job. I keep one eye open, feeling guilty as hell while she passionately calls down all the angels and saints from heaven to guide my path. When she's done, she places her rosary in my hand.

"For luck and safety," she says, tears glistening in her eyes. "Keep it close, *sana lwam*. It will always keep you safe."

I close my fingers around it and hold it to my heart, fighting back the emotions threatening to spill out. She's had this rosary for as long as I can remember, so it means a lot.

"You'll do well, my girl. The Lord will make it happen."

I desperately want her to stop with the holy talk because it feels like a curse. I blatantly lied, and because of it, she has prayed, ironed, cooked and given me one of her most treasured possessions. I feel terrible.

She walks me to the main road to find transport to Port Elizabeth, giving me Johannesburg survival tips along the way. You would swear I'm relocating to a war zone.

"Hold your bag close in the taxis there and keep your phone in your bra at all times," she says.

"I'll do that, Mama. I'll be fine, I promise."

Guilt is eating me up, but I'm grateful for the attention and love she has shown me all morning. All week, actually.

A car eventually stops, and I hug her goodbye.

I arrive at the airport in Port Elizabeth hours before my flight and instantly regret it. It's small and there is nothing interesting to do. I find a quiet spot on the viewing deck and watch the few planes outside. My mother thinks I'm making the right decision and I have nothing to feel bad about. My conscience doesn't agree, but well, mama knows best.

It's almost time for my flight so I find my way to the boarding gate and join the queue. I should be thrilled but unnecessary guilt is weighing me down.

I find my seat and snap a picture before sitting back and counting down to my first flight. I look out as we take off, so lost in my head I barely notice the cruise. I wish I could open the window, put my hand out and scoop a handful of clouds, but I know as solid as they look, they are just water and air, and would fizzle in my hand just like my relationships.

I sit back and scan through a magazine, with Chris Brown singing in my ears. But even his amazing voice fails to silence the noise in my head. I don't think I'm doing the right thing.

The captain's voice yanks me out of my head. We will be landing in OR Tambo in 15 minutes, which means I have less than 30 minutes to pull myself together.

I find Dalu leaning against a pillar. He only notices me when I throw my arms around him. I haven't seen him in a while, but we have been chatting so it's not too awkward. I'm overly chatty as we head to the parkade, and he keeps smiling at me.

I stand on my toes when we get to the car and receive his kiss. He makes it last longer this time, his hands tightly closed around my waist. I hold on to him when it ends, burying my face in his chest, not ready to let go yet.

"Let's go before we're arrested for public indecency," he teases.

He holds the door open and I take a deep breath before fastening the seat belt.

"You alright?" He throws me a quick glance as he drives onto the highway.

"I'm good. I was just sightseeing." I quickly smile and focus all my energy on him. I need to stop second-guessing myself!

I take his free hand in mine and smile at the beauty of it all. Things worked themselves out in the end after all. Who am I to argue with fate?

We park at the end of a long driveway and a man greets us politely and takes my bag. No introductions are made so I have no idea if he's a relative, friend or worker, although my guess is that he's a worker.

My eyes dart all over the place as we scale up the winding staircase. I'm trying to act normal but I'm beyond amazed. Some people are living!

"You grew up here?"

"Yes, I did. This is home."

I keep staring at him, feeling bad for all the times I didn't treat him right and for what he had to go through for a chance to be with me. But it was all worth it, wasn't it? In the end, he won. He has me all to himself now. It's actually romantic when you think about it.

"Where's everyone?" I ask because it's a ghost town.

"They're around somewhere... This is your room." He stops at a door.

*My room, not ours?*

When the door closes behind us, he pulls me into his arms.

"I've been dying to do this since we left the airport." His eyes echo his words.

A knock on the door robs us of the moment and we both sigh in disappointment. A girl that looks like she could be my age walks in and announces herself loudly. He has mentioned her before but I wasn't paying much attention, so I don't remember her name.

"Baby, this is my sister Zobuhle.... Zoe, this is my girl, Lotus."

"Nice to finally meet you, Lotus. I've heard a lot about you." She hugs me before I can catch up.

"Good things only, I hope."

"Of course! You're all my brother talks about." She exudes so much warmth, I think we will get along.

"I'm sorry for disturbing you guys. I came to say hello and to let you know that dinner will be served in 40 minutes, so you might want to dress up."

He locks the door behind her and we pick up where we left off. He's touching me in the right places, breathing on my neck and sinfully nibbling my earlobe. The urgency is taking away the gentleness, making it a bit clumsy, but I savour it all and drift into space. I surrender to the sensation of his hands, each touch sending lightning through my veins. It's been a long two-month drought, so my body is overreacting.

"Don," I moan into his ear and he goes cold as if a switch went off.

Flip!

"Don' stop, baby," I quickly moan damage control.

"We don't have much time. We can't be late for dinner."

"Baby..." I keep my arms around his neck, trying to reignite the flame.

"Let's dress up, Lotus." He peels my hands off.

"So I'll be seeing your parents in a few minutes?"

"Yup. They're probably dressing up as we speak. Let me also go and dress up."

I keep hearing this *dress up* and I'm starting to think it doesn't mean putting clothes on.

"What do you mean dress up?"

"Freshen up, put on something decent, fix your hair and look clean, nothing hectic."

"You guys do that? You doll up just to eat?"

He looks more shocked that I asked that, and again it registers to me - worlds apart.

"Let me go and shower. Please get ready. We can't be late."

"Okay." I guess I have to shower too.

As the water runs down my body, Don crosses my mind. He would lather my skin, clean me up, then turn me around and do mind-blowing things to me. I shake the thoughts away and finish up.

I slip into a dress and pair it with heels, then powder my face and settle for a natural pink lip gloss to create the illusion of naturally rosy lips. I plait a French braid, then bobby-pin it into a bun, and complete the look with a necklace, earrings and a cute bracelet. I look put together; his parents would be crazy not to like me.

"Ready?" Dalu walks in and stops as if time stood still. "You look... perfect."

*I know.* "Thank you."

He eyes me hungrily before pulling himself together. "Thank you for doing this with me."

"The pleasure is all mine."

A smile plays on his lips. "Shall we?"

"Yes, sir."

I follow him out of the room and down the stairs, trying my best to keep my breath in check. I know I look gorgeous but I don't think that's enough to win over an entire family.

We walk into the dining room and I'm mind blown. The stunning tapestry and beautifully set table make it feel like a dinner party straight out of The Real Housewives. I knew his family was rich; I just had no idea how much. If this is what my future looks like, then I accept. I belong right here, and who knows, I might make the cast of The Real Housewives one day.

"Hello, welcome. You must be Lotus." A woman walks to me.

Her hug makes it impossible for me to reciprocate. It was brief, light and gone in two seconds.

"Thank you."

"Come and say hello to our old man."

"I'm not old," a man, who I'm sure is Dalu's father, says.

He really isn't old. He isn't lively either. He looks indifferent and somewhat bored by life itself.

"But you are, darling."

"Don't mind her. Some people think calling others old makes them young." He shakes my hand and goes back to looking disinterested.

I greet everyone around the table, and it's a relief to finally take my seat. I was tired of smiling. If I didn't love Dalu before, I do now. A wholesome family has always been on my wish list. I grew up dreaming of such a family unit. With a mother and father, and importantly, money. I have enough savings to get by, courtesy of Don, but money that's not constantly replenished quickly runs out. Also, I don't know how much will be left after the renovations are complete. This right here is old money, and I'm all for it.

They ask about my flight, Eastern Cape, Cape Town and food allergies. That last one was quite random. His mother asks if I'm by any chance vegan, lactose intolerant or gluten-free. I tell her I have no qualms with wheat and dairy. I also say I'm a flexitarian and today is my eat-meat day. I heard that term on TV and I have been running with it since. I'm glad it impressed her.

His mother sits the way she speaks; with a poise and grace I can only aspire to attain. I think she's the one I need to impress because the father looks like he doesn't care about much. Zoe already likes me, unless she's good at pretending.

"Start from the outside in," Dalu whispers when he sees me trying to figure out which fork to pick up.

I take my phone, open Notes and type, *'I don't know how to eat these things'* and pass it to him.

He types, *'Watch me, it's easy.'*

*'Cool. You look hot by the way.'*

I watch him smile as he reads.

*'You too. I can't wait to take that dress off you.'*

It's my turn to smile. *'I can't wait.'*

He bites his lip and types, *'I'll appreciate your body properly tonight.'*

*'I'm all yours, Mr Mthethwa.'*

"Dalubuhle. Phone away," his father says sternly.

"I'm sorry." Dalu fake-coughs.

He's not sorry, and he should get his hand off my thigh because his father is looking in our direction.

"Don't overindulge on that. We have four more courses to go," he whispers in my ear.

I'm sure his parents think he said something naughty because of my reaction. Can he stop?! I'm trying to impress my in-laws here! I need to earn a seat at this table.

It's all going well and the conversation is easy until I'm put back in the spotlight.

"So, Lotus, what do you do?" his father asks.

"I'm a quality control manager for a food manufacturing company in Cape Town." That sounds better than saying I'm unemployed and having them think I'm after their son's money.

He humphs.

I don't like how condescending it sounded. He grills me with question after question, looking straight in my direction. It's starting to feel like an interview. I'm sure next he'll ask, "Why are you the right candidate for my son's heart?"

"Stop interrogating the poor girl. Ask her less serious questions like how she met our Dalubuhle," my mother-in-law comes to my rescue.

"I'll let Dalu tell that. He tells it so much better." I reach for his hand under the table.

I melt inside as he talks about this gorgeous, intelligent, funny, adorable girl he met during an audit. I watch him come alive as he talks about me, saying he just knew I was the one from the get-go.

"So, Lotus, where are your parents?" His father catches me off guard with the abrupt change of topic. I was still enjoying hearing about myself.

"My mother is in Eastern Cape."

"And your father?"

"Well, umm..." I look to Dalu for help, but he doesn't know, so he can't save me.

"I don't know. I've never met him."

He humphs again and I feel terrible inside. I'm getting a feeling that he doesn't approve of me.

Dinner ends with dessert and more questions about what drives me in life, my hobbies, whether I prefer pilates or yoga, my thoughts on the unrest in the Middle East and where I see myself in five years. It's like they are trying to assess if I'm worthy of their son. I answer to the best of my ability but I'm not sure I passed.

I make it a point to let them know that I'm a steadfast Christian. Everyone likes a church girl, right?

# *THREE*

I'm getting out of my shoes and Dalu is saying his parents loved me. I don't know why he's lying because his father definitely didn't. His mother maybe, but his father did not.

"We've been avoiding the inevitable, so maybe let's get it over with," he says.

I was worried this time would come, but he's right. We said we would talk in person and here we are. I'm the one who messed up so I do most of the talking. I come clean about my relationship with Don. Well, I modify details here and there because whoever said the truth shall set you free either had a death wish or a weird urge to live life miserable and alone.

"It wasn't a solid relationship. I was afraid to break up with him. I messed up and I regret it every day. You were always the one for me, but you were so good, you scared me. I'm not used to men being good to me. Donavan didn't love me, that's why I was with him. I didn't think I deserved to be loved. But more than that, I didn't think I deserved you. You were perfect and kind. You had your life together. You had the looks, the body, the education - you had everything. You could get any girl you wanted and I didn't believe it could be me."

"You always deserved me, pretty girl. Don't ever think so low of yourself again. I love you and you love me, that's all that matters. I'm also sorry that I didn't try harder to keep you."

If he had tried any harder, he would be six feet under right now.

"How did you end up with that guy, Lotus? How did you end up mixed up with gangs? I'm not blaming you or trying to make you feel bad, I'm just trying to understand. I want us to talk about everything and move on."

"I didn't know he was part of a gang until it was too late."

His eyes narrow and he scans my face. "Do you still love him?"

"What? No, never! That chapter is closed. I love you." I reach for his hands and he looks at me with glassy eyes. "I'm sorry for what I put you through. You didn't deserve any of it. If I could go back, I'd do things differently. I'd never have taken you for granted."

I don't know if he believes me or not.

"I have one last question. Your tattoos; he forced you, didn't he? He branded you with his name, right?"

I find myself nodding, glad he phrased the question the way he did because I wouldn't have known what to say. He looks away, blinking back tears. I hate how much I broke him.

"All I wanted was you and they tried to kill me for it... But I forgive you."

*Phew!*

"I'm sorry that I couldn't protect you from those savages, but you're safe now. We'll get through this."

Hearing his voice break and watching his eyes flood hurts me. I hold on to him and bury my face on his shoulder. I have never felt this close to him before. There is hope after all that we can be something.

We are in each other's embrace, exchanging promises to never hurt each other again, when the door swings open. What happened to knocking?

"Did I interrupt something?" Zoe peers into the room.

Dalu and I exchange glances. Talk about bad timing!

"No, come in," Dalu says with a forced smile.

"Great! What were you guys up to?"

"We were just, you know, catching up." Dalu rubs the back of his neck awkwardly and I curse silently.

"Ah, I see. Well, don't let me stop you. I'll go and chill in the jacuzzi. Maybe you guys can join me when you're done."

I don't even know why she's still here. Can't she read the room? I want to stay in and catch up with Dalu in my own way. I'm nursing a bruised ego and a guilty conscience. Bad-mouthing Don left me feeling some type of way.

"Yeah, sounds good." Dalu gives me an unsure glance.

"Alrighty then. See you soon." She closes the door behind her.

Dalu eyes me shamelessly as I change into a bikini. I stop him from taking his clothes off when the heat becomes too much. We need to go before his sister comes back and ruins everything again.

I really needed this - good company, funny stories, bottomless drinks and a boy smitten with me. The more the wine goes down, the more I gawk at Dalu's body. Right now, I need him more than he will ever know. We are laughing louder as the alcohol hits the right nerves and a third bottle is inevitable. I haven't had so much alcohol in a while!

We have been in the jacuzzi for quite a while and I'm starting to feel dehydrated, so we move to the loungers.

"Lotus, you got mad tats. What do they mean?" Zoe asks when my wolf comes into full view.

*Damn you, bikinis!*

"This one is a wolf."

"Duh! What does it symbolise?"

"Strength? Loyalty?" I sound so unsure *shame*.

"Oh, so you're like a follower? You run in a pack?" She laughs even though it's not funny.

"Oh, please! I'm not a follower, I'm an alpha. Alpha females don't run in packs." I saw that on Pinterest. I hope she doesn't ask me what it means.

I quickly move on to the one on my wrist. "This one is..."

"...her father's name. It's beautiful," Dalu finishes my sentence and places a kiss right over the tattoo of Don's name.

WTF!

"Oh, sorry. I thought it was an ex's name or something stupid like that. But I must say, getting a deadbeat's name inked is equally weird."

"Who would be so stupid as to tattoo a boyfriend's name on their body?" Dalu sniggers.

"You'd be surprised how brainless some people are!" Zoe laughs. "I need the bathroom. Be right back."

Wow! Just wow! I need a top-up.

"Don't mind Zoe. We can always get you laser surgery to remove the tattoos. You're mine now; you have no business carrying another man's name on your body."

I feel a chill down my spine, but for peace's sake, I let him believe what he wants to believe. I'm not getting rid of anything.

"I read up on the Wolves after they threatened my life. Those are animals, baby. They are brutal criminals. I hope the army wipes every single one of them out. The world would be a better place without them."

I take a long sip.

"Don't worry, they'll never bother you again. They'll all die like the dogs they are."

Why is he saying these things? I feel bile rising at the back of my throat but I suppress it and push it down with wine. No need to spoil my perfect weekend.

It must be around 11 pm when Zoe says she's going to bed, leaving Dalu and me alone. We get cosy and our conversation becomes more personal.

"I'm sorry about some of the questions my father asked you. He shouldn't have asked you about your parents."

"It's fine. I'm sure he meant no harm."

"Still, there was no need for him to make you that uncomfortable.

But thank you for being perfect tonight."

See, I knew it was worth it.

"So, about your father, I sensed that there was something you were not letting out. Do you want to talk about it?"

"No, not really."

"Why?"

"It will spoil the mood."

"Whatever it is, you can tell me. I just need us to be honest with each other. Let's start on a clean slate, with no secrets or lies. We should be able to talk about anything, no matter what it is."

I look away, debating with myself. I don't want that. I prefer keeping my secrets to myself. I want us to leave the past where it belongs.

"I need to be able to trust you, Lotus."

Oh, here we go! But you know what, it's fine.

"I know my father. Well, I know who he is. Who he was, rather. I never really met him."

"He died?"

"Well, yes, it's complicated. I don't know where to start."

"Start anywhere." He wraps his arm around me and pulls me closer.

"I really don't want to talk about it."

He pauses, and I let out a silent sigh of relief when he says, "I understand."

"I don't get it, Dalu. I'm not a bad person. I don't understand why I never had a father. I know what my mother said, and I know he was a bad person and all, but why wasn't I given a chance to make my own decision? All my life I just wanted to meet him."

His tighter embrace tells me he sympathises.

This right here is what I manifested, yet I suddenly feel sad. I feel like I shouldn't be here. Tears roll down my face and I close my eyes and pep-talk myself to get it together. This is my future, I can't mess up.

We wallow in the sad aura until we return to talking about nothing. I top-up my glass one last time and fake being okay. My head is so light, I can hardly keep my eyes open, but I keep bringing the glass to my lips and drinking the wise waters. We keep talking and opening up to each other.

I needed this.

"I think it's time to call it a night." Dalu takes my glass and balances me when I stagger.

"My parents' room is closer to yours. Mine is at the end."

"Your room it is then." I giggle and hold on to the towel he wrapped around my shoulders.

As soon as the door locks, the towel falls off and his mouth comes down on mine. I'm floating so bad, I'm barely feeling anything. His hands are all over me and mine are disturbing more than they are helping. My bikini leaves my body and I fall back onto the bed and pull him down on me.

\* \* \* \* \*

I wake up with a splitting headache. I guzzle the water on the pedestal and wince the lingering ache away. I still have Dalu's scent on me. I think we had sex but I don't quite remember the details. I don't know if I can ask. Oh, *mann*, I need to get a grip. This desperation to earn him back needs to die. I'm starting to act beside myself. Good heavens, my head!

I put on his T-shirt and pussyfoot to the glass door that opens to a balcony. A rush of cold runs up my feet as I step outside. The wooden floor is wet and freezing air is seeping into my bones, but I don't care. I need to process my feelings.

I lean over the railings, taking in the surroundings, ignoring the wind slapping my face. A few ripples are disturbing the perfect layout of the blue water in the swimming pool, but besides that, there is nothing interesting in sight. This reminds me of the peaceful mornings in Gordon's Bay. I wish I could go back there, but I also know that I need to close that chapter and focus on getting back on my feet. Don really forgot about me! I can't believe it. What did I do wrong? It's still very early to be overthinking like this, yet my mind is already on overdrive.

Dalu's arms close around my waist and I lean back into him. I hate that I'm thinking about another man with his arms around me. We stand in silence for a while, then he turns me around and looks at me with a warm glow behind his eyes.

"I love you, Lotus. I'll always love you."

*Is that a promise of an eternity?*

"I love you too."

"Last night was special. I hope no one heard us."

*Oh, so we did have sex! Good to know.*

My heart settles as I take in his kind eyes and calm face. We really can be something if I focus.

It's starting to rain again and a few showers are spraying us. I turn back to face outside. It's getting too misty to see far. His kisses on my neck get heavier and his hands close around my breasts, squeezing, prompting me to arch my back. I'm getting wet, and not just from the rain. The fear that someone might see us is long gone as I stand on my toes to receive him. He pulls my panties to the side and I gulp at the entrance. I close my eyes and float around in my head, welcoming every thrust and embracing every moan. I hold on to the slippery railing as he goes deeper and faster until he groans and pours himself into me. We stay there for a while, merged into one, breathing in unison.

Healing is coming faster than expected.

\* \* \* \* \*

Time flies! I can't believe it's Sunday already! Yesterday was amazing. Exhausting, but really amazing. Dalu has been good to me. He treats me like a princess, pays me attention and makes love to me every chance he gets – he's just perfect. Something is missing though; that deep connection, but like my mother said on the phone, I need to look at the bigger picture and keep my eye on the ball. She said if I mess this up, I'll be the biggest fool to ever live.

I follow Dalu downstairs for breakfast. I'm happy that I don't have to share a table with his family today. I ask the chef for a toasted croissant with eggs, bacon and cheese, and a cup of tea.

Dalu says he needs to go and talk to his father, so I'll have my breakfast outside. I need some alone time.

I don't remember the last time I felt this good. This is how my life should be. The only delicacy available to me in the last two months has been *vetkoeks*. The *spaza* shop wouldn't stock croissants if they were the last food on earth. Also, UberEats doesn't cover our area and I can't go to town as I please because my car is in Cape Town - another promise Don broke.

Out of habit, I dial Don. As usual, it says the number doesn't exist. I curse in my throat and try again. I don't know why I'm still doing this to myself.

I wish I could stay here all month but Dalu already booked my return flight. I wanted to ask him to change it to a later date but I restrained myself. I need to let him set the pace until we are at par, then I can start with demands and whatnot. Also, it might soon get weird with his parents around.

"What are you up to?" Zoe startles me and I almost drop my phone. She has no timing at all!

"Nothing. Just going through people's statuses on WhatsApp." The truth is I was trying to call Don for the umpteenth time.

"Oh, great. I never go through that nonsense. I don't understand some people's constant need for validation. It's ridiculous."

I'm not quite sure what I'm expected to say, seeing how often I update my status.

"Where's Dalu? I haven't seen him this morning."

"He said he'll join me soon."

She folds her legs on the chair and looks at me. "I hope you're not playing games with my brother this time. Do you love him or is he a placeholder for someone else?" She goes all serious on me without warning.

"I love him." Like is more apt but not everything deserves to be said out loud.

"That's good to know. Be good to him, Lotus."

"If he keeps being good to me, I don't see how I could possibly be bad to him." I try to laugh it off but her jaw doesn't budge.

"I know he can be difficult, but all I'm asking is that you take care of him. I know it's not easy loving someone like him, so if you're not up for the long run, don't string him along. I'm serious."

What does she mean *difficult* and *someone like him*? He's a lamb and a total yes-man. There is no sweeter man on earth!

"I love your brother, Zoe. We're good, and we have a good thing going. I'm in a good place now and I've never been more sure in my life."

"I hope you mean that. I know about your ex. That really messed Dalu up. Don't do that again." She gives me a threatening eye.

*Now why would Dalu tell his sister my personal business?*

"Are we clear?"

"Yes, we are."

"Great. Enjoy your breakfast." She pats me on the shoulder and walks away.

*What was that?*

I only see Dalu when he sits next to me. I want to ask him why he disclosed my secrets to his sister but I decide to smile instead and tell him I missed him.

"We have a few hours before we go to the airport. Think we can take it upstairs?"

"I would love to but I'm not feeling too great."

"Do you want to lie down? Should I go and get you water?"

"I'll be alright. I just need some air. Actually, I was thinking we should go past Sandton and get a few things before going to the airport."

"I see." He looks disappointed so I foresee my shopping spree not turning out well or not happening at all, so a girl's gotta do what a girl's gotta do.

"Actually, I know what will make me feel better." I bite my lip and he brightens up instantly.

## Heart in Two

I lean in and whisper, "Your room or mine?"
"Mine. I need your scent on my sheets after you've left."

# *FOUR*

Being back home sucks! I'm right back on my grandmother's verandah, wallowing in depressing thoughts. The rush of the weekend I spent with Dalu is gone and it's like I hit a new low. Dalu was supposed to be my sweet escape. I just wanted to feel better and salvage whatever was left of my life. Yet I feel worse than I did before I went to see him.

"Lotus!" my grandmother yells.

*What now?*

"There you are. I've been calling you!"

Great, she found me! I bet if I was living in Dalu's home, no one would find me for weeks if I wanted to hide.

"Really? I'm sorry, I didn't hear you."

She shakes her head and stands with her hands on her waist, looking at me like I'm unbelievable.

"There's a car that's been driving up and down in front of my house. Who is it?"

I shrug and go back to my phone. I need all the sun I can get before it gets too hot, with some peace on the side.

"Who is it, Lotus?"

Is she being for real right now? How would I know? The road belongs to the municipality. Since when am I a representative?

"I asked you a question! All those demons you invited into your body are messing you up. I'll slap them out of you one by one if you don't know me!"

She believes tattoos are portals through which demons enter a human body. It doesn't help that I have faux locs. She says locs are the devil's preferred hairstyle.

You know what, it's fine. Let me indulge her. I'll never know peace if I don't do this.

I follow her to the side of the house facing the road. A black car drives past and she points, "That one!"

"I don't recognise it."

The car reverses and stops outside the gate. They probably want to ask for directions. Look at my life now; I have been reduced to a GPS.

My grandmother is behind me, talking to herself and scolding me for loving men too much. I don't even know where that is coming from. I cross my arms and watch. Nothing much entertains me around here so my curiosity is piqued. It shouldn't be anyone I know because I would die! A whole me seen in these yesteryear pyjamas and an old bonnet on my head! I would die an excruciating death.

"Hilton?" I find myself asking out loud when he steps out of the car.

My heart skips a beat and I feel my chest closing up. It can't be!

I walk fast towards the gate and signal Hilton to get back in the car.

"Who is it?"

"It's no one, Mama. They want directions."

"Are you going to men dressed like that? How are you not ashamed?" she harrumphs.

I ignore her and rush out of the gate, open the car and jump in.

"Drive!" I say as soon as I close the door.

The engine kicks off and I dig my nails into my palms. I'm shaking in my seat and my heart is palpitating, but I feel frozen. I don't know how to process this. I catch Hilton's expression; he looks like he wishes he was anywhere but here. He's not behaving like someone who hasn't seen me in months. Well, he never liked me anyway.

We turn into what used to be a communal football field. I spring out of the car as soon as it stops and storm around to the driver's side. Don gets out of the car and looks at me like he's seeing a ghost. My anger just spills out and flares up like wildfire.

"Why, Donavan? I just want to know why!" I jab a finger into his chest. I want to slap him across the face but I'm practising self-restraint.

"*Skat.*"

"*Skat?* Is that all you have to say to me right now? *Skat?*"

"Calm down."

"Calm down? Are you serious right now?" I pace in small steps and rest my hands on my waist when I stop. I don't have the words to express all the emotions boiling inside me. I'm livid, yet a huge part of me wants to jump into his arms and stay there forever.

"*Skat*, please calm down."

"You abandoned me! You never bothered to keep in touch and *skat* is all you have to say?" I jab him again, forcing him to step back.

"You're overreacting. Can we talk like normal people?"

"Wow! You know what, I'll walk home. You can return to whatever hole you crawled out of."

I turn away and he grabs my arm and turns me around. His touch sends electric waves through my skin, bringing back old memories. I catch his eyes and my anger deflates like a balloon. He's still everything he was; sexy as hell, with the most beautiful eyes I have ever looked into. Pride is the only thing keeping me rooted. I so desperately want to be in his arms, but I won't make the first move. He doesn't deserve it.

"I'm sorry, my angel," he mumbles.

His words hang in the air, and for a moment I'm torn between the intensity of his look and the storm of emotions inside me.

"I'm sorry, my *skat*."

"You're sorry? You disappeared without a trace. Do you have any idea what it was like for me?" I went through the most because of him.

"I didn't want you worrying about me."

"You didn't want me worrying about you? Well, I was worried anyway! Over two months, Donavan! Do you have any idea what I went through thinking that something had happened to you? I was worried about you every day! Every single day, I worried about you! I'd call you even though I knew your number wouldn't go through. I'd watch the news and even buy newspapers hoping to get information about you. I was worried sick! All you had to do was pick up the damn phone!"

He starts to speak and I raise a hand to stop him. "Don't bother."

I need a moment to gather my thoughts and sort through the mess of emotions I'm experiencing all at once.

"Lotus, please."

"I can't believe you did this to me!"

"Stop yelling. Give me a chance to explain."

"Fine. Explain, but don't expect me to forgive you."

He keeps quiet and looks down.

I walk to the back of the car. It's like my heart is shattering in real-time and I'm feeling every cleavage. I hold on to the car, trying to pull myself together before I can walk home. What I really want is to break down and cry, but I don't want to be that girl right now.

His footsteps approach and he stops behind me. I silently beg him to say something.

"Hey," he says softly, as if he heard my thoughts.

I turn around to face him. "What?"

He looks at me deeply, probably doing it on purpose because he knows the effect his eyes have on me.

"I hate seeing you like this. I feel terrible about it."

I squint, trying to gauge his sincerity.

"I'm really sorry, my *skat*."

I unfold my fists. I want to fight some more but I know if I keep pushing, things will go south. Besides, I don't have any strength left in me. If he doesn't love me anymore, it's okay. I'm loved elsewhere, so I won't beg for crumbs.

Who am I kidding?

"Don..."

"I said I'm sorry, Lotus."

How is he the one getting annoyed right now?

*Deep breath. Rein it in. Give him a chance to give you closure.*

He pulls me into his arms. I resist, but as the warmth of his arms reminds me of the nights he would hold me almost like this, I begin to relax. I lose all restraint and break down, quietly at first, then I shudder, trembling in his arms, my tears soaking into his hoodie. He holds me close until I feel like I'm melting into his body. I missed him so much.

When I eventually get it together, we stand there for a while, the tension between us slowly dissipating. When we finally pull apart, he gently rubs away a tear from my cheek with his thumb, then leans in and presses his lips to mine. My hands go around his neck to lock him in. He kisses me with such passion and intensity, it makes me feel alive again. I'm lost in his arms, feeling as if time has stopped and nothing else in the world matters. It's as if he's pouring all his apologies into the kiss and his hands are imprinting his DNA onto my skin. He is evoking emotions I'm not sure I can contain. I wish we were in a room right now; the reunion sex would be fire!

When my feelings overpower me, I start crying again. He brings me to his chest and holds me tightly, his chin resting on my head.

"I'm sorry, my angel."

I sob some more because his voice reminds me of everything that was. I'm heartbroken and happy at the same time.

"I'm sorry I took so long. Thank you for waiting for me. I thought about you every day, but I had to keep you safe."

I have a lot to say but I'll say it on the way to Cape Town. If I keep talking now, I'll break down all over again. I'm not sure what I will tell my grandmother. Maybe I can say I got the job in Johannesburg and they said I need to start tomorrow, so I have to leave right away.

"Let me go and pack my bags so we can go."

Guilt flashes across his face and he looks down.

"What is it?"

"I'm not going back with you. I got a call on our way here. We're under attack. I need to get back to Cape Town."

The words hit me like a physical blow and I look away to hide the new wave of pain. The harsh truth of another abandonment sets in and I panic. "You can't leave me here! Take me with you, please, Don. I'll stay out of the way."

"I'm sorry."

This can't be happening to me. So why did he bother coming all this way? I want to curse him and kick the car, but I close my eyes and cuss him out in my head instead.

"Fine. Let's spend the night in Port Elizabeth and you'll go to Cape Town tomorrow."

"I want to, but I can't."

"Please don't leave me." My grip on his arm tightens.

"I have to. Give me some time to sort things out. I'll come and get you, okay? Just a bit more time, my angel." He cups my cheeks and his eyes search mine. "Do you still love me?"

"I do. I love you."

"Thank you."

"Tell me you love me too." I let go of the last shred of pride. I desperately need reassurance.

He frowns a little and squints his eyes. "Since when do you tell me what to do?"

"Please, Don."

"I wouldn't be here if I didn't." He pulls me into his arms and holds me as I bawl my eyes out.

\* \* \* \* \*

What was supposed to be the best day of my life has turned out to be the worst. I waited for Don for a long time, and then he just popped up and said hi and bye. All I have done today is cry and beat myself up about everything. Why do circumstances always make me the bad guy? I'm the victim here! If he had called me, I would have never gone to Dalu.

I have to do the right thing but let me wallow in my grief a little longer. I need to find the least brutal way to obliterate Dalu's heart. I should just block him and hope he forgets I ever existed, but I can't bring myself to. He's always there when I need him. He kept me alive when Don disappeared on me.

I can't postpone this any longer. Let me rip off the band-aid.

*'There's no easy way to say this, D. I can't be with you anymore. You deserve better. Take care.'*

I almost delete the message but the grey ticks turn blue before I can. He immediately starts typing and I want to block him before his response comes through, but I'm not that cruel.

*'Don't do this to us, baby. Whatever it is, we can talk about it.'*

I should have blocked him because what is this now? Does he not have an ounce of pride?

*'Please don't make this harder than it already is.'*

*'At least tell me why.'*

I'm not sure how to respond, so I keep staring at my phone. Maybe I should use the old-and-tried *'It's not you, it's me'*. Maybe I should tell him the truth.

*'Call you in a bit,'* he texts.

That's not a good idea. *'I think it's best if we don't talk.'*

*'YOU OWE ME THAT AT LEAST!'*

Whoa! Caps? Incoming call? I really should have blocked him!

Deep sigh. I answer the phone and my "Hello" comes out thinner than intended.

"Baby, what's wrong?"

I close my eyes and curse his kind voice. He should yell at me and tell me he hates me. He should call me names. He should tell me straight up that he thinks I'm stupid and he hopes I fall into a sewage and drown.

"What's going on? Talk to me."

"Dalu, I, we, I need time out. I thought I could do this but I can't. I'm sorry."

"Why? I thought you were happy. Did I do something?"

"No, you didn't. I just need time to heal."

"I'm confused. What changed? After everything, why would you wake up and suddenly want to break up? I don't understand."

"I'm really sorry."

"At least tell me why."

"I'm in a bad place. My mental health is in shambles. I need to sort myself out."

Silence follows and I pinch the bridge of my nose in regret.

"It's him, isn't it?" He drops his voice.

"No, of course not!"

An awkward silence follows, and I look at my screen to make sure he's still on the other end of the line. "You there?"

"I'm here. I just needed a moment to let the knife you drove into my heart sink in."

"Dalu..."

"It's okay, Lotus. I won't force you to be with me. I'm used to you doing this to me." The pain in his voice tears through my gut.

"I'm sorry."

"I'll live. I survived before, didn't I? ... I was going to call you later, not that it matters anymore. I have an audit in Port Elizabeth on Friday, so I was going to ask you to spend the weekend with me, but I guess that's out of the question now."

"Oh, Dalu."

"You'll refuse, I know, but let me ask anyway. Can you meet me on Saturday for lunch? Maybe I can give you the phone I got you, that one you wanted in Sandton. How far are you from PE?"

Now that is enticing! I can afford the phone, but spending my own money hurts so much, it's unbearable. Funny how it didn't hurt one bit when I bought my mother the latest phone, but when it comes to spending on myself, it hurts like a mother.

"I really don't think that's a good idea."

"Please, Lotus. We'll have lunch, then part on amicable terms. You just dropped a bomb on me without warning. I think I deserve an explanation. Please have lunch with me on Saturday. Just lunch, nothing else."

I close my eyes and envision the iPhone and Instagramable food. I regret the words before they even leave my mouth.

# FIVE

I'm the biggest fool on earth. Don has been AWOL since that day. He didn't even give me his phone number, and I was too caught up in my emotions to ask. I'm back to waiting indefinitely. I feel so stupid and I'm so angry! I dumped Dalu for nothing. Maybe this trip to Port Elizabeth is what I need after all. I'm tempted to spend the whole weekend with Dalu. Anyway, we will see.

I'm waiting for my grandmother to go to the shops so I can sneak out. She knows I'm going to PE for an 'interview', but I don't want her to see me leaving in this outfit. I'll deal with her when I get back. She gave me hell the other day for going outside in pyjamas to meet 'strange men'. Then she asked why the interview is on a Saturday, and I said the food industry doesn't close, so Saturday is a normal workday. I'm getting good at thinking on my feet.

I look at myself in the mirror one last time and I'm glad that I don't look like my problems. A voice in my head tells me I'm making a huge mistake but I manage to silence it.

I walk to the main road and flash a placard written PE to passing cars. This is the epitome of *'how the mighty have fallen!'* Hitchhiking does not align with my brand at all, but what's a girl supposed to do? Sell the drugs under my bed and buy a car? Hijack people at gunpoint? I don't think so.

A Golf GTI with three guys inside, blasting loud music, stops. I thank them for stopping but refuse to get in. I don't want to be on the news tomorrow and be part of the statistics. Their remarks about my thighs were enough to repel me.

I'm about to text Dalu that I won't make it when a bakkie pulls over. Maybe I shouldn't be going to PE and this is the universe punishing me for doing things I shouldn't be doing. A whole me at the back of a bakkie? The world must be ending!

I sit on a scarf, with three other people that don't exactly smell sanitary. I put on my shades and look away from the wind, cursing Don in my head for reducing me to this. He should have sent my car already! It's uncomfortable, so I can't even sleep.

I take a picture of the road behind us and it comes out looking rustic. When I'm done doctoring it, it looks like an image from an 80s movie. I post it on my mother's Instagram profile with a philosophical caption about the challenges of embarking on new journeys. I close my phone and sit back, wishing the bakkie would go faster.

I'm relieved when I jump off in town. It's pretty empty and most shops are closed, which is expected on a Saturday afternoon. I stand on the side of the road and send a location pin to Dalu. While waiting, I scroll through posts on Instagram, wishing it was me in a bikini on an island somewhere. I smile a little when I see *'Seen'* under the last message to Chelsea. She might not respond but at least she reads my messages.

Dalu finally arrives and gives me a long hug. I ignore the sadness in his eyes and mentally pep-talk myself to stay in control for the next two or so hours. If all goes well, I might grant him breakup sex, so let's see how it plays out.

"You look beautiful." He kisses me full on the lips before I can react. Such a violation!

As we drive, not once does he bring up the breakup. He's talking more than I am and over me, I guess to stop me from addressing the elephant in the room. It's uncomfortable but I keep my eye on the prize. After lunch, we'll go shopping in Boardwalk Mall and I'm going to buy the most expensive items in whatever boutique we end up in. I deserve it after sitting in that bakkie.

We drive into a hotel and I give him a questioning eye.

"I'm staying here, but there's a restaurant on the other side. Gorgeous views and even better food."

Fair enough.

We walk from the parking lot like a couple. He's still out-talking me and gripping my hand tightly. It's awkward. I have mixed feelings about all of this, but the rewards waiting for me at the end outweigh my internal conflict.

We are ushered to a table at the edge, with unobstructed views of the ocean. The gentle breeze fans my face and the smell of the sea brings back memories of the dinner we had at Brass Bell. I was smitten with him then, and he looked as good as he does today. A memory of Gordon's Bay joins the party and I look out into the sea, feeling a familiar sadness creeping in. I promised Don I would wait... again. Flashbacks of him stepping out of the car looking fine as hell, wrapping his arms around me and kissing me deeply, flood my mind. He drove all the way from Cape Town for me. The least I can do is wait for him a little longer.

The waiter draws my attention, and Dalu gives me a funny look when I order a mocktail. I tell him I need to be sober to navigate my way back home. The truth is, I don't want to get tipsy and end up doing something I'll regret. As the waiter walks away, I play with my fingers under the table, fighting with my thoughts.

I find the perfect lighting and snap a picture of my beautiful drink with the ocean in the background. I'll post it later on my mother's page. At this rate, she has to pay me for this content.

Dalu is nice as always. He's having an Old-Fashioned and taking his time with it. He asks about home and my family, and he tells me about his family and how everyone keeps asking about me. He's talking about everything except the damn breakup.

My oysters arrive and I take a picture before I dig in. I don't have much of an appetite because I had a big breakfast, but I won't let good food go to waste.

It must be the oysters' aphrodisiac effect, or maybe my brain has finally come to its senses, because I find myself loosening up and engaging more. I desperately want us to address the obvious but I don't know where to begin. Plus we are getting along quite well, so I don't want to mess it up just yet.

"Taste this." He holds a spoonful of chicken livers towards my mouth.

I don't know what happened but the spoon empties on my chest. Just great!

"Oh, baby, I'm so sorry." He tries to dab me with a napkin.

"It's okay. Let me go and clean myself in the bathroom."

I'm so annoyed! Why did he try to feed me those stupid livers? *Yerrr!* At least my blouse is dark-coloured so it's not too bad, but still, how can he be so clumsy?! He was sorry and remorseful, but isn't he always?

I walk back to the table and ask him not to feed me anything anymore. I eat the rest of my oysters in silence and down the rest of my drink, listening to him going on and on, wondering if it's too early to ask about the phone he promised me.

"Are you alright?" His brows knit together as he looks at me.

"I think I'm going to puke." I don't know what's happening in my stomach but it's not good.

I run to the bathroom and throw up. I stay a little longer in front of the sink, asking my mirror image what the hell I'm doing. The universe is giving me every sign not to be here. I feel so sick, I don't know what's happening to me. I need to get that phone and find my way home.

I find Dalu waiting for me outside the toilets. My head is spinning and I'm feeling a bit faint.

"You alright?"

*Do I look alright?* I nod.

"I think we should go to my room so you can lie down for a bit."

I don't think going to his room is a good idea but I need to lie down before I can think of hitchhiking back home. My vision is blurring and my stomach is cramping badly. I can't ask him to drive me home because it's far and I don't want him to know where I stay. I also can't risk my grandmother seeing him and having to explain who he is. I don't need the drama. I could ask him to drop me around the corner, but better safe than sorry.

I hold on to his arm as we head to the elevator. He probably mistakes it for affection, but I just need support so I don't fall flat on my face. I catch my reflection in the elevator's mirror and I can't believe how pale I look.

We walk slowly down the corridor, my arm on his shoulder, and his around my waist. I feel like I'll fall down any second. We eventually stop at a door and he finds his key card.

On a normal day, I would have marvelled at this room, and maybe taken pictures of the view and selfies in front of the portrait behind the couch. But right now, with the way my head is spinning, I could even sleep on the floor.

He takes my shoes off and helps me lie down on the bed. I try to protest but I'm losing control of my body and I'm fighting hard to stay awake.

"Try to relax," he says.

I feel faint-headed; everything is beginning to blur. I can barely see and I'm hearing him talking but as if from a cave. I want to say something but my eyelids are so heavy, they close on their own. My head is spinning and my body is shutting down.

He pokes me and I slowly turn my head to face him.

"How are you feeling?"

"Like death."

"Good. Me and you are going to have a chat." His concerned look disappears.

"Dalu." I reach for his hand but he roughly swats it away.

"Shut up! You'll answer my questions. Understood?"

I find myself nodding against my will.

"Good girl. The intel you gave me about Gordon's Bay paid off big time, so I need more."

What intel? I don't remember telling him anything. Was it that night in Joburg? I must have been *kak* drunk!

"Tell me the truth about your father."

I shake my head, the motion causing sharp pain.

"Now!" he bellows.

My lips move, forming words without my consent. "He's gone."

"What do you mean?"

"He died."

"How did he die?"

"Donavan killed him."

His mouth opens and closes, and he runs his hand down his face as if wiping away invisible sweat.

"No way! Donavan killed him? Your boyfriend, Donavan? Why?"

"He was the General of the Wolves."

"Geez, this is good! You mean to tell me the General of the Wolves was your father? Wow, Lotus! Who would have thought? Go on. Why did your boyfriend kill your father?"

Tears well up behind my eyes but I fail to stop talking.

"I wanted him dead before I knew he was my father."

"Go on."

"He ordered a hit on Don and he wanted to take me out as well. I didn't know he was my father."

"Wow! This is gold! Tell me everything."

I tell him everything I know about the General and the Wolves, tears trickling down the side of my face. Why can't I stop talking?

"Now tell me, where do the Wolves get guns from?"

"Police armoury." I close my eyes and feel myself drifting away.

"This is good stuff... Hey, hey, don't sleep on me now, wake up!" He pours water on my face and I jerk up.

"We're not done yet. Sit up straight and tell me everything." He forces me up.

"Please stop."

"Oh, pretty girl. We're just getting started," he says, a chilling smile spreading across his face.

# *SIX*

I wake up feeling like a truck ran over my head. I wince as pain slices across my face and squint my eyes to avoid being blinded by the light. I reach for my phone first. Shit! It's almost 7 pm!

Dalu is sitting on the one-seater couch by the window, looking out into the ocean.

"Dalu."

He turns around and I can't read his expression.

"You're awake. How are you feeling?"

"Much better." I sit up and cuss under my breath.

*What happened? Why am I naked?*

"Did you sleep with me?" I panic at the thought.

"You know I'd never do that. I took your clothes off because you were sweating."

How did I not feel him undressing me? Even if I was sweating, why would he take off my underwear? Why is the bed not wet if I was sweating that much? Warning lights are blaring in my head and all sorts of worst-case scenarios are playing out. I cover myself with the sheet and ask him to pass my clothes.

"How far along are you?" he asks, handing me my bra.

"What do you mean?" I look up at him.

"You're pregnant." He clasps my hand and my heart drops to my stomach.

"Why didn't you tell me we were having a baby? You should have told me the moment you found out. Is that why you wanted us to break up? Were you scared I'd think you were trapping me with a baby? Come on, Lotus, I'd never abandon you and our child."

My eyes widen as he clings to my hand.

"People throw up all the time; it doesn't mean they're pregnant. Even men throw up."

"Yeah right! I knew you were out of character. It must be the hormones. I knew you wouldn't break up with me like that. You'd never do that. You're mine, pretty girl, till death do us part."

The tone he used for that last part gives me chills.

"Umm, can I dress up?"

My heart is thumping in my throat as I pull up my shorts. I struggle with them and end up taking longer than I would have if I was calm. Memories of what happened before I passed out are slowly piecing themselves together, intensifying my fear with each passing second. I need to get out of here now.

I pick up my handbag and grab my phone.

"Where are you going? Stay the night, baby. Let's celebrate." He blocks my way.

"Celebrate what, Dalubuhle?"

"Our baby."

"Please *mann*, it's not yours." Can he be serious!

His smile disappears and a scary flicker fills his eyes. I step back as he steps towards me until I bump into the closet.

"I'm going to ask you questions and you're going to answer truthfully. Can you do that?" He pins my arms to my body.

Not this again! Who is this guy and what has he done with Dalubuhle?

"When did you last sleep with that thug that killed your father? No lies."

"Over two months ago."

"When did you sleep with me?"

"In Joburg."

"Good girl. I asked you if you loved him and you said you didn't. You said you loved me. You hate him, don't you? You hate how he forced you to get tattooed, how he degraded you and how when he was done using you, he dumped you like garbage and continued with life like you didn't exist. Am I right?"

*What is happening?*

"Am I right?" He raises his voice and bangs the closet door near my head so hard, I screw my eyes shut.

"Dalu, please," I whimper.

"Whose baby is it?"

"Let go. You're hurting me."

"You're delusional, Lotus! You want to give my child to a low-life, good-for-nothing scumbag? If you were already pregnant when you came to Joburg, you would have told me. Remember, we agreed on no lies and no secrets?"

"Please stop."

"What do you see in him? Tell me. What is it about that dirty scum of the earth that you can't let go?"

"Dalu..."

"Is it the sex? Is it money? I can give you both if that's what you want."

"Why are you doing this?"

"Who do you love between me and him? Tell me the truth."

"Him. I love Donavan," my mouth betrays me.

His hand closes around my neck and squeezes till I'm gasping for air.

"Wrong answer. Let me ask again. Who do you love between him and me?"

"Da...lu..." I try to claw his hands off my neck.

"You see! I knew it. It's me you love. You're just confused... We need to do better, baby. We're going to be parents for goodness' sake. We must communicate better and stop playing games."

*Can he snap out of it already!*

"I don't want you anywhere near that criminal! Do you hear me? I don't want my child anywhere near that filth."

*What the hell is happening?*

"We'll be alright. I hate it when you cry like this. It hurts me." He pulls me into a hug so tight I can't move.

I want to knee him in the balls but I doubt I can deliver a good enough impact, so I remain frozen, trying to figure out if I'm dreaming. My ex said I bring out the worst in people and I induce psychopaths. He blamed me for everything he did to me. I don't know if I did this to Dalu but I won't stay long enough to find out how this one ends.

He pulls away a little. "What do you want for dinner? We should order in, and you know, talk. We really need to talk."

"I have to go home," I whisper.

He looks at me as if I'm being unreasonable. "You're not going anywhere. I'm ordering us food."

How is he managing to appear this normal while acting so deranged? It's like a totally different person is in front of me. I have to get out of here before it gets worse. Maybe I can act equally deranged, knock him unconscious and run away. I would do exactly that if I wasn't so terrified.

He lets me go and pulls out his phone to order food, I guess. I dash for the door, leaving my handbag on the floor. His hand closes on mine when I reach for the handle, and he twists it so hard, I'm afraid it will snap.

"Let go! Help!"

The speed at which his hand covers my mouth is as if he was anticipating my scream. I bite his hand and kick him, but before I can break away, he pushes me so hard, I fall on the floor. He kneels over me, and I watch helplessly as he reaches into his pocket, takes out a small bottle and disperses two tablets into his palm. I want to scream for help but I'm afraid he'll silence me if I do, maybe permanently.

"I hoped it wouldn't get to this, but you're acting crazy."

I try to fight him but he shoves the pills into my mouth and tells me to pick between swallowing them on my own and him pushing his hand down my throat.

"Look what you made me do, pretty girl."

\* \* \* \* \*

I'm buzzed when I wake up. It takes a second for my mind to figure out where I am, and when it eventually does, it works itself into a frenzy. It's 7 am! Was I out all night? What the hell did Dalu do to me?

I tiptoe to the bathroom, armed with a vase, ready to bash Dalu's head in. The shower is wet and there are used towels on the floor. I hate feeling weak and being at the mercy of someone. I swore to myself I would never go through this again.

A blinding pain cuts across my forehead and I drop the vase, sending it splattering into pieces. What the hell did Dalubuhle do to me? Whatever it is, I hope it doesn't harm my child. I would never forgive myself otherwise. I wasn't thrilled when I first saw the two lines on the pregnancy test. It was a big inconvenience at the time. It still is, if I'm being honest. I haven't decided if I'm keeping it or not. I don't think I have the strength to go through pregnancy and then take care of a baby I didn't plan for on my own. I don't have it in me to be a mother. I was supposed to get married and do things right, but here we are. So much for breaking generational curses.

I hold on to the toilet seat and retch, then wash my mouth. I need to get out of this place right away.

There are footsteps outside the door as I leave the bathroom. I look around for a weapon, but there isn't anything in sight that could crack a skull. I arm myself with a boiling kettle and stand ready near the door.

"Room service," a voice says.

I open the door with a shaking hand and find a guy in a uniform holding a tray in his hands.

"Good morning, ma'am. I'm sorry for disturbing you. Your husband said we should deliver your breakfast."

"My husband?"

"Yes, ma'am. He ordered breakfast to be delivered at 7:15 am. I'm sorry I'm late, there was a delay in the kitchen."

Exactly how unhinged is Dalubuhle?

"Ma'am, are you alright? Is that blood on your wrist?"

Bloody hell! Dalu used something red to 'erase' the tattoo of Don's name. What else did he do to me? I feel sick just going through the possibilities.

"Oh, this? It's nothing. Just a bad henna job." I put my hand behind my back. "So where is my husband now?"

"I'm not sure, ma'am. He left with two bags."

I thank him and take the tray, balancing it with the boiling kettle. When I set it down on the table, I see a note with my name on it.

*'My love,*
*I have an 8 am flight. I didn't want to wake you and our baby up. Thanks for coming over. I love you.'*

Good Lord! I don't know what game this guy is playing but I need it to stop. I'm feeling sick again but I'll have to manage. I rush out as if I stole something and I'm glad no one stops me. I'm sure Dalu is watching me right now and enjoying his sick game. I want to go to the police station and open a case, but knowing the police, they will probably laugh at me.

I have missed calls from my mother and an unknown number. I open WhatsApp and find messages from Dalu.

*'One day you'll look back and thank me for doing this for you and our child. I'm saving you from yourself. You look beautiful when you're sleeping, by the way.'*

*'You're not going to tell Donavan about us. You're going to stay away from him like you promised. You may think this is to hurt you, but trust me, it's to protect us. I'm doing what a man you deserve should do.'*

*'If you tell Donavan anything, or if you disrespect me by going back to him, I'll send him these.'*

I sink down towards the dirty pavement. He took selfies of me and him in bed, stark naked. His one hand is groping me so ungracefully, it's making me sick. I feel so violated. I can't shake the feeling that he did worse to me while I was out. Others are pictures we took at his parents' place. We were kissing in one and he had his hands on my ass in another. There are two videos as well. One is a full tour of my naked body. In the other, I'm in a tiny bikini twerking on him in the shallow end of the pool. Midway, I turn around and kiss him before he lifts me and carries me out of the water. It's the Roland situation all over again, without Chelsea to hold my hand this time. I want to scream down the walls of the earth! People are passing by and looking at me, but my mind is so far from here, I couldn't care less.

*Breathe, Lotus, breathe.*

My phone vibrates and an unknown number flashes on my screen. I feel cold inside. For my sanity, I won't answer it. I hold my bag so tight, my nails are digging into it. I'm struggling to remain composed. I can't hitchhike in this state, I have to get an Uber.

I finally find one willing to take me home. I don't argue when the driver says he wants R2000 and won't be running the ride on the App.

We stop at a fuel station so I can withdraw money from the ATM.

It's a long way home and the driver won't stop complaining about the bumps and potholes. It's like he's accusing me of digging holes on the road in my spare time. I fidget with the hem of my blouse, blatantly ignoring the driver's attempt at conversation. When what happened yesterday starts replaying in my head in slow motion, I clench my fist and shake my head vigorously. I must look like I'm having an ancestral visitation.

"Are you alright?" the driver asks.

I don't respond, not trusting the scream I'm suppressing not to burst out if I open my mouth.

It takes every last bit of strength to thank him when he drops me off around the corner, although he should be thanking me because I'm sure he makes R2000 in a month.

I force a relaxed face and greet two ladies from my street, trying my best to act like everything is normal. I walk faster after passing them to avoid meeting more people. I feel like someone is following me. I wish I could run the rest of the way but I can't afford to draw attention to myself. I should have let the Uber drop me off in front of the house.

I find the keys under the brick where we usually leave them. I let out a heavy sigh of relief when the door closes behind me and lean against the inside of the door, still trying to get it together. Paranoia jumps at me again and I quickly lock the door and make sure all the windows are closed. Middle finger to Dalubuhle Mthethwa for messing me up like this.

I'm glad there is no one at home. I need to be alone so I can process everything and get myself together without an audience. My grandmother must be in church and my mother is probably in a tavern somewhere downing her third beer. I can finally drop the guard. I'm so dumb! Memories of Roland flood my brain without warning and I slide down until I'm sitting on the floor with my face on my knees. So much is happening all at once, I feel like I'm going to explode. Regret, uncertainty, fear, anger, hurt - they are all torturing me. I rock myself back and forth, hugging my knees, trying to calm myself with positive affirmations.

My grandmother will be home soon. She will be mad that I slept out yesterday. I just hope she doesn't throw me out as she sometimes threatens to. I'm out of strikes with her; another stress I need to digest. I went from being in her black book to her good books, right back to her black book.

Eventually, I manage to stumble to my feet, still feeling a bit dazed. My head is pounding from the side effects of whatever Dalu roofied me with. Not knowing what exactly he did to me, or what I said, is driving me nuts.

I drag myself to the bathroom and fill a bucket with cold water. I'm trying to convince myself that it's not that bad, but I know those pictures would end me. I've been through this before and I don't know if I can survive it this time. I feel dirty; I need to scrub that psycho off me. Thankfully, my tattoo is unharmed, but my wrist is inflamed and itchy from whatever he used to 'erase' Don's name.

Why do all my relationships end in such deep regret?

My skin is barely-dry but I put on pyjamas anyway. Care is something I don't have at the moment. I don't have an appetite but I need to eat before trying to sleep. I haven't eaten since yesterday. If it wasn't for the life in my stomach, I would go on a hunger strike. I ransack the kitchen and end up settling for a bowl of cereal because everything else requires cooking, which I don't have the energy for.

I sit back on the couch, staring blankly at the TV screen, hardly hearing what the news anchor is saying. I'm absentmindedly picking at the muesli drowning in milk, already regretting my choice of cereal. In my defence, there was no yoghurt. I'm startled by a loud noise outside the window and I almost drop the bowl in my lap. Splashes of milk land on my pyjamas and on the couch. I listen for any other sounds. After a few moments of silence, I put the bowl aside. I can't live like this. I'm probably imagining things but that doesn't make it less torturous. Even the shadows in this room seem darker than usual.

Fuck you, Dalubuhle Mthethwa!

# *SEVEN*

My grandmother didn't yell when she came home from church on Sunday. She just said I was on my own and she had nothing left to say to me. I tried apologising but she started singing and continued with her chores like I didn't exist. My mother wasn't thrilled either but she helped me because I was sick. Whatever Dalu poisoned me with really messed up my system.

My mother went with me to the clinic, and the nurse said it's normal for pregnant women to feel sick. I wanted to tell her my situation wasn't normal but I didn't know how to with my mother sitting right there. I asked if she could draw blood and test for everything and she said they don't do that there.

"Is it Madonna's or Dalu's?" my mother asked when we left the clinic. "Don's."

She couldn't hide her disappointment, but thankfully she kept her words to herself. She's rooting for Dalu; I don't know how to tell her what a monster he is.

"Have you decided what you want to do with it?"

"Not yet."

"Decide fast before it's too late. Don't pin your hopes on adoption; it's a difficult process. I don't think you have the strength to go through it. And don't you dare think of leaving your child at home and running off!"

I found it interesting that me raising my child was not an option she considered.

I have nightmares about what happened in that hotel room but I have no one to talk to. It's driving me into a dark hole. I can't text Chelsea about it; it's not something to casually text someone who doesn't talk to you. I don't know what Dalu drugged me with. I can't rest until I know exactly how much damage was done. I have a doctor's appointment in Port Elizabeth tomorrow and I'm not looking forward to the journey there. I have no option though because I need to know if the baby is fine in case I decide to keep it.

I make an omelette and a cup of tea. It feels good to finally sit down. I've been on my feet all morning. I switch to the Cape Town news channel. It's the usual - court cases, road accidents, weather and sports. I keep drinking my tea, scrolling through Instagram and occasionally looking at the screen.

The news anchor's voice catches my attention when it says, *"Breaking news: Cape Town gang war continues."*

I put the cup down and increase the volume.

*"Breaking news coming in from Gordon's Bay.*

*A house suspected to belong to one of the leaders of the Wolves gang was raided by a rival gang in the early hours of this morning. The incident is said to have resulted in a violent shootout, leaving residents of the quiet suburb shaken.*

*According to the latest reports, two fatalities have been reported, and several others were injured.*

*This is the second gang-related incident at this house.*

*The South African Police are currently investigating the incident and will be issuing an official statement later today.*

*The suburb is currently on high alert and residents are advised to remain indoors and report any suspicious activity to the police.*

*We will be bringing you more updates on this developing story at 8 pm."*

My heart sinks to my knees. Just when I thought life couldn't get any worse! Is Don one of the fatalities? They would have mentioned it, wouldn't they? It can't end like this. I need to yell at him one last time for coming back here, giving me hope and taking it away again. I need to slap him and scream at him. I need to kiss him one last time and tell him he was always the one for me. I need to hold him in my arms and tell him that we made a baby.

I scroll through Twitter, searching for any news about the incident. I try all possible keywords and hashtags, but I get nothing. I text Chelsea, begging her to let me know if Don is alright, even if with a thumbs-up emoji. *Seen. Ignored. Yerrr!* I almost smash the TV with my phone.

Why is all this happening to me?

I rush to the bedroom and grab a notebook. As I sit on the bed, pen in hand, tears streaming down my face, I want to scream. It feels like the world is crashing down on me. Everything is going wrong all at once. If it's not Dalu, it's my grandmother, if it's not that, it's my reflection in the mirror calling me stupid, and now it's this. The hope that Don would come to get me kept me alive this past week. If he's dead, I don't know what I'll do. The chaos in my head intensifies and I write faster, in my worst handwriting. I can't find the right words to say goodbye and ask for forgiveness. I wipe my tears with the back of my hand and continue writing. I need my grandmother to know how much she means to me. I know I have been nothing but a disappointment ever since I met Don, but

I love her with all my heart.

I carefully fold the letter and place it next to the brown envelope filled with money. It's the least I can do. I address the money to my mother because there is no anger strong enough to make her say no to money. My grandmother, on the other hand, would probably burn it with incense and put the ashes in an urn so I can join them the day I die.

I change into sweatpants and throw on a jacket before packing my bags. I stash some money in a bag and hide the rest in an old suitcase. I cradle my gun, wishing I'd had it with me in that hotel room. I put it back in the teddy bear and place it next to the duck in my duffel bag. I quickly cram clothes and shoes in my suitcase until it can barely close. I hate that I'm leaving like this. I doubt my grandmother will allow me back after this. It sucks because we were close to rekindling our relationship and getting back on track.

I look around the room, taking in the familiar sights for what could be the last time.

The potholes on the road are making it very difficult to drag my suitcase. I could have packed fewer clothes, but if I end up banished then I might never be able to recover some of my valuables. I'm out of breath by the time I reach the *spaza* shop.

"Yellow bone, are you going somewhere?" the shop owner asks through the window.

*Well, hello to you too!*

"I am."

"Are you going on a holiday? I bet you'll look juicy in a bikini! I can almost see you shaking it in water."

*Eeww!*

"I need your help." I meant to start with small talk but his trashiness didn't take long to surface.

"What can I do for you, gorgeous?"

"Please drive me to town."

He laughs at me like I told a good joke. "And why would I do that? I'm running a business here!"

"I'll give you R500."

He laughs at me again. "R500 is not something I'd close my shop for. Unless you're thinking of other ways to top up." He licks his lips and eyes me with disgusting lust.

"Okay, R1000!"

"No. Try Bra Terra down the road. He might be able to help you."

I hate how people always refuse to help by referring you to someone else. Just say no with your chest!

"Please, I'm begging you. I'm really desperate."

He scoffs and goes back to writing in his ledger.

"Okay, here, it's about R2000, take it." I offer him all the money I have in my handbag, hoping it will be enough to make him change his mind. That's what the Uber driver charged me, so I hope it's the going rate for the greedy.

His eyes widen. Fingers crossed that means he will take me.

"I'm very busy but I suppose I could help you. Give me a minute to lock up."

Once again, the love of money saves the day. I look around as I wait, praying that no one sees me.

He packs my suitcase into the boot and I find my way into the passenger seat with my duffel bag and handbag. The overwhelming scent of the cinnamon air freshener is making me sick, so I roll down the window, but dust gets in, so I'm forced to roll it up again.

We struggle along the bumpy road until we reach the main road, which is also bumpy but wider, allowing us to swerve around the larger holes. He chats to me excitedly and confirms that men really gossip more than women. It stops being okay when he starts asking me questions I know everyone is asking themselves. Too many assumptions have been made about why I came back home. I tell him I needed a break from Cape Town, to take care of my mental health.

"Is that so? Are you depressed because you were fired from work and evicted from your apartment because you couldn't afford rent anymore?"

"What?"

"It's okay, sweetheart. It will pass. It must have been humiliating when the bank repossessed your car. I heard they did it at work, in front of everyone. That must have been embarrassing. But it happens. Next time, don't rely on a man to take care of you. They will leave you high and dry! Just buy a small car, something you can afford. Live within your means and you won't have problems."

*Oh, wow! Is that what everyone thinks?*

"I don't know where you got all that from. It's news to me."

"It's okay. Don't be embarrassed. Cape Town is a jungle. Many young people fall into the trap of living above their means. Just learn your lesson."

I have no words.

"Why do you keep to yourself so much? I never see you with anyone. Why don't people want to be friends with you?"

I check the GPS to see how far we are. If I remain in this car for too long, I might be the only person who makes it out alive. I focus on my phone to distract myself. I need him to leave me alone, but since when do gossip mongers read the room? It's a miracle I don't snap.

He drops me off at the bus station and complains about how much I inconvenienced him. Mxm! He knows he wouldn't have made R2000 in a week! He should be thanking me, just like that Uber driver should have. Ungrateful men worldwide! He doesn't even have the decency to help me with my luggage. We really have the worst crop of men in this generation.

I struggle with my suitcase across the dirt to the ticket office. It's crowded and noisy, with vendors selling all sorts of things, and touts loudly calling out for passengers. I wait impatiently at the back of the slow-moving queue, fighting a war in my head. My duffel bag feels heavier by the minute on my shoulder. When it's finally my turn, I ask for a bus to Cape Town. The earliest one leaves at 3 pm but I'm told it's not as comfortable as the luxury coaches that leave at 8 pm. I couldn't care less about luxury right now. I would ride a cactus to Cape Town if it were the quickest option.

I go around the corner and dig for money in my bag since the *spaza* owner took all the money I had put aside. When I go back to pay, the rank marshal, or queue prefect, or whoever this man keeping 'order' is, rudely tells me to go to the back of the queue. He saw me here; what the hell? I stand my ground and refuse to go to the back. Anyone with a problem should speak up. No one says anything, so I get my ticket. People make me so angry, *yerrr*!

The wait is brutal. Time is crawling across the clock with no care for my anxiety at all. I have paced the entire station, punched the air and spoken to myself to the point of looking crazy, yet it's only 2:20 pm. I resort to sitting in a corner, alternating between willing myself not to cry, calling Don's number that I know doesn't exist and checking if Chelsea responded on Instagram.

At 3 pm, I join the crowd of passengers pushing each other through the door of the bus. Whatever happened to order? I'm pretty sure there is space for everyone, so no need to act so barbaric. Only when I'm on board do I realise the seats don't correspond to what's written on the tickets, so it's first come first served, hence the scramble. I end up somewhere towards the back of the bus, on a broken seat, next to someone smelling like they crawled out of a flooded tavern. I should have waited for 8 pm because this is not it. This is a classic example of '*you get what you paid for*'.

The bus only takes off an hour after its scheduled time. *Ja ne!* It's going to be a long ride. I try to convince myself that it's not too bad and we will be in Cape Town in no time. I'm hoping my headphones will somehow save me from the torture, but the state of the bus tells me I'm lying to myself. It's a nightmare; never mind how slow it's going.

One of the windows near me can't close and the wind is blowing harshly on my neck. I pull up the hood of my jacket and curse out loud. This is so messed up.

Some passengers start complaining about how slow the bus is going and the driver takes offence and floors the accelerator. I hate reckless drivers with a passion. He's going at speeds I don't think are legal for buses, worse on such a windy road. He's overtaking recklessly and swerving around sharp bends. At this rate, it will be my funeral people will be attending, not Don's. The motion is making me sick and I grip my bag hard, trying not to throw up.

The other passengers don't seem to mind. They are laughing and talking as if nothing is wrong. Am I the only one worried about this bus's road unworthiness and its speed? I should have waited for 8 pm!

It gets real when I close my eyes in a sad attempt to summon sleep. My nerves are frayed from all the worrying, my throat feels raw from yelling in my head, my mind is spinning and I'm yelling at Dalubuhle, Donavan, Chelsea, the bus driver and all the passengers for doing nothing - in my head, of course.

The hours drag by and it's getting dark outside. At least the driver has regained sense and we are now moving at an acceptable speed.

We stop at a pit stop and I follow the other passengers out. I'm starving but I only buy water and mouthwash, then force myself to throw up.

I put my headphones back on when the bus kicks off again and eventually doze off.

# *EIGHT*

As I get off the bus in Bellville, it suddenly feels too real. I might have been too impulsive coming here. If Don is dead, what am I going to do? I didn't think that far. I'm mad at him because all this would have been avoided if he had just communicated like an adult. If only he had given me Caleb's and Hilton's numbers so I could call them in times like these. But more than anything, I'm afraid. If he's dead, I don't know what I'll do.

I feel like I haven't been here in years. It was right here that Don told me for the first time that he loved me. I want to replay that moment but I'm so caught up in my feelings, it isn't coming off as a pleasant memory. I can't afford to fall apart and end up trending on Twitter with strangers making all sorts of fucked-up assumptions about why I was crying.

I keep requesting Ubers and they keep cancelling. Why doesn't anyone want to go to the Cape Flats? Don't answer that. Initially, I wanted to go to Gordon's Bay, but after thinking it through, the Cape Flats made better sense. I try Uber again with fingers crossed but still no luck. Bolt, same story. I hate metre taxis, but what choice do I have? I resort to haggling with a taxi driver, and after begging him as if he'll take me there for free, he reluctantly agrees. He charges an exorbitant amount, almost four times what Uber estimated, saying he's risking his life by driving into the heart of a crime zone. Men and robbing me of my money! What a shameless gender.

I take a picture of the number plate and send it to my mother so that if I go missing, the police will have a lead. She's mad at me but at least she's talking to me.

I cringe as the driver tosses my suitcase with zero decorum into a boot full of tools, a blanket and other things that just look smelly. I hop in and immediately roll down the window. It's stuffy and disgusting, but again, what choice do I have but to endure?

The drive is as chaotic as that bus ride, if not worse. The driver is weaving through the back streets of Bellville, hooting and flipping off other drivers, even though he's the one at fault, and recklessly accelerating down narrow streets. He's dodging people and cars, almost hitting a man pushing a trolley, and missing the curb by an inch. I don't understand why he's rushing. It's not like he has clients lined up or something. Speeding like this can only lead to broken limbs and RAF disputes. The thought of getting a lot of money from the Road Accident Fund briefly crosses my mind, but I snap out of it quickly.

"Can you slow down? Are you trying to kill me?"

"My sister, buy your own car if you want to control the steering wheel."

"*Tshini!* I'm a paying client. Drive like you have some sense!"

He mumbles something but he starts driving like a normal person. I wonder what went up his ass that's causing him constipation.

We stop outside a house I know too well. My palms are clammy and I'm taking deep breaths to calm down. Maybe I should have gone to Gordon's Bay, but it seemed like a bad idea, you know, with the recent shooting and all.

"Are you going to get out of my car or what?" the driver says, pulling me out of my thoughts.

Mxm. Such an insufferable stranger.

I pay him after he has removed my suitcase from the boot and he smiles, suddenly cheerful. Money *ne!* Did he think I wouldn't pay?

"Thank you, my sister."

What happened to being rude? But as we have established, money is the cure for all stress.

Thankfully, the gate is unlocked. I struggle with my suitcase until I make it to the door. My heart is drumming so loud, I have to blow air out of my lungs to breathe properly. I hesitate for a moment, my hand poised to knock. I'm scared of what's waiting for me on the other side. I thought I was ready for anything but I didn't think this through at all.

Before I can knock, I hear footsteps on the other side of the door. He must have seen the taxi dropping me off. What's the first thing I should say to him? What if it's not him? What if it's no longer his house? Do I slap him after greeting him or before? What if rivals took over the house? My mind is still racing when the door opens.

A guy eyes me unwelcomingly and greets me dismissively. His ink leaves no doubt that he's a Wolf. He looks familiar. I think I have seen him before, right here in this house and on my birthday. I'm sure he knows me but watch him act like he has never seen me in his life.

"Can I help you?" he says when I don't respond to his greeting.

He's rude but I don't care too much about mannerisms right now. Men I have encountered in the recent past have proven that they are the worst gender ever created.

"Is Donavan around?"

"Who's asking?"

"Duh! Am I invisible?" I've had it with this dimwit.

He scoffs but thankfully doesn't say anything stupid. I was gearing up to take out all my trauma on him.

"Let me go and find out."

"Wait... So he's alive?"

He raises an eyebrow. "Why wouldn't he be?"

"Mxm!"

He goes up the stairs with a lazy spring in his step and I follow him. My nerves are killing me so I won't just stand by the door and wait. I want to punch a hole in the wall. I want to yell, headbutt someone, kick a rock - anything but stand outside. Why am I not excited? I wanted Don to be alive. I prayed for it even. Yet I'm not excited. I'm just so angry! None of the things I have been through would have happened if he had never sent me away in the first place, or if he had come back for me as he promised, or if he had just picked up his damn phone!

I hear Don's voice before I see him, and I run up the rest of the steps.

"Oh, she's here. I'll be outside," Rude Boy says.

I push him aside, ignoring his protest.

"What are you doing here? I thought I made myself clear," Don says. "Donavan!"

"I told you not to come to Cape Town!"

"Well, I came anyway!" I snap, tears pricking at the corners of my eyes. I don't want to cry; it will stop me from properly expressing my anger.

His jaw tightens and he looks at me with no love in his eyes. "You disobeyed me. You shouldn't be here."

"Are you serious right now? I'm here and this is your reaction? What do you mean I disobeyed you? I did what you asked of me! I gave up everything, Don! But what did I get? No messages, no calls, nothing. I got nothing! You could have been dead for all I knew!" I'm in his face and he keeps pulling away.

"I'm not dead. There was no need to be reckless."

"I don't care! I just wanted to see you, to make sure you were okay!" How can he not understand that?

I expected a better welcome; open arms, tears, apologies, kisses, the whole nine yards. I'm not even getting a chance to be relieved that he's alive. Why is he not wrapping his arms around me and kissing me a thousand times? Why is he not crying, tearing up his clothes and rolling in hot ash because of the regret he feels for abandoning me, not once but twice? Why is he not happy to see me? Why is he not apologising and begging me for forgiveness? My voice catches when I try to yell at him some more and I feel my heart breaking into pieces.

"You know what? It's fine! Why am I not surprised? It's just like when you came to Eastern Cape. The joke is on me for thinking this would be different."

He hesitates and I see a flicker of guilt in his eyes. "Okay, fine. I probably should have called you."

*Probably?* I'm the clown of the year.

His phone rings, and when he turns around to answer it, I'm defeated. Maybe this was the closure I didn't know I needed. I should have known that his not reaching out was communication itself. He came, saw me and was done with me, but I was too much in denial to see it.

"Let me get my jacket. We'll talk on the way," he says after hanging up the call.

"On the way?"

"Yes. I'll take you to the bus stop."

It's like a knife drove through my heart. I look at him and words fail me, so I shake my head, turn around and walk away. I should have never come here.

I get to the bottom of the stairs and look around the living room, memories crashing down on me so hard, I can't restrain the tears. I struggle with my suitcase; one of the wheels is broken and it won't move. I push it away and it falls on its side. I screech and kick it hard. Stupid bag!

Of all the possible outcomes, I didn't foresee this one. He doesn't love me anymore. He couldn't even pretend. So why did he go all the way to see me at home? I know he's detached from his emotions but I don't understand why he's so cold.

"Lotus."

"What?!"

He grabs my arm firmly and turns me to face him. "You don't have to leave."

Really? I know he didn't expect me but I'm here now. *'You don't have to leave'* is not good enough.

His eyes keep searching mine and I'm fighting back words. I'm boiling; I'm sure my nostrils are flaring. Fuck him deeply! Fuck him to hell and back!

He opens his mouth to say something but he stops himself.

"What was that?" I fold my arms.

"You caught me at a bad time. Tris is waiting outside. I have to go."

"Where are you off to?"

"Something needs my attention."

He doesn't give me a chance to say anything.

He locks me inside the house. Good, because I might have just left.

I dump myself on the couch and bury my face in my hands. I have a feeling I'll go crazy within the next hour if I don't occupy my thoughts with something else. I wish Chelsea would talk to me; she would cheer me up, and maybe we would go out later or something. I call my mother and I'm surprised when she answers. She keeps her phone on silent when she's at work.

"Did you travel well?"

"I did. I'm at his place now."

"That's good. I don't have much time to talk. I'll call you after work."

I sniff back a sob.

"Are you alright?"

"I'm good." I clear my throat and try to sound okay.

"What's wrong, Lotus?"

"He's shutting me out, Sisi. I shouldn't have come. He doesn't want me here." I fight back the pain in my voice.

"Did he throw you out?"

"Not really. He said I should stay, but it's the way he said it. It's as if he just said it."

" *Yho, amadoda!* Give him some time, he'll come around. How about everyone else? Are they treating you better at least?"

"I haven't seen anyone yet. But you know they go with Don's flow, so I expect a shitty welcome from them as well." I didn't mean to sound so pitiful.

"Oh no. I'm so sorry, my baby. Maybe you should get everyone together and catch up all at once. Host a small dinner or a braai or something. It will be alright, you'll see."

"I don't know."

"Don't worry. He'll come around. Everyone will. If they don't, come back home."

"I really hope so." I'm afraid to go back and face my grandmother.

"They will. I have to go now. Some of us have jobs."

"Thank you, Sisi. I love you so much."

"I love you too. Let's talk after work."

She has no idea how much she made my day. I needed to hear kindness for a change. Now I can go upstairs, take a bath and get some much-needed sleep.

# *NINE*

It's been three days and I have never felt emptier. Don is hardly around, and when he is, he's either sleeping, watching TV or on his phone. The closest thing to affection I have received so far is a quick kiss on the cheek when he got home the night of the day I arrived. He's already leaving and it's not even 7 am yet.

"What are you guys doing tonight?"

"Why?"

"I was thinking of making dinner for you, Hilton, Caleb and you know, anyone else you want to invite."

"I don't think that's a..."

"Please, Don. I need this." I need to reintegrate into our little society, and the sooner the better. I feel so left out. I need to get back to normalcy as soon as possible. Plus, I need to keep busy to stop from going out of my mind.

"Okay fine. Text me all the things you need and I'll have someone drop them off."

"I don't have your number." My throat tightens and I swallow hard.

"Right. I have yours. Let me buzz you and you can text me the list."

He has my number and never once thought to call? Wow! I suppress my emotions and save his number. I'm sure he got it from Chelsea, which means she talks to him but won't talk to me.

"Later." He walks out without looking back.

I feel like shit but I dump myself on the bed and write the basics for a meat-based dinner and send it to him. I stayed awake many nights thinking of reuniting with Don, and now that I'm here, I wish I had never come. It's worse than the last time I saw him. Last time, he just popped in and out, but he held me, kissed me and made me promises. He cared about me. Now I feel like an inconvenience to him.

I head to the bathroom and I look at myself in the mirror as I take my clothes off. I look really good, so why is he not touching me? Is there someone else? I push back the pain that comes forward as I shower. Dalu keeps creeping into my mind. Thoughts of my grandmother's disappointment and how she must have felt when she found out I left, join the party. I do my best to push them back and try to focus on the life growing in my stomach. I can't even tell Don about it. I don't even know if everything is fine in there since I didn't end up going to Port Elizabeth for a doctor's checkup. Maybe I should just get rid of it. I don't see how it will fit in my life.

I dress up and find my way downstairs. There is no wine in the house or I would have opened a bottle. I end up on the couch, scrolling through the channels, not finding anything worth watching. I make an appointment on the Marie Stopes website for an abortion and then settle for an old chick flick. I pull the throw over my legs and cradle a cup of tea. Rooibos with a dash of cinnamon and lemon is the best combination ever discovered.

I must have fallen asleep during the movie because I'm woken up by a loud knock. A documentary is now playing on the screen. I'm not sure whether I should open the door or not. It could be Don's enemies, although I doubt they would knock. The knocking persists until I decide to just open the door.

The rude guy from that day walks past me, looking annoyed, and dumps bags of groceries on the kitchen counter. I wonder what could make a stranger this hostile towards me, but I'm going to be the bigger person and play nice. After all, I'm rebuilding all my relationships from the foundation.

"I don't think we were properly introduced that day. I'm Lotus."

"Cool."

"And what's your name?" Don called him Tris but that sounds more like a pet name than a real name.

"Tristan."

"Nice name. Can I call you Tris or Tri or T?"

"Tristan."

O-kay! "Do you want a beer?" I could use some company, and maybe we can be friends.

"No."

Ouch! "Umm, okay. Do you want to hang out a bit?"

"No."

How rude!

He walks out without saying goodbye and I make a mental note to give him the smallest portion if he shows up this evening. I'm so done with him.

I better start cooking and hope it's true that the way to men's hearts is through their stomachs. I put on Chris Brown and sing along as I chop the vegetables. I'm nervous but I'm going to be optimistic and cross my fingers for the best. I haven't seen these guys in months, and the way things are awkward with Don, I can only imagine what it will be like with all of them around. Well, I saw Hilton back home but he was ice cold, so it doesn't count.

\* \* \* \* \*

I went all out with the food and put beers in the freezer so they can be ice-cold by the time the guys arrive. I really hope they appreciate it. I even made two different desserts to give people an option.

I put on a nice dress and heels, and fix my face and hair to perfection. I know that other family, whose son turned psycho on me, would have appreciated the effort.

Don arrives with Caleb and Hilton, chatting and laughing like the good old days, except for Hilton - his face is blank, like the good old days.

"Welcome! It's good to see you." I put on my best smile.

Caleb hugs me warmly and I'm relieved. At least someone still likes me.

"Welcome back. You look amazing, as always," he says.

I blush and thank him. I haven't received a compliment in a while. Then I turn to Hilton and brace myself.

He looks at me like he doesn't recognise me, his eyes narrowing slightly as if trying to figure out who I am.

"Hilton." I smile at him nervously and open my arms for a hug.

"Lotus," he responds with a clipped tone and no sign of a hug.

He can't even pretend! So why did he come? I didn't expect roses and kisses from him, but I didn't expect him to be this cold either. There was a warmth to his coldness that day he came with Don in Eastern Cape, but it's not there today.

Don steps in to diffuse the tension and it frustrates me how he talks to Hilton and not me. He doesn't even check if I'm alright!

I had planned it out to be a buffet so everyone could dish for themselves, but they went straight to the couch and are not showing any signs of coming to the kitchen. I guess I have to dish up for them.

No one bothers to help as I serve the food.

I finally sit down, next to Don, with my own plate. I don't have an appetite but I don't want them to think I poisoned them. I can feel Hilton's eyes boring into me but I'm ignoring him. I keep hoping someone will include me in the conversation and talk about things I know, or maybe thank me for the food, or tell me how empty Don's life was without me. Anything to reassure me at this moment will be welcome.

"Why are you back?" Hilton asks with a frosty tone.

"Umm." I look at Don for help but I get none, so I ignore the question and focus on my plate.

I can't let Hilton get to me. I know how unkind he can be and I don't want to be reduced to tears in front of everyone. He asks again, and thankfully Caleb chimes in this time, changing the subject to how great the food is. I thank him in my head. Such a lifesaver.

Hilton waits for a gap and he's at it again!

"Why are you back? Why did you show up here uninvited?"

This time I'm saved by a knock on the door. I quickly volunteer to answer it.

Great! It's Tristan. He might as well sit next to Hilton so they can tag team on making me uncomfortable. He gives me a curt nod and lights up when he greets everyone else. I don't understand his attitude. I only interacted with him twice, and it was brief on both times, so I really don't get it. He doesn't know me from a bar of soap to dislike me like this.

He refuses my food but accepts a beer, which he takes from the fridge himself. The way he's so free with everyone but gives me dismissive answers makes it clear he wants nothing to do with me. I can only wonder why, but I'm done trying. I have enough problems to deal with, so he can join the line.

This dinner is a disaster. I thought alcohol would be flowing and we would all be laughing and catching up, but it's just one awkward moment after another.

"At some point you guys need to leave my house. My girl and I have plans," Don says.

At another time, that would have made me blush, but he hasn't paid me any meaningful attention since I came or bothered to include me in anything. So plans could easily mean me sleeping and him being on his phone.

"Of course, we all know you'll choose a woman over your pack any day," Hilton says. "Your world is burning but all you care about is playing happy families with a girl that doesn't respect you. And now we're all forced to be part of the circus."

I did not expect that at all. I know Hilton is not very fond of me but that was harsh. Don's lips tighten and he clenches his fist but he doesn't say anything. I don't know why I even expected him to defend me. Can he grow a backbone already!

Tristan looks amused and I hate him for it. I hate all of them except Caleb.

Hilton stands and pauses, as if he's about to say something, but then decides against it and walks towards the door.

"Alright, Tris, I think we should also go now. Alpha, see you tomorrow. Lotus, thank you for the meal and welcome back." Caleb puts his hands together and bows slightly.

"It's a pleasure. Thank you for coming."

I try to say goodbye to Tristan but he barely acknowledges me and heads out the door. Don walks them out and says he will be back soon. Is he mad at me? What did I do? You know what, screw him!

He finds me washing the dishes. I silently hope he'll join me, or at least talk to me while I finish up. I will even take an apology for his friends' behaviour.

"You'll find me upstairs," he says.

I close my fists and gather my courage.

"Don, can I talk to you for a second?"

He leans against the counter, looking like a distant friend, if anything.

"Did I do something wrong?"

"What do you mean?" He looks genuinely surprised.

"You've been weird towards me since I got back. I know you didn't want me here, but I thought maybe you understood where I was coming from. I don't feel welcome and it gets worse every day. So I think I should go back home. I can't do this anymore."

He looks down as if carefully choosing his words. "I told you I'd come and get you, but you decided to do your own thing. Now I look like I can't control my woman. I don't have time to be babysitting you, Lotus. I have one crisis after another to take care of."

"So my presence is an inconvenience?"

"Something like that," he mutters, avoiding eye contact.

I feel a knot tightening in my stomach. "I see. I understand. In that case, I'll be on my way back home tomorrow." I try to keep my voice steady but I can't mask the hurt.

He stays quiet while I return to the plates, the weight of his words sinking in.

"I didn't expect you to come here, but that doesn't mean I don't want you here. You're here now and I'm cool with that. I just have a lot going on."

I deserve better than that.

"*Skat*, please." He turns me to face him.

"You've been ignoring me and treating me like you don't want me here. You couldn't even stand up for me tonight."

He looks down and I swallow the lump in my throat.

"I'm sorry."

"I'm sure you are."

"I mean it. What can I do to make it better?"

I know what I want to say but I don't want to say it. I don't want to complicate things further.

"I'd like us to spend time together. I'd like to get back to what we were before I left."

"I hear you. I'll try my best."

"Promise?"

"Promise... You're going to hate me but I have to go somewhere. I'll be back tomorrow morning. Please be okay for me."

I'm not fine with it, but what can I do?

"That's alright. I'll see you tomorrow." I try to mask my disappointment with a smile.

He gives me a quick kiss on the cheek, and as he goes upstairs, a familiar loneliness settles in.

# *TEN*

I regret asking Don to take me with him. I thought it would be like the good old days, you know, making out in the woods, eating wings on the bonnet of his car or driving across town to a secluded spot. I did not have this in mind, but you know what, I'm going to suck it up and enjoy it. I need to bond with my man, and if this is what it will take, then so be it.

I asked what I should wear, and he said "anything", which wasn't very helpful, so I settled for comfort. We drive in his red car that I don't particularly like. When I suggested we take my car instead, which was really my way of asking about its whereabouts, he insisted that this was perfect for where we were going because everyone needs to know when he's approaching. How that's a good thing, I don't know. Shouldn't he be laying low considering the situation at hand?

"And my car? Where is it?" I guess I have to ask directly.

"At Elik's house. I'll send someone to get it when Elik comes back. Unless you want me to break in and take it."

I can't tell if he's joking or serious.

"Please don't. I can wait." Although the truth is I can't wait. I need to be mobile and stop being stuck in the house all the time. I had to postpone my appointment at Marie Stopes, so maybe when I get my car, I'll finally go and get it over and done with.

I'm chatty today. We are finally making progress. That talk after the disastrous dinner really helped. It didn't end in strokes and kisses, but at least I bared my heart and clearly he heard me because we are here now.

"You know, I was watching you earlier and I realised how lucky I am that you're mine."

His words catch me off guard, and a blush creeps up my cheeks.

"I've been a bit tied up and there's a lot going on, but I'm glad you're here with me and I'm sorry I haven't shown it. I'll do better from now on."

I think I'm going to cry.

"You look really good, my *skat.*"

Okay, now I'm really going to cry.

He holds my hand when we join the highway and I steal glances at him as he drives. This right here feels like how it's supposed to be.

We drive towards Mitchell's Plain taxi rank and park in a dodgy place, across from a burning pile of litter. There is a thick stench in the air that makes me want to get back into the car, but I'm spending every minute with my man today and no smell is strong enough to stop me.

"And if someone breaks into the car?" It looks very unsafe.

"You think anyone would do that?" He gives me a corny look.

"The truth? Yes!"

"I guess we shall see."

"Okay." I'm learning to let a lot of things go. Asking usually gets me answers I'm not emotionally ready for. Besides, like I said, I'm not going to let anything spoil this day.

The taxi rank is packed with people going every which way, talking loudly. Some of them seem to be in a hurry, while others are taking their time. Some taxis hoot as they speed off and others remain parked so close together, I don't know how they are not bumping into each other. It's so grimy, I'm repulsed. I hate crowds. Being surrounded by too many people makes my skin crawl, that's why Chelsea let me use her car back then. Trains used to make me want to unalive myself. Chelsea - I quickly shake thoughts of her out of my head. Nothing will spoil my day.

We stop near the long rows of taxis and Don pulls me closer, his arm on my shoulder. "People in those two rows owe me three days' worth of money. I need you to collect from the drivers. Each one should give you R1500. I'll handle the rest."

He walks away before I can object. I'm frozen in place, wondering where to begin. This is definitely not my style. I'm about to run after him when he starts roughing up a big guy, holding him up by the collar and pointing a finger so close to his face, it's like he wants to drive it right through his eye. I'm traumatised. It's one thing knowing what he does, it's another seeing it live and direct. I don't like it one bit. Does he expect me to do the same? What if they have guns? We know taxi drivers carry guns.

Deep breath in. Deep breath out. Let me try. "Hello, excuse me," I greet a small group of men, with a small wave and an unsteady smile.

"Where to?" one of them responds.

"Umm, no, I'm not going anywhere. I'm here to talk to you." Courage deserted me the moment they addressed me in Xhosa.

"I'm sorry to disturb you. Don, I mean Alpha, asked me to come and ask you for R1500 each. He said you know what it's for."

"Who?"

"Alpha."

"Who's that?"

"Huh? Him." I point at Don.

"Who is he to you?"

"Ehm, can we focus? He asked me to collect some money from you. Could you please hand it over so I can be on my way."

"*Sies!* The nerve! Coming here all dolled up with blood money. You're disgusting! We work hard to put food on the table for our families and you just come and take it like it's nothing!" The man closest to me shoots me a disdainful glare.

"I'm sorry for offending you. I'm just doing what I was asked."

"*Sies!*" The man spits on the ground and looks at me like I'm scum. I recoil but do my best to fake nonchalance.

"Fine. Here!" He throws an old plastic bag and it lands at my feet.

I bend down and pick it up. They each throw me a plastic bag, deliberately throwing them on the ground. I can tell they hate me, but they are mad at the wrong person. I don't want to be doing this either.

I'm still wondering if I'm expected to count the money when Don approaches and the men look like they are staring at the face of death.

"Are we good?" He stands next to me, his hand resting on my shoulder.

"I think so."

"Good."

"Boss, I think I'm R200 short. I'll do this trip, then I'll bring it to you," the talkative one says with a shaky voice.

I have no idea when Don drew out his Okapi knife. I just find myself catching my breath.

"Baby, wait," I say without thinking, holding his arm to stop him from cutting the man's face for R200.

"He says it's R200 short!"

"It's just R200."

"It's not about the money, it's about the principle."

"I know, my love, but he says he'll bring it."

He folds his knife and I see his gun flash as he puts it away. "Next time, don't make me come for my money because you know I'll leave with more."

The "Yes boss" is perfectly synchronised.

A tinge of guilt washes over me again. I didn't want to witness this side of him. I don't know why he felt the need to expose me to it.

"Let's go. We'll collect in Bellville, Crossroads and Hanover Park, then we'll be done with taxi drivers. Are you hungry?" He walks away without waiting for me.

I have three R100 notes in my pocket, and as I turn away to catch up with Don, I pull them out and drop them on the ground. I look back and nod at the men.

This isn't what I had in mind when I said we should hang out. But since we are here, I might as well enjoy the ride. Bellville is worse than

Mitchell's Plain, but thankfully, it goes quickly. After that earlier ordeal, I'm not getting my hands dirty. I can't go through that again. The words of those men stung.

Crossroads is as buzzing as Bellville. Don fits in effortlessly and the guys seem fond of him. A few call him Alpha and the rest call him Boss. I used to think those who called him Alpha were in his gang and those who called him Boss owed him money or something, but too many people call him 'Boss'. Not everyone can owe him, he's not SARS.

He laughs and jokes with the taxi drivers as he collects his money and I stand at a distance, half on my phone, half watching everything.

"The food is ready. Let's go and eat," he says when he's done with his rounds.

I lock hands with him and walk across the rank. The *food* is three heads of sheep surrounded by spices, all placed on old newspapers. Before I know it, I'm sitting on a dirty pavement, sharing meat with a group of guys. I don't pay any mind to the questionable hygiene of the place and the health hazards of what I'm doing right now. This is an application for food poisoning. I pass on the drink. There is no way in hell I'm sharing one straw with strangers. I would rather choke on dry meat than do that. Some of these mouths look like they kiss ghosts for a living.

I catch Don staring at me. I don't know why he's smiling but it makes me blush.

When I've had my share, my shirt is marred with oil stains and has fingerprints where Don touched me. I ask him to take a picture of me so I can capture this moment.

We say goodbye to everyone and walk hand in hand to the car.

"I thought you had people that do this for you."

"I do. But ever heard the saying *'out of sight, out of mind'*?"

"Oh," is all I can say.

Before we get into the car, I pull him in for a hug. It really has been a beautiful day, and although I'll never do this again, I did enjoy most of it. I have been lost the last few months, and him ignoring me since I came back has been killing me. I hold on to him a while longer, taking in his scent and savouring the strong feel of his arms around me.

"So Hanover Park next?" I ask when we finally let go of each other.

"No. I'll handle it another time. We're done with taxis for today."

That's perfectly fine with me.

We laugh and joke as we drive. He's so silly! He's telling me crazy stories that are unbelievable and I'm laughing my lungs off.

"Aren't we going the wrong direction?" I ask when I see signs for Kaapstad.

"Oh, you don't want wings from your club?"

"What! When did you become so thoughtful?"

"You're my girl. I love seeing you happy." He gives me a beautiful smile before looking back on the road.

I absolutely love this version of him.

I'm glad when someone meets us outside the club with a doggy bag. I didn't want to get out of the car.

He holds my hand on the drive home and I'm completely smitten.

"I missed you," he says.

"Me too. A lot!" This is the happiest I have been in a long time.

I jump into the shower when we get home so I can change into pyjamas and we watch a movie to end the day on a high note. I hum my favourite song as I scrub my body, and dance as the water washes me clean.

He stands to meet me when I walk into the bedroom. The towel falls and his hands run down my back until they rest on my bum. He kisses me so passionately, I feel myself drowning in him. His hands are all over my body, giving me the assurance that I'm still his. He lays me back and kisses his way down until he's in between my legs. As his tongue goes to work, wave after wave of sensation flows through my nerves. He holds me still, artfully eating me up until I erupt all over his face.

He gets out of his clothes and bites his lip, looking down at me. The blue of his eyes, the scars on his face, the hunger in his eyes - I love all of him. He plants wet kisses on my neck as if breathing life into my skin. I close my eyes, grab a handful of sheets and clench as I feel him ready to go in. I need to focus so he doesn't just fall in and think I was having sex the whole time we were apart. I need to be super tight. I'm going to repeat every Kegel exercise I've ever done.

I carefully control his entry and I know I'm doing something right when he gasps. I focus on the right balance between wetness and tightness to build my home. I hold on to him, remembering to moan through it all. He stays at it, struggling to hold back. I gyrate and work him until he loses control and comes undone with a loud groan.

"I love you so much," I find myself saying.

He responds by kissing me and pulling me into a cuddle. "You're perfect, my *skat*."

*That I am!*

# *ELEVEN*

I'm in a good mood today. I cleaned the whole house, cooked up a storm, baked a cake and binged on my favourite show. Sometimes I wish I was a reality show star. It feels criminal to look the way I do and live the life I live, and not be on TV. I set the table with rose petals, candles and champagne glasses. Slow music is playing in the background, the lights are dimmed for the ambience, the food is warm and waiting, and I'm wearing lingerie under my coat. I'm pulling all the stops tonight. I even got Don a gift: perfume and a personalised hoodie, and a card written: *'We are pregnant. You are going to be a dad.'*

I hoped Don would be home early but it's getting late now and I'm losing my patience. After yesterday, I have decided to keep the baby. I think it would be good for us. I didn't want to tell him without a ceremony.

Let me call him.

"Are you coming home tonight?"

"Nope. I've got things to do," he says coldly.

"What things?"

"Stuff," he says in an end-of-discussion manner.

"So your stuff is more important than me?"

"See you tomorrow, Lotus." He hangs up with zero regard for my feelings.

All my planning gone to waste! Might as well call it a night. He's blowing hot and cold, I can't keep up. I thought we were good; I don't understand the change in mood. *Stuff,* really? When it comes to his life outside me, it's like there is a thick wall between us. Even when I asked about the Gordon's Bay raid, he brushed it off and changed the subject. It was on the news for crying out loud!

As I grope for sleep after a trip to the bathroom, I hear footsteps coming up the steps. It's way past midnight. Shit! I quickly roll over, grab my gun in the drawer of my bedside pedestal and jump out of bed. I tiptoe to the door and wait. The footsteps seem to have stopped right outside the door. The door opens slowly and someone steps in. It's pretty dark, thanks to the block-out curtains.

"Don't even think of it!" I hold the gun to his head, ready to shoot his brains out.

"*Skat?*" He sounds somewhere between scared and surprised.

"Shit, Donavan! I could have killed you! What happened to calling?"

If I got a Rand for every sigh of relief I let out, I would be a millionaire by now.

"It's late and I have keys." He switches on the light. "Put that thing away before someone gets hurt."

"I thought it was an intruder... What happened? Are you hurt?" I put the gun on the bed and attend to him.

"Hilton was shot."

"Oh no. Is he dead?"

"Not really."

I won't ask what 'not really' means in this context. It's a yes or no question.

"He took the hit for me. I've been letting things slide for too long. It's time to put an end to it."

I've heard that tone before and I know heads are about to roll. I want to hold him but he's soaked in blood.

"Let's get this off you."

I lead him to the bathroom. I take my time washing the blood off his skin, listening to the sound of water steadily falling from the shower. We don't exchange a single word as I clean him up.

I let him step out of the shower first because I have demons to face on my own. I wash myself, fighting back emotions. Tonight was supposed to be special. I was beginning to think the war was over and that maybe I had exaggerated the whole thing in my head. Everything seemed normal when we went to the taxi ranks and to Longstreet. There were no signs of chaos, and I haven't heard gunshots since I got back.

I find him resting his forehead on the wall, water dripping from his body onto the floor. I hand him a towel and he roughly dries himself. We are hardly speaking; it's just body language and passing things to each other.

He sits on the edge of the bed and I kneel behind him, massaging his shoulders.

"Hilton can come and stay with us. I'll take care of him." I have a self-awarded degree in nursing and bullet wounds are my speciality.

"You hate Hilton."

"I don't hate Hilton!" *Hilton hates me.* There's a difference.

He looks back at me suspiciously. "Are you serious?"

"Yes."

He reaches back, his hand finding mine on his shoulder. "What would I be without you?"

"Miserable, sad and maybe dead?" I trace a scar on his face. I usually find myself doing that. Sometimes he lets me, sometimes he takes my finger away.

"Are you really cool with Hilton crashing with us?"

"Of course!" I'm determined to mend fences and to earn brownie points.

Silence returns and I go back to kneading the knots on his shoulders.

"I need to tell you something. Swear on your life you won't do anything about what I'm about to tell you. I shouldn't be telling you this."

I'm not sure I want to hear whatever he has to say but I make the promise anyway. He's letting me back in and I won't pass at this first chance.

"Promise we won't discuss it further and you won't overreact. Promise you won't breathe a word to anyone this time. Give me your word."

"I promise. You have my word." I'm hating this more by the second.

"We don't have a General."

"I know that. Your father will be the next General." I think that was the plan. He doesn't tell me their business anymore, so maybe things have changed.

"We can't have two Generals."

"I'm not following."

"The General didn't die."

His words hit me like a ton of bricks. "Are you telling me that my father is alive?"

"Yes."

"You knew this whole time but you didn't say anything? How, Don? Why?"

"I knew you would overreact."

Wow! I'm so pissed, I could punch a hole in his back.

"But the news said he was dead. You told me he was dead!"

"Me? I didn't say that. Did I?"

His casualness is driving me crazy.

"Get out!"

"What?" He looks at me vividly surprised.

"I said get out!"

"What do you mean?" He returns to being calm. "Where should I go? It's my house."

I let out a bitter laugh, laughing at myself really. I'm so stupid.

"Don't tell anyone. You gave me your word."

Is that all he's worried about? That I'll run my mouth?

"I'm going to sleep," he says so calmly it further breaks me.

How can he expect me to just be fine after dropping such a bomb?

I storm out of the room and collapse on the floor in the next bedroom. I cradle a pillow with trembling hands. He knew my father was alive all this time and he chose to keep it from me. He knew what it meant to me and how gutted I was when I found out who he was and thought he was dead. How could he do this to me? I had finally made peace with his absence. I had accepted that he died without ever loving me, and I'd acknowledged my role in his death.

For years, I built walls around my heart to shield myself from the pain of his absence, but now Don has opened the wound. He knew how much being ignored and feeling unworthy, just like my father made me feel all my life, affected me. Yet after sending me to Eastern Cape, he did exactly that. He abandoned me and left me grovelling, talking to his voicemail day after day. I took the first bus out when I thought something had happened to him, hurting my grandmother in the process, because I cared that much for him. Yet even then I wasn't worthy of his apology or even an explanation.

It hurts so bad, my chest feels like it's burning. It's like every bit of pain I've ever felt in my life is crashing over me in waves. All the things Dalu did to me, some of which I will never know, and everything Roland put me through, flood my mind all at once. I bury my face in the pillow and scream until my throat hurts. How was I so naive to think Don would ever love me fully when my own father couldn't?

It was in high school that I decided I was going to find my father. I was tired of my mother failing to parent me, and the curiosity of my roots got the better of me. I wrote to *Khumbul'ekhaya*, pleading with them to help me find my father, but they never wrote back. Maybe they didn't receive my letter, or my case was not good enough, I don't know.

After my first heartbreak, I confronted my mother again, demanding to know who my father was and where I could find him. That fight turned ugly and nasty things were said, some of which never left my heart because I believe my mother meant every word. She never really loved me; I always had to force things and she learnt to tolerate me as the years went by. I needed my father to explain to me why boys behaved the way they did. I just needed someone to love me unconditionally. I wanted the relationship my then best friend had with her father. I envied how he would come and watch her play sports, cheer her on, lift her up on prize-giving day and kiss her on the forehead when he picked her up after school, which was every day. On weekends, they sometimes went to the car wash, just the two of them, and I will never forget how much her face lit up every time she spoke about him. He protected her and loved her.

Then Chelsea came along and I admired how her father doted on her. How she laughed on the phone with him, and all the pictures of him at all her milestones, all the way from her birth. He always showed up for her. I needed that. I craved that. I had no idea what it felt like.

Then I almost had it, but impulsive decisions and recklessness led to my father being shot. It hurt deeply when I realised what we had done. I knew what a terrible person he was, but I couldn't stop wondering if he might have loved me anyway. It hurt so much more because I couldn't openly grieve him. I had no one to turn to. Even Don left me then.

The door creaks open and I close my eyes.

"*Skat.*"

I remain still as he lifts me into bed. He gets in next to me and spoons me. My sobs resume, spreading through my body like an earthquake, each convulsion rattling me to my core. He pulls me closer and wraps his arms tightly around me.

"I'm sorry, my angel."

# *TWELVE*

I wake up alone in bed. Confusion creeps in when I realise I'm not in our bed, then my thoughts assemble and an ache settles into my chest. I close my eyes and affirm myself.

*I'm strong. I'm beautiful. I'm sexy. I'm the prize. Positive vibes only.*

I repeat the mantra until I feel better and then I drag myself out of bed. I shuffle to the master bedroom and Don is not there. I check my phone, hoping for a message from him, but there is nothing. I try calling but it goes straight to voicemail. I have a missed call from my mother but I won't call back now. I need to get into a better headspace before I can talk to her.

My gun is on my bedside table, and for a split second, I imagine pulling the trigger and the bullet finding its mark on Don's forehead. I dismiss the disturbing thought and put the gun away. I take a deep breath and recite out loud, "I'm strong. I'm beautiful. I'm sexy. I'm the prize. Positive vibes only".

I make the bed and fluff the pillows, then pick up Don's clothes from the floor and tidy up the room. I wish there was a TV and fridge in here so I wouldn't have to walk down the stairs. I'm doing my best to keep my head up and not dwell too much on the voices in my head.

I switch on the TV on my way to the kitchen to make a cup of coffee. I need to eat something, but caffeine will kickstart my system and give me the strength to toss an egg.

I shriek when I see a figure standing next to the staircase.

"What the hell?! What are you doing here? How did you get in?"

"Relax, will you?" He walks towards me.

"What the actual fuck!"

"I need to talk to you."

"About? What could be so important that it warranted breaking and entering?"

"Dalubuhle."

"What?" My heart stops and I instantly go into defence mode.

"He's planning to tell Alpha about you."

"What about?" My hands fold into fists at my sides.

"Stop it, it's not cute. I'm doing you a favour by telling you this, so don't act dumb with me. I don't owe you shit, and I don't have to be sticking out my neck for you like this, so pull yourself together."

My insides are twisting. At this rate, I'll go into labour in three months. It's as if the whole world is conspiring against me.

"Why are you telling me this? What do you want from me?"

"What could I possibly want from you, Lotus?" he says condescendingly. "I'm going to ask the questions and you're going to answer truthfully. That or I tell Alpha myself about your little rendezvous. Is that clear?"

I scoff and cross my arms on my chest, trying to mask my fear with defiance. "Whatever!"

"Did you sleep with Dalu?"

I did not expect that question! "That's none of your business."

"It is if it affects my life. So I'll ask again. Did you sleep with him?"

"How does it affect you?"

"I'll ask one last time. Did you sleep with Dalu? Yes or no?" He steps closer as if to search my eyes for the truth.

"If you must know, no, I did not." I try to keep my voice steady.

"Is the child you're carrying Alpha's or Dalu's?"

Good Lord! Don doesn't even know I'm pregnant yet it's already public knowledge! I can feel a migraine building up.

"How did you know?"

"Answer the question."

"It's Don's."

"I hope you're not lying this time because your first answer was a lie. I know you fucked Dalu."

"How do you..."

He hardens his expression and I stop mid-sentence. "Just get your shit together and stop dragging all of us into your mess."

He searches my eyes again and I want to recoil.

"I won't tell Alpha but I'll need something from you in exchange."

"What do you want?" I will do anything.

"Two things actually. One, you don't tell a soul about this conversation or mention to anyone that I know your dirt. Two, I'll collect in the near future and you'll deliver without questions."

I nod.

"Good. I knew you'd see things my way. Now that that's out of the way, I need you to go and pack your bags. We're leaving."

"Sorry, what?"

"I need to take you to the other house."

"You want to take me to Gordon's Bay?"

"Are you always this slow or is it just today? Go pack a bag. Alpha's orders."

"He didn't tell me anything about that."

His eyes narrow as if I'm frustrating him or annoying him, or both. "That's not my problem."

"But there was a shooting there. It's not safe."

He shrugs. "If Alpha says it's safe, then it's safe."

"But..."

"But I don't have all day."

He's so unbearable; I can't stand his stinking attitude. I'm just keeping it together because he knows about Dalu, otherwise I would have flipped both my fingers in his face. I haven't recovered from the trauma Don put me through last night, and now this? Where am I supposed to get the strength to deal with everything all at once? I don't want to go to Gordon's Bay but I also don't want to get into it with Tristan right now.

"One last thing," he says.

I stop on the second step, wondering what now.

"There are people who know about you and the General. I suppose that's a piece of information you would like to share with Alpha before he hears it from other sources."

"What General?" I keep my eyes fixed ahead.

"If you're going to be intentionally dumb, then improve your acting skills. Now get your bags, let's go."

Damn it! I thought that was a well-kept secret. And if he doesn't know that I already know and that Don knows everything, then it might not be coming from the Wolves. Don will be so livid! How did he get that information? Could it be whoever told him about Dalu? Is that why he hates me? I'm royally screwed.

I toss a few things into a bag. A part of me wants to lock myself in here and go to sleep, but I'm not about to poke a bear. I struggle with my bag down the stairs. Tristan doesn't give me a hand; he watches me struggle with it all the way to the car. I don't know why he parked so far down the street. There was ample parking outside the house.

"Seatbelt," he says as we drive off.

Duh! Does he think it's my first time in a car?

I don't ask where he's taking me because it doesn't look like he's approaching the highway. Maybe there are shortcuts; I won't ask. I want to ask him about Dalu and what else he knows about me. I also want to ask why he's choosing not to tell Don. I thought they were sworn to loyalty since that's all they preach.

"Does Don know?" I risk it and ask.

"Would I have said I won't tell him if he already knew?"

I curse him in my head and turn my attention to my phone.

He pulls over in front of a house in a neighbourhood I don't recognise.

"Go to that car. He'll take you."

"Who is he?"

He looks at me and scoffs before getting out of the car. What a jerk!

I'm relieved when *he* turns out to be Caleb. He smiles at me and I almost walk into his arms. He's the only person who's nice to me lately. He gives me a pat on the back before turning to Tristan.

"Why did you bring her here?"

Tristan shrugs as he did to me earlier. "Just following orders. Alpha said I should pick her up and drop her off, but since you're going to meet him, I figured you could take her. He thinks she's better off in Gordon's Bay."

"And you agree with him?"

"Honestly, I don't know and I don't care. I do what I'm told, that's all."

"Why didn't you tell me you were bringing her?"

"I told you to wait, you waited. You're going to Alpha, so take her with you. Why do you like complicating things?"

He walks back to his car without waiting for Caleb to say more.

"Is he always so rude?" I ask, getting into the passenger seat.

"Most times, yes."

"That's messed up. He's so mean!"

"He can be like that sometimes. He's just not good at sugarcoating things. But he's not a bad guy. He's just direct, you know, a lot like Hilton." He laughs at that last part.

"But why is he mean to me? I've never done anything to him."

"If it's any consolation, he's like that with a lot of people, so don't take it personally."

It's hard not to take it personally.

I'm happier driving with Caleb. It was going to be a very long drive with that demon. The fact that he's so volatile while holding my deepest secrets is terrifying. I wish I could talk to someone about everything going on, but with Chelsea gone, I have no one. All the people I can remotely trust are Don's friends, so there are lines I can't cross before things backfire. I guess I could talk to my mother, but I don't want her to panic and tell me to come back home.

"So, how do you know Tristan?" I try to redirect my thoughts.

"He's a Wolf. Isn't that obvious?" Caleb glances at me.

"No, silly. Of course he's a Wolf. I just thought you knew each other beyond that because of how familiar he is with you. Plus he seems to be around you and Don all the time now. Is he Don's protégé or something?"

He looks at me and then back on the road. "He's my little brother."

"No way! Really?" I would have never guessed. But now that he mentions it, I see the resemblance.

"How come you've never introduced him to me? How come he wasn't around much before?"

"I don't know. Maybe the opportunity never presented itself."

Fair enough but I sense that there is more to the story, so I probe. "I was around you guys a lot before I left. Where were you hiding him?"

"He's more available now because he has time. He went back to UCT for an MBA. We need more hands on deck, so he's helping out where he can."

UCT, as in the University of Cape Town? That's where Dalu studied! Am I overthinking things?

"Did he do his undergrad at UCT?"

"Yes, he did. A few years ago. Why are you so interested in him? Do you have a crush on him? Do you want Alpha to kill my brother?"

"Don't be silly." I make a face. "He has been mean to me since we met, so I was wondering what his deal is."

I wish I could ask more about Tristan but I think it's enough for now. I even wish I could ask about the General but I gave my word.

"Caleb, can I ask you something?"

"Sure, what's up?"

"Why is Don being so distant? He brushes me aside every time I try to be deep with him. Am I missing something?"

He looks at me and back on the road. "He's upset that you didn't trust him. He wanted you to stay away from here, for your own safety."

"But I had to come back. I thought he was dead!"

"I know... But he came to see you, that should have meant something. Give him some time, he'll come around."

"Do you think he'll ever truly forgive me?"

He smiles warmly and gives me a kind glance. "Of course he will... So, I hear you're going to be nursing Hilton."

"Yup." I'm nervous about that but I'm going to do my best. Maybe if I get it right with Hilton, Don will let me in again.

"Good luck with that."

"I'm already traumatised. Is he already in Gordon's Bay?"

"Yes. He's waiting for you," he chuckles.

"I can't wait!" I do not even try to hide the sarcasm in my voice.

"Come on, he's not that bad. I'm sure you'll be fine."

"It's not like I can opt out now. I just have to do my best."

"That's all anyone can ask for. Hilton may not show it but everyone knows he likes you, so you'll be fine."

*Hilton likes me?* I hope I live long enough to see the day.

The house comes into view and nostalgia grips my heart. I remember my first time here. The kids were super excited to see Don and they warmed up to me. We had the best time on that trip out of town. Life was so much simpler then.

Caleb kills the engine and turns to me. "Look, there's nothing Alpha hates more than secrets. So don't keep secrets from him because he always finds out. Start by telling him you're pregnant. Why are you keeping that from him?"

*Damn you, Tristan!*

"I haven't found a good time to tell him. I'd planned to tell him over a romantic dinner but he didn't show up, and when he eventually came home, Hilton had been shot, then we had a big fight and *ja*, I never got the chance."

"Just tell him. You don't need a fancy dinner to do that."

"I will. I guess I'm afraid because he never wanted a child. So I feel bad, you know? I feel like I'm trapping him or something."

I don't tell him how bad the timing is. After what happened last night, I don't want to tell Don. I'm not even sure I want to bring a baby into this world. I don't want to become like my mother and scar the poor child for life. But now that people know about my pregnancy, going through with the abortion will be tricky.

"You're overthinking it. Take it one day at a time and try to understand where he's coming from. A child might actually be what he needs right now. Just tell him."

"I will."

If only all of them were as kind as Caleb, my life would be great. He takes my bag and carries it into the house. Look at that! Chivalry is not dead after all. Tristan can learn a thing or two from his brother.

# *THIRTEEN*

I wake up from a much-needed nap, feeling like I was hit by a truck. My body feels heavy and sluggish as if I have been carrying a weight on my shoulders all day. When Caleb and I got here, Don was in a meeting in his office, so I went straight to bed without even looking around the house. All I wanted to do was curl up and cry, and that's exactly what I did. The whole mess with Don and the General, and Tristan and Dalu is too much for me. Even thinking hurts at this point. It feels like I'm living on borrowed time, and sooner or later, the truth will come out. My hand rests on my stomach and I sigh. Let me just get it over and done with.

I find Don with Caleb and Hilton in the living room. Their laughter abruptly stops when I walk in, making everything suddenly awkward.

"Hi. Can I steal Don for a minute?"

He seems annoyed by my request but he follows me to the bedroom anyway. I don't get it at all. How is he the one who's upset? He's the one who kept the fact that my father is alive from me. What's with the attitude? I'm so over it.

"What's up?" He closes the door behind him.

I really wanted to tell him about the baby but I don't feel like it anymore.

"I want to meet the General."

"Eish, Lotus." He runs his hand over his hair.

"Five minutes with him is all I need."

"That can't happen."

"Please, Don. I need this."

He sighs and sighs again. "Fine. I'll make a plan."

"Really?" I expected more resistance.

He looks at me and I feel myself drowning in his eyes. He looks so good, I want my child to look at me just like this. That is if I don't *fetus deletus* and send it back to sender.

"I shouldn't even have told you, but I thought you deserved to know. Sorry."

Yeah right!

"What exactly are you going to ask the General?"

Oh, have we moved away from feelings already? I thought he'd offer a more genuine apology or some kind of explanation.

"I don't know." I look down and play with my fingers. "I want to ask him why he mistreated my mother. Why he never looked for me. Why I had to grow up the way I did while he was out there living his best life. I guess I want closure."

"I'll take you to him soon, but there are things you must know and promises you must make before I agree to this."

"Okay."

"You won't mention anything about that shooting. As far as he knows, Hilton and I saved him, so he's indebted to us. I'd like to keep it that way. You won't say anything about the Wolves. You're my woman and that's all. Don't mention anything you shouldn't. Ask what you want to know and keep your answers to his questions short."

I can do that.

"But there's something, I don't know, your mother might have lied to you."

"About what?"

"About you and the General. He never knew you existed until he saw a picture of you with me. You look a lot like him, you know, so he says he knew you were his child the first time he saw your picture. He could have killed me that day if he wanted to, but he wanted a relationship with you and he's not stupid. Killing your daughter's boyfriend is not the best introduction in the world. So yeah, he'll tell you the whole story, but someone is not telling the truth and I doubt it's the General."

I remember things differently. He didn't kill Don because the other Wolves stepped in and saved him.

Don really needs to stop dropping bombs on me like this and expecting me not to explode.

"Why wouldn't it be him?" Everything in me is refusing to accept the possibility of my mother lying to me. We have a good relationship now and she is the only one there for me. I don't have friends or anyone anymore. I don't want to lose her; she's all I have left.

"The General is many things but a liar is not one of them. I questioned him under a blood oath and none of us lie under a blood oath."

"Why not?"

"We just don't."

I want to ask what a blood oath is but my head is spinning. I would rather the General be the bad guy. I can live with that. I accepted that a long time ago. I can't accept that my mother lied to me. What would have been the motive? She shouldn't even try to say 'I was protecting you' if any of this is true.

"Don't worry about it. You'll get the answers from him."

I bury my face in my hands and keep shaking my head.

"*Skat?*" He peels my hands off my face.

I take a deep breath and realign myself. "Can we talk about the time I was gone." I run away from what I really want to say.

"Are we back to that?"

"Yes, we are back to that!"

He runs his hand down his face and makes that *not-this-again* expression.

"I did what was best, Lotus."

"Best for who?"

"For everyone. We've been through this. Why are we talking about this again?"

"Because we've never really spoken about it."

"I don't know what you want me to say."

He never really apologised when I came back. He said sorry but he never poured his heart into the apology.

He reaches for my hands but I pull them away.

"You've been shutting me out ever since I got back. I know we agreed that I'd wait for you to come and get me, but I panicked when I saw the news. You didn't reach out after you left, Don. Not even once! You changed your number again! I had to come and find out if you were okay. I was terrified, Donavan! And now I'm here feeling like shit every day because you don't hide how much you don't want me here. Then about the General..." I break down and fail to complete my sentence.

He holds me tightly without saying a word, just keeping me in his arms while I sob. When I calm down, he loosens his grip and looks at me.

"I know I haven't been there for you as much as I should. I was so angry at you for coming to Cape Town, I didn't realise how much you risked for me. I never mean to hurt you, my *skat*, even though I somehow always end up doing so. I'm trying. Please don't give up on me."

I needed to hear that, but now I'm going to cry again.

"I'm miserable, Don. I'm just stressed out all the time. It's a lot, and being pregnant doesn't help. I just wish things could go back to normal."

"Wait, wait, pregnant? What do you mean? Are you pregnant?" His eyes widen in shock.

"I am pregnant." I look down, trying to keep it together.

"You are... Are you..." He stares at me, still processing.

I nod. I know he said I shouldn't take the morning-after pill that last day but he never wanted kids.

"You're pregnant? As in, you're carrying my child?"

I nod again and look at my feet.

"My angel, look at me. Are you saying I'm going to be a father?"

Finally, a bit of excitement!

"Are you really pregnant, Lotus? This is not a bad joke, is it?" He lifts my chin and looks at me, tears forming in his eyes.

"I am. I've wanted to tell you since I came back. I even had a whole dinner planned, but you didn't show up."

"You've been pregnant this whole time? How many months now?"

"Three."

"Why didn't you tell me?"

"You haven't been easy to talk to since I came back, and before that, I couldn't get hold of you on the phone."

I hope that's guilt in his eyes.

He pulls me in, hugging me so tightly he's squeezing air out of my lungs.

"I love you," his voice breaks. "I never thought I could love, but I love you. I want to be with you. As scary as it is, I love you, my *skat*. I want to be a good father to our child."

I can't find the right words, so I just hold on to him, clinging on as if he's the only thing in the world that makes sense.

# *FOURTEEN*

Hilton is driving me crazy. I swear he's doing everything in his power to give me one headache after another. It's like he's playing some twisted game; trying to see how much he can push me before I snap. He's lucky that I'm a Christian, otherwise I would creep into his room at night and throttle him to death. I'm trying my best to take care of him but he makes it so damn hard! One moment he's not talking to me at all, and the next he's being rude and dismissive. See what happens when little boys are not given enough hugs? We end up with guys like Hilton.

How rough was his childhood exactly? I know he had it rough but I'm interested in the details so I can properly psychoanalyse him. Rumour has it that he killed his own father, and not by accident. And now I'm stuck with someone like that. The situations I put myself in!

I know we shouldn't judge people but I'm judging him. He has the darkest tattoos I have ever seen. His wolf has red eyes and it looks alive. On his back, he has a grave, complete with a tombstone and **R.I.P.** Apparently, the grave is the destination of anyone who 'stabs him in the back'. Absurd if you ask me. In what universe does that make sense? He has a coffin over his right breast, and when I asked what it meant, he said "It's to bury you in it" with a blood-chilling tone. He has another of a hand with broken fingers because apparently he prides himself in his ability to break four of a man's fingers with one snap. How twisted is that? I honestly don't think he's all there, if you know what I mean.

Every day, we spend up to twenty minutes of awkwardness together when I wash his wound and change his bandages - never underestimate the power of YouTube. I always talk him through it and I enjoy it when he gets annoyed. At least he's nearing the end of his antibiotics course. He refuses to take pain pills. He says he gets off on pain. I told you he's crazy.

Google said he needs physical exercise to strengthen his arm but the doctor said there will be no need for that because there is no one in the world who exercises their arms more than the Wolves. It took me a day to understand what he meant. Speaking of which, I need to let him know that the doctor will be coming to check on him today. As the resident nurse, I found it fitting to schedule the appointment. He's healing well but you can never be too sure with these things. I'm not taking any chances and risk suffering the consequences of Hilton losing an arm.

"You look pretty. Turn around let me see," Don says when I join him in the kitchen.

I indulge him and laugh when he whistles. Ever since I told him I'd like more compliments, he has been showering me with them. He has been perfect since I told him about the pregnancy. Maybe that should have been the first thing I said when I got back to Cape Town. It might have saved me a lot of stress. My mother still thinks I should go ahead with the abortion, but I think I might just keep it.

I pull out a barstool and he rushes to my side and helps me sit as if I can't manage on my own.

"I've got it, baby. You're always so worried these days," I laugh, even though I'm charmed.

He's sweet, but he's been treating me like I can't do things by myself. I can't imagine what it will be like when I start showing.

"It's, I don't know, I just want everything to be perfect for you and the baby."

"I know, my love. I appreciate it, but I'm fine, I promise."

"Okay... so I was thinking maybe we should go to the doctor again this afternoon."

"*Ha a,* Don. No. We've been to the doctor twice this week already."

I'm not going for a scan three times a week. I agreed to the second visit because it was with a different doctor. I wanted more tests and a second opinion, considering everything that happened with Dalu in Port Elizabeth.

"I know, I know. But I was thinking maybe we should go again. Just to make sure everything is going well."

"We don't need to go to the doctor every day. They said everything is great so everything is great."

"I'm just making sure. I want our baby to be okay, you know?"

"I know you love us, baby. And we love you too. But you need to relax a little. Please trust the doctors."

"Alright, alright, I'll try to chill out. But you have to promise me something," he places a hand on my stomach.

"What?" I look up at him and I bite my lip. I can never get over how beautiful his eyes are.

"Promise you'll let me worry, even if it drives you a little crazy. Please let me worry. I just want both of you to be okay."

"I promise. I love you." I place my hands on his.

"I love you too, my *skat*." He kisses me on the cheek. "I made breakfast. Let's go and eat with Hilton."

"Thanks, baby, but I think I'll eat right here."

"I made you tea as well," he says, like that should change my mind.

He hands me a cup of tea brewed to perfection, and I can't help but melt. Since words of affirmation are not exactly his style, he compensates with acts of service.

"Come, we're eating with Hilton."

"No, baby, I don't want to." I make a puppy face hoping to soften him up.

"We have to eat as a family. Come on."

I roll my eyes.

"I'm going to pick up your car from Elik today. Now can we go and eat?"

"Really?" I get up and throw my arms around him. Finally, I'll get my car!

Eating with Hilton is not something I want to do today but I grab a tray. Dating bullies sucks.

"Good morning, Hilton," I smile at him.

He looks at me then turns to Don and starts talking like I'm invisible. See why I didn't want to eat here? I have no idea what they are talking about. They are speaking Afrikaans slang so I would have to really concentrate to understand what they are saying and I don't have the energy.

When we are all done eating, I collect the empty plates and head to the kitchen. I'll load the dishwasher later. For now, I need to clean Hilton's wound before the doctor arrives.

"Right! Let's see how we're doing today," I walk back into the room with a basin and a clean cloth.

I actually enjoy doing this - changing bandages that is, not spending time with Hilton. It makes me feel useful.

Hilton already has his T-shirt off. His body is perfectly chiselled, like the rest of them. I'm sure sex with him would be a near-death experience. He strikes me as the type that ties you up, then goes in without foreplay and chokes the living daylights out of you while fucking you senseless and saying "What's my name?" What do they call them? Sadists? Christian Greys? Don't ask me why I'm imagining sex with Hilton. I didn't mean me per se.

Don is standing at the corner, the way he usually does when I carry out my nursing duties. They know their medical bill is coming, right? I don't work for free.

"Let me get the scissors. One second."

I'm just outside the door when I hear Hilton say, "How do you handle her? She talks non-stop!"

"She keeps me alive," Don says.

Hilton scoffs and I walk away. I return and carry on from where I left off. I work skilfully until he's all patched up. In hindsight, I shouldn't have bandaged him since the doctor is coming. Oh well.

"Okay, we're done. This is the part where you say thank you, Lotus."

He looks at me like I said something stupid. "Thank you for what?"

"Hilton..." Before I can finish, he starts talking to Don.

My jaw drops. He's allowed to be ungrateful, but I won't tolerate disrespect. I've had it with him!

"Why do you hate me so much?" I stand with my hands on my waist.

"Hate you?" He looks at me with a patronising eye.

"Yes, Hilton. Why do you hate me?"

"Hating you means I have to recognise you, which I don't. What's your name again?"

"Cuz, come on," Don steps in.

I'm glad he did because I was about to slap the ink off his cousin's face with my backhand. I'm doing all I can to help him and this is the thanks I get?

"*Skat*, wait for me outside."

"Stay out of this, Donavan!" I snap.

Shocked doesn't even begin to describe his look.

"Lotus..."

"Actually, please leave. I want to talk to Hilton alone."

He reaches for my arm and I shake him off.

"Now, Donavan. Leave."

He gives me a wide eye, looks at Hilton, then lifts his hands in surrender and walks out. Hilton chuckles and gets up.

"And then? Where are you going?" I block his way, ready to push him back into the chair if I have to.

"What?"

"Did I stutter? Sit down. We're having this talk today. It's long overdue."

He sits down, crossing his good arm over his chest and holding his injured one. I have balls of steel today. Squaring up to Hilton is one of the million ways to die in the Cape.

"I know you don't like me, and that's alright. I don't care about that. But what I won't tolerate anymore is your disrespect. I try with you, Hilton, but you jab at me every chance you get for no reason at all."

"You..."

"I'm not done talking. We have to live together, so there should be some respect between us. Have you considered what this tension between us does to Don? Do you even care? Do you care about anything?"

Blank face. No response.

"I care about you. I asked Don to ask you to stay with us because as much as you scare the shit out of me, I want us to build some sort of relationship. We're family. I'm carrying your blood. You're going to be an uncle. Are you planning on hating my child too?"

I'm shocked that he hasn't walked away yet or shot me in the mouth to shut me up.

"Ok look, you don't have to like me..."

"Who said I don't like you?"

*Did he say he likes me?* That caught me off guard.

"So you love me?"

"Don't push it." His look softens and I feel my anger floating away. He loves me!

"So are we good?"

"We're good."

"Great! See? Talking solves everything. You boys should try it sometime."

Okay, now I'm pushing it for real because I wrap my arms around him, careful not to hurt his arm. He doesn't hug me back but he doesn't push me away either.

"I forgive you," I say with a grin.

I'm sure he doesn't know how to apologise so I'll forgive him for that too.

# *FIFTEEN*

The past week would have been perfect if it wasn't for Dalubuhle sending me texts from different numbers. I have tried ignoring him but the threats keep coming. He's hell-bent on making my life miserable. He's not normal in the head.

I text Chelsea on Instagram and ask her to contact me at her earliest convenience. *Delivered - Seen - Ignored.* That was my last attempt at saying sorry. I don't even remember what I'm apologising for anymore.

A message pops up just as I finish texting Chelsea. Agh, *mann*! Can he stop!

*'Hey, baby. Can I come over?'*

Eye roll.

*'If you switch off your phone today, you'll leave me no option but to tell Donavan how you're working with his rivals. I wonder how he'll react to that.'*

*'What are you talking about?'* I send without thinking it through.

*'You told people that he abused you and branded you with tattoos? Did you not?'*

Good Lord!

*'Dalubuhle, please leave me alone. You know I never said that.'*

*'Do you remember when you told the rivals about the drugs in Gordon's Bay and they raided the Wolves?'*

What is he talking about? I curse the day I met this boy.

*'How about how you told everyone how Donavan murdered your father, the General?'*

*'I didn't tell anyone that!'*

I didn't give him all the details. I just confirmed that Don was in a gang and that my father died, so how does he know all this? I want to pull my hair out.

*'Does he know that you're carrying my child?'*

I wish I could throw my phone across the room. Why is he doing this?

*'If you tell him anything about me, just know that I'll tell him everything. I'll tell him that you're spying for another gang because you want revenge for your father.'*

This can't be happening.

*'You're willing to lie just to punish me?'*

*'Guilty as charged.'*

*'That's too low, even for you.'*

*'Nothing is too low for me, honey child. I don't pretend to be a saint like you.'*

How did I miss the red flags?

*'Whatever, Dalubuhle.'*

*'Good girl. You don't want to test me.'*

*'How do you even know all these things? I didn't tell you all that.'*

*'The recordings I have say otherwise. Have you forgotten everything you told me in Port Elizabeth?'*

Oh, no, fuck! I bury my face in my hands and cringe at the memory. I still don't know what exactly he did to me or what I said.

*'One last thing, why did you lie about the General being dead?'*

I'm done entertaining him. I need to fulfil that promise I made to never suffer at the hands of a man again. I'm over being delusional that he'll get tired at some point and stop. He has shown me who he is and I would be a fool not to believe it. I'm done making excuses for people who abuse me. Remember how I made every excuse in the book for Roland? How did that end? So if Dalu wants to play, then let's play.

I dial the one number I stole from Don's phone for times like this. I probably shouldn't be doing it but I don't have many options at my disposal.

I'm about to hang up when he answers.

"Please don't hang up. It's Lotus. Donavan's Lotus."

"Lotus? Surprise surprise! Is everything alright?"

"Nothing is alright."

"What's wrong?"

"Umm..."

"Look, can I call you back? I need to take this." He hangs up before I can say anything.

Alarm bells go off in my head and I'm praying that he doesn't call Don and ask why I'm calling him. I have been betrayed enough this year. Don made it crystal clear that his friends are out of bounds.

It feels like forever before my phone rings.

"Sorry about that. I was talking to my girl. What's up?"

*Phew!* "No problem. I need your help."

"What can I do for you?"

"It's a lot. I don't know where to start."

"The beginning is usually a good place to start."

I search my head for the right words to present my case without sounding like a liar, a whore, a cheater, or all the above.

"You sound frightened. What's going on? Are you sure you're

alright?"

"Don doesn't know I'm talking to you right now. He should never know. Please promise me that whatever we discuss will stay between us."

"Okay! What is this? Are we planning a surprise party for your man?"

"I wish. I'm in deep shit. I wouldn't bother you if I had a choice, but please, you have to help me. Don is going to kill me." I hope he's not a snitch like Caleb.

"What did you do?" he asks with an accusatory tone.

"Please give me your word that you won't tell anyone." I hope he takes his word as seriously as the Wolves do.

"I'm not promising that I'll be able to help, but shoot, you have my word. I won't tell your man about this phone call, unless of course he holds a gun to my head and threatens to chop off my balls."

Deep sigh. It took a lot of courage for me to make this decision. Who better to understand that I cheated than a serial cheater?

"I accidentally cheated on him."

"You what?"

"It wasn't deliberate. I was just trying to move on."

I can feel him judging me and I want to wither and die.

"You know what? Why don't you come over? I have some time to kill. Some things are better discussed in person."

It's past 2 in the afternoon. Don won't be happy that I went out, but I have to do this. I tell the two Wolves in the living room that their Alpha asked me to bring him something and instructed me to come alone. They are sceptical but I'm not their friend, they shouldn't try me.

I drive in meandering routes, to lose any tails, driving all the way to Milnerton while I'm going to Newlands. I get to Elik's house almost two hours later. He's shocked to see me, as if he didn't know I was coming.

"Last I heard, you'd been banished to the rural areas."

*Banished?* Wow!

"Well, I'm back."

"I see that. I just need one moment and I'll be with you."

It's not like I can refuse although I would prefer he attends to me right away since I'm chasing time. I text Don an '*I love you*' and he responds with a thumbs-up emoji.

I have been waiting in this large room for what feels like an eternity. He said he was taking a quick call. I'm not sure what 'quick' means in his dictionary.

He finally walks in and hands me a box of chocolates, as if that makes up for the time he has wasted.

"Sorry about that. I was talking to my girl."

*Again?* "How is she?"

"She's awesome. Zimbabwe is treating her well but I need her back now. It's empty here without her."

He sits opposite me and I shift in my seat uncomfortably, feeling like I'm being judged.

We catch up and I appreciate how chilled he is. He is so easy going. I almost ask him if he has been with Chelsea since I left but I stop myself. I can't risk ticking him off.

"Thank you for agreeing to assist me at such short notice." I immediately hate how formal I sounded.

"You cheated on Lemon! Are you mad?"

I hang my head. I'm not very proud of it, and I'm not particularly fond of Don being called Lemon. I also don't think I cheated if we're being fair.

"Wine? Prosecco? Beer? What can I get you?"

"Are you trying to get me drunk?"

"No, never! Unlike you, I kind of really love being alive."

"You're not funny... I'll have water, thanks."

He disappears to the kitchen and returns with a bottle of water. "You sounded frightened on the phone. What's going on?"

"Don doesn't know I'm here. He shouldn't know I was ever here."

"He won't hear it from me. Scout's honour."

I explain everything as best I can, telling him how Dalu has been threatening to tell Don about our little affair.

"Yeah, Lemon will kill you for real when he finds out."

"I know that already!"

"So how exactly can I help you?"

"Well, last time Fierce told me that you once hacked into her phone. I need you to hack into Dalubuhle's phone, or get me information on him or something, anything I can use to stop him."

"She told you that?"

"Amongst other things, yes."

"I won't ask what else she said." He laughs as if a joke went through his mind.

I tell him more about my situationship with Dalu and the drugging, stalking and harassment that followed. It feels good to tell someone, even though I might be oversharing and digging my own grave. Some of his questions are invasive but I answer honestly. I feel like he's now just snooping and laughing at my pain.

"Show me the pictures he threatened you with. I want to see if they can be passed off as photoshop."

"You can tell if a picture is photoshopped?"

"Of course. It's not rocket science."

O-kay.

"So, will you show me the pictures?"

"Umm, no, I can't. Like I said, I'm kind of naked in them."

"Put emojis on the essentials. Let me see one. Besides, if they end up on the net, everyone will see them anyway."

Fine, I get it. I need him on my side because I know Don will most likely run to him to validate the images when shit hits the fan.

"There's a video as well. Can a video be photoshopped?"

"You can edit anything. Let me grab my laptop."

I decide to trust him blindly. He's my only hope. I put stars on my privates, airdrop the pictures to him and try to read his expression as he goes through them.

"What information do you need on this guy?"

I'm disappointed that he doesn't comment on my pictures or, you know, go into cardiac arrest because of being overwhelmed by my sex appeal.

"Any dirt on him I can use as leverage. It's not just my pictures hey. He said he has information that could bring down the Wolves. I'm not sure what exactly he has."

"I don't know why but I'd like to see him try. It would be fun to watch." He laughs as if Dalu is a stupid child trying to kill a lion with a sling. He's not taking this as seriously as he should.

"Don't laugh! He wants to frame me for it. I kind of told him some things and he wants to use that to frame me."

He makes me repeat what happened at the hotel, what Dalu said, and his obsession with my baby.

"He sounds sick."

"I know, right! It's scary."

"You created a psycho. You must be good at whatever you do."

He doesn't look at me so he doesn't see the face I made. *'You induce psychos, Lotus. It's all your fault!'* my ex's voice rings in my memory.

"Okay, let's start with the basics. Change your passwords for all your social media accounts and enable two-factor authentication. Actually, first check if there are other devices logged in and then we'll take it from there."

Good heavens! Someone else is logged into my Instagram. Could it be Dalu? That would explain why he knew my every move! He read all my messages to Chelsea. *Yho!* I feel so violated.

"Don't log him out. Start sending false information to Chelsea. Play him."

"Chelsea, huh?"

He blushes and looks away, and quickly changes the subject. "What kind of phone is this boyfriend of yours using?"

"I think it's a Samsung, and he's not my boyfriend, please."

"Perfect."

"Bring your phone, let me install something."

He holds it up and looks at the screen before he draws my pattern and is granted access.

"How did you know my pattern?"

"I'm shocked that people think drawing lines on their phones is a security feature. Try iris recognition, fingerprints or a PIN code at least, so that we can take longer to gain access to your phones."

"So you could hack into a password-protected phone without formatting it?"

"Too easy. You can even put soul recognition and we'll still open it if we want. It's just a device at the end of the day, made by human beings."

Confident or arrogant? I can't decide.

I sit back and wait for what seems like forever and a day.

"Okay, we're all set. Here's what I need you to do. You need to meet up with this guy in a place with public WiFi."

I cringe at the thought of spending time alone with Dalu. If any of Don's people see me, I'm dead on sight. Besides that, I just don't want to be anywhere near that loony.

"See this?" He points to a funny App that he installed on my phone. "Make sure it's running when you meet him. Then find a way to make him connect to the WiFi wherever you are. Be creative. Then have him 'share WiFi' with you by letting you scan the QR code on his phone. Got it?"

I stare at him blankly.

He comes and sits next to me.

"WiFi... Settings... Current network... Share... See? It pulls up the code. He'll have to authenticate it with his lock screen password or whatever he uses, then you scan it and we're in."

I see now.

"So, with your permission of course, I'll have to run your phone on my laptop. So whatever you do on your side, I'll see on my side. As soon as that boy bites the bait, I'll get into his phone. Got it?"

No, but it's okay, he can clone my phone. He can do anything at this point honestly.

"Just stay online no matter what. Have a power bank handy because your battery will drain faster than usual. And for this week only, please don't send nudes to Lemon."

"I don't send nudes anymore." I purse my lips. I never learn. I always send my boyfriends nudes and it never ends well.

"You should. King David saw Bathsheba naked and he married her and made her a queen."

What a narrative! It sounds like something Chelsea would say.

"Thank you so much for this."

"Don't mention it... seriously, don't mention it to anyone!"

"My lips are sealed."

"One last thing, I'm sending you a file right now. It's malware, so don't open it. I need you to forward it to your boyfriend. Maybe send him a couple of files and have it in the attachments as well. As soon as he opens it, it will corrupt his data and make it easily accessible. So when you scan that QR code, my job will be as good as done."

"But won't he know that you're hacking him?"

"No. Everything runs in the background. Just do what I told you and leave the rest to me. And no offence but I don't think he would ever expect you to hack him, so he won't have his guard up."

Offence taken but I'll let it slide.

I don't wish to be Fierce. Can you imagine having a man that can gain access to your phone just like that? The horror!

"So what's your endgame? What do you want done to this guy?" he asks without looking up.

"I don't know. Killed, I guess. I need him gone, preferably permanently. I wish there was another way but it's either his life or mine, and as selfish as it sounds, I choose mine. Think you can help me with that?"

"Oh, hell no! I'm not a hired gun. I don't touch blood. We have your man for that."

Oh, wow!

"For interest's sake, how much would you pay me?"

I only realise it's a trap after I say "R5000". He laughs so hard I want to melt and flow away. That was my entire monthly salary at Dr. Dirk's company! People need to start respecting money.

He's going through my phone on his laptop and I don't really care. What's the worst he can see? He has already seen my body and knows my deepest secrets. We cheaters have to stick together.

"Someone has been keeping tabs on you and monitoring your online activity. Let's fix that for you."

Sheesh! That's unsettling. How did all this happen?

"Right, we're good. Should I send the bill to Lemon?"

"Oh no, please, no. I'll settle it myself."

"Relax, I'm kidding! This one is on the house."

*Phew!* He shouldn't joke like that!

"Can I ask you something?" he says as he walks me out.

"Sure."

"Why did you come back? When I heard you left, I was happy for you. You got out. I thought you would start over far away from here."

"I had to come back... and I'm pregnant."

"Even more reason you should have stayed away, no?"

I'm confused. "And raise a child on my own?"

"That's better than being here. Don't you want better for your child? The world you are in is no place to raise a child, especially now."

I don't know what to say, so I thank him and promise to keep him updated.

*The gloves are off now, Dalubuhle. Let's go all out.*

# SIXTEEN

Today is all about me, myself and I. Since I got back to Cape Town, all I have done is stress. I haven't relaxed or had a peaceful day to myself. It's just been a rollercoaster. I'm going to make a cup of tea and read the Wolves' Creed. I've been obsessed with it lately. It has all the secrets of the Wolves: their history, beliefs and the rules they live by. I stumbled upon a copy while spring cleaning in the Cape Flats one day.

Before I get off my phone, I send a message to Don. *'I love you, Donavan. I'm making dinner tonight. Please be home early.'*

I'm not expecting a response; I just needed to somehow let him know that I'm no longer mad at him. We had a fight before he left. He disappeared for two days and my poor heart couldn't take it. I kept thinking the worst. Then he showed up casually in the morning like nothing happened. I wasn't having it, so we got into an argument and he did what he does best - took off. His phone has been off ever since. I have no idea where he is, what he's doing or who he's doing it with. I'm learning the subtle art of not giving a fuck.

My phone chimes and I reach for it.

*'Sorry, Lotus. I missed your call this morning. What's up?'*

Let me call her again. Texting takes longer than necessary to get information.

"Hey, Zoe."

"Hey, Lotus."

"It's been a minute!"

"Life happens to the best of us. I saw your missed call. What's up?"

"It's Dalu. Have you heard from him?"

"Umm, yes, he's here at home. Why?"

"I haven't heard from him and I was worried. The last time I saw him, he umm, he hurt me really bad."

"What happened?"

"He drugged me, beat me up and left me in a hotel. He has been stalking me ever since. I just need him to leave me alone." I hope she will talk to her psychopath brother.

"Not again! I had no idea it had gotten that bad. I'll speak to him."

"Not again? What do you mean?"

"Can we switch to video?"

"Sure."

She's by the poolside, wearing a cute bikini. As I come into frame, she sits up on the lounger and takes off her shades.

"Oh, there you are! I needed to say this to your face."

"Huh?"

"You know, Lotus, my brother made it through the worst. After years of pain, he had finally healed. Then he met you. He wanted to give you the world, the moon, the stars, the whole Milky Way, Lotus! He wanted to make you happy, and he was ready to let everything go and build a future with you. Then you left him for another guy. Do you know what that does to someone's ego? You obliterated him! You sent him right back to square one. Do you know that we found him just in time and rushed him to the hospital? When he came out, he wasn't the same. Something was different, and now we know what it was, don't we?"

*We do?*

"He found a way to protect himself from the likes of you. To make sure people like you never hurt him again. You hurt him for no reason, Lotus! Then against his better judgement, he took you back, and you finished him off. I was against it but I gave you a second chance and hid the truth from our parents. I was actually rooting for you and standing up for you. I thought you had changed. I don't know if you ever loved my brother, but I promise if anything happens to him, I'll never forgive you."

"Wow, Zoe..."

Did she hang up on me? That went south unexpectedly. What was all that? Did she not hear the part where her brother was the abuser? I feel a familiar ache in my chest and I look out into the ocean. A part of me wonders if I'm somehow responsible for what Dalu did to me. Maybe I provoked him. Maybe I deserved what he did to me. Maybe if I had just left him alone. Maybe if I hadn't gone to Port Elizabeth. Maybe this is my karma. I hate that I'm here again. After Roland, I swore never to go through this again. It took a long time to feel remotely well.

Maybe it's something in my bloodline, a curse of some sort, a legacy of suffering passed down through generations. Maybe it's my turn now and I have no choice but to go through it. My grandfather treated my grandmother like shit for years and kicked a baby right out of her stomach in front of my mother. My mother was just a child then, and for years, she watched helplessly as her mother suffered. When she was older, my grandmother tried her best to repair the damage, but she landed in the arms of my father. He dealt her the same hand my grandfather did my grandmother. He wanted to kill me before I was even born. He threatened to claw me out of my mother's stomach with his bare hands if she didn't abort me. She was just a clueless teenager. She escaped him but he had set a precedent. For years, I watched men treat my mother like she was nothing; talking to her anyhow, beating her up as they pleased, calling her all kinds of names. She brought all sorts of men into her life. One guy even tried to force himself on me. Those were the days I yearned for my father the most. I wanted to find him so I could escape home and live with him. I wanted him to protect me and be kind to me because my mother took out her frustrations on me. For years, I watched her drown in the bottle and hide bruises with makeup. I vowed never to let men treat me that way. I thought I would be the one to break the cycle, but I guess the joke was on me. You can't escape fate.

I wipe a tear running down my face and try to drift to happier memories. My plan to relax is ruined, maybe a nap will help.

I walk into the living room and just great! Can this day get any worse? I don't know why he likes creeping up on me so much.

"I'm not staying long."

"Good to see you too, Tristan."

"Remember when I said I'll collect in future? I'm here to collect." He says it like a crossroad demon coming to collect a soul.

"Not today, please." I look at him, trying to keep the tears at bay.

"It's not negotiable."

"What do you want, Tristan?"

"I need you to get into Dalu's place."

"What?" I almost drop my phone in shock.

"In and out."

"Have you lost your mind? I can't do that!" Breaking into someone's apartment is way beyond my capabilities.

"We leave in ten minutes. Go and change."

"What if he's home?" I protest, even though I know he isn't.

"He's in Joburg." He grabs my hand, places a key in it and walks away before I can ask how he got it or why I have to be the one to break in.

"Ten minutes, Lotus!" he says without looking back.

My anxiety shoots up and panic courses through my veins. After that call with Zoe, I don't need this. I remain rooted to the floor, fighting back all the emotions swirling inside me. He doesn't give me a chance to catch my breath; he stops by the door and turns around.

"By the way, I need to know everything you discussed with Elik."

What the heck! He must be out of his mind! I'm not breaking into anyone's apartment or snitching on myself. He's crazy! He can join Zoe and Dalu on my blocked list. How does he even know about Elik?

I hold onto the couch, trying to steady my shaking hands. He couldn't have chosen a worse day. This can't be my life. I stand up straight and there he is! He's such a pest.

"Let's go," he says, his tone leaving no room for negotiation.

"I told you I'm not doing that."

"Suit yourself. Let me dial Alpha and tell him everything." He pulls out his phone and my heart sinks. How long are people going to hold Dalu over my head?

"I can't do it. Why don't you do it? Isn't breaking into people's houses and committing crimes your area of expertise?"

He raises an eyebrow but remains quiet.

"Ask Caleb or someone else. Don't you have people for such things?"

"Go and dress up. You're wasting time."

His dismissive tone upsets me. The audacity of this guy! I cross my arms and stare at him defiantly.

"Now, Lotus."

I hurl a string of insults at him in my head as I head to the bedroom. So much for not letting men abuse me anymore.

I have watched enough movies for this scene: sweatpants, trainers, a beanie and a hoodie - all black. This is a terrible idea. I won't think this through because I'll get cold feet.

I get into his car and fidget, failing to find a comfortable position. My palms are sweating and I keep wiping them on my sweatpants.

"Can you stop tapping your foot?" he says under his breath.

He starts the car and my stomach tightens into knots. I feel like I'm going to be sick. I try taking deep breaths and digging my nails into the palms of my hands to calm my racing heart. He ignores me and gives me instructions with undertones of threats. Why is he like this? I'm pregnant for Pete's sake! I might not be showing but I'm almost halfway in. It's as if he enjoys making me suffer, and for the life of me, I can't figure out why.

He parks a street from Dalu's apartment block.

"Ready?"

I nod, pulling the hood over my beanie-clad head. He hands me a pair of gloves and I shove them in my pocket. I get out of the car, holding the plastic bag with the wine and chocolates tightly, so I can pretend to be going to see my boyfriend if I'm caught. I look around as I walk, staying alert but trying not to be too obvious. My shoes feel heavy and I feel like someone is watching me.

I stand across the street, pretending to be on my phone while scanning the building. My focus keeps being disturbed by people passing by and the noise of traffic driving past. Every sound seems heightened and I'm trying my best not to be jumpy. The basement gate is open, and by the looks of it, it's not closing anytime soon. Two cars have driven out so far and it didn't move.

I cross the road and pretend to be texting as I enter the basement and approach the staircase. My heart is pounding with each step; I bite my lip to keep my breath in check. The door leading to the apartments is open, held back by a makeshift holder. That's very odd but very much appreciated. I hurry down the passage, keeping my head down until I reach Dalu's door. I breathe a silent sigh of relief when the key turns smoothly and I step into familiarity. It's still as gorgeous as ever. Memories slap me in the face, leaving a bitter taste in my mouth. I quickly pull the gloves from my pocket, urgency pushing aside the flood of memories.

A bottle of whiskey and a glass on the kitchen counter tug at my emotions but I shake off the sentiments. They remind me of the night Dalu hosted Chelsea, Hulk and me here. I leave the plastic bag on the counter and rush to the second bedroom. There is a computer on a desk cluttered with papers, and a dirty coffee mug left unattended on a coaster. I type my name when the screen prompts me for a password as Tristan instructed. Good Lord! What a psycho! Even the wallpaper is a picture of me. What the hell!

*Focus Lotus!*

I transfer a folder on the desktop to the flash drive. He isn't very smart. How can he name it *'Bloody Wolves'*?

I look around the room, my breath catching with each subtle movement, but nothing catches my attention. As the files copy across, I go to the master bedroom. What the actual fuck! When I get over the shock of the large portrait of me on the wall, I get to work. There are documents spread all over the bed. I take pictures of everything. It's mostly pictures of Don with different people. There are financial statements of Club Lotus and SARS files of the several clubs in Longstreet owned by the Wolves. I snap as fast as I can and jump at every sound, real and imagined. There is plenty of proof of tax evasion, money laundering and other crimes against the state. There is enough evidence to build a strong case against the Wolves and have them serving twenty life sentences each. Extortion, torture, racketeering, kidnapping, possession of illegal firearms and all the illegal stuff going on in that Wolves family are documented. This is worse than I thought. I thought he was just stalking me, but this is bigger than me.

There is a blog article alleging that one of the Alphas of the Wolves opened fire a few months back and gunned down three men point-blank but walked scot-free. Apparently, the docket miraculously disappeared and the two witnesses who came forward died unexplainable deaths. One jumped off a building, how original, and the other disappeared without a trace. There is a printout of a list of police officers and soldiers on the Wolves' payroll. No wonder the army didn't win the war. The operation was doomed from the get-go.

I do a quick sweep of the rest of the apartment to make sure I didn't miss anything. I'm about to leave when I see a brown envelope under a stack of books. Inside, there is a picture of Don with Elik and documents about Elik's businesses. This can't be good. I take pictures and put them back.

I head back to the bedroom with the computer, and as I check the screen, I hear footsteps outside. Shit, shit, shit! I grab the flash drive and shove it into my pocket before powering off the computer. There is nowhere to hide here, I need to dash to the other room. I listen for the footsteps again and I don't hear them anymore, but my heart won't stop racing. I yank off the gloves, grab the plastic bag from the counter and roll down the sleeve of my hoodie to open the door.

I can't get out of the building fast enough!

I take a detour to make sure I'm not being followed. I only allow myself a proper breath when I'm satisfied that I have lost any potential tails.

I get into the car, and as soon as the door closes, Tristan drives off.

"What did you get?" He asks when we join the highway.

I hand him the flash drive, my hands still shaking a little. I hope this is the last time I have to do something like this.

"You sure there are no cameras?" The thought of prison makes me weak.

"Everything is off. You're good."

"You sure? I can't afford any of this coming back to haunt me."

"100%."

I hope he's telling the truth.

"I'll airdrop you the pictures... Tristan, do you know how obsessed he is with me?"

"Sort of... I guess we'll find out just how much."

"I can't shake off what I saw. He has a whole portrait of me in his bedroom, my name is his password, and he has all this intel on the Wolves. It's a lot!"

"I know. Don't stress about it. I'll handle it from here. You have nothing to worry about."

This is the first time he has shown me any kindness since I met him. But, also, he could be pretending because I just committed a crime for him.

I find myself looking at him as he drives, and an image of Dalu behind the wheel flashes across my mind. He was always excited and nervous around me, and would make me blush when he called me pretty girl. He would play Chris Brown and sing along with me. A sad feeling washes over me and I look away. Life really comes at you fast.

"You did great," Tristan says as he parks outside the house.

No comment from my end. I just want these pictures to finish airdropping so I can leave.

"What are you planning with Elik?" His eyes shift to meet mine.

"Nothing," I respond flatly.

He adjusts his position, turning his body to face me. "Look, I get that trust isn't exactly our thing, but we have to team up on this. I want Dalu wiped off the map as much as you do. The guy's a menace to my family, and I'll be damned if I don't protect my brothers. Please, Lotus."

I cross my arms and look straight ahead. I don't trust him one bit.

"I'll go through these files and I'll give the flash drive and pictures to Elik to go through. How is that?"

"Do that."

"I will. Now please tell me what you discussed with Elik. You don't have to tell me all the details, just the essentials. Do it for Alpha then, if not for me. Dalu's out there plotting to bring my whole family down. I can't let him win."

I play with my fingers, fighting the voice telling me to trust him.

"I'm giving you my word. I won't betray you." He sounds so sincere, it's almost convincing.

He continues begging until I give in. He gave me his word after all.

When I'm done telling him, a sense of relief washes over me as if a heavy burden has been lifted from my shoulders.

"I can get you close to Dalu. The sooner we move, the better. And if it somehow blows up, I've got your back. So arrange a meeting with him and I'll watch your back."

Whoa! What's with the accent? Since when does he talk like the Dons? What happened to his UCT twang?

"I got you. Just keep your mouth shut and act normal."

"Sure. Can I go now?"

I slam his door and strut to the house. I head straight for the fridge and guzzle juice directly from the bottle. When I'm quenched, I go to the bedroom and dump myself on the bed. This is not the life I signed up for. I take a deep breath, pep-talk myself to keep calm, then set my caller ID to private and dial the last number Dalu messaged me with.

"Hey, D. It's Lotus. Do you have a minute?"

"Hey, sweetheart. For you, I have all day. To what do I owe the pleasure? Do you miss me?" he says cheerfully.

"I was wondering if we could meet in person. I feel like we need to talk face-to-face. You know how things sometimes get lost in translation over the phone."

"You're in luck. I'll be in Cape Town in two days. Let's do brunch at Canal Walk."

"That's perfect."

"Great! I'll make the reservation and send you the details. I can't wait to see you, pretty girl."

I clench my fist. "Me too. Bye."

What a mess!

I kick off my shoes and get under the covers, fully dressed.

# *SEVENTEEN*

I'm late for my meet-up, if I can call it that. Tristan picked me up late. I hope Dalu didn't get upset and leave. We all know how unpredictable he is lately. We are meeting for brunch, but brunch makes it sound affectionate and enjoyable, so let's go with 'meet-up'. I'm trying my best to look calm. I haven't seen Dalu since Port Elizabeth and PTSD has me by the tits.

I have been walking! I just hope I'm not being followed by Don's minions; you know him and his paranoia. He hasn't been home for the past two days but he left me guarded, thankfully by stupid people. They let Tristan leave with me without many questions. This is the first time I'm grateful for Don neglecting me. At least I can focus on fixing my messes without him getting in the way. I keep looking over my shoulder and walking in and out of shops to lose any tails, if any. I'm sure I look like a thief, but who cares?

I finally reach the end of the Mall and I see the restaurant. I text Tristan the number of the entrance closest to it because Dalu most likely parked on this side. My anxiety is rising but I have to keep it together. My life depends on it.

Oh, there he is, with a glass of something on the rocks. We truly are an alcoholic nation. Who drinks at 11 am during the week?

I try my best to push back the trauma. Seeing him is triggering. I had wished to never see his face again, both in real life and in my nightmares. I also keep thinking he knows I broke into his apartment.

"Good to see you. It's been a minute."

"Likewise, sweetheart."

"I'm sorry I'm late. I underestimated the distance. I parked far away and had to walk all the way. These shoes are so uncomfortable, I should have... worn trainers." Flip, I'm blabbering.

I can feel the tension in my shoulders so I take a deep breath, re-organise myself and sit up straight. I'm doing such a terrible job at looking relaxed.

"You never could be on time, so I didn't expect you to be today." He smiles, and flashbacks of Port Elizabeth cross my mind.

"You look pretty."

"Thank you. You don't look bad yourself."

I'm starting to hate this *you look pretty* compliment. It makes me wonder if people actually see beyond my face.

I hold his gaze and feel my heart skip a beat, and not in a nice way. There is a dark glow in his eyes. I need to tread carefully.

The waiter shows up with a rehearsed smile to take my order.

"I'll have freshly squeezed orange juice and a bottle of sparkling water, ice and lemon." I ask for five minutes to decide on food.

"So, how have you been? You've been dodging me," he says.

"Did you leave me an option? It's difficult to want to see someone who threatens you every day."

"Threatens you? Is that how you see it?" He sips on his drink.

"Yes! How would you feel if roles were reversed?"

He shrugs and swirls his drink.

I lean forward so no one can hear our conversation. Only heaven knows why these tables are this close to each other.

"We need to talk, D. Like I said on the phone, we really need to talk."

"I know. Do we have to do it here though? Can't we take it to my place?"

"Here's good... If it goes great then we can take it to your place." I just had to throw in that last part as an incentive for him to behave.

"That's fair I suppose. Does that mean you'll spend the rest of the day at my place? Maybe spend the night?"

"I don't think that's a good idea."

"Why not?"

*Is that a trick question?* "Well, you know..."

"You know you're going to pay for everything, right? Every little thing, you're going to pay, Lotus." He quickly downplays the dangerous tone by signalling the waiter. "Relax, will you? I'm kidding, I'll pay. Order whatever you want." He flashes me a smile and a chill runs down my spine.

I get a chicken salad, and because of my cravings, I ask for pickled gherkins on the side and sweet potato fries.

"So, what did you say? Can we hang out later?"

I thought we already addressed that.

"I don't know. Let's see how this goes, then we take it from there."

He looks satisfied with my answer.

"Do you have WiFi?" I ask the waiter when he returns with the condiments.

"Yes, we do. AfriFud, and the password is afrifud@123, small letters, no spaces."

"Thank you."

I find the network and keep intentionally failing to log on.

"Is yours connected? Mine is refusing."

"I don't use public WiFi. There's data for that," Dalu says with a low-key brag I had gotten used to.

"Not all of us can afford data hey," I drop my voice.

"Your boyfriend can't buy you data?"

I shift uncomfortably and sip on water.

"Let me tether you... Look for Dalu's Samsung."

Shucks! I'm getting it wrong. I don't need him to tether me, dammit, but let's go with that. He turns on his hotspot and calls out the password. Thank heaven he never changed the default password. It's lengthy, with random letters and numbers, so it's easy for me to say I didn't get it. I'm not even typing, I'm just pretending. I have my barcode scanner open and waiting for a chance. When he calls the password out for the third time, I voice my feigned frustration.

"Sometimes I forget just how slow you are." He laughs and passes it off as a joke.

That's not nice. Tristan said the same, and Elik implied it too. People need to hang it up.

"Let me see for myself. Did you say z8ey4 at the end? Let me see."

He hands me his phone, and never in my life has my left hand been more effective! He's distracted by the waiter asking how he wants his steak done and what sauces he wants to accompany his meal.

*Brain, please cooperate. Remember every step Elik told you.*

I go to WiFi, get the AfriFud WiFi, type the password, then quickly pull up the QR code and scan it with my phone. I almost squeal in pleasure when it connects.

"What are you still doing?" He snatches his phone.

"You know I'm slow. Change that password to something easier."

I quickly WhatsApp Elik, *'I'm in.'*

"Done. Sorry, I had to send a quick message to my grandmother. No more phones now, I promise."

I need him to put his phone away just in case he realises he's being hacked. I put mine in my bag to lead by example.

"Don't you get tired of using your grandmother as an excuse?" He raises an eyebrow.

Oh, dear. At this rate, I'll need something stronger.

I ask about his parents, and he says they are doing fine. I'm on edge, expecting him to ask me questions that might make me lose my head.

"How is Zoe?" I risk it and ask.

"She hates you. She thinks you're a gutter rat."

"Ouch!"

"What? You asked."

That hurt, but we move.

"Dalu, what's going on? I'm genuinely worried about you." I hope my face relays my concern. This is the act of my life and I'm gunning for an Oscar.

I take it up a notch and reach for his hands.

"You hurt me, Lotus. You knew you didn't want to be with me but you kept making me believe you did. Whenever things weren't going well with your boyfriend, you would come to me. You had sex with me without protection knowing you were sleeping around with other guys. Why did you do that to me?" He frees his hands from mine.

"I'm sorry."

I'm embarrassed but I have to see this through. For what it's worth, I didn't give him any diseases. The gynae appointment confirmed that.

"Sorries aren't cutting it anymore. You let me introduce you to my family. I opened my heart to you. My home, Lotus. I introduced you to my parents. You let me into your body and told me you loved me. And right now you're sleeping with another man while pregnant with my child. You did all these things to me and sorry is the best you can do?"

This is going to be harder than I thought. For the life of me, I don't understand why this boy thinks I'm carrying his baby.

"I know. I was confused and I'm sorry that I did that to you. For what it's worth, I loved you... But D, you changed on me. It's like I don't know you anymore."

"Sweetheart, you didn't know me even when you knew me."

I don't like both his look and his tone.

"What do you want, Lotus? You want us to get back together?"

"No. I just..."

"You want a free meal so you can post on Instagram?"

"You think that little of me?"

"Trust me, you don't want to know what I think of you."

I hold the glass with both hands and mentally count down from ten.

"So why did you ask to meet me? I have another appointment, so get to it. Say whatever you want to say so we can eat and I can leave."

Didn't he ask us to hang out at his place after this or did I not hear him correctly?

"I wanted to apologise, Dalubuhle."

"You could have done that over the phone."

"Yes, but I needed to look at you when I said it so you know I really mean it."

"The same look you gave me every time you faked your orgasms?"

My eyes pop open.

"Come on. Do you really think I don't know these things? Funny because I thought you faked it because you loved me and wanted me not to feel bad. I thought we would work on it, but I now know that I wasn't the problem. Your mind was never there."

We changed subjects too quickly. This is uncomfortable. I can't justify that without offending him, so I let it slide. The funny thing is I wasn't exactly faking. I didn't always get there but that's normal.

"You know what would make me forgive you?"

"What?"

"Seeing you dead." He chuckles like it's funny. "I'm kidding. I'm not a murderer like your boyfriend."

"Then what, Dalubuhle?"

"I'll forgive you if you let me have full custody of my child when you give birth and have no contact with us at all. Taking that much away from you will soothe my heart, and only then will I forgive you. You can even go on with your criminal and I won't bother you. You two deserve each other anyway."

I don't think he's joking. He really believes I'm carrying his baby. Does he honestly think I would give my baby to him? I know I'm not going to be mother of the year, but hell would freeze over before I give my child to him.

"So? What's it going to be?" He leans towards me.

"I'm sorry for everything I put you through. Believe me I am, but I was already pregnant."

"You will burn, Lotus," he says under his breath.

He laughs and makes it look like we are having fun when the waiter places our food in front of us. I lost my appetite a while ago. I'm now just sitting here wondering how I missed all the signs. I liked him at some point. If Don hadn't come back, I would have built a future with this guy. When they say you can never know a person, this is what they mean.

"You'll give me my child. Simple as that. You know what I'm going to do? I'm going to tell your Alpha, whatever that means, how you squirm in bed and how you love it when you get on top of me. I'll show him the pictures and the videos. Let's see how he takes that. I hear they don't deal too well with betrayal. Then I'll bring them down one by one, starting with your boyfriend. They won't know what hit them. They won't even see it coming. When I'm done with them, they will beg for death. Let's see who'll have the last laugh."

"You think you can bring them down? You have no idea who they are, do you? Please let it go, Dalubuhle. What do you have on them anyway?"

"I thought you'd never ask!" He grins so evilly, my insides twist into knots.

He details the gruesome things Don has supposedly done. I saw some of it in his pile of evidence but most of it is new and I don't believe it. I know Don does some questionable things from time to time, but I don't believe he's capable of such extremes. Even the devil himself wouldn't do half the things Dalu is accusing Don of.

"You did well by cancelling all those abortion appointments. Don't even think of getting rid of my child!"

My jaw drops.

"So run and tell the mighty Wolves what I told you, and they'll know you spied on them. I made sure it all leads back to you, pretty girl. They will believe me better when I tell them how I'm still screwing you, and how you're pregnant with my child, and all the cute dates we go to, like this one. Maybe they can cut off your grandmother's neck for fun and you can stop lying on her name. Isn't that what they do in their spare time? Terrorise people and such?"

Now he has crossed a line.

"You're crazy, Dalubuhle! You need to get thrown in the loony bin where you belong."

His eyes flicker with a dangerous flame.

"I'm not crazy! Don't say that!" He bangs his fists on the table, drawing attention from everyone around.

"You're crazy! Go to a shrink and get pills for mad people."

"Stop saying that!" he shouts louder this time and pushes the table.

The glasses fall on the floor and break, and the salad bowl empties on my lap. He gets up and I stand up in time to hold his arm.

"Please sit down." I'm embarrassed but I need to keep him.

He looks at me long and hard, his upper lip twitching. "Fuck you, Lotus!"

He walks away and this time I let him. I'm so humiliated.

I quickly take out R1000 from my bag and leave it on the table before chasing after him. That should cover it. He's walking in long strides and not looking back. At least the salad wasn't dressed yet so my clothes are not entirely messed up.

I duck into a boutique as he stands in the queue to validate his parking ticket. I text Tristan, *'Come to Entrance 3'.* A sales lady asks if she can help me but I brush her away without even looking in her direction. I didn't mean to be rude but I'm playing Nancy Drew and I can't afford any distractions.

I walk out of the shop when he walks out of the revolving doors. I'm praying that he doesn't look back. I follow him while calling Elik.

"Did you get into his phone?"

"Yup. Almost done downloading."

"Great. Can you see his location?"

"Yeah... He has a lot of porn, damn!"

"Focus, Elik! I need to follow him. Guide me."

"I'm sharing his live location with you right now. Coming through... Done... Be safe, Ma. You're playing way above your league."

I open the link on WhatsApp and start navigating.

"Get in." Tristan's car stops with a screech. "We're losing distance. Get in!"

I jump in and he drives towards the exit before I can even fasten my seatbelt. He shamelessly tailgates and overtakes as soon as the road splits.

"What do you have? Quick, summarise."

"I have his location. I'll direct you."

Dalu has put in a bit of distance between us but Tristan drives like he has a death wish, so we close in. He's over speeding, doing 160 on a 120 zone. He only slows down when we off-ramp.

"What will we do when we catch him?"

He ignores me and keeps his eyes fixed on the road. We turn around a corner; it looks pretty deserted and run down. There is no one in the street, not even kids playing. He drives to the end, and as he turns, there is Dalu's Mustang. What could he possibly want on this side of town?

"Get down. Call Alpha or Caleb quickly. Send them our location."

He parks behind a bakkie. We have a view of Dalu's car but we are far enough not to be spotted. I dial Don... voicemail. Caleb... voicemail. Oh shit! Elik can't help with this one. Who to call?

Okay, here goes. "Hilton, it's Lotus, don't hang up."

"Why would I hang up and rob myself of a chance to be annoyed?"

"Eish, your arm. Are you able to drive? Is there a car at the house?"

"Ask what you want to ask."

"I need your help. Please, this once, don't cut me short or be mean. It's very urgent. Which safe house is the General being held at?"

He laughs a not-so-nice laugh before he says, "So Alpha told you about the General? Sweet."

"Snap out of it, Hilton! I wouldn't ask you this if it wasn't life-threatening. I'll explain everything in detail, but for now please just work with me. I'm begging you, please."

"He's in Manenberg. What's going on?" Finally, a sense of urgency in his voice!

"I need you to trust me blindly."

"Speak!"

"There's a guy I know. He has information on you guys that could send most of you to prison and expose your dealings. He's in Manenberg right now. I'm not sure but I think he's working with the General. I may be wrong but..."

"Where are you right now?"

"Manenberg."

"What?"

"I met him earlier for brunch and followed him."

"Are you that stupid? Go to a safe place right now! I hope this isn't one of your games or I swear, Lotus, I'll break your neck."

That has me breathing out of my mouth and I find my hand touching my neck.

"I'm not alone. I'm with Tristan. Long story."

"Give him the phone."

"Please don't tell Don any of this. I'll tell him myself."

"Give Tristan the phone!"

I hand over my phone and bite my nails. This is way bigger than me, and at this pace, someone is going to end up dead, and right now the odds are against me. Did I just throw myself under the bus?

"I need to stay here and keep an eye on Dalu till backup arrives, but I also need you far away from here," Tristan says when he hands me back my phone.

"So what do we do?"

"I don't know. Can I drop you off at the main road and you take a taxi to Town, then Uber from there?"

I don't think there is another way, so I agree.

"Tristan, look!" I point. "That's Dalu's father! What is he doing here?"

"Who?"

"Him!" I point at a man in a suit standing with Dalu near the gate of the house the General is in.

"It can't be! That's Viper, the General of the Hard Livings. There's no way that is Dalu's father. Are you sure?"

"100%. I've been to his house in Joburg. It's him."

"Fuck!"

This is way deeper than I thought.

Tristan drops me off by the road and promises to call me. I have to believe that blindly trusting him and Hilton is a good thing, for my own sanity. I feel like I built my own gallows and asked to be hanged.

*Great going, Lotus!*

I'm trying to wrap my head around Dalu's father being the General of the Hard Livings. I've heard of Viper and all the dealings he's involved in. I'm talking gold mines, government officials, human trafficking, organ harvesting, oil smuggling and prostitution rings. For him to turn out to be Dalu's father is a complete mindfuck. I sat at the same table with him! Did he know who I was? Was I a project to that family?

I get into a taxi and find my way to the back to avoid hopping on and off along the way. The taxi takes its time, looking for passengers, allowing me the time to wallow in my thoughts. I don't even mind how crowded I feel in this packed space. How did things get so messed up? Was Dalu using me all along? The fact that Gordon's Bay was raided because of my big mouth and that the General probably knows Don was behind his hit is making my stomach churn. I need to tell Don everything soon, but where will I start? What am I even doing? I wonder if it's too late to go back to Eastern Cape. It just keeps getting worse, and people wonder why I occasionally drink.

# *EIGHTEEN*

It's like when I got off in town, I knew I had to come here. I needed someone who would listen without judging, and since I'm running low on friends, I didn't have much of a choice. It's days like these that I really miss Chelsea.

Elik lets me in and hands me a bottle of water to calm me down. He's quite the patient one. He hands me a box of tissues when I start bawling my eyes out and keeps assuring me that it's going to be alright. I don't see how it will be alright. Too much has happened. Everything is blowing up and I might just be in heaven before the sun sets. He was right. I had gotten out and I should have stayed out.

"Cheer up. You did great and your man is going to see it that way. Let's see where that boy is at."

He leaves and returns with his laptop and sits next to me.

Elik is a breath of fresh air. I feel like he understands me more than anyone. He's easy to talk to and he makes everything better effortlessly. I understand Chelsea *shame*!

"He's still in Manenberg. He's not moving."

I'm not sure why exactly I'm nodding.

"So do you have a plan?"

"Meaning?" I look at him.

"I mean, you're not exactly Hilton's favourite person, and from what you said, neither are you Tristan's. So the probability of them telling your man about this is somewhere between 0.8 and 0.9. So my question is, what will you say in your defence?"

I shrug and clasp my hands. I'll just lie, I guess.

"Besides, if Hilton doesn't tell on you but they catch your little boyfriend, they'll make him squeal. So the probability of Lemon finding out what you did just shot up to 0.95."

Can he stop with the Maths! Busy making gambles with my life. I'm holding onto that 0.05 chance that a miracle will happen and I'll be saved.

"Look, Ma, when they ask you about all this, please leave me out of it. I don't want to be crucified for sins I didn't commit."

That goes without saying. He has helped me a lot, so incriminating him is the last thing I would do.

"Don't you want a glass of wine?"

"I'm pregnant, remember?" Drinking is my personal secret, the only one I'm going to keep to myself.

"That won't matter if you die. Are you sure you don't want to go out in style? Get to heaven feeling a little tipsy and nice?"

I wish he knew how much I'm suffering inside. Such jokes are not funny at all.

He returns with a beer, and juice for me. I pass on the juice because I can't stomach anything.

"So if you wipe everything from his phone, will everything be gone?"

"Yes and no. Yes, if he stores everything on his phone, which is highly unlikely. No, if he saved his data somewhere on his laptop, hard drive, cloud or anything like that, which is most likely the case. But let's be optimistic, shall we?"

There is no winning. Dalu has printouts and a PC with the files.

"Where did you find this guy, Lotus?" He laughs at me and I pout. Can he ever be serious?

Lightbulb moment! "I need to go and see him tonight."

"What?"

"Even I know that you don't leave a job half done. He asked me to come over tonight, so maybe I should go." That was before he went off the rails.

"I don't think that's a good idea. Besides, how will he make it home if Hilton lays his hands on him?"

"There's that by the way. Help me out here. I'm running out of ideas." I'm getting frustrated and he's not helping.

"You're really pulling me deeper and deeper into this. Do you know how much I charge your man for these kinds of jobs?"

I don't know and I don't care.

"Just help me through this, please." I can go on my knees if he wants me to.

"Fine. Let's just say somehow they don't catch him and he makes it back to his apartment. Then somehow the Wolves don't raid his place and take care of him. You meet him tonight, then what?"

"Well, I have a gun."

The shock on his face when he realises I'm not joking is amusing.

When he recovers, he says I'm punching above my weight. Deep down I know he's right, but it's either Dalu or me, and I'm determined to not take this one lying down.

"Get an anaesthetic or something. Try propofol. Get it in his drink and knock him out. Get creative, sweetheart. You're too pretty to be shooting people in cold blood."

He's condescending but I'll forgive him because he's on my side.

"Can I get propofol over the counter at a pharmacy?"

"Are you for real?"

I hate how people treat ignorance as stupidity. How am I supposed to know where to get a drug I only learnt about two seconds ago?

"The Doc can get it for you, but the only problem is that he's the Wolves' doctor, so his allegiance lies with your man, not you."

"I'll take my chances."

"Way too many people know your secret now, do you realise that? Hilton, Tristan, me, and now you want to add the Doc? All of us are Lemon's people. Not that I'll snitch but I'm just saying it's not much of a secret when you run around telling everyone."

"Do you have a better idea?" My turn to give him the eye.

"Nope. Just leave my name out of it."

"Of course... What's Tristan's deal anyway?" I hope someone can finally tell me about that guy.

"You really don't know? Actually, what do you know?"

"Not much, clearly."

"You didn't hear it from me but come on, isn't he everywhere you are? Your man likes having someone follow you and that's Tristan now. He's your tail."

It all makes sense now!

"Speaking of which, has Tristan given you the flash drive yet?"

"What flash drive?"

I tell him how I broke into Dalu's apartment and how Tristan was supposed to give him the flash drive and pictures.

"For a pregnant woman, you're very busy!"

Am I a joke to this guy?

"I honestly think you have taken this too far. Leave it to the Wolves. This is above your pay grade."

"I know, but I need to get out of this hole and I can't leave that to luck. I have to work my way out."

"I'm just saying. Anyway, tell Tristan to give me that flash drive soon so we can try and fit the pieces and hopefully solve the puzzle."

I wonder why he hasn't delivered it in the first place.

"It's quite poetic though when you think about it."

"What is?"

"You being the Wolves General's daughter and dating an Alpha of the Wolves, whose father was the General of the Wolves before yours, and two-timing him with the son of the General of the Hard Livings. All three of you have something in common. Children of the Generals of the two biggest gangs in Cape Town!"

I wish I could throw something at him. There is nothing poetic about that. It's a horror story, if anything. I laugh with him anyway because it is quite something when you think about it.

My phone rings and it's a private number. I choose to ignore it because I suspect it's Dalu.

"Answer it. Put it on speaker," Elik says.

"Where are you?" a voice on the other side says.

"Hilton?"

"Where are you?"

"Well, umm, let me send you my location."

"Just tell me where you are."

Oh, good Lord. I was hoping I could request an Uber to the nearest mall and send the location from there.

"Umm, what's this place by the way? Newlands. I'm in Elik's house. You know Elik? Don's friend?"

"Yeah, sure. I'll be there soon... What are you doing there? ... I'll be there, stay put."

"Dude!" Elik looks unamused when I hang up.

"What was I supposed to say?"

"Fine, traitor! Damage done. Let's do damage control."

He's quite the character!

"How good do you lie?" He looks like he's cooking up a master plan.

"I think I lie decently enough."

"I'll need you to do better than decent today."

"Do I have a choice?"

"Nope. Alright, here's the script. Dalu called you and told you he had intel on the Wolves and that he would create fake evidence against you if you didn't show up. So that's why you met up with him. Let's get that done right now."

He does something on his laptop, and a few moments later, my phone chimes and an SMS comes through. It's from Dalu. The time sent is 8:22 am. Huh?

"Show them that message to justify why you went to meet him without telling them. I'm sure they know you're not a geek, so don't say you tracked his phone or anything like that."

"Tristan knows I was tracking him. He was in on it."

"By the way there's Tristan. Damn! Since when are you cool with Tristan? Leave that out then. Don't volunteer too much information and don't confess things you were not asked."

He walks me through my story, making sure it makes sense. I nod, holding on to every word as if my life depends on it, because it just might. I need to manage Tristan so my story doesn't fall apart.

"Right. So when Tristan told you to go somewhere safe, you went to town and waited for his call. When it didn't come through, you decided to come and be with your friend, Fierce. You got here and I told you she wasn't around. You wanted to leave but you were in a bad state so I told you to come in and get it together before leaving."

I nod again, letting every word stay with me.

He makes a call. I can only hear his end of the call.

"Lemon, my guy. Think you can come through to my house?"

"Your girl showed up and she's in a bad state. She was looking for my girl but she's not around."

"Couldn't let her leave, man. Can she wait here for you?"

"Anytime. You would've done the same for me."

He hangs up and I'm thinking, *he's such a smooth operator!*

"You rehearse that and I'll keep going through this boy's files. We need to know who he's talking to. You've got to love the trust people have in phones. They store their entire lives and darkest secrets on these devices, can you believe it?"

He gets busy on his laptop while I remember my script and mentally prepare myself for my Liar of the Year performance.

"He has emails from his psychiatrist urging him to come for his sessions. He missed eight sessions! Did you know he sees a shrink?"

I shake my head. He was right when he said, *'You didn't know me even when you knew me'.*

"He has a shrink in Joburg and here in Cape Town. Getting to the bottom of this will be easier than expected. No one holds the deepest secrets of a human being than their shrink."

"How will you get the information?" I don't want an innocent doctor dying because of me. I have caused enough chaos in this world.

"Oh no, please! These hands don't kill people. Everyone has a price. For the right price, that shrink will drive herself to you and give you the file."

I'm getting a headache trying to process everything.

"Oh, this is not good."

"What? What did you find?"

"His auditing firm is a laundromat. He was onto you long before you met him... Why do guys stalk you so much before asking you out?" He tries to make light of the situation as he goes through whatever he's going through on his laptop.

"What do you mean?"

"You know how the Wolves clean their money through Club Lotus and such? It looks like the Hard Livings clean some of their money through DM Auditors. Smart move, I must say."

"Really? But where do I come in?"

"I think this guy used you to get close to Lemon. He needed an inside person in the Wolves, and I think that's you."

"What? I would never snitch... willingly."

I move closer to him. I'm not exactly sure what I'm looking at. There are email threads and pictures from before I met him, court proceedings of Roland's case, and pictures of me with Chelsea. He even has a picture of my ID. That's so creepy.

"What is this?"

"Well, someone tipped him off that Lemon had his eyes on you, so he became interested in you too. I guess he wanted to get close to you, hoping you'd volunteer information down the line. He studied you for a while, waiting for the right moment. When your company was due for an audit, he offered your ex-boss a good discount. He gave you the pass you needed and here we are today."

I can't believe this. What a mindfuck.

"So he never loved me?"

Elik looks amused as he smiles. "Is that what you're worried about?"

"Well, yes, no, everything! ... Wait, what the hell is this? Open that."

He clicks on a file labelled *'Lotus Profile'* and opens a picture of me surrounded by the words, *'Ambitious. Easy. Insecure. Needy. Impressionable. Liar. Pretty.'*

"Well, at least he called you pretty."

"Not funny, Elikplim!"

"Sorry."

He sifts through more files. Dalu is tracking my Period App; that's probably how he knew I was pregnant. What the hell!

"I think he meant to use you, but he fell in love with you. I believe he loved you, and he probably still does. Ever heard of crimes of passion? ... But damn, he hates your tattoos! He was planning on sedating you and getting them removed. That's so fucked up."

Good Lord! A memory of that hotel room in Port Elizabeth flashes through my mind and I shudder.

"Okay, there's nothing else here. We'll see when we get the flash drive... Are you alright?"

"No." I'm far from alright.

He looks at me pitifully and tries to say it's not that bad. It's beyond bad!

I get up and pace. I'm so gutted. I don't know what's worse - Dalu using me or me falling for it. When I say men are trash, this is what I mean.

"Elik, flip, I almost forgot. I saw something while I was going through Dalu's apartment. It was in an envelope, separate from the rest of the documents, so it might mean something to you."

"What did you find?" He looks up from his laptop.

"Let me airdrop the pictures to you. It's you and Don and your company records, I don't know. Accept my airdrop."

"What the hell?! This was in his apartment? He has these?"

"Yup. He has more actually, you'll see when you go through the flash drive and the rest of the pictures."

The furrow in his brow deepens as he studies the images. I don't know what it is but it must be bad. He's usually composed and easily laughs things off, but right now he looks almost as stressed as I am.

* * * * *

The intercom rings and I find myself clasping my hands and saying a prayer. Did they find Dalu? Did he tell them about me and him?

"Keep it together and remember what we spoke about." Elik gives me a stern look.

Don, Hilton and two other Wolves walk in through the main door. I get up and run to Don. I'm glad when he opens his arms.

"Are you good?" He holds me so tight, he's squeezing life out of me.

"I'm good now that you're here. I was scared. I couldn't reach you so I called Hilton."

"Come." He takes my hand and leads me outside.

"What happened?" There is so much concern and kindness in his voice, I almost feel bad narrating the lies I rehearsed with Elik.

"I'm going to kill that boy with my bare hands. I'm going to make him beg for death."

At this point, I want nothing less. He must execute him in a kill first, ask questions later style.

"He's working with the General. They were gone by the time Hilton arrived. Tristan got some pictures but couldn't close in on his own. We'll find him and he'll tell us everything, don't worry. You shouldn't have gone there."

I hold him closer and bury my face in his chest.

"You should have called me when you got that SMS in the morning. What did the message say?"

*Thank you, Elik.* I pull out my phone and show him.

"I tried calling you but your phone was off." I didn't try in the morning, so I'm hoping his phone was off as usual.

"Yeah, I always forget to charge it."

Hilton joins us before I can answer his next question. Didn't anyone teach him not to interrupt private conversations? These guys were raised by wolves, excuse the pun.

"I need a moment with Lotus."

"You can ask her anything, it's cool," Don says.

"Alpha, I need a moment with her alone." His voice is hoarser than usual and my fear rises.

"What's wrong?" Worry spreads across Don's face.

"I need to ask her something."

He gives Hilton a long look then begrudgingly agrees.

"Why did you call me?" He gets straight to the point.

"I couldn't reach Don, and after Don, you're the second person I trust." Fingers crossed for brownie points.

"Trust? Anyway, your story checked out and Tristan backed you up. How did you know where he was going? How did you know anything actually?"

"I met up with him earlier and he mentioned the General. That's when I knew."

"I didn't tell Alpha anything, yet. I just called him and told him to come through without explaining. I won't tell him, but you have to tell me everything you know about this boy and his connection with the General. I know you're not telling me everything."

I'm sure he can tell I'm scared. He steps forward and looks down at me, "Do it for the survival of the pack".

Yeah right! Only now that he needs information, he considers me one of them. But you know what, I need Dalu taken care of so here goes. Sorry Tristan and Elik for not consulting with you first. I tell him everything Dalu said and has hinted at in the past. I leave out parts where I'm dating Dalu, parts where I'm in photographs in my birthday suit and parts where I'm the one telling Dalu family secrets. I save the best for last - Dalu's father is the General of the Hard Livings.

"Viper? Are you serious?"

"I wouldn't lie about that." I'm actually shocked that Tristan didn't tell them that already.

"Shit!"

"Will you tell Don? I don't want him thinking that I was cheating on him."

"Are you cheating on him?"

I shake my head without hesitation. Right now I'm not cheating on anyone and that's the answer to his question.

"He's the Alpha. Ultimately, we have to tell him everything. But leave that to me. I'll only tell him what he needs to know to solve this, nothing more, nothing less. Information is what's important; it doesn't matter where it comes from."

"Thank you, Hilton."

He places his hand on my shoulder and gives me a gentle squeeze. It was so quick, I might as well have imagined it.

# *NINETEEN*

I'm woken up by the ringing of my phone. By the time I reach for it, it has stopped and I can't call back because the number was private. Who the hell is calling me at this time of the night? I turn to Don's side of the bed and he's not there. I remember his face before he left and a chill grips my stomach. We came back from Elik's, he went out with the guys, and when he returned, he looked at me long and hard before storming out. I ran after him but he drove off before I could reach the car. He knows, doesn't he? But what exactly does he know? I'm going to go crazy very soon. And like Elik pointed out, too many people know my secret, so I can't even guess who snitched. Were they playing me the whole time then ran to Don and sold me out like it was Black Friday? After how Dalu played me, I should have known better than to trust anyone.

My sleep is ruined so I go through my messages. Oh there, Fierce says she's coming back to Cape Town tomorrow. I'm not in the mood for her, but yay, I guess. I send dancing emojis and move on. Fierce is a good person but she's not the best communicator. We have never been that close anyway, so when she didn't put effort in our communication, I also let it go. It was starting to feel like I was forcing things. She's the queen of blue-ticking and she wants to talk only when it suits her. Everything must be on her schedule. We can't live like that. Elik probably told her he saw me, that's why she is texting me.

My phone rings again and I jump at it this time.

"Hello?"

"It's Caleb. Come and let me in."

"Where's Don?"

"I'm not his bodyguard. Come and open the door." He drops the phone.

What is he doing here at this time, and since when is he rude? It's after midnight. Weird visiting hour if you ask me. I find my gown and readjust my bonnet. At this rate, I'm going to start seeing a shrink like Dalubuhle.

"Can we talk?" He walks past without greeting me. His usual friendliness is absent. "Where's everyone?"

"Outside, guarding the house. I don't know. Did you see the time?"

"Great. No eavesdroppers then."

"Caleb, what's going on?"

"I don't know what game you're playing but it's sick and you need to end it."

"What are you talking about?" I hold my gown tighter. Because it's coming from him, I'm utterly shocked.

"Are you still sleeping with that cheese boy? Are you still cheating on Alpha?" He gives me a look I never thought I would ever see on Caleb's face.

"What? No, never! Where's this coming from?"

"Stop lying, dammit! Tell the fucken truth for once!"

"Caleb?!" I didn't even know he could raise his voice.

"Alpha knows you're working with that boy and your father. What the hell, Lotus! How could you?"

"What?"

"He knows everything! It's a miracle you're still standing here in one piece."

I try to say something but I end up gasping like a fish.

"You're not even going to deny it?"

"It's not true. That's not true, you have to believe me." I feel faint but I can't focus on that right now. I have to convince him that I'm innocent.

"Believe you? You lie to a man who's bent over backwards for you and I should believe you because you say so?"

"Caleb..."

"I never thought you had it in you. Seriously, I thought you loved Alpha. But hey, I guess looks can be deceiving."

"I love him!"

"No, you don't! It explains why you're friends with Chelsea. You two are the same."

I'm so confused. What has Chelsea got to do with anything?

"Caleb, I..." I feel a coldness in my womb.

"Save it. I don't want to hear it. But yeah, heads-up, Alpha knows everything."

I hold my stomach with one hand and grit my teeth. Where's this pain coming from? I feel dizzy and my vision is blurring.

"Are you okay?"

*What do you think? Do I look okay to you?*

He helps me to the couch, disappears to the kitchen and returns with water. I take short breaths until I can lift my head again. I have a feeling he thinks I'm faking it.

I take deep breaths until I feel better. I don't know what that was.

"I'd never betray Don like that. Ever! How could you think that?!"

He looks at me and sniggers. "Imagine my surprise when Chelsea told me about you and that boy, and everything you got up to in Joburg and Port Elizabeth. I decided not to do anything with the information because it's stuff you told her in confidence. I knew you were justified because Alpha abandoned you. But you betrayed the entire pack, Lotus. People died in the shootout after you gave away our hideout. They raided our stash. We lost a lot of money. We're losing to Viper, all because of you."

I would like to explain but I don't know where to begin. I won't address anything because I might dig myself into a deeper hole. Caleb is the sweetheart of the pack. If I lose him, then there is no hope of convincing anyone else to be on my side.

"Look, what you do is none of my business, but when it starts affecting Alpha, then you've made it my business. When it starts threatening my family, then it becomes my business."

"I swear I'm not working with Dalubuhle and I've never even met the General. I bumped into him outside the club that time and that was it. I didn't know Dalu's father was Viper, and as soon as I did, I told Tristan and Hilton. You can ask them. They'll tell you everything I'm telling you right now."

I can tell he wants to believe me but I guess I have lied so much it's difficult to give me the benefit of the doubt.

"Are you sure? Then what's the connection between you and that boy and your fathers? What's the deal between you and the General? How is Viper working with the General if you didn't put them together? What connects the four of you? What are you hiding, Lotus?"

He steps closer and I shrink back into the couch. I thought he would slap me. I have never seen him like this before. He went from upset to concerned and now he's back to upset. I'm starting to think all men are bipolar. I have to weave a lie fast but my brain is not cooperating. I wish I could tell him everything but I have told too many people.

"Speak! What were you doing in Manenberg? Since when are you tight with Hilton? Since when are you best friends with Tristan? You put my brother in danger, Lotus! What the hell are you hiding?"

"Nothing, I promise. You've got all this wrong. It's not what it looks like."

He laughs like I told a good joke. "Keep playing. I'm washing my hands of you. Just don't say I never tried."

"Caleb please..." I grab his arm and try to get up.

He shrugs it off and I fall back onto the couch.

"I like you, I really do. I want to believe you. In fact, I'm praying hard that you're telling the truth and this is just a big misunderstanding. I love what you mean to Alpha. But you have to understand, I saw the look on his face and it's not looking good for you. I thought I'd stay out of it but I want you to fix things before it gets ugly. Although I don't see how you can pull that off now."

His face softens as tears roll down my face.

"Go and find Alpha, and if you know what's good for you, tell him everything."

"Did he send you here?"

"That's not his style. I thought you knew him."

So he came to give me a heads-up? I think I should be grateful.

"Why are you telling me all this then?"

"Don't get it twisted. I'm doing this for Alpha, not for you."

Ouch!

"Where's he?"

"Probably in his club."

"It's late. I can't drive alone. Can you go with me?"

"No. I've played my part. Figure out the rest."

He looks at me, smirks and walks away. He even does that hand salute the Wolves do, with the thumb and first two fingers raised.

I ask some Wolves outside the house to drive me to Longstreet. I'm glad when they don't ask any questions. I look out the window, into the distant lights, appreciating the silence in the car. It's getting more complicated by the day.

Longstreet is like the good old days; buzzing with cars and people. It's alive every day of the week till the early hours of the morning because even if locals don't show up, tourists and backpackers crowd the scene. At this time of the night, the streets are still alive with flashing lights, blaring music, honking cars and people shouting as they find their way home or to another club. This used to be my life. *Phuza* Thursdays were something Chelsea and I looked forward to. I miss that life. I miss going out for drinks and dancing the night away. I miss the routine of work, the thrill of planning to do short courses to improve myself and the stress of preparing for audits. I miss that SMS on the morning of payday. Even though I was earning peanuts, they were *my* peanuts. I miss Chelsea and Hulk, and all their drama. Above all, I miss the way Don used to look at me like he couldn't believe he had me. That look has been gone from his eyes for a while now. I think he liked me more when I was doing my own thing.

"Madam." The bouncer nods at me.

He never used to call me by name back then. I was just Chelsea's friend. Now I'm 'madam', just Alpha's woman. I'm always someone's shadow.

"Is Alpha around?"

"Check in his office or ask the guys at the bar."

"Sure, thanks."

"Are you alright?"

"I'm good, thanks."

I keep going up the dark stairs so that he doesn't ask me any more questions. I stop at the top and look around at people dancing, talking too loudly and having a good time. Everyone seems happy and carefree. Me and my heavy heart envy them. I miss the me that used to be dancing on that floor.

I stop outside Don's office. It's so loud, even if he said, "Come in", I wouldn't hear, so I brave it and open the door.

"Get out!" Don points a gun in my direction.

"I'm sorry." I close the door and lean against the wall.

I shouldn't have seen that. I can never get used to this life. Why didn't they lock the door? Wouldn't that be better than shooting anyone who walks in?

The door opens after some time and the guy says a quick *aweh* before going down the stairs with a bag. I hate that I know what's in it.

"Get out." Don doesn't look at me when I walk in.

I close the door behind me and walk around the table.

"Leave before I do something I'll regret. I don't want to see you."

My breath catches but I thug it out and keep walking until my knees are touching his. I'm not sure whether it's hate or disgust in his eyes.

He pulls out the top drawer, takes a gun out and puts it on the desk. "It's loaded," he says without looking at me.

I don't know why that doesn't scare me. He can shoot me if he wants. Maybe he can put me out of my misery.

"I need to talk to you."

"Get lost."

"It's fine if you don't want to talk to me. You just have to listen."

He gets up and I push him back. "Sit down, Donavan. I have things to say to you."

He looks at me long and hard but I don't budge. He curses under his breath and sits down.

"I'll talk and you'll listen. I don't have time to be playing games with you. It's past two in the morning but see where you are!"

"You've got the nerve, woman," he mutters under his breath.

"I don't care if you're mad at me, or you're stressed out, or whatever. I told you that you have to tell me when you're not sleeping at home so I don't have to worry. One message is all I ask for. Is that too much?"

I can see his clenched fist and the vein throbbing on his face, but I'm thugging it out to the very end.

"Lotus..."

"No, Donavan, you don't get to speak. The baby and I should be sleeping right now. You just up and left and I've been worried sick. My BP is high and it's affecting the baby."

He frowns a little as his eyes follow my hand to my stomach. My stomach is starting to round out but it's not really showing. It just looks like I've put on a bit of weight.

"Being pregnant is not easy. This is my first pregnancy. I'm scared half the time and sick the other half."

I try to take his hands but he draws them back.

"Look, I haven't been completely truthful. There are things I've been keeping from you but with good reason. I'm going to tell you everything and I need you to let me finish."

"I knew you were lying."

"You did? How?"

"I have my ways."

"You know what, I don't want to know."

This is my Last Act and since I didn't get my Oscar last time, I have to get it tonight.

"I'm going to tell you the whole truth and hope you can find it in your heart to understand."

"I don't have a heart."

"We all know that. But can I speak before I get cold feet?"

He looks at me and I think I have his attention.

"I don't know where to begin. I should have told you from the get-go but I was scared you wouldn't believe me. I was scared you would leave me."

"I'll leave you if you don't start talking."

"Please don't be mad."

"You're making me mad by dragging this!"

Ready. Steady. Go.

"Dalubuhle has been stalking me. It's been going on for a while now. When you abandoned me in Eastern Cape, I resumed talking to him. You know we used to be friends since university. So we were just chatting on the phone, nothing much."

Don knows I know Dalu, and since I said he was my friend from university when he dropped me off in front of my old apartment that time, I need to maintain the lie. I just hope he doesn't remember that it's the same guy who called that time after the audit.

"Lotus..."

"I met him again briefly when I went for a job interview in Joburg. He was with his father and we all had lunch. I cut him off when he wanted more, and that's when the threats began. He said if I told you, he would expose the Wolves. He has a lot of dirt on you guys."

He closes his eyes and I know the question that's coming, so I answer it.

"I didn't cheat on you with him. I might have flirted with him here and there, but I never slept with him, ever."

I hereby denounce any sexual activities I had with Dalubuhle Mthethwa. May it be known from today henceforth that it never happened.

I hear him exhale. *Good going, Lotus!*

"He finally left me alone and I thought he'd gotten the message. Then he resurfaced not so long ago. I wanted to tell you but I didn't want to be the reason the Wolves got exposed. I wanted to protect you. I thought if I could somehow outsmart him and get the evidence he had and give it to you, then you would be proud of me. I wanted you to be proud of me. That's why I did what I did and got the evidence for you. I gave it to Tristan to give you because I didn't want you to know what I had done."

"You should have come to me. It's my job to protect you, not the other way around. It's me you should come to. Not Tristan, not Hilton, not Elikplim, not anyone else, me!"

"I know, baby, and I'm sorry. I just wanted to protect you and I didn't want you to be mad at me. Dalu said he had hard evidence to take you out and demanded that I meet him in Canal Walk. To be safe, I asked Tristan to go with me and wait outside. I begged him not to tell you because I wanted to tell you myself. When I got there, he started telling me things he claims you did, and he said he has evidence."

"What things?"

I recount the crimes Dalu accused Don of and everything I saw in his apartment. Of course, I don't mention that I was in the apartment. I just say Dalu told me everything.

I see his hand tense. Oh my goodness, he did all that?! Who am I sleeping with exactly?

"And then what happened?"

He's not going to address the allegations?

"He took off and Tristan chased him. We lost him somewhere in Manenberg. That's when I tried calling you but I couldn't get through. So I called Hilton, that's how you know I was out of options."

He sits up straight and I can't tell what he's thinking.

"I'm sorry I told Hilton and Tristan things I didn't tell you first."

He sighs, in relief I hope.

"Come here." He sits me on his lap and kisses my shoulder. His breath is laced with alcohol, but what's new?

"Dalu is working with my father. I mean, the General."

"That's what Hilton said."

"I'm not sure but I think he has mental challenges. That makes him unpredictable, so you have to be careful. He could hurt you."

"I'm always careful... You don't want to know what I thought your role in all this was."

"Baby!" I look at him as if a sudden thought just occurred to me. "Fierce told me that Elik is good with technology and stuff. Why don't you ask him to hack Dalu and track him down? That way you'll know everything. Beat the psycho at his own game."

"Great thinking. I'll talk to him."

I'll send a message to Elik later. He should share all the information he has on Dalu with Don but make it look like he got it after Don asked him. That way he'll get paid for his services and I won't be implicated. I hope Tristan has delivered the flash drive.

"I love you, Donavan, and I'm glad the secrets are out. It was killing me. I really thought I was protecting you. I'm sorry."

"Next time, tell me. Whatever it is, come to me with it."

"Yes, baby, no more secrets. Pinky swear?"

He laughs and it's so genuine, it melts my fear. He gives me his pinky and we swear.

"Baby, I don't know how to say this. I finally found out why Dalubuhle is obsessed with me."

"Yes?"

"It's to get to you. It's actually you he's obsessed with. His father is Viper."

"What? He's Viper's son? And no one told me? Fuck!" He pushes me off him and stands. "What the fuck, Lotus!"

"I didn't know. I swear."

"You didn't know? Lotus, isn't this the same boy you told me was a good friend of yours when you two were running around all over Cape Town? Isn't it the same boy Caleb threw out of my club? Isn't it the same boy you wanted to bring to my house to talk to the kids? The boy who dropped you off in front of me in a Mustang? Didn't you say you hung out with him and his father in Joburg? So if you were so close and such good friends, how did you not know? You had lunch with Viper!"

Shit! I don't know how to get out of this one.

"I don't know what to tell you. I'd never seen Viper in my life, so I didn't know that it was him. Come to think of it, Dalu tried getting closer to me after I started dating you. I was too blind to see it. It must have been his plan all along."

"I hope you're not lying to me, or I swear."

My heart is thudding again and I'm close to losing composure.

"I'm not. I have no reason to. I can try and get him to meet up with me, and then you come in and take over. We need to get him into a room and make him talk. It's the only way to get the truth out of him. I'm sick of his games." I have no idea what I'm doing. I just hope somehow Dalu disappears before that happens.

"Sounds like a plan." He sits back down and I sit on his lap.

*Phew!*

"They're trying to get to me by taking away the most important thing in my life."

*I like that angle. Let's go with that.* "No one can ever take me away from you."

"I hope so. This is not the kind of life I want for you. You and our child need to stay out of it. The streets are not for everyone, my darling, that's why they made pavements."

Awww. Aren't we deep sometimes?

"I love you, baby. I really do. I never should have kept secrets from you." I kiss him on the forehead.

"Don't do it again."

His phone rings, a welcome buffer. It's the Wolves who brought me asking if they should keep waiting or leave.

He's less tense when the call ends.

"Stop it!" I swat his hand away as it goes up my T-shirt.

"I need you," he whispers in my ear.

He kisses my neck, and the warmth of his breath on my skin makes me shiver a little.

"The door's not locked," I whisper when his fingers graze the right spot.

"No one will come inside."

"But you will," I chuckle and bite my lip.

"Of course I will."

He stands with me and his lips crash into mine. I taste alcohol on his tongue as I kiss him back just as hard. When I come up for air, his lips trail down to my neck and one hand squeezes my breast, making me moan with my eyes closed. He pulls my pants down, then lifts me onto the desk, gently setting me on the edge. His lips find mine again, deeper and wetter this time.

My breath hitches when he pushes in, sinking deeper with each thrust as my body opens up to him. He pauses for a second when he's fully buried inside me, and his mouth finds mine again, more demanding this time. Then he starts moving, faster, harder, deeper, pounding into me like he wants to claim every part of me. His hands grip my hips, and I open wider as my moans grow louder. I hold on to the desk, my head thrown back, his body slamming against mine, each stroke leaving me breathless. With one final thrust, he lets out a deep growl and his fingers dig into my skin as his warmth spills into me. I wrap my legs around him and pull him closer, my nails still digging into his arms. He kisses me, softly this time, before looking deep into my eyes.

"I love you, my *skat*."

"I love you too, baby." I hold on to him, my chest still rising and falling.

I wish I could stay here forever.

# *TWENTY*

We are wrapped up in each other when a voice booms through the corridor. We might as well live in a hostel with the way people come and go as they please.

"Alpha!"

"What the hell is Hilton doing here?" Don moves me out of his arms. "Stay here, I'll be right back."

I want to stay but I have my own issues, so I quickly grab a gown and follow him. If Hilton is here to undo all the hard work I did earlier, I want to be there to witness it.

"What are you doing here at this time?"

"Do I need a reason to check up on you? It's like that now?"

"Of course not. Is there something you want?" Don sounds impatient.

"Lotus, you good?"

"I'm good, Hilton. How are you?"

"Alright then. Guess I'll be on my way. I have a feeling my Alpha doesn't want me here."

"No man, I was just in the middle of something very important," Don says.

That's an interesting way to say he was about to have sex.

"I'm sure you were. Everything is more important than the pack these days."

"Come on, my bru, you know it's not like that."

"Keep lying to yourself. You're selling out and you know it. At least be a man and admit it. Step down and let those whose hearts are in it take over."

"Stepping down means death for me. You want me dead, Cuz?"

"At this stage, I don't give a damn. Babysitting you is getting tiring. Make up your damn mind or someone will make it up for you one of these days."

*I should have stayed in bed.*

"Hilton..."

I've heard that tone before and it's never good, but Hilton is not fazed one bit and he rudely cuts Don off.

"I'll see you tomorrow, Cuz." He salutes and walks away.

When did things get bad between them? They were fine yesterday.

"Baby, I'll walk Hilton out. I'll be right back," I say to Don.

I can tell he does not approve but I don't wait for him to stop me.

"Hilton, I have a proposition for you." I get straight to the point when I catch up with him outside.

"What could you possibly have to say that I would want to listen to?"

I ignore his rudeness. "I can convince Don to be the next General."

"We have a General."

"Not for long. You know you'll need a new General soon, come on."

He stops and turns to face me. "How exactly would you do that?"

"Leave the how to me. Just know that I can do it."

"What's in it for you? What do you want in return?"

"Nothing. I don't want anything."

"Try again. What's your price?"

"Fine! Since you insist, I'll name my price."

"See, I knew there was a catch. What is it?"

"If I succeed, promise me you'll go back to being my friend again."

"I was never your friend." He looks at me blankly.

"Okay, friend is kind of an overstatement. I want you to be what you were to me before all this happened."

"And what exactly was that? You're Alpha's bitch. What has that got to do with me?"

"Bitch, Hilton?" I'm so offended!

"Whatever, Lotus. Say what you want to say so I can go." I can't tell whether he's annoyed or indifferent. I see why people are scared of him.

"You were my friend. I want that back."

He looks at me like I'm delusional, or worse.

"That's my price. Take it or leave it."

"You want me to go back to not caring about you? Whether you're alive or dead really wouldn't make a difference, you know. Is that what you want?"

"Yes, exactly that. That's how you treated me before and I miss that Hilly who would never call me a bitch and who wouldn't shrug me off when I hugged him."

"Don't call me that stupid name." He frowns a little, and I might be imagining it but I think he's softening up.

"Fine, Hilly, I won't call you that."

"We have a deal. Can I go now?"

"Yeah, sure. Drive safely."

He looks at me like I said something senseless. He'll come around. I worked on him before; I'm sure I can do it again.

"Lotus," he calls as I begin to walk away.

"Yes, Hilly?"

"Do you understand why it's important for Alpha to become the General?"

I shake my head. I have my suspicions but I would be lying if I said I fully understood.

"Alpha has lost the plot. He better become the General when the time comes or he's dead. You too by the way. Dead, all of you. Do you understand that?"

That sent a cold shiver down my spine.

"I understand. I'll work on it... But who will be the next Alpha of the Cape Flats turf?" I realise I have never asked.

"That's none of your business."

Mxm. See how human beings are? They want your help but don't give you all the details. I know I offered to help in this case but still.

"You need to deal with Alpha urgently. You made him weak. Fix it."

"Excuse me?"

"I never should have allowed him to do all this in the first place."

"To do what?"

"To do this nonsense that the two of you are doing. It's made him weak. So he either becomes the General and restores his dignity, or they send him six feet under."

Wow!

"And that deal he's involved in with Elik will blow up in his face. When Viper finds out what's going on, he's going to think we're preparing for a full-blown war. Then what do you think he'll do?"

I'm not sure what he'll do. Call the United Nations? Fly to The Hague and file papers at the ICJ? I don't know, so I shrug.

"It's a miracle that Alpha is still alive, and that's because Caleb and I are out here busting our asses and working overtime to protect him! The only shot he has right now is being the General."

Makes sense, I guess.

"He'll get you, this baby he's obsessed with and himself killed. I might just kill him myself to spare us the headache."

I'm starting to feel cold. Hilton has predicted my death enough times in the last few minutes, I'm starting to believe that I'll die soon.

"So I hope you're not playing games when you say you're going to convince him to step up as General. He needs to want it so we can get him there."

"I'll do my best."

"Do that... Actually, tell me something. How are you and Alpha okay right now? Hours ago, he wanted you in the ground. How did you talk yourself out of it?" He blinks and I don't know what he and Caleb were thinking getting tattoos on their eyelids.

"I managed to talk to him, and thankfully, he understood."

"You lied, you mean."

"I did what I had to... Hilton, why exactly did you come here?"

"Caleb asked me to help you and make sure Alpha doesn't do anything stupid. So there you have it. He called in a favour. I wasn't going to waste my time otherwise."

"Caleb?" I don't believe it.

"Is there another Caleb you know?"

"No, there isn't."

"So why are you acting like you don't know who Caleb is?"

"What?" I'm so confused.

"Are you surprised that he still looked out for you after you and your friend screwed him over?"

"What do you mean my friend and I screwed him over?"

"You helped Chelsea cheat on him, didn't you? But it's none of my business, so don't explain anything to me."

"What? You know what, let's leave it. I'm just shocked that Caleb would ask you to do this for me. He hates me."

"Why do you like thinking that people hate you? Does it make you feel important? No one hates you, Lotus. People just don't care about you."

Ouch! I don't know what's worse.

"For the record, Caleb doesn't hate you. Unlike some of us, he has a heart. Too bad people like you play around with that. See what happens when you have a heart? Look at Alpha now, weaker than a woman."

If he calls Don weak one more time, I swear I'll smack him. I also want to protest and say women are not weak but the timing is off.

"Please thank Caleb for me and tell him I'm sorry."

"I won't do that. You have your own mouth."

He's so frustrating but I can't give in to the part of me that's itching to say something mean to his tattooed face.

"Can I go now?" He gives me an attitude I don't deserve.

"Of course you can."

"Let's hope your little plan works. Do whatever it takes."

"Will you help me? Please help me plan how to execute everything."

"Can I say no?"

"Not really."

"So why are you asking stupid questions?"

He steps into his car and shuts the door while I'm in the middle of a sentence.

Convincing Don to want the General's position will be tough because he has no interest in it. He's fine with letting the other three Alphas compete for the position. When the General dies, which is only a matter of time, his position will be up for grabs. Unlike becoming an Alpha, which involves earning stars, becoming a General is purely political. One of the Alphas will step into the role either by winning a campaign or by eliminating the competition, whether by killing them, digging up enough dirt on them to force them out, or sending them to prison. Even though the Wolves' Creed has strict rules against internal violence and forbids Wolves from killing each other, those power-hungry enough always find creative ways around it. An Alpha can opt out of the race, like Don plans to do.

If a former General, like Don's father, agrees to step back into the role, he automatically takes the position. But since no one can lead from prison, they had to keep the General alive until they could figure out how to get Don's father out. That was the grand plan, but it hasn't been going well. Now with the war looming, they need a plan B, and that's Don.

Yvonne Maphosa

# *TWENTY ONE*

I'm standing in front of the mirror, tugging at a pair of jeans that refuse to fit right. I hate how everything is starting to feel too tight.

I swear I ballooned overnight. It's like my body has been taken over by an alien. I can't believe I have carried this baby for almost five months. I haven't even taken the time to embrace being pregnant and enjoy the journey. Honestly, if it were up to me, I'd have the baby taken out and put in an incubator for the remaining months.

Don comes up behind me and wraps his arms around me.

"You look great," he says.

I glance at him over my shoulder, raising an eyebrow. "Great? I'm just getting bigger every day. Nothing fits anymore. I feel like a balloon."

He chuckles and pulls me closer. "We're pregnant, my *skat*, so obviously we're going to get a little bigger. But you look beautiful."

Did he say *we*? "Beautiful?"

"Yes! Look at you." He turns me to face him and looks at me like I'm soul food. "Do you ever hear me complaining?"

He's an idiot. He'll say I'm beautiful whether I'm big, small, or anywhere in between.

"You say that but I don't feel that way."

He cups my face and looks into my eyes. "You look gorgeous. You're perfect to me, my angel."

I blush, feeling chuffed. "Thank you, baby. You're the best."

He kisses my forehead. "You need to finish dressing up because if I keep looking at you like this, we'll not make it to the airport on time."

He lets me go and pulls out the sonogram from his nightstand drawer. Since our check-up yesterday, he's been looking at it an unhealthy number of times. I even caught him wiping away a tear and talking to it as if the baby could hear him.

"You're obsessed with that thing."

He chuckles. "I can't help it. I keep imagining what he'll be like."

*He*? I know he's hoping for a boy but I want a girl.

I don't want to know just yet; I want to save it for the gender reveal at my baby shower.

I finish dressing up and pick out sneakers that match his.

"Alright, let's go," I say, as if I'm not the reason we are late.

I'm trying to stay positive. When I first told Don my plan, he didn't like it. He said I was making a big mistake but he agreed to support me anyway.

We find Tristan sitting outside. He doesn't pay me any attention and barely looks up when I greet him. He has been acting weird lately. He claims not to know where Dalu is, but I don't believe him. I wish I could get Dalu out of my mind. It's been two weeks and he hasn't said anything. I keep expecting him to randomly pop up like a pimple and turn my world upside down.

I'm playing with my hands and shifting in my seat. I can't seem to settle down.

We park at the short-stay parkade at the airport, and I leave Don and Tristan in the car and rush in.

My mother squeals excitedly when she sees me and I run into her arms. I expected a harsher reaction considering how late I am, but I guess she's finally growing up. It took a great deal of bribing and begging to get her to agree to come to Cape Town.

"How's Mama doing?" I hook my arm to hers and walk with her suitcase next to me.

"She misses you. She wants you to come back home."

"Really? She's not mad at me?"

"No, she's not. You know how she is. But she will give you a very long lecture when you get home."

"Maybe we can go back together." I need to get out of Cape Town for a bit. I also really miss my grandmother.

"That will be perfect actually... How's the baby?"

"She's fine. She's not very fussy so I can eat whatever I want."

"So you still insist it's a girl?" she laughs. "You're carrying *her* well. You're glowing!"

I feel my cheeks flush with embarrassment and I stop myself from saying the inappropriate thought that crossed my mind. I can't tell my mother that nights with Don are probably the real reason I'm glowing.

"You look good too. Look at you!"

"I know! I bought this outfit from this other lady at work. I'll show you her catalogue later. She has nice things that would look good on you."

"I would love that. I need new clothes... How are the renovations going?"

"Slow, but we'll get there. At least you'll be able to supervise when we get back home. It's hard for me. Between work and catering, I barely have any free time left."

"You're doing great with the catering. I'll help you when we get home."

I have been using her Instagram page to get her some business. I'm excited about the thought of wearing matching aprons and being hands-on with her. I'll start packing tonight. Don might not be thrilled about me leaving, but he'll have to understand.

We find our way to the car and she exchanges brief greetings with Tristan and Don. I can't believe she still calls him Madonna.

I join her in the backseat while Don puts her bag in the boot.

"Why are you so quiet now? Since when are you this quiet?"

I look at her and close-mouth smile to escape the question. "Hormones."

I take her hand in mine and rest my head on her shoulder. A thought of what lies ahead has drowned all my excitement.

"Are you alright?" she asks because I keep taking deep breaths at intervals.

"I'm fine. I'm just worried about how Mama will react when I get home."

"Don't worry about that. She'll come around. We'll talk properly in private. There are too many prying ears here."

The drama never ends!

We leave the main road and it's like we have entered a different world. There is graffiti on walls, dirt on the side of the road, crowded buildings and run-down double-storeys. It looks worse than the other time I was here. It's the Wolves' turf though so we should be okay.

"Is this where you live? You need to do better! Come back home because this is not it." She looks mortified.

I want to tell her that I don't live here but I'm too edgy to talk.

We turn into another street and park behind Hilton's car.

"Stay in the car," Don instructs.

"You live here? *Tjo,* better you than me! All this for a penis, Lotus?" She turns up her nose.

Well, my grandmother's house wasn't any better before I started renovating it, so she's one to talk.

Don opens my door and gives me a hand. "Are you sure about this?"

"I've never been more sure."

He's not convinced but he keeps his words to himself.

"Hilton, Caleb... Hi."

Caleb nods and Hilton stares at me blankly. I decide to annoy him. I'm doing it more for myself if anything, as a distraction to calm my nerves. I give him a bear hug and rest my face on his chest. He needs love, and lucky for him, I'm overflowing with it. Loving the unlovable is my humble contribution to society.

"I'm not letting you go until you say something." I grin, my hands still locked behind his back.

"Leave me alone. Run to Alpha and give him headaches."

"That I will do, but after you say something."

"I said leave me alone. Isn't that something?"

"Fair point."

I let him go and find my mother biting Don's head off for making me live in such horrid conditions. He's not listening to her, which is making her even more furious.

"You don't have to do this," Don whispers as we walk through the gate.

"I do."

Don walks in first, then my mother and I follow. I don't know what I expected a safe house to look like, but this is not it. We are standing in a normal living room with couches, paintings of wolves and other animals on the wall, a dining table with a full set of chairs, and a ceiling with an old-fashioned chandelier. I expected bulletproof walls, no windows, burglar bars, fingerprint access and military lasers.

"Come on," Don calls from the other door.

I hesitate before grabbing my mother's hand. The door leads to a bedroom with floor-to-ceiling built-in closets, a double bed with a headboard and matching pedestals. It's a normal bedroom. My mother thinks it's her room and she exclaims how she has a king-size bed waiting for her back at home. Not true by the way.

Don opens the closet doors and moves the jackets aside, revealing a door. I'm as surprised as my mother.

"What is this? What's going on?"

I raise my hand to signal her to keep quiet. She has been yap-yapping non-stop, and no disrespect, but if you think I'm annoying, then clearly you've never met my mother.

The door opens to a flight of stairs that lead down to a dimly lit room. A younger Wolf I don't recognise walks through a door at the opposite end, pushing a wheelchair. My mother shrieks and I remain frozen in my step. I thought I could handle this, but coming face-to-face with him has thrown me off. All the lines I practised for days have completely slipped my mind.

"What is this?" My mother grabs my arm and hurls a string of insults too explicit to repeat. Her face is filled with terror and her anger is vivid in every expression.

As she turns to walk away, she bumps into Hilton. He blocks her path until she pulls her hair and screams. I hate that it had to come to this. I had to put an end to all the secrets and the 'he said, she said'. I got tired of walking through life with too many unclosed chapters and different versions of stories. Judging by her reaction, we might not have much of a relationship left after this. Don assured me that nothing will happen to her, physically at least. No one can ever promise anyone emotional security. She calms down a bit, but her face still looks like she's staring death in the face.

"But why, Lotus?"

I look down and clasp my hands. I hope deep down she understands that she left me no choice. For years, I begged her for answers and all she did was lie. She has her version of events and my father has his, so I had to put both of them in the same room without warning them. That way, they wouldn't have a chance to prepare their stories. I have waited for this moment my whole life; a chance to ask my father why he abandoned me. And who knows? We might unite and be one happy family. Okay, I'm taking it too far.

I have never seen my father properly. The first time I saw him, I was hiding uncomfortably at the top of the stairs at Don's house, watching him slice Don's face. The second time was on my birthday, outside Club Lotus. It wasn't a pleasant encounter either. Then he got shot and died, yet here he is in the flesh, a few steps away from me, looking at me and my mother with an eye I don't like. He is still heavily scarred, his eyes are still empty and his hairline is still divorced from his forehead. He looks older than I remember and the lines on his forehead have deepened. Also, one of his legs is gone. Don didn't tell me that part.

He looks nothing like me. I'm insulted that Don even suggested it. Maybe a bit of his eyes, lips, eyebrows, jaw and nose, otherwise nothing else.

Why isn't he shocked that we are here? I hate people who don't react.

"Well, well, well. If it isn't my favourite Alpha and his lapdogs bringing me my long-lost daughter and the bitch that got away. Christmas came early this year." He smiles, showing beautiful teeth.

My mother's lips are trembling and I'm sure if I listen closer, I'll hear her teeth rattling. Tears are streaming down her face and she's clutching her dress with both hands. Maybe I shouldn't have set this up, but it was a necessary evil. She knows that I have wanted to meet my father my entire life.

Don's presence behind me is reassuring. At least if I lose everyone, I'll still have his arms to fall into. Hilton is standing behind my mother, Tristan is by the corner and Caleb is standing on my right hand.

"To what do I owe this honour, my sweetheart? You haven't changed one bit. You're still drop-dead gorgeous. Come give daddy a kiss." He wheels himself towards my mother.

She looks at him with what I think is a mix of disgust, fear and rage. Why did I do this to her?

"Did you miss me?"

"How are you not dead?"

"I suppose dead people are not always dead. I also thought our child was dead, yet here she is."

I'm glad the conversation is starting itself. I thought I would have to play judge, jury and executioner.

"The Source kept me alive until the day I saw a picture of my child. I lost my leg in an unfortunate situation involving a disgruntled son-in-law, but I'm recovering well." He shoots Don a knowing eye.

"I wish they had killed you!" My mother's voice shoots like it was squeezed out of her.

"The way you killed my daughter?"

"Don't do this. You know I couldn't be around you."

"You knew who I was. I never lied to you. When you told me you were pregnant, I asked what you wanted to do. You said you wanted an abortion and I gave you the money for it. You said you knew a doctor. You came back to me and said you had the abortion. Then you disappeared from the face of the earth without a trace."

The knots in my tummy tighten. He didn't abandon me. He just didn't know about me.

"I had to protect her from you! I found out I wasn't the only one. You had dozens of us!" Her voice is raw with pain.

"You knew that. You thought what? That we would get married and live happily ever after?" He laughs mockingly and I feel chills in my stomach.

"I don't care anymore. I never wished to see your face ever again. I had to protect my daughter from you and your life! I gave up everything and went back home a failure just so my daughter could have a chance at life. I gave up everything for her. So don't think for a second that you will waltz in and undo all that."

"Should we clap hands for you or do you have an address where we should send your medal? You want to sound like a hero, yet she turned out just like you. She's sleeping with the Alpha of the same Wolves you despise. Just like you, she fell for an Alpha. You must be very proud."

By the way, he was still an Alpha when he was with my mother. Don's father was the General then.

"Oh please, don't even begin to compare what she has with Madonna to the pathetic relationship we had! He loves her and takes care of her.

He doesn't beat her or hold a gun to her head and force her to do things she doesn't want to! They share love, something you'll never know. I never loved you. I feared you! I hated you then and I hate you to this day. I would gladly dance on your grave, and I will!"

He doesn't address anything she alleged and that's how I know it's true. Why didn't she trust me enough to tell me all this?

"So yes, here's your daughter. I gave up everything for her. And if I had to do it again, I would."

"Shut up! You raised her with money you made on your back."

"Stop it!" I speak up for the first time. I won't let him talk to her like that.

"My child, your mother lied to you. I didn't know about you. I would have given you the world itself. But don't worry, we can start from today."

That easy, huh?

"I'd be damned!" My mother pulls me back, her nails digging into my flesh.

"Don't listen to her. She's a liar. She kept us apart. I'm your father. I'll make up for all the time we lost."

I close my eyes and ask the universe why. Do you know how long I longed to hear those words? Except after everything I know now, I wish I never heard them. He broke her. She was just an impressionable teen and she gave up everything to give me a chance. She resented me because I reminded her of him, but she didn't hate me. She never once missed my birthday and she would get me something every time she got paid. She loved me in her own way, and when my whole world collapsed, she was there for me.

"Lotus, go outside!"

"Sisi..." My voice comes out thin. I wish she could rip my soul open and see how sorry I am.

"Outside, now!"

I look at her helplessly.

"I'm going to tell Mama what you did today, but I need you to get out right now."

In a different time, this would have been cute: running to my grandmother to tell on me. We used to do that a lot when I was in high school. We would bicker like siblings and tattle on each other. We were both scared of my grandmother, so saying 'I'm going to tell Mama' was a big threat.

"I'm sorry."

"What did I ever do to you, *sana lwam*? How would you feel if I told your dear boyfriend about your shenanigans with that Zulu boy? Would you like that?"

I'm glad she's speaking in Xhosa.

"Do you know what you've done? Now he knows how to find me. I hope you're happy with yourself."

"Sisi..."

"Don't sisi me!"

"I'm sorry."

"You know what? I'm leaving. Stay with your father, and don't you ever contact me or come home again, you hear me? You've made your choice."

I want to say something but my lips tremble and I can't form words.

She bumps into Hilton and hurls deep insults. Thankfully, he didn't hear a word she said.

"Move out of my way or I'll kick you." She pushes him but he doesn't budge. She pushes him again and he remains still.

"If you don't move out of my way right now, I'll slap the tattoos off your face one by one!"

"Let her go, Cuz," Don says.

Hilton steps aside and she scurries up the steps.

"Caleb, follow her," Don says.

"Lapdog. Running everywhere the master tells it to." The General adds a bone-chilling laugh.

I didn't want this to happen. I just wanted us to talk and get to the truth once and for all.

"Sisi, wait." I run after her.

I get to the top and find her sitting on the bed. Her chest, stomach and throat are heaving but she's not making a sound.

"I'm sorry, Sisi. I needed answers but I see now that I went about it the wrong way."

I try to hold her but she pushes me away so hard I almost fall. She stands up, straightens her shirt, and wipes the tears off her face.

"I'm leaving."

"I'll go with you."

"No, you will not. I can't look at you right now."

"Please, Sisi, let me come with you."

"Which part of you are no longer my daughter did you not understand? Go to your father!"

She instructs Caleb to drive her or else she will find her own way.

The pain I'm feeling is disturbed by a sudden fear. I run back down and stand frozen on the last step as the words hit me like a heart attack.

"You're going to tell me about this Dalu boy. I asked what your connection with him is. Tell me everything."

"And why would I tell you?"

"Because you're under a blood oath."

I sure know how to dig my own graves. All I wanted to know was what exactly happened. I found out, but at what cost? Now I know why they say ignorance is bliss and curiosity killed the cat. But also, had my mother just trusted me enough to tell me the truth, all this would have never happened.

If I had to describe the state I'm in right now, I would ask you to imagine trying to walk down the aisle of an aeroplane that is nose-diving, then just before it crashes, you jump off and a bullet train hits you so hard you're tossed back into the air. Then you land in a pothole and a truck runs you over. That's how I'll describe my life in the next interview when I'm asked, *'Tell us about yourself.'*

"Don..."

"We're in the middle of something, Lotus."

"Listen to your girlfriend, Alpha. After all, you take orders from everyone. You're just a puppet. We all know who runs your turf," the General says with a mocking grin on his face.

"You're under oath. You'll tell me everything."

"You always were cunning. You're just like your father!" He wheels himself backwards.

I need to think fast. I know Don won't pay me any attention when he's like this. It will be like riding a dead horse.

"Father, can we talk? I need answers. What my mother said..."

"My darling, I know your mother did a terrible job raising you, but when men are talking, you don't interrupt."

My jaw drops.

"Lotus." Hilton points to the corner, and I have no option but to obey.

I wish I had written a will. What would I have put in it? Shoes, I guess. I shrink into the corner next to Tristan. I wish I had my rosary so I could summon a higher power. For the first time in a long time, I pray. It's the only thing I can do right now.

"Tell me everything about you and the boy. Lay it all out, every last detail."

I have never seen Don this menacing before. He has a gun in his hand and his voice sounds murderous. When did the plot change? I wasn't gone that long.

"Well, let's start with the juicy details to marinade you."

"Don't do it, Alpha. He'll play with your mind," Hilton says.

"Let him try. Let's hear it all and put an end to this madness."

"Don..." I call with my thinning voice.

"Stay out of it, *skat.* Actually, please go upstairs."

"I think you'll want her to stay for this one. How can we have a show without our main star?"

I wish I could kick him out of the wheelchair, squeeze his throat and watch him take his last breath.

"I don't know why, but I feel like I'm going to enjoy this. Your world now revolves around my daughter. She's all you care about, and that cursed baby growing in her stomach, which may not even be yours. I can't wait to watch everything you hold dear fall apart right before your eyes."

"How do you know about the baby? You know what, never mind that."

"Are you sure you don't want to know? I'll tell you anyway. And when I'm done, remember you made me do it."

I can't breathe. I'm sweating rivulets. I feel like I'll pee myself.

"Fine, tell me. What do you mean the baby might not be mine?"

"He's playing with your mind, Alpha. Leave it," Hilton says, with a tinge of desperation in his voice.

"No, let him talk. I need to hear this."

"Very well then. Let the party begin. I'm sorry, my child, I don't mean to hurt you, but since Alpha shot me and took away my leg as a personal favour to you, you deserve this. Believe it or not, I want a relationship with you. We'll play father and daughter later and forgive what can be forgiven and live with what can't be. For now, I'm sorry in advance for everything I'm about to say."

My life flashes before my eyes and I part my lips to breathe. I didn't mean to sabotage myself like this.

Tristan grabs my wrist. "Keep it together," he whispers.

I look at him and he nods so subtly I might have imagined it.

Hilton pulls out his gun and points it at the General. "Speak or I'll get rid of your other leg!"

I thought Hilton was on my side. What is he doing? Why is he provoking him?

"Speak!" He taps him at the top of his head with the gun. "You're wasting our Alpha's time."

The General shoots me a disdainful look. If he could spit on me, I'm sure he would. I flinch, and Tristan's grip tightens.

"*Sies!* She should have aborted you!"

"I'm glad she didn't abort her. We'd have missed all of this. Your daughter is Alpha's now. She'll have his child and he'll always be your son-in-law. The one man you hate the most is who your daughter loves the most. I bet you right now, your own blood will choose Alpha over you if we made her pick."

Such betrayal! I turn to Don for help but he doesn't even look at me.

"I'll not have my child shagging this filth! You're useless as an Alpha and as a man! You're a sissy! You'll not insult me like this!" The General's face changes to something dangerous as he reaches for something on the side of his wheelchair.

Everything happens so fast yet as if in slow motion.

"You'll die like the dog you are!" He aims the gun at Don.

I cover my ears as the gun fires. I feel it more than I hear it. My lungs seem to give up all air and my gut squeezes painfully. My ears ring loudly before everything goes silent. I might have lost my sight as well because I can't see anything.

"Get up!" Tristan shakes me.

I stay on the floor, folded into a bundle.

"Get up!" He pulls me up.

My father is sitting with his head drooping to the side, blood trickling out of his mouth and from the hole in his head. His eyes are open, and I know it's too late to look away. The image is imprinted in my brain forever.

I follow Tristan up the stairs, trying not to look back. It's like I'm swimming underwater. I can't hear anything and my vision is blurry.

Hilton catches up with us and says something to Tristan in Afrikaans. Tristan goes back down while I shudder and hold on to the wall.

"I'd love to stand here and listen to you crying all day, but I have more pressing things to do. Follow me," Hilton says.

He says we must hurry in case someone heard the gunshots and called the police.

As he drives, he calls his 'guy' in the police force to give him a heads-up if anything comes up. At least it's Manenberg, he says, gunshots could literally be coming from anywhere. I want to ask if the walls are not soundproof and how the sound would have been heard outside all the way from underground, but I can't find my voice.

The image of my father's lifeless body soaked in blood will never leave my head. I feel like screaming with everything inside of me, but that would be a bad idea, so I keep whimpering instead.

"You wanted him dead before you left Cape Town. Shouldn't you be happy?"

"Happy?"

"Yes."

I close my eyes and curse him. "No, I'm not happy, Hilton. Despite everything, he was my father."

"He wasn't much of a father to you. You lost nothing. Now stop making that noise."

I sniff again. I know he has a point but I don't need to hear it right now. I feel hollow, like I lost everything.

"He was not a man you'd want to call a father. He'd have killed you without thinking twice."

"Why did you say all those things? You pushed him!"

"I know you don't think right, but shock me for once and get this one."

"Please don't do that. Not today."

He looks at me and back on the road.

"I did it for you and Alpha. The General was going to tell Alpha everything he knew about you and Viper's son."

"Oh my word, Hilton! Thank ..."

"Don't say it," he cuts me off.

I silently thank him a million times and try to process everything going on in my head.

"What if he had killed Don, or you?"

"Wolves take the bullet for their Alpha. I knew that boy would jump in front of Alpha. As for me, he wouldn't have killed me. The angle was wrong and I wasn't the one fucking his daughter."

"But..."

"But nothing. All this mess is your doing. I saved your ass, now stop making noise."

"So you did it for me?" I need to hear it again.

"And Alpha. Did you not hear that part? Alpha would have never forgiven you. I give everyone three chances. You're on your third strike that's why I'm burying your story with that boy. Losing you would kill Alpha, and I prefer him alive."

"Why do you care whether I live or die?" And who is he to play a god? Giving us three strikes and all.

He looks at me before looking back at the road. "Without you, who would annoy me and make my life unbearable?"

I want to smile, but I cry harder instead. If he wasn't driving I would hug him.

"You'll be safe here." He parks outside Don's house in the Cape Flats.

I look at him and continue hugging myself. He looks like he's fighting a losing battle with his thoughts and he finally gives in.

"Do you want me to stay with you?"

"I'd love that, but you have to go and take care of business."

"You sure?" He's soft-spoken and warm, a very strange contrast to his nature.

"I'll be alright."

"Alright then. Be good. I'll see you later."

"Thank you, Hilton. I truly appreciate everything." I hold on to his arm. I don't know how I will ever repay him.

"Don't mention it."

He waits until I'm inside the house before driving off.

I double-check that every door is locked, then take out the key so Don doesn't wake me up when he gets home.

# TWENTY TWO

I'm trying to sleep, but every time I close my eyes, I see my father's face. I will never get the chance to talk to him, or ask him why, or hold his hand. I try to focus on deep breaths, but it's like trying to catch the wind with my bare hands. The memories of my father's final moments come crashing over me, each one like a punch to the gut. I curl up and hug my knees. My stomach is making it uncomfortable, but I stay there, rocking myself.

My breathing eventually steadies, but I still feel like death and my throat is parched. I slowly get up and find my way down the stairs, balancing on the wall for support. I fill a glass with water and gulp it down in desperate swallows, then splash the rest on my face. It does nothing to soothe me.

*Aaarrrggghhh!* I throw the glass against the wall and it shatters into pieces, the crash echoing through the house. The noise feels like a release, but it's short-lived. It falls silent again and gunshots ring in my head. I hold on to the sink and scream until I feel my voice drying up. I wish I could call Don, but he is out there cleaning up my mess.

When I feel better, I make my way back upstairs. I had it all mapped out, but things took a wrong turn and went south very fast. If it wasn't for Hilton, I don't know how it would have all played out. I finally found my father, only to discover things I wish I never did. He was ready to throw me to the wolves, in the literal sense. He didn't care about me. He knew telling Don about Dalu would have been a signed death warrant, but he was willing to do it anyway. Can I blame him though? He was under a blood oath and had no option. I wish I had gone to see him on my own. Things might have worked out differently. Maybe I should have listened to my mother and let it go. Maybe I should have listened to Don when he told me it was a bad idea. Now I must live with the knowledge that I was sired by an abuser.

I find my grandmother's rosary in the drawer and sit on the floor, clutching it tightly, the silver cross feeling cold against my skin. Tears are rolling down my face, but I'm not making a sound.

My phone rings and I ignore it. I keep focusing on the space between the door and the corner, reciting Hail Mary in my head. It rings again and I sigh and reach for it.

"Alpha's on his way. Take care of each other, alright? Call me if you need anything."

"Thank you, Hilton."

I dry my face, get off the floor and try to look normal.

Don walks in looking exhausted, and I put on a brave face.

"How are you doing?"

"Good," I say, even though anyone with eyes can see that I'm far from it.

"That's good."

He sits on the edge of the bed, looking away from me. I move closer and rest my head on his shoulder.

"If anyone finds out what happened today, I'll be on death row. I want to live long enough to see my face on our child. I need to hold him in my arms, even once."

"You'll be around long after she's born. You'll drive her on her first day to university." I'm still insisting it's a girl.

He looks back at me and I see tears in his eyes.

"Let's lie down, baby."

We huddle together. The silence is too loud and the echo of gunshots keeps ringing in my ears.

"I also can't sleep. Let's go downstairs; I could use a drink."

I need a drink myself but I won't even think of drinking in front of him.

He grabs a beer then lights a joint. I'm relieved when he passes it to me.

"Who else knew that the General was still alive? I thought he was a kept secret."

"He was, until Viper and his son got to him. Now the real question is, who let them in? Someone close to me is a rat."

I can't think of anyone close to Don who would betray him like that. They would all die for him. There has to be another explanation.

"Could it be the young Wolf who was taking care of him? The one who died?"

"Could be. Everyone thinks so."

*But would he still have sacrificed himself?*

We return to smoking in silence.

"*Skat.*"

"Yes?" I'm glad to be talking again. The misery that was seeping through the silence was starting to drive me into depression.

"What did the General mean the baby might not be mine?"

I feel cold, like a blizzard attacked me without warning.

"I... umm..."

"Yes?" He raises an eyebrow.

"I have no idea. I think he assumed Dalu and I had a thing. Who knows what lies Dalu told him? There was nothing between us. Just because we were friends doesn't mean there was anything more. We chatted a little when I was in Eastern Cape, but I cut him off when he started crossing a line. I'd never be involved with him like that. I don't even understand why people think that. I've always been honest with you, baby. You know I'd never do anything to mess up what we have."

His phone rings, and I say a silent thank you to heaven. I need to get it together and sound as normal as possible. I shouldn't over explain.

"Who was that?" I ask when he hangs up.

"Elik."

I've always wondered how a guy like Elik is involved with the Wolves. He's educated, well off, owns companies, and is a straight up smart guy. Why would he get mixed up with the Dons and Hiltons of this world? But right now, I need to stretch this conversation so we stay as far away as possible from that question he asked.

"How exactly does Elikplim Nkrumah fit into the puzzle?"

"Cameras in the safe house and the General's phone."

"Huh?"

"He had to take care of the evidence and go through the phone to see if there was anything useful in it."

"What did he find?"

His phone rings again, and by the time he's done, he has moved on from the chat.

*Phew!*

"If everyone believed the General was dead, how are you going to explain holding his funeral now?"

"All the key players knew he was in recovery and laying low in the safe house. Alphas had access to him, but he was such a shitty person, no one bothered to check in on him."

"Oh, that's a relief."

"As long as no one finds out we did it, we're in the clear. We'll give him a decent funeral and move on."

Tears suddenly well up in my eyes and I'm too slow to catch them. Emotions caught me off guard.

He reaches for my hands. "Hey, don't cry. I know he was your father. I'm sorry for how it went down. Talk to me, my angel. How are you really feeling?"

"I hate him so much. I've lost my mother because of him. You were right. I should have listened to you. I messed up."

He sits me between his legs and wraps his arms around me.

"I care a lot about you, my *skat*. Seeing you like this hurts me. But in a way, I'm happy you confronted both of them. I know it wasn't the closure you hoped for, but it's a step. You don't have to be strong around me, okay? I'll never judge your feelings. Let it all out. I'm here for every bit of it."

He keeps me in his arms until I calm down.

"I love you so much," I say when I find my voice again. "Please promise you'll never leave me."

"I'll never leave you. You have no idea how much you mean to me, do you? You and our child are my entire world. Every beat of my heart belongs to you, Lotus."

My emotions burst out of me and I bury my face in his arm.

When I feel better, I untangle myself from him and straddle him. Our eyes lock and I nod. I need this. He leans in and kisses me, his hands going under my top and skilfully unhooking my bra. I lift my arms and he makes short work of taking off my top. His mouth takes in my nipple and the sensation surges through every cell in my body as if I'm about to explode into a million stars. He comes back to my lips and I hold on to his arms, struggling between moaning and kissing him.

He stands with me, and my legs wrap around his waist. My belly gets in the way, so he lays me on the couch and pulls off my leggings and panties. My breath catches when he takes off his T-shirt. Those chiselled abs, those muscles, those arms, that ink on his skin – I need him inside me right now. I get up and help him out of the rest of his clothes, then push him back on the couch and get on top of him. I gasp as he enters, and the soft moan that escapes his lips makes me even wetter.

I move slowly, my breasts on his face, his hands on my ass, my head thrown back. As the rush intensifies, I lose the rhythm and hang onto his neck as he drives into me until I'm screaming his name. His hands stay plastered onto my back, holding me steady as I tremble from head to toe.

When I finally catch my breath, he takes over, his strong arms balancing me until I'm steadily bouncing on him. The slippery sound of him sliding in and out, and the soft slap of my ass against his thighs, drive me wild.

"Don..." I moan, feeling every inch of him, each thrust stealing a piece of my soul.

I arch my back as he picks up the pace until he comes undone with a deep growl, his body shuddering against mine. He stays inside me for a while, his arms tight around me.

When he finally regains his strength, he kisses my forehead, lays me down, and curls up behind me, his hand resting on my stomach.

"I love you, my angel," he murmurs sleepily.

\* \* \* \* \*

I woke up feeling better today. I need to reach out to my mother, but I don't know what exactly I'll say to her. She said I was dead to her, but she can't have meant it. I don't even know if she's still in Cape Town or if she left already. Caleb left her in town. Apparently, she said she would sort herself out from there.

I dial her number before I get cold feet.

"What do you want?" she snaps.

"Sisi, where are you?"

"Why?"

"I was hoping I could come to you and talk."

"Talk about what?"

"Everything. I need to explain. I'm sorry about what happened."

"Is that it? You're sorry? Then we're done here."

"Sisi, wait. Okay, fine. Can you come to the funeral?" Fingers crossed. At least then I can force her to talk to me.

She keeps quiet and I hold my breath.

"When is it?"

"I'll text you the details. Sisi, I'm really sorry. Please don't hate me. Please ..."

"Goodbye, Lotus."

Ouch! I hope she makes it to the funeral. I desperately need to make things right with her. I hate how she doesn't see that everything that happened was her fault. If she never lied to me, we wouldn't be here right now. But I'll be the bigger person.

I want to text Chelsea, but that boat sailed and I can't keep chasing someone who doesn't want to be caught. I'm beginning to make peace with her absence. I have apologised, begged and done everything but show up on her doorstep, and she has blatantly ignored me every time. It hurts, but I need to accept it and move on. And she told Caleb everything I told her! She obviously wanted Don to find out about Dalu. I feel so stupid for always texting her. I don't even know what I did that was so bad that she couldn't talk to me about it.

Don is still sleeping and the silence is driving me crazy, so I call Fierce. We might not be close friends, but I need someone to talk to. She cheers me up and makes me laugh in no time. She and Elik deserve a reality show! For a moment, I forget all my problems.

Don's phone rings, and he grunts and covers his head with a pillow.

*Shame*, he was sleeping so peacefully. I wish he didn't have to answer it, but I kind of set the world on fire, so he has to.

I shake him gently until he grumbles and takes the phone.

"I have to go. Meeting with the Alphas," he says after the call, forcing himself up.

Yesterday was a horror-thriller-action movie. The guys had to act fast to cover their tracks. So now, as far as the rest of the Wolves know, Dalu and the young Wolf are responsible for the General's death. They also know that Dalu is Viper's son, which means this is going to spark another gang war. This is not what I had in mind when I planned to question my parents.

The young Wolf was an easy target because of his ties to Viper's gang. His brother runs with the Hard Livings, so it was easy to make it look like he led Dalu to the General. I don't know why they didn't expose that the General was working with the Hard Livings to bring down the Wolves. Don said it was the least he could do to give him a hero's funeral instead of letting him be mutilated and burned as a traitor. I think he did it for me.

Elik erased all traces of us from the CCTV footage and falsified texts between the young Wolf and Dalu. The phone was then planted back on the Wolf's body, where it was conveniently 'discovered' during the search. To seal the deal, Elik fabricated several payments from Dalu to the young Wolf. The flash drive I got from Dalu's apartment that time was also slipped into the Wolf's pocket.

Hilton used a gun that couldn't be traced back to *us* - a type commonly used by the Hard Livings. Tristan planted the gun in Dalu's apartment and removed all traces of me from there. He also left behind pictures of Dalu and his father to confirm he was Viper's son. I'm not sure how he pulled it off, but I'm thankful he did. So when the Wolves raided Dalu's place, they found the gun, pictures and documents that made him look guilty.

Don and another Alpha took the gun to their police contacts and had it dusted for fingerprints. As expected, the report came back with Dalu's prints, thanks to a brown envelope and some creative persuasion on Don's part.

It's all set, but I can't shake the feeling that it's too fragile. Maybe it's just paranoia, but I'm scared this will come back to bite us. I also really hate how the young Wolf, who sacrificed his life for Don, has been branded a traitor. His body will be mutilated and defiled, and his family will be denied any compensation. But like Don reminded me, 'In every war, there are casualties'.

I feel like the weakest link in this chain. If anyone discovers my involvement and questions me, it's over for everyone.

# TWENTY THREE

Black really is my colour. I was tempted to put on black lipstick, black eyeshadow and winged eyeliner, but Goth is not my style.

I wish I could post this look on Instagram. I'm sure I would get 1K likes in no time, but that life is behind me. I take the picture anyway because what Instagram cannot do, WhatsApp status can.

I hop on a video call with Fierce to show her my outfit. She hypes me so much, I feel like the hottest girl in the world. She assures me that I don't look pregnant at all, which is a relief since I don't want my stomach showing. I chose a mid-length dress that flows gracefully from the waist, with a gentle flare that skims my legs. The soft crepe fabric drapes beautifully and adds just the right amount of fluidity to hide my little bump. The flutter sleeves give it an elegant touch, and the Louboutins pull the whole look together. I kept it simple with gold earrings and a small necklace. I feel like a million bucks.

I hate to say goodbye to Fierce, she keeps me alive these days, but we have to leave now.

I do one last check in the mirror and give myself a distinction. Now we can go. Don looks like a god in black. Don't ask me a god of what. Probably of death or thunder, something lethal like that. I step up to him and smile my way to his lips. He turns away and my lips land on his cheek.

"I'm not showing up with lipstick," he whines.

"You'll show up with it on your cheek then."

I take a wet wipe and clean it off.

"You look gorgeous." He makes me twirl around as he whistles and showers me with exaggerated compliments.

He holds the car door open for me and I smile to myself as I get comfortable in the passenger's seat. It's the little things *mann.*

"Remember to stay calm. You can't act out or say anything to anyone. He wasn't short of enemies, so you don't want the only thing you inherit from him to be his sins. It's already bad enough you have me." He gives me a side eye before focusing back on the road.

"You're nothing like him, baby." I reach for his hand.

We drive in silence for the most part, and I stay distracted by my phone.

We approach the cemetery and I can already tell the type of crowd that's here. Dropped cars, expensive mags, weird colours, gold-plated Mercs - why do they violate their cars like this? Two police vans drive past

165

as we park and I spot a group of police in riot gear moving into the cemetery.

"Cops?"

"They're going to lurk to make sure nothing shady goes on. Don't worry about it. The top dogs are on our payroll, so if things go south, they conveniently won't witness a thing and will need to investigate further."

Caleb comes to meet us. He's nice but I'm still a bit funny around him.

"Take care of her for me, my bru," Don says.

"Always."

"*Skat*, please keep it together. Stay with Caleb."

I promise and smile as his fine-self walks away.

"You look good," Caleb breaks the ice.

"Thank you. You too."

"So, how are you feeling?"

"I'm not sure. I think I'm good."

We walk side by side, our footsteps falling into a steady rhythm.

"Caleb, I just want to say sorry for everything. I swear I had no part in whatever Chelsea did. I'm also sorry for putting Tristan in harm's way. It was not the intention at all."

"I talked to Tris and I owe you an apology. He said he's working with you and I misread the whole situation. He explained everything... I'm sorry for getting on your case."

"It's cool. I understand where you were coming from."

"So are we good?"

"We're good... And thank you for sending Hilton to check up on me."

"That cost me a lot!"

I try to ask what exactly it cost but he laughs it off.

I didn't expect so many people at the funeral. I often forget that gangsters are human before they are criminals. I thought Hilton was scary, but looking at some of the guys here, I've decided he's very normal. Some of the Wolves look young *shame*; my heart goes out to them. They probably had no idea what they were signing up for when they got in, and now they are stuck.

There are four distinct groups, each representing a pack. A few of the guys in each pack are standing with their women. They call their girlfriends bitches; it vexes me. Don is standing with Hilton and Tristan. I don't know why I'm with Caleb and not him. Maybe it's to confuse the enemy. Don whispers something to Hilton before walking to the front. I think Alphas have to represent their packs. Although the leader of each of the four packs is called an Alpha, only Don is called Alpha. The rest use their nicknames.

We have the best Alpha, hands down. Look at him! I'm blushing inside, just remembering what those lips can do. The Alpha across our pack looks like he eats human flesh for breakfast and washes it down with blood. He sharpened his teeth to look like fangs. They call him Skinner. The other one, Dust, looks like a sociopath with a history of serial killing. He looks like the type that forces his victims to chop themselves up into pieces like they are on the set of a *Saw* movie. The other Alpha looks like the face of extreme childhood trauma. He looks dead just like his name - Ghost.

"There she is," Caleb whispers in my ear.

I follow the direction of his eyes and I see my mother approaching, swinging her hips side to side like Arianna Grande is singing in her head.

"I'll be right back."

Walking on high heels on grass is the pits, but I keep my head held high. I go around the guys and towards her. Thankfully, she spots me because I can't shout and draw all the attention to myself. My mission today is to blend with the shadows.

"Did I miss anything?"

"Not really. We just got here."

"Good. We have to see that bastard lowered into the ground. I don't trust him. He could be faking his death, again."

"He's really dead this time. I watched him die."

Concern floods her face but she quickly shakes it off. "Are you alright? Where are the tears? I know you love being the main character and getting all the attention."

I'll pretend I didn't hear that. "I'm good. Happy even. He deserved it for what he did to you." I'm walking on eggshells around her because I'm desperate for her forgiveness. I didn't think she would come and I'm happy she did. Just like her, I'm not here to mourn. I'm here to confirm that he's truly dead, and maybe dance on his grave. I'm even considering setting up camp here for a few days to make sure he doesn't claw himself out of the ground. You can never trust the devil.

Who am I kidding? I'm bleeding internally. My heart is shattered and I'm weeping inside, but I'm determined to fake not caring long enough until the next bathroom break where I can bawl my eyes out. Me and him never got a chance, and that's not fair.

"You!" My mother greets Caleb with a sharp eye.

"Hello, Ma." Caleb extends his hand for a handshake.

"Where's your jailbird?" she whispers.

I look towards Don's direction since I can't exactly point.

"Mmm... He's not that bad today."

I smile a little. That's a compliment.

The coffin is lying on the casket jack, ready to be lowered into the ground. It's not a typical funeral. There is no wailing or anything like that. It's as if everyone is attending a stranger's send-off.

The four Alphas step forward, each on either side of the grave, and they take turns giving eulogies on behalf of their packs. It's fascinating to watch, and almost touching.

I don't quite understand what Skinner and Dust are saying. I just know they are angry and that Viper and Dalu should be very afraid, wherever they are.

Ghost is next. He clears his throat before giving a long speech in Afrikaans, ending it in English.

"Those Hard Livings think they can just take one of ours and walk away like it's nothing? General Ryan is gone! He's marching with the bones before his time! We're not letting this shit slide! We're coming for every last one of those motherfuckers! They want a war? Let's give them hell. Those cockroaches will be begging for mercy before we're done, and we'll show them none! Viper and his crew better start running because we're going to grind them into dust. When you spot a Hard Living, take *it* out with no hesitation. Show them what happens when you fuck with us. Let's wipe them out! Do it for the General, and for every drop of blood they've spilled from our brothers. Rest in power, General."

What was that? Who declares war so openly? Don was right when he said Ghost will do anything to be the next General. Because, honestly, what was that? But it got the Wolves riled up so I guess it worked.

Don is the last to speak. He raises his hand and the Wolves fall silent. I feel a sense of pride and I smile to myself. There is something about a man with power and status.

His accent is a bit off, yet I find it beautiful. It makes me cling on to his every word.

"Today we lay to rest a legend who was more than a leader to us. A man who lived and died on his own terms. Who never took shit from anyone. Who always had our backs no matter what. I remember the first time I met the General. I was just a kid looking for a way out of the streets. He saw something in me that no one else did. He showed me that there was more to life than just surviving. He welcomed me into the family with open arms.

He was a boss, a king, a goddamn force of nature. He made the Wolves into something that people feared and respected. He was a tough one, but he had a soft spot somewhere underneath that leather jacket he always wore. He was a true Wolf. If anyone crossed him. If anyone dared to disrespect him or his family, he would come down on them without mercy. But most of all, he was a man of honour. He lived by our code: loyalty, respect and strength. He knew what it took to survive in this world, and he taught us all how to do it. He made us strong and kept the packs together.

He'll forever live in our hearts, our memories and our actions. Now that he's gone, we are left to pick up the pieces and carry on his legacy. Rest in power, General Ryan. You were a real leader. You'll never be forgotten."

He raises his gun in the air and shouts, "We are GIFTED!"

The other Alphas raise their guns heavenward, while the rest of the Wolves point gun signs with their fingers. I raise mine, ignoring my mother's judgemental look, and I say with them, "And Gifted I Fight Till Eternal Death!" our voices echoing throughout the cemetery.

Silence follows, fingers still steadfast in the air, and I don't know what signal was given but the Alphas shoot their guns in perfect synchrony. So beautiful yet so reckless!

The moment I have been waiting for eventually arrives - body viewing - my chance to be 100% sure that he's truly in the box and not drinking rum on a beach in Jamaica and making us bury a stunt double. A lone tear betrays me and Caleb squeezes my hand. I look forward, focusing hard on not falling apart.

"It's okay to feel," he whispers.

I bite my lip and push my emotions back. It's not okay to feel in a space like this.

There is a method to the madness. Small groups from different packs approach the coffin, perform salutes and return to position. We, the nobodies, go last. I keep my mother's hand in mine. A woman and two girls in front of us are wailing like the General meant everything to them. The younger of the girls turns around and my breath catches. It's like I'm looking at my younger self. I almost lose composure but I fake-cough myself back into position.

I finally come face-to-face with the sperm donor that contributed to my creation. He looks terrible. He was shot in the head so he's deformed. They tried their best to put him back together and shape him up, but he looks abnormal. The skin on his face is loose, with visible eye bags hanging like granny tits. They slicked his hair back, making his protruding cheekbones stand out. When I see past the deformities, I come face-to-face with myself, and reality hits home hard. My mother lets go of my hand

and walks away, leaving me alone right when I need her the most. I stand there a little while longer, grappling with the finality of it all. This is the end. I'll never sit down with him and really understand. I will never get the answers to the million questions I have.

When everyone has viewed the body, a priest comes forward for the last words, complete with a collar around his neck. A priest? Now I have seen it all. Many of the Wolves believe in the Source. I know if I ask Don, he'll say, "The Source is everywhere and is for everyone. Even sinners like us deserve redemption".

The coffin is lowered into the ground and no one in sight is in tears. I feel my heart snap when the last of the coffin disappears.

*Goodbye, Daddy. May you have the afterlife you deserve.* I'm not going to wish him peace. I'll leave it to afterlife karma.

I say a prayer as we walk away, asking for forgiveness, and without meaning to, I ask that God hears my father out and shows him some grace when he shows up before Him.

"Aren't you coming to the after-party with us?" Caleb asks my mother as we walk towards the exit of the cemetery.

"Your problem is that you think we're friends. You think because you're the nicest and most human of them all, it automatically makes you likeable. I'm not one of those impressionable girls that trip and fall all over you because you look unnecessarily handsome. Shave that beard before you give girls heart attacks!"

I can't help but chuckle. She's a special kind of special. Caleb looks confused and tugs his beard, making everything funnier.

We walk towards the parked cars and my mother takes Caleb's hand and stops him.

"Listen to me. Chelsea did not sleep with that Elik. She made a mistake by going to see him. She was very wrong for that, but she did not cheat on you. She deeply regrets hurting you. That girl loves you, Caleb. She has been through a lot. Please be kind to her. Hear her out."

Caleb swallows and looks down.

"I'll be on my way now. Chelsea is taking me out for lunch."

She's staying with Chelsea? Wow! I feel so betrayed. I can't even explain the pain that cuts through my heart.

"Sisi, can we talk?" I reach for her hand.

"No, we can't."

I'm taken aback. I did not expect that response.

"Please."

"No. I'm leaving now. I'm happy that your sorry excuse of a father was put down like the dog he was. You asked me to come to the funeral and I came. Now I'm asking you to give me space and I expect you to respect that."

I open my mouth and close it again. She looks at me, and for a moment I think she'll open her arms and hug me. Tears stream down my face as she disappears into a cab. Something inside me dies. She really chose Chelsea over me, knowing very well how much Chelsea not talking to me broke my heart. I wipe my tears and take Caleb's hand when he offers it.

"Did your mother insult me?"

"She complimented you actually."

"She did?"

"Yes! She called you handsome and all those nice things."

I can tell he's flattered.

"Thank you for today." I look at him sincerely.

"It's only a pleasure."

I guess we won't be touching on what my mother said about Chelsea or anything she said before she left. I prefer it that way.

As Caleb drives, I look out the window, watching houses roll past. I'm fine for the most part, but there is a part of me that's broken. It's more trauma than pain. Nothing could have prepared me for the sound of gunshots close range, and of seeing not one but two dead bodies. The images haunt me every time they cross my mind. I can't even sleep with the lights off anymore. Then my mother came and gave me hope, only to shatter it at the snap of a finger.

"Are you still here with me?" Caleb's voice pulls me out of my head.

He says something else and I look at him deadpan. I have no idea what he said.

"Excuse me?"

"I said earth to Lotus."

"Oh, I'm sorry. Where are we now?"

"We're here. We won't stay long. Alpha doesn't want you here, and with good reason."

"Why? Am I in danger?"

"You roll with us, so you're always in danger. But that's not it. The Wolves get rowdy at these after-parties. Shootings break out, people stab each other, some get drunk and get out of line, some get high and lose it, the whole mess. We all grieve differently. And you know how they treat some girls here. Alpha would lose his mind if any of the guys started groping you. So we'll go in, pay our respects and get out."

I agree. I don't exactly want to hang out with strangers that have criminal records.

I powder my face before leaving the car and apply a layer of lip gloss. Bereavement does not mean I must look homeless. I straighten my dress and fix my hair. When I'm satisfied, I walk with Caleb into the house.

The Wolves have weird beliefs, I must say. Don explained to me the other day that after a funeral, it's customary for Wolves to have an after-party to toast to the dead. They don't grieve like the rest of us. Instead of mourning, they celebrate the life of the departed. To them, death is an honour, not a tragedy. It's like earning a medal. They call it 'marching with the bones', meaning they carry the spirit of the deceased with them, making sure their energy strengthens the gang. It's about never showing fear, even in death. If they were to grieve, it might make them question their way of life and feel more human than wolf, which would be bad because a conscience is the last thing a gangster should have. So instead of crying or feeling sad, they throw a party and have a jol. They raise their glasses, share stories, dance, and cheer, all to keep their fallen's legacy strong. Showing sadness or pain is seen as a weakness, something no gangster admits to. Partying instead of grieving helps them manage their fear of death, so they can face it bravely when it's their turn to go.

There is alcohol everywhere, loud music pouring out of speakers and girls dressed like they are selling their bodies.

"Tequila, whiskey, brandy... pick your poison," an overexcited girl, who reminds me too much of Chelsea, says.

"Tequila, please, and a slice of lime."

Caleb takes whiskey. We toast and empty them into our throats. I screw my eyes shut and bite hard on the lime as the tequila burns its way down. I had forgotten how strong a shot of this stuff can be.

"Should you be drinking?" Caleb asks, as if it just crossed his mind.

"I have a broken heart to soothe." I down another shot.

He looks at me disapprovingly but lets it go.

"Do not tell Donavan!"

"Not my place."

I excuse myself when I spot Hilton talking to some guys. I hook my arm around his and smile up at him. He looks down at me with that '*What did I do to deserve this?*' eye I'm used to.

"*Aweh*, my bru." I grin at him.

"I'm not your..."

"But you are my bru, my bru. Just say *aweh* back."

He sighs deeply. "You can let me go now."

"Not until you say '*Aweh*, my bru' and do the hand salute like this." I demonstrate with my free hand.

"Lotus!"

"Just say it! People are watching now."

"Fine... *Aweh*, my bru," he says with a dropped voice but doesn't salute. He sounds so irritated, it's hilarious.

"See! Did you die?"

"Get lost. You're such a nag."

I chuckle and keep my arm around his. He tells the guys to disappear and they dissipate like dust. They fear this big bear? Poor things.

"I came all the way to say hello to you, Hilly, and this is the thanks I get? Fine! Be like that." I purse my lips and fake a sad look.

It doesn't faze him; he still looks annoyed.

"I'm leaving. Stay here with your miserable party. I'm going to do better things at home like watch TV, pray for you, or sleep. Anything but this crazy party."

"Goodbye, Lotus." He untangles himself from my hold and walks away.

They don't make them like him anymore.

I'm ready to leave when the wailing woman from the funeral catches my eye. She's standing alone near the door, with a glass in her hand.

"Are you going to drink that or will you swirl it the whole day?" I attempt to break the ice, but it falls flat and she gives me an awkward look.

"I don't drink."

I want to ask why then she has alcohol in her hand but she starts talking.

"I can't believe he's gone. How could he do this to me?" She looks at me as if she wants an answer. "Why would he leave like that? He promised to take the girls on a trip. That's all they looked forward to, and then he was shot and we were all devastated. He was recovering well in hospital and then he vanished without a trace. For months, I searched for him. I looked everywhere. And then he was found dead. It doesn't make any sense. No one will tell me anything."

"Was he your..."

"Husband, yes. He wasn't the best husband, but he was an amazing father. He lived for his girls. They loved him more than anything. He was always there for them. Now they're lost and confused. I don't know what to tell them."

I feel a stab in my heart. Why couldn't he be that to me too?

"I'm sorry for your loss. I just came to pass my condolences. You were standing alone and I thought you could use an ear." I can't stay longer and listen to her describing that monster as a hero.

"Thank you. Who are you again? You look familiar. Have we met before?" She squints and I look down. I don't want her to pick up the resemblance I have to her husband and put two and two together.

"I don't think we've met."

She looks at me suspiciously and returns to ranting.

"They killed him like a dog, and you know what makes me angry? The fact that nothing will happen to them. There's no justice for the likes of him. The memory my children have of their father is him with a bullet in his head. I know who he was, and it was always bound to end this way, but he was my husband and he took care of us. He deserved better."

She throws the drink down her throat and gulps down every drop. I'm tempted to ask what happened to not drinking, but without warning, she starts crying and I have no option but to embrace her. I fight back the tears welling in my eyes. I'll not cry; not in front of strangers.

"If you're who I think you are, give me a call sometime. Take my number." She dries her face.

I hand her my phone and she punches in her number. No promises to call but we'll see.

Caleb calls me and I say goodbye to the widow.

"I see you and your stepmother were bonding well."

I almost start ranting about how the General was an amazing father to his other children but never bothered with me, but I decide not to. I'll open up to my man instead.

Caleb drops me off at home and says he's going back to the party.

"That party you said gets rowdy and is full of radical Wolves?"

"Yes. I'm part of the Wolves. Rowdy and radical is in my nature."

He knows he's nothing like them. His heart still beats in his chest. Don always says Caleb is the Mahatma Gandhi of their family, all for peace and non-violence.

# TWENTY FOUR

The past week has been hard for me. Half the time I don't know if I'm coming or going. Don has been so supportive, he might be the only thing keeping me sane. He sleeps at home almost every night, holds me every chance he gets and he's so kind, I forget my problems half the time. He communicates and respects my feelings so much, I feel like staying in mourning for a long time. I'm finally getting the man I ordered.

It wasn't my father's death that hit me the hardest. It was my mother walking away from me and choosing Chelsea over me. She's still not taking my calls; I don't know what else to do. Tristan drove me to Chelsea's apartment the other day, but either no one was home or I was ignored. I wonder what I did to that girl. How can she stay with my mother but not talk to me? I stalked her Instagram and I couldn't believe my eyes. The audacity of posting 'Girls' Night' - she and my mother in pyjamas, laughing and having wine! I thought she was going to come back to me one day, but now I'm mourning all of them at once: my father, my mother and my best friend.

Tears fall onto my phone screen and I quickly wipe them away with the sleeve of my coat. I type paragraphs to my grandmother, pouring my heart out. I don't know if she'll respond but I just hope she at least reads them. I hold my grandmother's rosary to my chest as I often do. I never imagined going through life without my family. My grandmother means everything to me and I regret not spending more time with her when I had the chance. I regret every word I never said and every emotion I never showed. She did her best with me, but somewhere along the way, I lost my path and now here we are. I should have said goodbye the right way, but would she have understood? Maybe I should go home or give her a call, but where would I begin?

I can feel a dark cloud settling in, so I shake it off, grab my phone, scroll to Hilton, and text, *'Please come in an hour or two so we can start.'*

I drag myself outside so I can clear my head before Hilton arrives. I watch the waves splashing lazily against the rocks before slowly flowing back into the sea. I wish I could put on a bikini and go into the ocean, but I'm too lazy to even get up and go to the kitchen to get juice. This house is perfect for my mind. I have even forgotten how it was raided months ago and made the news.

I'm still lost in my thoughts when a voice startles me.

"You gave me such a fright! Don't ever do that again. Do you want to give me a heart attack?" That's so not cool. Sometimes I don't even know why I try with him.

"Shall we get down to it? I have things to do."

No greeting, no apology, no nothing. I close my eyes and take a deep breath. 'Inner peace' like Master Shifu in Kung Fu Panda would say. That's much better. I feel less violent now.

"I said come in an hour or two."

"I'm here now."

I give him my hand so he can help me up but he just looks at me before turning around and walking into the house. I guess it's time I gave up on him for my own peace of mind. Clearly, he's one problem I'll never be able to solve.

He has already made himself comfortable on the table and is tapping his fingers impatiently. Who created this guy and why? Surely, he wasn't made the same way the rest of us were. One day I will cut his chest open and check if there is a heart in there. I pity the woman who was made from his rib. Imagine being made from Hilton's rib? The horror!

"Want a beer?"

He just looks at me.

"Suit yourself. I'm going to make some tea. Do you want some?"

He looks at me like I'm crazy.

"Oh well, I offered."

I head to the kitchen to make a cup. I'm nervous because I don't have a plan B if this doesn't work.

I find Hilton looking somewhere between annoyed and frustrated.

"I'm aware that you don't like me much, and you're probably going to think what I'm going to say is stupid, but please hear me out." I know he likes me but I enjoy pretending like I don't know.

His face relaxes and he looks down for a split second. If I didn't know any better, I would say he looks guilty. But Hilton guilty? Hell would freeze over! The man is practically made of stone. I can sense his patience running thin, so let me get on with it while I still have a head on my neck. Rumour has it that he once killed someone for looking at him for too long.

"Don only listens to two people in the world. You know he's just like you. He doesn't like being told what to do. And once he's made a decision, he sticks to it. So here's what I'm thinking..."

"Spare the sermon for the church. Get to the point," he cuts me off.

"Okay, so you have tried convincing him to be the General and you have failed dismally."

"I'm listening."

I'm disappointed that he didn't take offence.

"Don will listen to his father."

"I'm listening." He sits up straight.

He really needs to add more words to his vocabulary!

"Don's father must be the one who asks Don to be the General. He's the only one who can convince him."

"Alpha forbade me from talking to his father about it. You think I didn't think of that?"

"He forbade you but he didn't forbid me. And like you always say, I'm not one of you. I can have direct contact with whoever I want."

"You want to go behind his back like that?"

"Yes. I'm willing to protect him from himself."

Is that an impressed look on his face?

I explain the plan to him, and when he nods, I know I'm on the right track. It's important that this happens.

"Alpha will be mad. He'll be very mad."

"I know he will be, but he'll be alive." I guess this is what they mean when they say sometimes you have to give up your life for the one you love. I stand to lose him but he will keep his life. I can't think of a greater sacrifice.

He thinks about it for a moment, then says, "Friday. I'll take you to Pops on Friday."

"Then we better get to work. Let's go to the study."

"I'll have that beer now."

"Coming right up."

I head to the kitchen to grab a beer, a soda, chips and some sweets. With our snacks in hand, we make our way to the study and sit next to each other.

"Tell me something. Why did Don's father rejoin the Wolves?"

"He had to rejoin before he went to prison. No one survives Pollsmoor without a number. He needed the protection."

"Interesting... Ok, shall we?" I open the Creed.

The Creed has two parts; the original voices of the Founders and parts written generations after. We need to go over the rules and conditions for an Alpha to rank up to a General. I'm sure the other three Alphas are gunning for the General position as well, so we need to find a way to outsmart them. I know they say 'It's simple politics' but nothing is ever simple with the Wolves. Funny enough, I have never bothered with the first part. The word '*History*' put me off the first time I saw it. Every time I went through the Creed, I would just scroll to what I wanted to read.

*The Wolves Gang was founded by four brothers. Their surname was Wolf. They regarded themselves as more than just a gang, but as a tight-knit brotherhood. The brothers established a structured organisation that evolved into one of the biggest gangs in Cape Town. Anyone who joined was seen as a family member, not a gang member, hence they were called Wolves.*

*In the beginning, the eldest brother assumed the role of Alpha, while the other three managed different turfs within the gang's operations. However, internal conflicts emerged among the brothers, prompting the division of the Wolves into four packs. This division granted each pack autonomy over its respective turf and ensured equality among the brothers. To maintain unity within the family, they recognised the need for a single leader and convinced their father to assume that role. And so the General title was born.*

*The brothers also recognised the need for a set of rules to govern their actions and maintain order within the family. So they established the Creed as the Law, outlining the principles and guidelines that every member of the Wolves gang had to adhere to. To emphasise the significance of the Creed, the brothers sealed the original five copies with their blood, imprinting a thumbprint on each document. This was the birth of the Blood Oath, which members of the Wolves cannot break. These copies were safeguarded, with one entrusted to each of the brothers, and the fifth kept by their father. Over time, as leadership changed from one General to the next, and from one Alpha to the next, copies of the Creed were passed down.*

We continue reading about how they went about taking over turfs and deciding which tattoo meant what. We end up on a page with the most blood chilling punishments.

"The General enjoyed torturing young Wolves. He said it made them strong."

My mood dampens at the thought of my father. "Why was he so cruel?"

"Rules are rules. Your fath... The General was a leader. It takes someone like him to understand what that means. You can't be soft and lead animals. You have to be tough, even seen as heartless, because that's the only way to keep hundreds of blood-thirsty animals in check. He had to be brutal to earn respect."

"But Don's father was not like that, from what I hear. So my father chose to be a savage." ... *and to abandon me,* I add in my head.

"You only know Pops from his son's point of view. I'm sure if you asked other people, they would describe him differently. Your father believed in making sure everyone knew who was in charge. He believed in doing whatever was necessary to keep everyone in line. Pops, not so much. He was like, well, like Alpha."

"Is that a bad thing?"

"It depends how you look at it."

"Who was a better General?"

"I don't think it was a competition."

"Wow, Hilton!"

"Power is like poison. It consumes until there's nothing left. Pops was different. He knew when to stop. Your old man was once a good leader, but he went out without any integrity left. He conspired to kill his own brothers and broke too many unbreakable rules. He betrayed us to our oldest rival. That's unforgivable in my books."

"So the Hard Livings have been around that long?"

"They were around long before the Wolves. The Americans came first, then The Hard Livings, then us."

"How come no one has ever told me this?!"

"Maybe because you're not one of us?"

I have nothing to say to that. He loves pointing that out.

I want to go back to talking about the General, maybe defend him a little, but I swallow my words and change the subject.

"Why did you choose to be a Protector? From what people say, you could have been the Alpha."

"I didn't choose to be a Protector, and I would not make a good Alpha."

I give him a 'continue' look.

"Unlike my cousin, I wasn't initiated into the Wolves. My father was an Alpha, so I was born a Wolf, more like what your child will be if it's a boy."

"What? How? How come Don wasn't born a Wolf even though his father was a General?"

He flips through the pages until he finds what he is looking for. "Read this."

*Any male offspring born to a Wolf leader is born into the pack. They become a Wolf by birthright.*

The next line says, *All sons born of leaders are Wolves and they should be marked when they come of age.*

"Okay, hold on. If Don was born a Wolf, why did he tell me that he joined the gang? He said he signed up and went through all the initiation stages." Also, wouldn't he have mentioned that our child could be a Wolf?

That's a piece of information he should have shared with me.

"He was born a Wolf but Pops got out before he came of age. Pops gave up the General title and all its perks, not because he was tired of being a Wolf, but for his son. He did it so his son wouldn't be a Wolf anymore. Donavan was still young and hadn't been marked yet, so when Pops got out, so did all his bloodline."

"Oh wow!" It's also one of the few times Hilton has called Don by his government name.

"So Don's father's sacrifice was for nothing?"

"Yes."

"Why did Don do that?" Don told me his reasons, but people often omit details when discussing themselves.

He pauses as if considering whether to tell me or not.

"He was a soft kid, so he got bullied a lot. He wanted people to leave him alone. Plus he was always around me and wanted to be like me. Then the General got to him and he signed up. He didn't think it through. He thought he could easily get out if he wasn't feeling it anymore, like his father had done."

"So when he joined the gang, you felt guilty? Is that why you took it upon yourself to be his Protector?"

"Yes and no. My father groomed me to be the General's Protector, but when Pops left, I needed plan B. Then my little cousin signed up and I had to keep him alive. I had to realign my focus. I made it a point to make him the Alpha and become his Protector. We had to be at the top, no matter who fell to make way for us."

That last line!

"Wait, Hilton... Don has four stars. I thought those were for Alphas. Why do you have four stars?"

"Four stars are for Alphas, so the Alpha's Protector gets them too because his life is tied to his Alpha. Being a Protector is an absolute honour, or a pain in the ass in my case."

He flips the pages of the Creed and shows me some text.

*A man hungry for blood should quench his thirst, not lead the pack.*

**Qualities of a Protector:** *Heartless, fearless, merciless, ruthless.*

They might as well have written *'Hilton'* because those words describe him to the T. I'm fascinated by all this. I didn't see most of it when I was going through the Creed on my own. I was too focused on the parts that would make Don a General.

"Wait, wait. So there can be many Protectors in a pack? Isn't that chaotic?"

"There are only five Protectors in the Wolves, one for each Alpha and the General, but there are many Guardians. The first Guardian in a pack to get four stars becomes the Protector. An Alpha can only have one right-hand man after all, it's not like he's an octopus."

He's so unintentionally funny.

"So you became the Protector?"

"I received my fourth star on my 16th birthday. The youngest to ever receive them. I could have been the next Alpha, but Protectors never rank up to Alphas. I made it a point to raise my own Alpha. One I would be loyal to for life."

I'm enjoying this. None of them have ever let me in this deep. Now I understand the bond between Don and Hilton.

"Donavan was a scared little boy when he joined the pack. He had no idea what he was signing his life away to, and by the time he realised what he'd done, it was too late. He made a mess with Candice, and when they excused her from life, he lost his mind. I knew it was only a matter of time before they got annoyed by his whining. They would have put him down had I not forced sense into his head. With his father in prison and his mother in the ground, he was wounded and terrified. I took it upon myself to train him into the soldier he is today. I worked that boy like a full-time job. They bullied him because he looked, spoke and acted like a cheese boy. It didn't help that he was pale and had blue eyes. He was just a wrong fit. He spoke pure English and school-type Afrikaans. He went to church every Sunday and was part of those little boys in the front dressed like small priests. He would say stupid things like please, excuse me, I'm sorry. He even prayed before eating. Who does that? I had to undo all that for him to survive."

What he described is what I want my child to be like.

"I saw this future years ago, so I suppose you can call me a prophet."

"Now you're pushing it. A prophet of what? Of doom?"

He laughs a little and it's beautiful to witness.

"I can foretell someone's death and see it through."

I don't even know why I'm laughing at something so dark. We go back to taking notes and I read a section on tattoos.

"Do you regret any of your tattoos?"

He looks at me and I know the answer is yes, but he's probably afraid of being vulnerable.

"Maybe the ones on my face. My father forced most of them there."

I sense that there is something deeper with his father, but I don't know if I can ask. I don't want him to shut down.

"I had my first tattoo before I knew what a tattoo was, and I had my first body in the ground when I was six. My father was a tough man. He punished weakness severely. He punished failure, so I don't fail unless I choose to. Have you seen my back?"

I have seen his back. I thought he survived a torture chamber or something. His own father did all that to him? How cruel!

"Father used to say the strongest steel goes through the hottest fires."

"I'm so sorry." I place my hand on his.

"My mother would try to protect me. She did her best to give me some sort of a childhood. So when she left, I had to grow up. There was no one left to run to."

"Where did your mother go?"

"Father killed her when I was eight." He swallows. "I'll never forget her dying face, or me begging my father not to do it, but hey, it is what it is."

This is the first time I have seen Hilton in pain. I stand from my chair and hug him from behind, tightly closing my arms around his chest.

"You remind me a lot of my mother. She was beautiful, warm, sweet, talked a lot and tried too hard to fix everything. She was very kind too."

Now he's making me emotional. I wish there was something I could do to make his pain go away. I excuse myself for a bathroom break so I can cry in peace. He asks me to bring him another beer on my way back.

We carry on with the Creed, flipping through the pages. I share stories of my childhood; the good, the bad and the ugly. I confess how the General's passing has affected me but I'm afraid to completely express my feelings considering what a horrible person he was. I tell him the things my grandmother endured, my mother's life and my childhood traumas. I have never even told Don some of this stuff.

"No one can decide your future for you. It's all up to you. You and your family are not cursed. You just crossed paths with bad men, that's all."

"I try my best but sometimes I can't help it. I messed up, and I'm constantly scared that Don will find out."

"You need to let go of things you can't control. Fear is worse than the thing you are scared of. You need to let it go. My cousin knows no one is perfect. He's a mess himself. But you two make it work, so make it work."

I look at him and he flips a page.

"You worry too much, Lotus."

"Wouldn't you, if you were in my shoes?"

"Not one bit. What's the point of worrying?" He looks up as if he expects an answer. I just shrug. "In future, use your gun when people bother you."

I don't know what to say.

"Tell me something. Why is being on your own such a problem for you?" He stops reading and leans back.

"It isn't." Where is he getting that from?

"It is. You're always crying about Chelsea. She doesn't want to be your friend. Time to let it go and move on. And Elik's girl? Does she ever visit you? Let people who don't want you go. Stop trying so hard. And that boy, Viper's son? You couldn't go two months on your own. It was too long for you. You had to have someone around. You hate your own company... Shame, daddy issues."

Are we in a therapy session? Is he psychoanalysing me right now?

"I need a smoke, keep reading." He gets up and heads out.

When he returns, our conversation takes a new direction, thankfully.

"Can you get me another beer?"

"Sure." I could use a break.

I get up, and in a clumsy attempt to reach across for the empty bottle, the Creed falls off the table and lands on the floor with a thud. As I pick it up, the jacket slips off. On top of the book is a folded paper. It must have been under the jacket. Hilton picks it up and unfolds it as I watch in anticipation. It has a page number, and when we flip to where it was, it was indeed ripped out.

*If ever only one leader, whether a General or Alpha, remains alive at any given time, the family must revert to having only one leader. This leader will be The Alpha. If this comes to pass, the four packs must merge into one as originally intended by the Wolf brothers.*

*After the passing of the Wolf brothers, their eldest sons became the next Alphas, and their sons after that. Then a war with the Hard Livings wiped out the entire Wolf bloodline, and new Alphas and a General had to be voted in. If the one-leader-only ever comes to pass, the family lineage will resume. The son of The Alpha will be The Alpha after him, and his son after that.*

I can't believe this!

"This is it, Hilton! Don doesn't have to be a General, he has to be The Alpha!"

He's as stunned as I am. It explains why someone removed and hid the page. It holds the ultimate secret. I can't believe the answer just presented itself. I think the spirits of the Founding Brothers wanted us to find it because why didn't the person shred it?

We read the page after where this one was and we stop at the part where no Wolf is allowed to spill another's blood. Hilton looks at me with concern-filled eyes, and it hits me that none of them can carry out the most important part of the plan because they are bound by the Creed.

"You don't have to," he says as if he read my mind.

"I do."

He looks like he wants to argue but decides against it.

"Goddamn! The General wanted to get rid of all the Alphas and be the only leader standing for the one-leader-only rule to kick in. He had it all figured out."

"Oh, wow!" I'm equally shocked. Deep down though, I'm impressed. He was smart after all.

"This means someone else out there knows this information and might use it to their advantage. We must move fast before the other packs beat us to it." I'm sure the other Creeds have the page intact.

"We have some time."

"We do?"

He flips a few pages and stops at a section detailing the death and mourning of leaders.

*When a leader, a General or an Alpha, passes away, the Wolves must adhere to a three-month mourning period, during which the designation of a new successor is prohibited.*

I feel a deep connection with Hilton. He let me into parts of his soul I'm sure he's never shared with anyone, and I did the same.

Don has to be The Alpha, come hell or high water.

# TWENTY FIVE

Hilton is on time like I knew he would be. He holds the door open for me and I struggle into the back seat. Why can't they just buy big cars?!

"You ready?" He looks over his shoulder. He gets too serious where Don is involved.

"As ready as I'll ever be."

"Don't mess up." It sounds more like a threat than encouragement.

I nod and lean back. I'm used to him now. You know when someone thinks you are going to fail but they have no option but to work with you? That is the case between us. Although I would like to think we have bonded on a deeper level and he believes in me. I just wish Don trusted me as much.

While he drives, I sink into my thoughts. The happy ones are quickly replaced by a familiar uncertainty. I'm drowning in could-haves, what-ifs and would-haves. What if it doesn't work out? The only weapon I have is hope - hope that things will work out well, that Don's father will be understanding, that at the end of it all, I won't be thrown out into the cold. I find myself cradling my stomach because I'm sure Don will take our child away if it ever comes to it, and a small part of me knows I'll be relieved. I'm failing to bond with it. It's an inconvenience, if anything. I'm bringing an innocent soul into the world; to suffer like I did, like my mother did, like my grandmother did. I never should have made a baby. The cycle should have ended with me. I should have been the last generation.

When I see the sign to Pollsmoor, fear takes over and I hug myself to stop from shivering. I hate this place; my worst memory lives here.

Hilton signs in at the gate and parks at the far end of the parking lot.

"Stay here. I'll be right back."

I nod and keep hugging myself. He disappears behind the tall walls, leaving me alone with my thoughts. I'm trying my best to calm my nerves so that I don't panic and mess up. The last time I was here, I came face-to-face with my ex. This place is triggering bad memories.

Hilton returns sooner than I expected.

"You're up. Make it work, Lotus. Lie if you have to, you're good at it anyway."

Was that last part necessary? I promise to give it my best shot. I would like to also give him a piece of my mind but I'll do it later, when I have more time.

"Do I look nervous?" The last thing I need is to panic and forget what I have to say. I need to be bold and unwavering.

"What does a nervous person look like?" he asks sincerely.

"Oh, good heavens! Never mind." Why do I bother with Hilton again?

"See that guy there? He'll be your escort."

I secure the bag across my shoulder. It's not too big but it's quite heavy. If I'm caught, I'm done for. You don't want to know what's in it. I adjust my oversized coat, making sure it hangs just right to hide the bulk underneath, then I drape a scarf around my neck to cover the view from the front. The coat is far from flattering, but it does a decent job of disguising both the bag and my growing tummy. Don's reaction if he were to show up right now crosses my mind and I quickly blink it away. I need to focus.

My escort greets me with so much respect, I wonder who Hilton told him I am. I hesitate when we get to the security checkpoint. My teeth chatter and I quickly close my mouth when I'm told to walk through the body scanner.

As I walk away, the bag still with me, I know crime will never end in South Africa. The Wolves have the police and prison staff on their payroll. Obviously, other gangs have the same plants in these law enforcement departments. So if the criminals run the law, who enforces it?

I expected to be led into a waiting room like the one we went into that time with Chelsea. I quickly swat away that memory. Absolutely nothing should distract me. I have worked too long and too hard to get this plan together. I run a hand over my belly and remember that I'm doing this for Don's child.

How big is this place? We are still going down a long corridor with a few doors on either side. My escort is walking in long strides ahead of me and I'm trying my best to keep up. I feel so heavy these days. Even though my bump is not that big and I'm still very agile, I feel like I swallowed a house. I wish I could just skip to the end and get this baby out of me.

We eventually stop outside a door.

"Madam, you have 15 minutes. I'll wait outside."

*You've got this! You can do this!* I mentally pep-talk myself.

The coldness of the handle catches me by surprise. I open the door and immediately wonder if I should have knocked. The room is not what I imagined. I expected a typical prison cell, you know, small bed with tattered grey blankets, a bucket at the corner for a toilet and a small window that looks like an air vent. This is homely. It's like a small bachelor flat. Is this what prison life is like? Not bad at all. It's very quaint and pleasant for rent-free living. No wonder some people enjoy getting arrested.

There is a three-quarter bed with fluffy blankets on one side, a bar fridge in one corner with an electric kettle on top, a packed bookshelf, and a cupboard doubling as a table. On the wall above the bed is a portrait identical to the one in Don's house in the Cape Flats - of little Don and his father laughing with the wind as the sun kisses their faces. Next to it are two smaller portraits, one of Don's mother and another of the three of them. It hits me that Don once had a complete family and a normal life.

"Good morning, young lady." Pop's voice is calm and calculated, I find myself standing up straight. It has a tinge of command without being too hard.

"Good morning, sir. How are you?" My hands come together in front of my chest.

"I could be better, but I'm alive and that's what's important. How are you?"

"I'm alive too. Thank you."

"That's good to hear. Please take a seat." He gestures.

I'm not sure where to begin. I look up at him hoping he will start the conversation, but his eyes bore into me and his lips remain together. He doesn't have many visible tattoos like some people we know. Grey hairs dot the black of his head and his beard, but he doesn't look that old. There are traces of Don on his face, especially in the shape of his nose and the curve of his lips. At least now I know that my man is going to age like fine wine. I suppose if you're in prison, all you can do is work out all day and enjoy taxpayers' money.

"My name is Lotus Janse van Rensburg. I'm..."

"... Donny's girlfriend," he finishes my sentence. "Donny has shown me pictures of you. He's always excited about you. It's a pleasure to finally meet you, Lotus."

My heart melts and I smile to myself.

I was hoping he would speak some more but he returns to silence. What's wrong with the Wolves? They have a way of looking at you without blinking much. It's intimidating and creepy.

"I don't have much time, sir." I have 15 minutes and I'm sure I have used three minutes already.

"I have all day."

Is he being sarcastic or what?

"I know if it comes out that I was here, it will cost me Don, and he'll probably take our child away from me. I love Don and I love our child

with my life. So me coming here to see you means I have no other option."
I look up and I'm pleased to find him listening attentively.

"Don wants you to be the next General. But you're in here, and without a leader, it's a matter of time before the packs turn on each other. Everything is volatile at the moment. Every Alpha wants to be the next General, except Don of course. That's the reason I'm here." I stop and swallow because I'm not sure how he will take what I'm about to ask him.

He looks at me in a 'continue' fashion and I swallow again.

"I need you to lie to Don." I play with my fingers. Innocence, or the appearance of it at least, is what I'm going for.

"I don't tell lies."

I internally make a face. Everybody lies.

"Don is afraid that if he steps up, he won't be able to rank down, and he doesn't want you reporting to him when you come out. I need you to lie to him and say you have no intentions of getting out anytime soon. Tell him you're running something in here that you can't just abandon. Make up something."

"Are you telling me that you know all our secrets?" he sounds unimpressed.

"I don't know all your secrets, but what I know for sure is that Donavan will be dead in six months tops. You'll come out of prison into a world without your son. I'll probably be dead too, and your grandchild."

Concern floods his face and I breathe silently.

"I know you've been begging Don to make peace with his mother's family. I can make that happen."

I catch a glimpse of his Adam's apple bobbing. Hilton didn't let me walk in here unequipped. He told me that Don and his father get along very well but they disagree on one thing - his mother's wish for peace between them and her family. Her family didn't approve of her marrying a gangster. She loved them dearly, but she loved her husband and son more. So her wish was that one day her son makes peace with her parents. But Don being Don just won't reach out. Hilton said it would mean a great deal to Don's father if Don fulfilled that wish.

"Are you sure you can make my son do that?"

"I can make your son do whatever I want him to." I catch my mouth but I have already spoken.

Thankfully, it makes him smile, which makes me smile back in relief.

"You drive a hard bargain, young lady. I can see why my son loves you. You're quite delightful."

My smile widens at the compliment.

"So do we have a deal or not?" I need to know. Time is not on my side.

His face goes back to serious and my smile fades.

"No, we don't have a deal."

*Tjo!* Why are people so difficult? I really didn't want to play this card, but it's now or never. If he refuses to go with this, then I don't know.

"I'm carrying a boy." I run a hand over my stomach.

"So?"

"So my son is going to be christened a Wolf, then he's going to become an Alpha. You were the first General of the family and we're going to keep the legacy in your bloodline. It's time your family led the Wolves. You had your chance, it's Don's chance now, and after him, our son will rank up, and his son after that. Don has to be The Alpha to protect his son."

"And how exactly would you accomplish that?" He looks amused.

"The Creed states that if ever only one leader remains alive at any given time, the pack has to go back to having only one leader, The Alpha. So to fulfil that, the other three Alphas will fall, and the four packs will merge into one as the Creed dictates. It's time the Wolves had only one leader."

His body language tells me that I struck a chord, but I have a feeling he already knew that law. I can only wonder why he kept that information to himself.

He's maintaining eye contact, waiting for me to cower, but I stand my ground and look him straight in the eye. I'm not dropping the ball. We can stare at each other till kingdom come if that's what it will take. I'm uneasy because I didn't want to reveal the grand plan without knowing if I could trust him, but desperate times call for desperate measures. When we are done, every Wolf will bow down to Donavan.

"That's not how it works. You're in over your head." He finally drops the hard stare. "You're in way over your head!" he repeats, as if warning me.

"That's what everyone thinks. They underestimate me, and that's what makes it easy." I keep my face straight and my eyes locked on him. Confidence bordering on arrogance is what I'm aiming for.

"Do you know how difficult that will be?"

I shrug in an uppity manner. "It won't be difficult. Not everyone is a Wolf bound by the Creed. The other Alphas will fall. Wolves are followers and they stick to the rules. With their leaders gone, the other packs will need to follow someone for direction. Don will save them, unify the packs, and be The Alpha as the Creed dictates."

"The Wolves, a family legacy, passed down from generation to generation, just as the Wolf brothers intended. You're right, I underestimated you."

Yay!

"Tell me, Lotus. Why would you want that life for your child? You have seen what it does to people. Is that what you want for your child?"

*I don't know. Being the mother of an Alpha sounds cool.*

"His fate has already been sealed. He's an Alpha's son. Power runs in his blood, so his path has been paved."

"I see. I just hope you know what you're doing."

"I do... Sir, unfortunately, I have to leave now. Are you in?" Being out is not an option I'm willing to give him, but it's good to be polite.

He thinks about it and I give him a moment. When I have counted to ten, in my head, I stretch my cutely manicured hand towards him. He looks at it, then at me, then back at it. I'm not moved, literally and metaphorically. I'm tempted to smile when he stretches his hand and shakes mine. This marks the day our family owned the Wolves. By the law in the Creed, the four packs will become one.

Do you now see the perks of being unemployed? You have all the time in the world to plot and study the Creed which they misquote so much. I don't think any of those guys ever read it; they rely on word-of-mouth. Don is lucky he has me and Hilton. Now I have to go back out there and resume acting clueless. When no one suspects you, no one keeps an eye on you. You strike unexpectedly and savour the priceless look on their faces.

"I didn't come empty-handed."

Time is ticking, and I don't have much sand left in the upper half of the hourglass, so I present my parting gifts. This is just me showing off. I managed to pull off the one job Don has been failing to for the past two weeks. I, Lotus, pulled off a job an Alpha has been failing to pull off! If that's not one for the history books then I don't know what is. I gave Hilton fresh ideas on how to get the new 'uncooperative' prison staff on their payroll. When the Minister went on a clean-up campaign, many 'dirty' people lost their jobs. The Wolves struggled with the new staff, but everyone has a price, and it's not always money. My ideas worked like a charm.

"I know you're broke because Don has been struggling to send you things. So I brought you enough currency to keep you afloat for a little while."

His face lights up with curiosity.

I place the bag on the table and slowly work the zip as if I'm in a *Charlie's Angels* movie. I empty the contents one by one. A brick of the good powder, a carton of cigarettes, a bag of weed, wads of cash and a Swiss army knife. I hesitate on the next item and he leans in and reaches for it. My hand grabs his and our eyes clash. I almost let go out of respect.

"That's mine."

"Was yours. I'll have it."

My hand tightens around his. If he wanted to, he could easily flip me over; he's obviously stronger than me.

"Don gave this to me and I won't be parting with it."

"Young lady..."

"Not open for negotiation, sir, with all due respect."

He loosens his hold and I let him go. He can have it all, just not my gun. Funny because I put it in the bag in anticipation of this standoff. I needed him to see that I have a gun. Ordinary girls don't carry guns.

"Keep it. Don't ever give away anything that means everything to you."

It's funny how he said 'keep it' as if the permission was his to give.

"I made this for you." I hand him a lunchbox with a home-cooked seven colours meal.

He brightens up and his smile grows. I pack the gifts back into the bag, leaving the knife on the table, then tuck the gun into my waist and cover it with my coat.

"Sir, I'm counting on you to stick to your end of the deal."

He gives me his hand to shake. "You have my word. Should we make a blood pact?" He picks up the knife and I pull my hand back. What is he smoking? I'm not exchanging blood with anyone!

"I may have the wolf on my skin and another in my stomach, but I'm most certainly not a Wolf. I don't need blood to cement a deal. Your word is enough for me."

"I have to say, from the way Donny spoke about you, I never would have guessed you would pull such stunts. Who helped you bypass all the systems to get to me? How did you do it?"

"If I told you, I'd have to kill you."

"My son is rubbing off on you!" He laughs. "Make sure to bring my grandson to see me when he arrives."

"I'll do that."

My escort knocks twice on the door before opening it. "We have to go before the shift change," he says.

I say goodbye one more time.

"I never would have expected this from you," Don's father says, sitting back in his chair.

"What can I say, I'm my father's daughter."

That's the facial expression I wanted to see!

"Who is your father?"

"Ryan, the last General."

He tries to say something but I bid him farewell. The shock on his face is exactly what I was going for. Although I'm surprised that Don didn't tell him.

I turn around when I reach the door. "Remember, I was never here."

"I've never met you in my life. If I'm lucky, I might meet you for the very first time when I get out."

This is the first time I've ever seen Hilton nervous. He's pacing and rubbing his hands together.

"How did it go? What did he say? What happened?" he bombards me with questions.

"Can I get in first? It's freezing out here."

He does not mask the exasperation on his face, and it makes me happy. It's my turn to torture him.

"Please get me out of here." I hang my head.

"You fucked up, didn't you?" He bangs the steering wheel hard and the hoot goes off loudly.

I'm laughing hard inside, but I have perfected the mask around him. I told you I would get him! He starts the car and reverses so harshly, the wheels screech and scrape the ground.

When the prison is well out of sight, I ask him to stop the car but he ignores me.

"I want to throw up. Stop the car."

"Throw up inside my car and I'll cut your head off to make sure you never throw up again," he says it so coldly, he might actually mean it.

I blow raspberries at him and he looks back, obviously confused by my sudden change of mood.

"What are you grinning about?"

"Don is going to be The Alpha."

His face softens into emotion, like he's actually alive like the rest of us. I think he's happy but the feeling is too foreign to him, he doesn't know how to react. He gets out of the car, comes around and tells me to get out.

"Look me in the eye and tell me you're not lying."

"I don't tell lies, Hilly, you know this." I chuckle because according to him, lying is my whole persona.

I tell him everything, exaggerating here and there.

I don't know how or when, but his arms close around me. I catch my breath in shock. He quickly pulls away and snaps back into character.

"Still want to throw up?"

"I didn't want to throw up, silly. I was just pulling your leg."

He shoots a frown before he goes back into the car.

"Guess what..." I smile happily as he drives.

"What?"

"My father-in-law totally adores me! He said I'm the best daughter-in-law he's ever had."

"You're the only daughter-in-law he's ever had."

"Candice?"

"Doesn't count."

Talk about bursting my bubble!

"You have to admit though, we make a great team, Hilly. Look at us, Batman and Clyde."

"Batman and Robin? Bonnie and Clyde? Maybe you and this Hilly make a good team, I don't know. Leave me out of it."

I can't help laughing. He's so precious, he doesn't even know it.

"Before I forget, can you get me Don's mom's parents' phone number, and maybe an address?"

"Sure. But like I told you, they're very difficult people, so brace yourself."

"I got this!" Honestly, I'm a bit worried I won't be able to get through to them, but I'm optimistic.

"Good luck. You'll need it."

He opens my door when we get home and gives me a hand. Today just keeps getting better.

"Thank you. You see you can be a gentleman when you put your mind to it."

"Don't get used to it." He helps me stand up straight and pats me on the shoulder. "You tried."

"We tried." I smile at him.

I place a hand on my stomach, silently praying it's a boy. It better be a boy or else I'm royally screwed. I had to improvise to solidify my case. The plan was to get rid of the other Alphas, make Don The Alpha, make the Wolves one family, then hand the reins over to Don. If my child turns out to be a girl like I have been wishing for all along, I'll be forced to have a sex change done on her at birth. Can someone remind me again why my life is so complicated? Why can't it be easy-peasy like other people's lives?

# *TWENTY SIX*

I haven't heard from Don in four days. It feels like forever. So much for agreeing to check in every day. He went to Pretoria with Elik for only heaven knows what. When I asked, he told me, "It's best not to know some things, *skat*". I tried pushing it but he wasn't budging. See why I should have mourned my father longer?

His phone has been off the entire time, and the uncertainty is driving me insane. When his phone doesn't go through for days on end, my mind spirals out of control. I haven't heard from Caleb or Hilton either, so I'm really worried. I want to call Elik, but it might be best to call Fierce instead. If Elik is also missing, me and her can bond over our abandonment issues. Maybe she can invite me over for frozen yoghurt and a movie.

"Hello, Lotus." Her tone is oddly cold.

"Hey, babe. Are you okay?"

"Why wouldn't I be?" She scoffs.

What's with the attitude? You know what, let me just get straight to it and leave her to deal with whatever crawled up her ass.

"Have you heard from Elik? I can't get hold of Don."

"I was talking to him before you called."

"Oh. I thought they were in Pretoria together."

"They are. Maybe your man doesn't want to talk to you." She adds a little laugh.

I don't know what's going on with her but it's beginning to annoy me. "Fierce, are you okay?"

"Lemon is not missing, Lotus. They're busy. Stop being so clingy!"

Why is she being such a bitch?

"It's easy for you to say because clearly Elik has been calling you. Don's phone has been off the whole time!"

"Like I said, maybe he doesn't want to talk to you. You know how he is."

"Are you saying you know my man better than me?" I've had it with her condescension.

"Did I say that?"

"It's the second time you've suggested it. What's wrong with you today?"

"I thought we were friends, Lotus."

"Huh? We're friends, aren't we?"

"You tell me. You, my beloved friend, knew that Chelsea was seeing

Elik behind my back but didn't tell me. So tell me, friend, what kind of friends are we exactly?"

Oh goodness, Chelsea! This is exactly what I didn't want. How do I keep getting blamed for things Chelsea did with her body? You would swear I was holding her down and offering commentary as she was actively cheating because I keep being accused of having 'helped' her.

"That's unfair, Fierce."

"What's unfair? You pretending to be my friend or you helping your BFF meet up with my man?"

That *helping* again!

"It's unfair to blame me for your man's inability to keep it in his pants. He slept with Chelsea, not me!"

"He slept with her? He actually slept with her?! That's not what he told me. He said he never slept with her." Her voice cracks.

Shit! Well, they had a whole trip to Dubai back then and I'm sure they were not spending the nights counting sand in the desert.

"I don't think they slept together the last time she made a move on him. He made her sleep in another bedroom from what I heard."

I was in another province so I don't exactly know what happened. Don told me something about Chelsea going to Elik's house and trying to sleep with him while I was in Eastern Cape. I asked him after my father's funeral because I didn't understand why my mother said her precious Chelsea didn't sleep with Elik and was trying to get Caleb to reconcile with her. I don't even know the full story, yet I keep getting blamed for it.

"What? Chelsea slept in my house?" she shrieks.

Shit! I think it's best if I hang up now and give her space to calm down. People usually lash out at the wrong people when they feel betrayed.

"Was I ever your friend, Lotus, or were you and your BFF making fun of me the whole time?"

"I wasn't a part of it. I wasn't even in Cape Town."

"But you were more than happy to tell me about it. Why did you decide to tell me now? I'd have never found out."

"What are you talking about?"

"You told me on Instagram. Can you stop it, it's not cute."

Oh fuck, Dalubuhle! Elik should have let me change the password.

"Fierce, listen..."

"You were supposed to be my friend."

Weak girls that date serial cheaters surprise me. She can't be such a cry-baby while dealing with a guy like Elik.

"Ey, look. Elik slept with Chelsea not with me, so please leave me out of it."

"Wow! You know what? Lemon will have a field day when he hears about you sleeping with Dalubuhle and taking cosy pictures."

"Oh no, baby, you're late to the party. The Dalu card expired a while ago. Go ahead and tell him. I'm tired of this shit! I hope you know that he'll kill Elik first for it before he touches me."

"What do you mean?" She calms down and suddenly sounds like she will cry.

"Why don't you tell Don and find out?"

"Lotus..."

"Don't be that person, *mann*. My Instagram was hacked; ask your man. I didn't text you anything. Elik cheated on you with Chelsea years ago. Be angry at him, not me. When they had their fling back then, I didn't know you or Elik. He left her and made things right with you. This last time, I don't know what happened. I was in Eastern Cape and Chelsea was not talking to me. So don't blame me for any of this. I literally just called you to ask if you'd heard from Elik because I'm worried about Don." I hang up before she can respond. I don't have time for this. I never should have called her to begin with. Hilton was right, I was forcing things with her.

I need a drink. I can't do this life thing sober. I dump my phone on the kitchen counter and chase a shot of gin with grapefruit juice. I'm about to take a second shot when my phone vibrates. It's a reminder to call Don's grandparents. I don't need this right now. I tried calling last week but the phone rang and rang, and no one answered.

I pace the kitchen, with the phone ringing in my ear. Who still has a landline in this day and age? A part of me wishes they don't answer, but I made a bargain and I have to hold my end.

"Hello?"

"Good afternoon, ma'am." My voice quivers with nerves.

"Who's this?" The voice on the other end says.

"My name is Lotus. I'm calling about Donavan, your grandson."

There's a pause, and I can almost hear the rapid beating of my heart as I wait for a response.

"What do you want?"

"Uh, well, I meant to call earlier. I was wondering if maybe I could come and talk to you in person, please."

"What do you want to talk about?"

"Donavan."

"I have nothing to say to him or about him."

"Please, ma'am, hear me out." I sound as desperate as I am.

"I want nothing to do with that criminal. Keep him away from us!"

"Perhaps if you could just meet with me..."

"Are you deaf? I said I want nothing to do with that criminal! I have nothing to say to him, and I have even less to say to you. How dare you! Who are you anyway?"

"I'm Donavan's girlfriend."

"Girlfriend, not wife? You have no shame, young lady! Don't ever call this number again!"

"I'm sorry, ma'am. I was just hoping..."

The line goes dead.

Wow! I will take another shot now.

* * * * *

"Follow me. We need to talk." Don walks right past me like he left in the morning.

What the hell? I wait a bit so I can rein in my emotions before following him into his office.

"What took you so long?" he snaps as soon as I enter.

"I'm pregnant, you know, so I'm pretty slow."

He makes a disgruntled sound. What can he possibly say? He loves this child in my womb more than he loves himself.

"You said you wanted to talk to me."

"Oh, so we should get straight to the point? You're not going to ask me how my trip was?"

"No, Donavan, I'm not going to ask you how your trip was. If you wanted me to know, you would have told me."

"Come on, Lotus. Are you trying to pick a fight?"

"Oh no, baby, I'm not trying to fight with you. You decided that you didn't want me to know what was going on with you. Why should I fight you about it?"

"I'm tired. Can we do this later?" He pinches the bridge of his nose.

"We're going to do this right now!" I'm so pissed off by his disappearing acts.

"I was busy. I couldn't call you."

"Oh really? Good for you. Were you not working with Elik?"

"You know I was working with him. Why?"

"Because he had plenty of time to call his woman and update her on whatever was going on, but you couldn't reach out to your pregnant girlfriend. Do I mean that little to you?"

He gets up, paces, then sits down again.

"So you're mad at me because I didn't talk to you? It was just five days, geez, Lotus!"

"Just five days, you say. Just five days! You know what, I'm done talking about this." I fold my arms over my protruding belly. "Let's give you all the attention, my king. What did you want to talk to me about, your highness?"

"It doesn't matter anymore."

"No, let's talk right now. Come on, let's talk."

He sighs again and looks at me. "Fine. Elik was upset with you. He said you told his girl that Chelsea gave it up to him."

I hope that's all Elik said or help me Lord!

"And you're mad because of that?"

"I'm not mad. I just need you out of people's business. Why are you going around making enemies of my friends?"

"I didn't tell her anything. She already knew. I just didn't know that she didn't know the finer details."

"And you thought to tell her everything and cause trouble for them?"

"What are you saying?"

"I'm saying stay out of people's business. First, you messed up with Caleb, now you're messing up with Elik. Why can't you just stay out of people's relationships?"

"Are you for real right now?" Caleb and I made up, so why is he throwing that at me right now?

"Yes!"

"Okay fine. But first, let's discuss how you take everyone's side except mine."

"What do you mean? I'm always on your side."

"We have selective amnesia, I see. When I got back from home and Hilton was being mean to me, you took his side. When I complained about how rude Tristan was to me, you took his side. When Caleb got upset with me, you took his side. Now Elik is mad at me for something he did and you're on his side. All you do is take everyone else's side."

"You know that's not true. I always take your side."

"You think? See how you're already on Elik's side before you even hear mine. I bet if anyone came to you and told you something about me, you would believe it blindly without hearing my side first because everyone else is more important to you than me."

"Come on, you know that's not true. I just hate lies, you know that."

"We all hate lies, but it's our job to protect each other. We're in a relationship, Donavan. We're going to have a baby soon. This is not just us fooling around. When people speak about me, you have to defend me like I would defend you any day."

"*Skat...*"

"Do you even know how I ended up telling Fierce about Chelsea? I called her to ask about you. Your phone had been off for days and I was stressed out of my mind. I needed to know you were okay. So even though I got the feeling that she didn't want to talk to me, I asked her anyway. I desperately needed to know you were fine wherever you were. Do you know how it hurt me when she said she had been talking to Elik? He kept her updated the entire time, yet I didn't even get an SMS from you. So I'm sorry that the Chelsea bit slipped out, but had my man loved me enough to care about my feelings, none of it would have happened."

He looks at me with guilt-filled eyes.

"Now I lost the last friend I had, thank you very much. And she said she would destroy me. I don't even know what that means. Who knows what tricks she has up her sleeves? But I bet when it comes down to it, you'll take her side."

"She won't do that. What could she possibly do?"

He has no idea!

"I'm sorry. I'll talk to you next time. Please don't cry."

"And that's all I'm asking for. Please talk to me. I worry about you."

"Give me a hug. You're already fighting with me and I haven't even given you a hug."

The way he says it makes me mushy.

"So are you going to tell me what you guys were up to in Pretoria?" I ask after the soothing hug.

"Of course not."

"I bet Elik is going to tell Fierce."

"Then go and date Elik if that's what you want."

Wow!

He kisses the top of my head and lets me go. "I need to do something quickly. I'll be with you soon."

I walk away feeling light.

I sit on the bed and decide to get it over with. I call Elik and it rings till voicemail.

I text, *'Hi Elik. I just wanted to say I'm sorry for messing things up for you. It wasn't my intention. Fierce sounded like she already knew, but that's not an excuse. I'm really sorry.'*

Still unread after five minutes, so maybe he's away from his phone. I'm just sending this one to keep my conscience clear.

*'Hi Fierce. I'm sorry about the whole Chelsea situation. I never meant to hurt you. I didn't think it was my place to tell you, and I honestly didn't want you getting hurt. I'm really sorry.'* I press send before I change my mind.

Don said he will be with me soon but it's been an hour. He wanted to talk to me when he got home and I doubt it was about Elik. I was just too upset to give him a chance to speak to me. Now that I think of it, he looked drained, as if something was troubling him. Let me go and talk to him.

I knock but he doesn't invite me in. I knock again and decide to open the door. I find him with his head resting on the table and his bruised knuckles clenched. His shoulders are hunched and taut. I place my hands on them and try to get him to relax before I start kneading them. A moan escapes his lips and I continue working my magic, alternating between his shoulders and his neck. The knots are slowly dissolving and I can feel him starting to relax.

I don't know how he shifted so quickly, but suddenly I'm sprawled on his massive desk with my legs wide open. He makes short work of impaling me. Now I understand why some people refer to the great deed as 'nailing'. But I understand this is about him letting off steam more than it is about me, yet I find myself screaming his name as he shows me no mercy.

We really should have spontaneous sex more often. That was mind-blowing. We are lying on our bed, spent. He had to carry me here when I couldn't trust my legs to stop shaking, let alone walk. I'm drawing circles around his tattoos and listening to his thudding heart.

"Aren't you going to ask me where I've been?"

I don't stop drawing my circle and I don't look at him as I reply. "I have to trust that wherever you were, you had to be there to take care of our family. That you didn't call to check in on me because you had no other choice."

His sigh is sad. He moves me until we are nose to nose and I can see the tiny veins on his iris. He looks exhausted and troubled. There are lines around his eyes and mouth. I want to kiss him and make it better, but I know that I can't take his burden away.

"Remember when everything was going down with the General and the Hard Livings raiding us and we were all under threat?"

I nod and let him continue speaking even though my heart is picking up pace. I don't think I want to know.

"Elik was throwing around the idea of going legit in Pretoria. He was talking about a clean business that could stash some cash for us. He said it would help you when, you know, when I'm not around one day. It sounded great and all, but in my mind, it was our ticket out if shit hit the fan. Obviously, I didn't tell him that. He'd have never agreed. So I wiggled my way into the setup process and made it look like I was just being a good partner. I figured, why not use it for our side hustle, like we do with Club Lotus, you know? I also thought we could get our tools through it. We were in the middle of a war, we needed guns. I usually handle my business well but this time I fucked up. I can hold my own but I fucked up big for Elik. I really screwed up, *skat*."

"What did you do?"

"Everything was going smooth until the Hard Livings got wind of our moves. That, plus Ghost's speech at the General's funeral, has them convinced that we're preparing for another war, so Viper's trampling all over our turfs. He's pissed."

Viper being Dalu's father will never not give me chills.

"Isn't he in jail?" His arrest was a very public and flamboyant affair.

He scoffs and I feel stupid for even asking that. Of course jail is nothing to these people. They might even be safer inside than outside.

"It's just a ticking clock now before we have another war. I'm only telling you this because things are about to get ugly, and should anything happen to me, I need you to start over at the place that I bought for you. It's off-the-grid, far away from here, completely off the radar. Only Hilton and Elik know about it, and they'll make sure you get there safely. It will be a bit of an inconvenience for you but..."

Before he even finishes his speech, tears are making their way down my face and I keep shaking my head. I can't imagine a life without him. I refuse to imagine a life without him.

"Hey, hey, *skat*, look at me." He wipes my tears and holds my chin between his thumb and forefinger.

"I love you, and I swear I'll do everything in my power to always come back to you. But I need you to be prepared for this war. I need to go out there knowing that you will manage on your own if things go sideways for me. Our child needs at least one of us around to watch over him as he grows."

He sounds like he's saying goodbye and I completely fall apart at the thought of him leaving me. He tries to pull me in but my stomach gets in the way, so he gently turns me around so I can nestle into him. He holds me tight, kissing my head and not saying anything.

# Heart in Two

I know I signed up for this, but dear Lord, please protect my heart. Don can't die. I can't live without him.

# TWENTY SEVEN

## HILTON

"Hilton," someone calls my name.

Out of habit, I reach for my gun, tucked in at the small of my back, always loaded and ready to fire. Unlike Alpha, who carries his gun at the appendix, because he clearly doesn't care much about his toolbox, I carry mine at 6 o'clock because it's still an easy draw and doesn't force me to always wear hoodies. In a world where everyone is an enemy, alertness is crucial.

"Cuz."

I turn towards the door and relax my hand. This boy doesn't knock! He jumped over my wall, didn't he?

He is wearing one of my favourite hoodies. He likes stealing my clothes; I don't know how or when he gets them. I probably have myself to blame. After all, I'm the one who taught him how to get away with murder. I prefer the term culling or assisted suicide; murder makes it sound heinous.

"What's going on?" I address the shameless intruder.

He looks paler than usual, and although he masks his pain very well, I know when my boy is not fine. I practically raised him all by myself. I'm only a few years older than him but life is better counted in experience than the number of years lived.

"It's Mummy's birthday."

Mummy! Mummy? There we go again. Normally I would call him out for using such unnecessarily flowery words, but today is not the day. I never strike an injured animal. Where's the honour in that? I put out my cigarette and open my arms. I only do this once a year and no one should ever witness it. I hold him and he holds me back. Even Wolves have to feel sometimes, as long as no one sees their tears. I don't cry. What could possibly make me cry? The new crop of Wolves is weak. Don't get me started on Caleb. How that boy is one of us surprises me every time. He told Alpha that it was okay to cry when we found him crying for Lotus. It's never okay to cry!

I keep him in my arms, all the while wondering how he mastered crying so silently. Wouldn't it be better to not cry at all? But like I said, today, out of 365, is the only day I allow him to be as soft as he wants.

When he loosens his hold around me, I pat him on the back. I make it a point not to look him in the face. Whether he's shedding tears or not is entirely his business. I'll never look him in the face and make him ashamed of himself. Unless he's on his knees begging a girl not to leave him as if she's oxygen. Then he should be ashamed of himself.

"Let me grab a jacket." I leave him alone in the living room, probably to steal more of my stuff. You can never win with a thief.

I straighten the corner of the bed in my second bedroom; I must have touched it on my way out earlier. I sit near the head of the bed and look at my wristwatch. In exactly ten minutes I'll go back out. That's ample time for him to pull himself together.

I'll mess him up if he makes a mess in my kitchen. He likes putting his beer directly on the counter. I feel my fist clench at the thought and I quickly remind myself that it's only for today. He's in a dark place, I need to protect him.

Every year, he celebrates his mother's birthday, which is also the day she died. He killed her with one shot. Pops left a gun lying around and Donavan found it. Thinking it was a toy, he pointed it at his mother and pulled the trigger. Although it wasn't his fault, he has failed to forgive himself for it. Every year, he celebrates her birthday in the oddest of ways. I now drive him to the cemetery because he drinks himself stupid. He barely survived the accident five years ago. I bring him to my house every time so I can keep an eye on him. He always wakes up back to normal. He never wants anyone to see him in that state, not even his treasured Lotus.

Ten minutes on the dot, let's do this.

What did I tell you? Two bottles of beer are sitting carelessly on my counter. He has slowed down. Only two?

"Are we good?" I toss the empty bottles into the trash can and wipe my counter dry.

He nods and looks up at me with those devilish eyes. He used to give me that look when he was younger and not sure what to do. What's that in his eyes? Fear? Pain? Grief?

I walk out and he follows. My gate is still locked. I knew he jumped over my wall!

I can't believe he bought that girl this car with our hard-earned money. Does he think at all or should I retrain him?

We drive in silence all the way to Gordon's Bay Cemetery. I attended Donna's funeral, and all I remember is how Donavan wouldn't stop screaming. She's buried in the left wing, on her family's private burial site. I can't help but wonder how a family comes together and decides to buy land exclusively for burying each other. How does that conversation even go?

I have a six-pack of beers and a camp chair. Donavan is wheeling a cooler box and carrying a picnic basket. He looks like a TV advert.

He lays a rug near his mother's tombstone and starts unpacking. Usually, I don't look, but today I'm curious what his yearly tribute is about. A cake? Champagne? Two glasses? A Bible? A platter of food? You've got to be kidding me! Then he positions a large portrait of his mother near the cake! When he takes out the last thing, I can't stop cursing in my head. Now I have seen it all. What in the ninth hell!

"I think I'll wait in the car, Cuz. Take all the time in the universe." I'm not watching this.

"Please don't leave me, Hilton."

If I didn't know any better, I would say my ten-year-old cousin spoke to me.

"I'll never leave you, Donavan." I open my camp chair and sit back.

I'm on my second beer when he cuts the cake.

"You want a slice?" He looks at me with glassy eyes.

Do I look crazy? I'm just here to take him back in one piece, not to partake in this madness. I hate seeing him like this. Can the clock go faster?

Do I know where my mother is buried? It's been so long, her face is fading from my memory. I feel something like pain when I remember how cruel life was to her. I take a long sip of my beer and erase her memory from my mind. I know where my father is buried. I buried him myself in the middle of the night, with Donavan holding the torch.

It starts pouring without warning and all I can do is swear. I can't imagine what this will do to his cake. He carefully places the flowers on the grave as if he doesn't feel the rain and continues talking to someone he alone can see. I wait, drinking my beer. I'm already wet and it's not my car.

He tosses the empty bottle of champagne aside and I know he's sloshed.

"Let's go." He walks past me as if he's the one who's been waiting all along.

He staggers and balances on the wall.

I hate this part. I walk to where he was having communion with the dead and pick up the trash. The dead deserve some respect too. Donna was a good woman.

It's raining hard by the time I start the car. It looks like a storm is brewing.

"Play something." He reaches for my arm.

I press play, and I don't mask my shock. You call this music? I don't know who sang this song or why they sang it, and I have no desire to find out, yet he volunteers the information.

"Chris Brown is the shit! Turn up the volume."

Lotus has really gotten under his skin, it's pathetic.


Lotus told me to get an automated gate. I had considered it before but she ruined it, so I'm not going to get it anymore.

"Easy there." I steady him as he staggers out of the car.

He's singing along to a ridiculous song. If it was a different day, I would have clapped him back to his mind.

"I'm going to be a terrible father, Cuz. Look at me." He dumps himself onto the blanket I covered the couch with.

"No doubt."

What was he thinking? Where does he think he will raise the child? In a cooler box underground? They will use that child as leverage every chance they get. And that woman of his; it's only a matter of time before someone sends her with a message to her ancestors.

"I'm terrible, Cuz. I left her alone again."

"Yes, you are."

He's terrible for always leaving and not calling her to let her know where he is. It's a miracle she hasn't started blowing up my phone. Lotus doesn't have boundaries. When she can't find him, she calls me. What do I look like? An operator to put her through to my cousin? No matter how many times I tell her off, she calls again.

She's a good woman. Heavily flawed, but aren't we all? She makes him happy and gives him a purpose. He lives for her now. It's made him stronger and an idiot at the same time.

"I'll call her. Pass me a beer, let me sober up first."

I shake my head but pass him the beer anyway. Why would any man do this to himself? Attach his life to a woman knowing fully well how senseless they are?


Donavan has passed out on the couch. He needs to get out of those wet clothes, but maybe a little rest will do him good.

My phone rings and I already know who it is.

"Hey, Hilly. Is Don with you?"

"No."

She blabbers on about how she hasn't heard from him all day.

"He's good wherever he is."

"He left in the morning and he wasn't looking good at all. He said he would be back soon but he's still not back. His phone is off. I don't know what to do. He wasn't okay. I'm worried sick. Please tell him to call me if you hear from him."

"Sure."

It's a full-blown storm outside. The wind is strong enough to blow a person away and hailstones are getting bigger by the second. There is no way Donavan will be going home today.

# *TWENTY EIGHT*

I watch Don going through his T-shirts and I smile to myself thinking of yesterday. I was fuming because he slept out without communicating, then he walked through the door with flowers in his hands. He knelt down and apologised, like sincerely apologised. I didn't even ask where he disappeared to because he carried me to bed and apologised over and over again with his body, hands and mouth.

"How is this one?" He holds a plain T-shirt and I give a thumbs-up. When we are good, we are good.

He slips it on and tugs a sweater over it.

"Isn't that Hilton's sweater?" I continue fixing my hair.

"It is. So it won't be a big loss when it burns to ashes. Too bad because I like it."

I won't ask.

He finishes dressing up and pauses, looking straight at me as if he hasn't seen me in a long time.

"You're staring, baby." I put the brush down and straighten my dress.

"Am I? My bad."

"Yes, you are." *And I like it.*

I tilt sideways to check myself in the mirror. I'm pretty far along now, and this dress hugs my bump comfortably. I'm surprised by how nice it looks. It's so much better than the old-fashioned maternity dresses I remember from when I was a kid.

We had another scan yesterday and everything looks good. It took a lot of convincing, and a bit of emotional blackmail, to get Don to agree not to find out the baby's sex. I'm a bit on edge, you know, because what if it's a girl? I've been stressing about it and I really don't want to add any more worries.

After the scan, Don was in such a good mood, he took me out for lunch and called it a 'date'. That was such a sweet surprise. Can you believe it? Flowers, dates... what's next? Am I crazy to think that a wedding might not be so far-fetched anymore? He might actually drop down on one knee and propose one day. Okay, I might be getting a bit carried away.

After the date, he took me shopping for more maternity clothes since I'd been complaining that nothing fit anymore. With my body changing so quickly, it feels like I'm buying new sizes every month. This time though, I actually enjoyed shopping, maybe because he was being goofy but surprisingly helpful. Usually, he just says everything looks good on me, which is annoying when I need real advice. I ended up getting a couple of cute dresses, and this one is my favourite. It makes me feel like a sexy mama. Honestly, I hate being pregnant, but the pregnant aesthetic? I'm totally rocking it! If I ever get back to Instagram, my haters will be so jealous, they'll die.

Before we left the mall, we stopped for some doughnuts and ice cream. Don was being thoughtful the whole day, I fell in love with him all over again.

"Baby, do I look fat in this dress?"

"Yes, you do. Let's go."

Tears well behind my eyes. I was feeling great and now I feel like a hippo. He just had to be mean about it.

"You alright?" he asks as if he didn't just body-shame me. "You've obviously put on some weight, but you're still gorgeous. You look beautiful. Nothing's changed in the way I feel about you. Didn't I prove that last night?"

I try to push past him, but he gently catches me plants a kiss on my forehead before wrapping his arms around me, careful not to press too hard against my belly.

"I'm sorry. You look really good."

I feel better, but as much as I wish I could stay here forever, I know he's running late. He has to drop me off at the spa first before heading to his meeting. So we really need to get going.

He helps me into the backseat of his favourite car and Tristan jumps into the front passenger seat. Their voices fade into the background as I get lost in my own world. I scroll through Instagram, looking for inspiration for my pregnancy photoshoot. I screenshot a few pictures and bookmark some posts. I'm tempted to text Chelsea, and that's my cue to switch accounts to my mother's catering page. What? I'm logged out? Ouch, that stings! I close my phone and look out the window, trying to suppress my feelings.

"Shit, a roadblock," Don says.

I sit up. That's not good. There is enough contraband in this car to send him to prison for a long time. This isn't the Cape Flats where he owns the police. The thought of him behind bars scares me. Who knows how long he'll be in there for? I don't want him to miss the birth of our child.

"Make a U-turn!" I lean forward.

"Can't. Too close." He eases on the accelerator but keeps moving.

I cover my mouth with my hands thinking of all the things under the seats. Unlicensed guns, drugs, and if I remember well, the number plates on this car don't match its registration, so when they check the disc against the number plate, he's screwed. We are all screwed.

"Give me that!" I snatch a water bottle out of Tristan's hand.

Some officers are thoroughly searching the two cars in front of us and I know we are next. The police stop us as expected, and Don rolls his window down.

"Good day, sir. May I please see your licence," the officer says.

Don's reaction as he reaches for his wallet in his pocket tells me that it's over. I let out a piercing scream and they all look back at me. The officer leans in and I let out a sharper scream, fanning my face with one hand and holding my stomach with the other. My dress is wet on the front and I make sure the policeman sees it.

Don unbuckles his seatbelt and reaches back to me. "*Skat*? What's going on? Talk to me, my angel."

"Is she alright?" the officer asks, showing genuine concern while I take fast, deep breaths.

"The window." I frantically wave my hand.

Don rolls it down and turns back to me. Two female officers join the scene as I let out a third scream, tears now running down my face.

"Is she alright? She's pregnant! Who is she?"

"She's my girlfriend." Don is trying to hide the panic in his voice but he's doing a horrible job of it.

"Don... drive... hospital!" I scream in bouts.

"I think she's in labour. Her water broke already. Why are you still here? Get her to the hospital. Go!" one of the female officers says.

I squirm dramatically as the police scold Don for wasting time.

"*He wethu*! Do you know how painful it is to be in labour? Take her to the hospital!" one of them yells at Don like he's a small child.

"You can go, sir. Get her to the nearest hospital," the male officer says.

Don drives off, stepping hard on the accelerator. I keep fanning my face until we have covered some distance.

"Stop driving like a mad person. You'll kill us." I laugh and sit up as he almost swerves off the road.

"I need to get you to the hospital!"

"Stop the car, baby."

"Okay, okay." He drives further and pulls over.

"But ..." he starts.

"I'm not in labour."

"You're not?"

"I wasn't going to let you go to jail."

His eyes widen and his lips part as if he's struggling to find the right words. He frowns as if trying to process what's going on, and then his face relaxes into what I think is a mixture of relief and adoration. I notice his hand trembling slightly as he reaches back to touch my face.

"Tris, come and drive."

Don joins me in the back and Tristan takes the wheel.

Without a word, he pulls me into a tight embrace. Even with my stomach in the way, he holds me close as if he never wants to let go.

"I love you," he says.

The words flow through me. I feel them more than I hear them. I wish he could say it again. Every time he says those three words, my life becomes complete.

"I can't go to the spa looking like this. You have to take me home." I rest my head on his shoulder.

"I'm late as it is. You have to wait in the car." He clings to me, I guess expressing what he's failing to put in words.

We finally make it to where they will be having the meeting. Tristan drives slowly between an interesting fleet of cars. I don't mean interesting in a good way by the way.

"Can I also go inside?"

"No!" they both say.

Oh, wow! Now I'm really curious about what goes on in there.

"Fine, I'll stay in the car by myself." I fold my arms and purse my lips.

"I'll be back soon," Don gives me a quick kiss.

There is no fence around the house and it's strangely close to the road. Three Wolves are smoking outside. They throw their cigarettes down, stomp them out and hurry into the house when Don and Tristan get out of the car. I remember Don saying, *'Don't let anyone fool you. Fear is stronger than kindness. Make them scared; that's how you earn respect.'*

I don't understand why they don't have security. I thought they would close the windows or post guards outside the house. What if their rivals ambush them?

As soon as the door closes, I get out and walk towards the window, looking around to make sure no one is watching me. I want to know what goes on in these secret meetings. If anyone sees me, I'll say I wanted to pee.

I peek inside, straining my eyes. It's dead quiet. Hilton is sitting with Caleb by the corner, some guys are standing, others are sitting on plastic chairs and others are sitting on the floor. Don grabs a beer from a bar fridge, and as he turns around, I retreat and press my back against the wall.

211

Actually, this is a better position. I can see if anyone approaches but also hear what's being discussed inside.

"Right, who's not here and why?" Don says.

Silence.

"Alright, I forgive you all for being early. Don't worry, I won't drag this out. Let's get straight to business... I know you've been stressing over the recent chaos. Not having a General is causing some unease. I need you to relax. The mourning period is almost over. But I'm not here to discuss that. Today, I want us to talk, Wolf to Wolf."

Silence follows and I feel like they will hear my heart beating through the wall.

"Very well, I promised to cut straight to the chase, so here goes. I understand some of you think I've been too quiet and I haven't been fully present. I'm not going to justify myself, but here's the deal. If anyone's looking for an exit, I'll make that happen for you. Not having a General means we're running as four independent packs. So here's a one-time deal. If for whatever reason you feel like switching packs, step up. I'll make it happen for you."

A long silence follows.

"Feel free. You don't have to tell me your reason."

I think one person stepped forward. Idiot!

The good thing about one person standing up is that it encourages those who are not brave enough to be the first. I think others are stepping forward as well.

"Anyone else?" I hear Don's footsteps and I hold my breath.

"So we have two dissidents among us. Alright, I see you. Tell me, which pack do you two want to join?"

"Woodstock," they say in unison.

No way! Even I know that Woodstock is their enemy. That's Ghost's pack.

"Woodstock it is. Kneel facing your brothers so I can release you."

My breath catches in my throat when I hear two successive gunshots. I recoil against the wall, feeling a heavy weight on my chest. It's like the ringing in my ears is stopping the airflow into my lungs.

"Why are you looking at me like that? I said they can go to Woodstock. I didn't say whether they'd be alive or dead when they get there."

I never should have left the car. I didn't need to witness this.

"Do me a favour. Pick up the shells and get my bullets back."

"The bullets are in their heads. How will I do that?" a thin voice says.

"I'm sure you have a knife on you. Get to carving."

"Yes, Alpha."

"Alright, let's get back on track. Where were we before some decided they didn't want to be with us anymore? Cheer up! We're just getting started... So I've caught wind that someone's been snitching, so now we're going to play a little game. Own up and I promise you won't end up dead. I know who you are. Stay silent and I'll come over right now, and well, let's just say your skull's going to take a hit."

I want to go back to the car but I feel paralysed.

"I'm going to close my eyes and count from five. When I get to zero, you better be in front of me. If you're not, well, when you make it to the other side, don't say you weren't given a chance."

He starts counting from five. I realise I'm shivering, so I close my fists and clench my teeth, struggling to breathe properly.

"Zero."

"You said you won't kill me, Alpha. I'm sorry. Please don't kill me."

I can't bear to witness another murder today. I'm already sick to my stomach.

"You'll tell me everything I need to know. Who you told, what you told them, when you told them, why you told them... Everything. But before we get to that, let's take care of you. Hilton, please demonstrate your famous finger-snapping move."

The guy pleads through chilling cries. I think Hilton slapped him or something. The sound of bones breaking is enough to make me break the silence. I quickly muffle my sounds and look at my hands shaking uncontrollably.

"The other hand too?" Hilton asks.

"No. That's enough. Let him go. I'll chat to him in a bit... To the rest of you, well, thank you for coming to my TED Talk. I hope you learnt a thing or two about loyalty."

TED Talk? I blame Elik.

I follow the wall until I'm far from the window, then I walk to the car as quickly as I can. If I wasn't so heavy, I would run. I bury my face in my hands and shake my head. I never should have left the car.

I look up when I hear the door opening. Don is no longer wearing the hoodie he had on.

"Good going, Alpha!" Hilton pats him on the shoulder.

"Don't encourage him!" Caleb says.

"You're back," Hilton says, ignoring Caleb.

"I never left," Don says.

They go on, laughing and chatting like nothing happened. It's so scary.

"*Skat*, Tristan will take you home. I'll see you later."

I nod, not trusting what I'll say if I use my voice. I just want to get home and forget what he did.

Caleb always says the problem with Don is that once he becomes trigger-happy, it's difficult for him to stop. He just keeps going; settling scores, correcting wrongs, instilling discipline, setting examples, sending out messages, until he doesn't need a good enough reason to pull the trigger. There is always one more person to take down.

It's the lack of remorse that bothers me. Last time, he was more upset about the sweater he ruined than anything else. When Caleb told him it was wrong, he said human beings can be replaced but a good sweater is hard to find.

# TWENTY NINE

I've taken it easy over the past month. I let the Wolves handle their business while I focused on getting some much-needed rest. I needed a break from all the chaos and the things I never should have witnessed. Being heavily pregnant has been horrible. I haven't had a single moment where I really felt great about it. I know that makes me a bad mother, but I can't force myself to feel things I don't. These nine months have dragged.

How long will it take to get back into shape after giving birth? *Yho!* I did not sign up for this. The back pain, swollen feet, heartburn, stretch marks, endless trips to the bathroom – it's exhausting. This wasn't in my plans at all. My boobs are sore and heavy, and sometimes the baby pushes up into my ribs, making it hard to breathe. I'm in hell! Everything is suddenly twice as hard, and even walking is a mission. I can't even sleep comfortably. And while sex is mind-blowing, we can only do it in one position. It doesn't help that I crave it all the time. Not that Don is complaining, but still, *yho!* Being pregnant sucks.

Lately, I haven't been okay, but I think I do a decent job of keeping it together. There's a deep-seated sadness I can't shake. My father's passing, especially the way it happened - gunshots, his eyes open, a gaping hole in his head trickling with blood, his body in a coffin. It all replays over and over in my nightmares. I wish my mother, grandmother and Chelsea were here with me. I need a woman to talk to every now and then. That's why I decided not to have a baby shower because who would I invite?

Hilton has been there for me in his own special way. He makes a good sounding board because he just looks at me blankly or grunts without commenting. Sometimes he shows up with random snacks and says, "Thought you might want these", before leaving soon after. It's like he's trying to show me he cares without being too obvious. He knows he loves me, even though he denies it. It makes me all mushy inside.

Don and I have grown closer over the last few months. He acts like he doesn't have much time left and wants to make every moment count. It scares me. He can't die and leave me alone with his baby. But he's been amazing *shame*. The way he cradles my stomach and lights up when the baby moves is everything.

At my last check-up, the doctor said everything looked good. My blood pressure was great, there was plenty of amniotic fluid, and the baby is due this week. I'm more nervous than excited, but I'm trying to stay calm. It's all a bit overwhelming. I booked a room in a private hospital, so at least I can look forward to some privacy through the whole ordeal.

My phone chimes and a WhatsApp message comes through. Chelsea? No way!

*'Hey, babe. Your mum asked me to reach out. I hope you've been well.'*

Wow! The audacity! You know what, fuck you Chelsea! Is this how you choose to approach me? After all this time, you come to me through a message dictated by my mother? You don't have the decency to approach me like an adult? Should I be grateful? Not even sorry for being a bitch, or your mother stayed with me when she was here and I never told you, or I heard your father died, or congratulations on your pregnancy? How about a reason for your silence? If my mother wants me checked up on, why doesn't she pick up the damn phone and call me herself? She's the one who lied to me all my life, then cut me off, ignored all my WhatsApp messages and logged me out of her Instagram. I'm done with both of you! You can go jump off a cliff for all I care.

I'm about to throw my phone against the wall when it pings again.

*'I guess we needed the break. We both had a lot going on. I don't know if we can ever get back to what we were, but I'm coming to your house now to talk.'*

So she won't even ask for my permission? She doesn't care if I'm cool with it? Fuck her! She will talk to the door when she gets here. I don't have time for nonsense.

*'I'm outside,'* she texts.

I take a deep breath and put my phone on silent. She must stay outside.

I hear voices, then footsteps. Fuck! Who let her in? I wipe my palms on my dress and give myself a quick pep-talk to play nice.

"Hi," she greets with a nervous smile.

I look at her deadpan, not exactly sure what I'm feeling.

"You look beautiful." She gives me an uncomfortable side-hug.

"Thanks."

Awkward!

"Come, let's catch up," she says like we last saw each other yesterday.

I was in the middle of reading but I guess it can wait since her majesty has spoken. I grab a packet of nuts so I can keep my mouth occupied, to avoid talking too much.

I join her in the living room, sitting a holy distance from her.

"Do you have wine or bubbles?"

I get up without saying anything, ignoring the ache in my feet, and return with a bottle of champagne, juice and glasses. She gulps the first serving and quickly tops up.

She goes on about her job, her life, new restaurants she has tried this month and the vacation she went to after I left Cape Town. It's a whole brag fest. I let her handle the conversation because I don't trust myself not to say the wrong thing. From the way she's laughing, I know alcohol has taken over. I feel like she was drinking fast to avoid facing me sober. One more glass and we'll be at the crying stage.

Don walks in and asks if he can talk to me in private. Getting up is a struggle so he helps me up and leads me to the kitchen. He asks if I'm okay with Chelsea being here. I assure him that I'm good. I didn't invite her but she's here now, so I'll just let it be. He says he'll be outside with his friends and I should call him if I need anything. He walks me back to the living room, helps me sit and kisses me on the lips.

"I love you, okay?" he says.

"I love you too, baby."

I watch him walk away. My smile fades when I see Chelsea sipping on her drink awkwardly.

There's a sharp pang in my heart that I keep pushing down with juice. An episode of *The Originals* is playing on TV but I'm not really watching.

"Elijah loves Hayley, but Hayley is such a bitch. She keeps pushing him away," Chelsea says.

"True." I sip on my juice while eyeing the champagne lustily.

"Hayley is so dumb. How dare she mess around with Elijah's heart like that! He's a good guy. Of all the vampires, he's the only one human enough to genuinely love. How could she do that?"

*I have no idea where this conversation is going, and honestly, I couldn't be less interested.*

"No guy will ever love her like Elijah." She bangs her fist on the arm of the couch and I roll my eyes.

She goes on a rant about how Hayley is ungrateful and messed up and wouldn't recognise love if it hit her in the face.

*Are we still talking about The Originals?*

She looks at me with glassy eyes. "I'm Hayley."

*Wow! It didn't take long for the dramatic side to surface.*

I look away to hide my irritation and I find Caleb standing by the doorway. How long has he been standing there?

Chelsea keeps talking, circling the rim of her glass with her finger. "I don't have a lot of regrets in my life, but losing Caleb is the worst of them all. That's my biggest loss to this day."

*Wow! Losing me meant nothing?*

"I wish I could go back and undo everything. He was the first guy to genuinely care about me." She takes a big gulp of her champagne.

Caleb is still standing by the door. I'm not sure whether to alert Chelsea or not. I don't know if she would want him to hear the things she's saying. I'm still trying to make a decision when she resumes. Oh, well, let it play out.

"Caleb treated me like a queen. Despite everything they were saying about me, he still chose me. He was very good to me. I'm not just talking about the sex, which was mind-blowing by the way."

I look at Caleb and he looks down. Great, Chelsea is back to crying. Fuck it! I reach for the champagne and make a mimosa. I can't deal with this sober. She didn't talk to me for months and this is what she chooses to start with? Why is she acting like she never ghosted me?

"He would text me paragraphs, call me, spend time with me, hold my hand at the mall and look at me like I was the most beautiful girl he'd ever seen. He would bring me lunch at work and say the most beautiful things. He wasn't afraid to show exactly how he felt about me."

I'm starting to feel sorry for her when I remember she did all this to herself. She messed up, not Caleb. And not to be self-absorbed or anything, but shouldn't she be talking about us? Did she come all this way just to vent? I thought she wanted to mend our friendship. She could tell me about my mother for a start. Obviously, they talk.

"Then I went and messed up for no reason at all. I hurt him."

"What did you do?" I might as well indulge her. I need to hear what exactly she did because I got blamed for it. It cost me Fierce and Elik, and it almost cost me Caleb.

"I got drunk and went to Elik's place. He wanted to kick me out, but you know how he is, he wouldn't let me drive in the state I was in. He let me sleep in another room and I left in the morning. He must have told Caleb another version of the story. I was wrong for going to his place, but nothing happened."

I look up at Caleb and I find his face expressionless.

"When was this?" I deserve the details.

"You were still in Eastern Cape. I wanted to, you know, hook up with Elik to make sure I really loved Caleb."

"Huh?" *In what universe does that make sense?*

"I know, I know. It was a stupid idea."

*See why I needed a stronger drink?*

"I miss Caleb so much. I thought he was eventually going to leave me like every guy does. Then he didn't leave and I settled in and let go of my fears. Then when I least expected it, he left me. He dumped me for something I didn't do!"

*Well, the intent to cheat is guilty enough in my books. Had Elik said yes, you would have cheated. How dare you blame Caleb for something you did, little whore?*

I take a long gulp of my mimosa and quickly top-up with champagne. The stronger, the better.

"I haven't been able to hook up with any guy ever since."

*Yeah, right! I don't believe that.*

"I wish I could go back in time and not go to Elik's place. Maybe I should have been honest with Caleb about everything. Do you think he would have understood?" She looks at me as if expecting an answer.

I shrug. *Frankly, I'm annoyed by your pity-party. Can you wrap it up already!*

"I just thought telling him that I slept at an ex's house wouldn't sound right, you know?"

I don't know what to add to this conversation. It's starting to feel like a therapy session, except no one is paying me by the hour.

"Those men destroyed me. Even when they went to prison, the pain never left."

*As heartbreaking as that is, how did we get here? This can't be the great reunion.*

"So you tell me, who would love a girl who went through all that? Would Caleb have loved me if I told him all that?"

*Oh, for fuck's sake. Cut it out already! Caleb knew all about it and still chose to be with you.*

"I lost the only man I've ever loved."

I take the glass from her hand and down it, then pull her into my arms. I rest her head on my shoulder and hold her. I feel terrible for what happened back then. My ex and his friends had no right to violate her like that. But right now I can't process it with the delicacy it deserves. I'm so angry at her, I can't move past that. I have to hold her to hide my facial expressions.

"Do you think he'll ever take me back?"

*I hope he doesn't take you back. You're a horrible person.*

"He wouldn't take my calls or respond to any of my messages. I came here because I knew he would be here."

*Aha! There it is - the real reason she's here. It was never about me.*

I don't know why it stings. I guess deep down I hoped she genuinely wanted to work on us. Is she aware he's standing by the door right now? Is she performing? I have no words.

"Lotus, please let me talk to Chelsea alone," Caleb says.

Chelsea starts bawling her eyes out and I shake my head. I can't believe she used me like this. You know what, let me go and spend time with people who matter. Damn this pregnancy! Standing up feels like moving a mountain.

I stand by the doorway, watching Don, Hilton, Tristan and the Wolves that are always around, drinking and playing music. I wanted to talk to Don but now I feel like lying down. My energy just dipped and my head feels light. I need to drink some water.

Chelsea walks into the kitchen and I almost choke on my water. She startled me.

"Let's go chill with the guys outside," she says.

I was still enjoying my alone time but it's fine. I don't want to be alone with her. I will leave her outside then go and lie down.

Just before we reach the door, she grabs my arm and signals me to be quiet. We stop and listen to the guys talking outside.

"Are you seriously considering getting back with that girl?" Tristan says.

"Bad idea, my bru. You can never wife a whore. She belongs to the streets," Don says.

"Don't call her that," Caleb says in a dropped tone.

"Well, I'm just calling a whore a whore." Don laughs and I feel my stomach churn.

I look at Chelsea and her face is fixed on the door.

"Do what you want. If you want her back, go ahead. Don't listen to Alpha. Wasn't he on his knees crying for a girl? Didn't he drag me across the country to go and see a girl? Do whatever you want to do," Hilton says.

"The thing is, I think I love her, but I can't get over what she did. Will I be foolish to make up with her?"

"You're always foolish. You make one stupid decision after the other. Why would you want to break that perfect streak?" Hilton says.

"Don't do it, my bru," Don says.

"I'm with Alpha on this one," Tristan says.

The water bottle in my hand accidentally slips and falls to the floor, drawing the guys' attention.

"Are you alright?" Caleb walks in.

"It's plastic, don't worry."

He picks it up and hands it to me.

"I'll be in the kitchen." I excuse myself so I can leave him with Chelsea.

They follow me and stop by the door. I don't know if they can't see me or if they don't mind my presence because Caleb pulls Chelsea into his arms. She clings to him and starts grovelling. It's pitiful to witness.

He lets her go and holds her shoulders, looking at her face. "I loved you and you betrayed me in the worst of ways."

*Loved? Past tense? Not good.*

She resumes crying and he pulls her into his arms again.

"I'm so sorry."

*So awkward.*

"If we're going to talk today, promise me you won't lie. No more lies. Give me the truth."

She nods vigorously.

"The thing is, I keep wondering why I wasn't good enough for you. You picked my friend, Chelsea. Of all people, my friend!" He's getting worked up.

*I thought you guys had this talk earlier. What is this? Love Back Repeat? And Caleb, Elik came before you, and Chelsea went back for more, so technically, you are second best. She loves Elik, not you. But she can't have him so she will settle for you.*

"You hurt me more than you can ever imagine, yet no matter how hard I try, I can't hate you. I can never hate you. I took out my anger on Lotus because I had to be mad at someone, and since I couldn't be mad at you, she took the fall. Hell, I punched Elik in the face and almost ruined a good friendship because of you. I lashed out at everyone except you. I couldn't be mad at you."

*You're forgiven, dearest Caleb. Chelsea, you're not forgiven.*

"I'm sorry. Please forgive me. I love you. Please, one more chance is all I'm asking for. Please, let's try again."

*Begging a man to love you? Bad move, Chelsea.*

"We need to talk before we can make such big decisions. We'll talk." He leaves her standing there.

*Oh, great! Now I must comfort her? Fuck, no.*

I turn away and pretend to be looking for something in the cupboard. A sharp pain slices through my stomach and I gasp, feeling as if my lungs are closing as it gets worse. It's like someone cut me with a knife. I grit my teeth and hold onto the bar stool.

"The baby is coming," I force the words out through clenched teeth.

"Like right now?"

"Yes, Chelsea!"

"Oh, let me get Donavan."

I push through the pain and manage to balance against the counter. "Lord, please grant me the Hebrew women's type of birth. Amen," I pray out loud.

They rush into the kitchen and Don is being dramatic.

"What's going on?" He tries to hold me, make me sit down and carry me, all at the same time.

"I'm starting to feel cramps, they're not that bad yet." They are very bad, but I don't want anyone to panic.

"Okay, so what now? Should I call an ambulance or take you to the hospital? What should I do? I'm calling Doc." Don dials the Wolves' doctor and puts the phone on speaker.

The pain is subsiding but I still feel weak.

"Alpha, it's a Saturday if you didn't notice. Can I please enjoy my weekend," the doctor's permanently nonchalant voice comes through the phone.

"Get here right now!"

"Why?"

"My girl is giving birth!"

"So?"

"I'm not playing with you. Get here right now!" Don sounds so lethal, I'm scared on behalf of the doctor.

"I'm not a midwife, Alpha."

Don stops and looks at the phone before looking at Caleb. It takes everything in me not to laugh when he innocently asks, "What's a midwife?"

"Take her to the hospital. Doesn't she have her own doctor? Why are you bothering me? Let me talk to her."

Don squeezes the phone so hard, I don't know how it doesn't break. He holds it to my face after his brief tantrum.

"How far apart are the contractions?"

"I don't know."

"You'll know when they're close."

"Okay. Doc..."

He hung up!

"We're going to the hospital right away. I'll grab the bag." Don dashes off to get my hospital bag.

I don't even know why he called the Wolves doctor because we have been going to a different doctor all along. I'm so anxious, I'm on the verge of a panic attack. I don't like pain, so I'm dreading the part where I have to push a whole baby's head out. I'm also not looking forward to meeting the baby, which makes me feel like a terrible person. I don't know how to explain it; I'm just not ready. I really wish my mother and grandmother were here to help me through this.

The kitchen feels overcrowded and everyone is exchanging nervous glances as if they are not sure what to do or say. They are acting like I'm going to burst at any moment. Chelsea is being so sweet, if I didn't know any better, I would think it's genuine. She's probably just trying to impress Caleb, you know, showing him what a good person she is. I wish everyone could leave me alone for a moment so I can catch my breath and centre myself.

# *THIRTY*

No amount of reading prepared me for this phase of my life. Giving birth is by far the worst experience I've ever gone through. It was excruciating! I guess it's safe to say we won't be making another baby. I'm reading up on tubal ligation as we speak. I completely hated being pregnant. I won't be repeating it in this lifetime or the next. My baby-making factory is officially closed for business.

By the time we got to the hospital, my contractions were hitting hard. The pain was so intense, I could barely breathe. When I started pushing, Don freaked out and ran away. Looking back, it's funny how traumatised he was. Chelsea stayed by my side through it all, holding my hand and coaching me through the worst of it. I'm so grateful she was there.

When Don finally came back, Chelsea stepped out to give us space. It was so surreal. Don stood next to my bed, with tears in his eyes, looking more vulnerable than I'd ever seen him. He looked at our child and I witnessed 'love at first sight'.

"He's perfect," he choked out and his tears spilled over. "Thank you, my angel," he turned to me.

I smiled through my own tears.

"He's so tiny," he whispered, like he was afraid to make any noise that might scare the baby.

I reached out and touched his arm. I was too tired to say much.

"I'm going to take care of you both, no matter what. I promise."

The baby gave a little yawn, and Don chuckled softly, fighting back more tears. It was such a beautiful moment to witness.

It's been a tough two weeks. Between the pain, paranoia, sleep deprivation and the baby's constant crying, I'm not sure how I'm still holding it together. All he does is cry; it's driving me nuts. I'm always exhausted and I can't remember the last time I had a good night's sleep. I'm glad we got a nanny because Don and I wouldn't have known where to begin looking after the product of our long nights.

The baby is tiny and pale, and he looks fragile. It was bothering me that after two weeks of breastfeeding him, he was still not growing, so we went to the doctor this morning. Thankfully, he's perfectly healthy. I got checked too, and my stitches are fine and there's no sign of infection; everything is healing well.

We were in a good mood after the doctor's visit, so we drove around. We passed by my favourite perfume shop, and eventually ended up in

Longstreet. It's such a normal place during the day, you wouldn't believe it.

We are on our way back home now. Don is driving and I'm in the passenger seat, stealing glances at him and at our baby snug in a car seat at the back.

"Have you noticed how stubborn he is?" Don says, as if it just occurred to him.

"We all know who he takes after."

We both laugh and Don turns his attention back to the road with a smile. I look back at our baby, sleeping peacefully. I think Don is as scared as I am about this whole parenting thing, but being who he is, he won't admit it.

"I still can't believe it. We're responsible for a whole human being."

"Yeah, it's kind of scary. But we'll figure it out, right?"

"We will." I take his free hand and intertwine our fingers.

His hand trembles a little as he tightens his grip. "We're in this together, *skat*. All three of us."

I smile, feeling a wave of contentment wash over me. Moments like this make everything worth it.

There are several cars in the yard and I can hear booming music coming from the house. We were only gone for five hours. I really hope it's not a party or anything like that. I'm not in the mood. They should go and play somewhere else. I spot Fierce's car and my heart skips a beat. I thought she said I was dead to her, and if I'm being honest, I'm not in the mood to be alive in the presence of her judgemental ass.

Don helps me out of the car and we walk arm in arm. N.W.A is blasting from the house, and usually I wouldn't mind, but do we really want *'Fuck the police'* to be one of the first phrases our child learns? We know he'll probably grow up to be a law-breaking citizen and probably fuck the police more than once, but can he at least have a decent childhood?

"Lotus, hi. Why are you walking alone?" Chelsea approaches.

I look at her judgingly. It's a public secret that she doesn't like Don, but can she at least respect him? Can she at least greet him instead of acting like he doesn't exist? Is that too much to ask?

"Is there a reason for that loud music?"

"Duh!" She makes a face.

I close my fist to stop my thoughts from forming into words. Don takes the hint and says he'll go ahead and shut down whatever nonsense is going on in there. I know he wants to get away from Chelsea and I'm glad he didn't address her. He doesn't have a lot of kind words in his vocabulary, so he might have said something offensive. They always had a love-hate relationship, and it got worse after she heard him say those things about her. I have decided not to get involved. It's not like she likes me anyway. I'm just her bridge to Caleb and she can't discard me before they are solid again. It's quite sad when you think about it.

"He's actually trying. It's cute," she says when Don is out of earshot.

"He really is. He loves his son more than anything."

"Shame. Too bad that little angel has you two for parents. It's a disaster waiting to happen."

I'll ignore that.

"I told your mother you had the baby but she wasn't interested. Sorry."

Wow! If the aim was to break my heart, she succeeded. But I won't give her the satisfaction. She goes on, giving me advice, cautions and tips on how to raise a baby, constantly hinting that I'm a terrible mother. I'm starting to get annoyed.

"He's so tiny! Are you feeding him enough?"

Why is she doing this? She knows how sensitive I am about his size. I need to change the subject before I get upset. I'm hyper-emotional these days, so if this conversation continues, it will end in tears and I won't be the one crying.

I walk into the house and curse out loud when they scream, "Surprise!"

What the hell!

Everyone considered family is here - Hilton, Caleb, Tristan, Elik, Merishka and a couple of other Wolves. I'm glad Fierce is not here. I guess Elik used her car.

Chelsea is over-excited as she flings her arms around me as if we didn't walk in together.

"I organised all this for you. You're welcome."

*Why?* Eye roll.

I think the Wolves didn't get the memo because they seem not to know what to do. They are huddled on one side of the room, beers in hand, looking nervous and out of place. Merishka takes the baby from Don and mumbles something about how wrong it is to expose him to so many people. She says we have abandoned the old ways. She is clearly upset about it. We all just watch as she works herself into a frenzy. Dramatic much?

Chelsea leads us like goats to the pen, to the living room. No one complains. I guess deep down we are all afraid of her domineering personality. She went a little overboard with this party of hers. There is a two-tier cake with the number zero on top. Is there such a thing as a zeroeth birthday? Is the absence of candles to blow out symbolising zero? You know what, I won't crack my brain over a mass of edible sponge and cream. I don't even want to be here right now.

More balloons? Yikes!

I sit next to Don on the couch. The baby is in his arms. He took him back when Merishka wouldn't stop suggesting we're bad parents. Chelsea is standing between Caleb and the Chucky-faced Wolf, with Elik behind her. It's funny because she slept with all three of them. I'm not judging, but her range is hilarious. I mean, Caleb is the best-looking of the Wolves and Chucky-face is, well, the ugliest. Chelsea clearly doesn't discriminate. I wonder if Caleb knows about her and Chucky-face. Elik, on the other hand, stands out. He's just different from everyone in the room, in a good way. A second look at Chucky-face and all I can say is Chelsea is brave.

I see Caleb's hand touching Chelsea's and I scoff. She doesn't deserve him.

There are balloons everywhere and gifts on the table next to the door. Don't people know that I hate gifts? I prefer cash. That way I don't end up with cheap picture frames and water glasses I don't need. Besides, when people give you cash, they give a significant amount, but when they buy gifts, they are not ashamed to buy stuff from China Town. Anyway, *positive vibes only* is the motto.

The theme of the baby-welcoming-party is Sleeping Beauty. It looks cute but kind of weird, considering that Sleeping Beauty was a girl and her birthday party was basically a horror story. She was cursed by an evil fairy and ended up in a coma. She fell asleep on her sixteenth birthday and took a century-long power-nap. I can't have my son passing out for a hundred years when he's sixteen! He'll be in his prime, and I won't be around when he wakes up.

I don't even know why we are having a party when the guest of honour has no idea what's going on. He's only two weeks old, but he already has the world revolving around him. Everyone is taken by him. Don was shocked when I celebrated him being a boy. I wanted a girl at first, but that was before I used my child as a dice. I was more relieved than excited, to be honest. It had everyone confused but it is what it is. It's a boy! Somehow, I believe he was initially a girl and my faith changed him into a boy to save me.

I'm not sure he looks like me, even though that's what everyone says. To me, he doesn't look like anyone. He just has his father's eyes. I wanted to name him Aiden but Don already had names picked out for him. He said I can name our next one Aiden. Next one? No way! I'm not doing that again. I can't wait to find a good plastic surgeon to snatch me back to my factory settings, then get my tubes tied. I can't look at my stomach without sinking into depression.

I always knew they were Wolves but I underestimated how much that meant to them. I think deep down they believe they are werewolves. Their obsession with wolves is not natural. Our baby was born on a full moon and they made a big deal of it. They said it was a sign; it was so weird. Don gave him his first name and Hilton gave him his second. I carried the baby for nine long months and I didn't even get the privilege of giving him a name! If I ever doubted how much Hilton meant to Don, I take it back. Now I know that if he had to pick between me and him, he wouldn't pick me. I don't know how to feel about that.

Our son's first name is Ulric, meaning the wolf ruler. A name fit for the next Alpha, I suppose. His second name is Alarick, meaning the fierce and supreme noble leader of all wolves. Who knew Don and Hilton could be so deep? I love the names. They are unique and have that special something. Ever heard the saying 'names are prophecies'? Like how I was named Lotus and ended up being as graceful and peaceful as the lotus flower. Seriously though, I have a feeling that my son's names are prophecies. He will be a noble and fierce leader. I can't pronounce Ulric well so I just call him Ricky. Do not judge me!

Chelsea's voice draws me back to the room. She's telling everyone to shush and listen to her, in her typical bossy stance.

"As I explained earlier, all you have to do is grab your present on the table, walk over to Donavan and Lotus, give them the gift and speak blessings over baby Ulric. Got it?"

I used to admire her confidence and wish I could be like her, but I think I'm good where I am. Being in charge all the time seems exhausting. She always was an alpha and I was a beta, and finally, it's okay.

I would rather be lying down right now but let's get through the theatrics.

"I'll go first so you can see how it's done. Watch and learn." She picks up a ridiculously big box and places it at my feet.

"Lotus, thank you for bringing such a beautiful baby boy into the world. I'm so happy for you. You've been my friend for a very long time and I'm honoured to walk this new chapter of your life with you. You'll probably make an interesting mother", she chuckles, "but I'll be there to mess up with you and to take the best pictures of you and baby Ulric. We'll spoil him rotten. I love you so much." She flashes a generous smile.

"Thank you."

Are those tears in her eyes? This baby is melting even the rocks. I thank her for the party because I'm courteous and I'm a good person. I'll ignore how she blatantly ignored Don's existence and made it seem like I made the baby all by myself.

Elik comes next with his bedazzling charm. Isn't it funny how everyone forgave him for having been with Chelsea but dragged Chelsea through the mud? I know she was wrong to try it again, but I feel like they let him off easily. Caleb, Don, Tristan, Fierce - all of them continued with Elik as if Chelsea forced him or something.

Elik looks back at Chelsea, for instructions I guess. I follow his eyes, and as Chelsea smiles encouragingly at him, I see Caleb's face turn into an unfriendly frown.

"I don't have much to say. I could talk to the baby I suppose, but I doubt he'll understand."

His perfume smells divine and there is something exotic about his accent. He's polite and lovable, and I'll never forget how he helped me when I had no one in my corner. For that, I'll forever be indebted to him.

"Okay, first of all, Lotus, we're good. I shouldn't have been mad at you to begin with. It's all water under the bridge."

"Really? Thank you." I'm genuinely relieved.

"And Lemon, my guy, you live life in the fast lane. You're good at what you do, but let's face it, you're not immortal. So here's an idea: why not set up a trust fund for your son? I can handle it for you. Whenever you have some extra cash, just give it to me and I'll put it in the fund. That way, your son's covered. His university fees, a car when he gets a licence, travel, sports expenses, everything. Because we both know that tomorrow isn't promised to anyone."

I like it, but I hate the dark undertone. My paranoia is rising again. Don can't leave me alone with a baby.

"Sounds good?" Don looks at me.

"It's an amazing idea," I say.

"Cool. Let's do it."

See! Gifts don't always have to be something bought. Sometimes an offer to help or even advice is a better gift than cheap, ugly things. I want to ask if the money will still be accessible if we end up in that remote place Don mentioned, but I don't want to dwell on those thoughts for too long and spoil the moment.

"Lotus, I remember you saying you only accept gifts in cash, so here's my humble gift to you." He hands me an envelope.

He remembered from my birthday? Wow! Can he teach Don how to remember important things?

My eyes widen when I see a fat stack of R200 notes. There is nothing humble about this amount. Now I understand why Fierce will never leave him. Money excites me, so I'm suddenly in a cheerful mood. I hope the others are taking notes.

Caleb comes next - calm and looking fresher than a pillow with a mint on it. He nods at me and takes the knee at Don's feet. This party is starting to feel like a cult. It's as if we are gods and people are coming to pay tribute. It's getting weird.

"Alpha, you're more than an Alpha to me. You're my brother and have been my closest friend since we were kids. I pledged to protect you with my life and to step in front of the gun so I can die before you do. I have nothing material to offer your son today, so I'm offering myself to him the same way I pledged my allegiance to you. I'll protect your son with my life, no matter the cost. I'll be loyal to him as I am to you. I'll die before he dies."

People are so reckless with their lives. I would never!

Don accepts and I smile my approval. It got too intense too fast.

The silence that follows is so loud you can almost hear it. I'm grateful when Chelsea's voice breaks it.

"Hilton, your turn." She nudges him.

"My turn to do what?"

"To give them your gift. We discussed this!"

"I don't have a gift."

"But why? I told you to get one! Fine, just go and say something nice to the baby."

"I'm not getting involved in this nonsense. Why am I even here?"

I catch his eye and he stares at me blankly. That makes me smile at him. His consistency is admirable.

"Hilton!" Chelsea whines.

"Alpha, call me after you're done with this circus."

The circus, as Hilton called it, goes on. Tristan gives us a plant that he says will ward off bad energies. It's the most random gift ever. I wouldn't have expected that from him. Maybe from someone like Elik, but him? No way.

One of the Wolves gives us an eighteen-year-old whiskey. It takes all my self-control not to point out how useless that is for a baby. People need to use their brains more.

Merishka gives us an Earth Child gift voucher and someone gives us a Woolworths voucher. Now that's what I'm talking about! See what happens when people use their brains?

The rest of the Wolves give useless gifts, which we accept gracefully.

The biggest gift they all give is their loyalty to my son. They all pledge to protect him and vow to lay down their lives for him. I guess I'll sleep better knowing that people will risk it all for my man and my son. But what about me? No one pledged themselves to me.

# *THIRTY ONE*

The party eventually ended and everyone left. I can breathe again. "I think he wants to feed," Don says, walking into the bedroom.

I don't feel like it but I don't have the energy to argue. I hold Ricky the way the nanny showed me, so he doesn't choke. I'm still getting the hang of it. Every time he smiles at me with that toothless mouth and looks at me with those big blue eyes, I feel like crying. I made this beautiful thing that drinks too much milk. I hate breastfeeding but Google says it's the quickest way to lose baby fat, so I guess I have to look at the bigger picture. I seriously need to get back into shape. Ricky really messed up my body.

Ulric Alarick son of Lotus Janse van Rensburg. Doesn't he sound like a medieval knight? His names go perfectly with his surname. Thanks to Don for that. Should he decide to go the corporate route, he will be very employable.

I finish feeding him, and Don takes him to the nursery.

I collapse on the bed, close my eyes, and take a deep breath. I can't believe Chelsea threw that whole shindig considering how shaky our friendship is. We haven't even talked, like really talked, and she is already throwing me parties. I can't decide if I'm grateful or annoyed.

I barely recognise myself these days. Everything is overwhelming. Ricky easily goes from soft crying to hysterical in microseconds and I'm expected to know how to calm him. I just need one day of uninterrupted peace. Hearing him crying in the nursery is frustrating. I can't remember the last time I had a moment to myself. I just need a break. Is that too much to ask?

My phone vibrates and it's a message from Hilton.

*'I'm outside.'*

My first thought is 'So?' but then I remember that Hilton never does anything without a reason. He wouldn't text me simply because he missed me, worse at this time.

I take the gift bag from the closet and slip out the side door.

"There you are." I hold my cardigan closed. "What's up?"

He looks up, and with a straight face says, "The sky, the last time I checked."

I don't even bother figuring out if he's serious or being silly. He drops what's remaining of his cigarette and crushes it under his shoe while I wait patiently.

"You need to tell Alpha about your visit to his father."

"What? Why?"

"Because you have a baby now. That's all you should be focusing on. Tell Alpha everything and let him take care of it."

"But I got this!"

"You got nothing. Tell him, or I will."

I don't like his commanding tone, but what can I say? He doesn't care.

"But..."

"But nothing."

I don't understand what's going on. Don and I have been doing very well. Telling him will undo everything.

"I can't tell him yet. I'll see this through, and when he's the only Alpha standing, I'll tell him and he'll thank me." That was the plan. Why is he switching up on me now?

"Who's going to take out the three Alphas?"

"You'll help me. You will, right? We had a plan, Hilton!" I sound as desperate as I am. Talk about classic betrayal.

"I take orders from one person only and his name is not Lotus."

My lips gap and I search his face for answers. We had a plan. Why is he doing this?

"Hilton..."

"Please don't ask me silly questions. Tell Alpha to call me. Before or after you tell him, I don't really care. You can go back inside now."

"Why are you doing this?" My voice has dropped so low, I'm close to tears.

"Do you always have to make everything difficult?"

"How am I making anything difficult?"

"Do you trust me?"

I shake my head.

"Good. I don't trust myself either. But you have to trust me on this. Tell him."

"But..."

"Before you go back inside, take this. Make sure Ulric reads it someday. Don't you dare read it, it's not yours." He hands me a sealed envelope.

"Sure." *Treacherous bastard!*

The mood is spoiled but I have to give him this.

"I got this for you." I pass him the gift bag.

He takes it but doesn't look inside.

"Open it, Hilly. Stop being so dramatic!"

He eyes me suspiciously, then reaches into the bag and pulls out the box.

"A perfume?" He raises an eyebrow. "Do I smell?"

"Of course, not. It's just a gift. I don't appreciate you enough, so I got you this. There's biltong in there too." That's his favourite snack.

For a brief moment, his blank look cracks; his expression softens and there's a glint of warmth in his eyes.

"You're welcome." I closed-lip smile at him.

He nods, and without another word, he turns and heads towards his car.

I can't help but smile a little. He caught me off guard but I know he always means well. Maybe I should tell Don, I don't know. I'll sleep on it. But I can't have worked that hard to give up now. I just need to heal, then I'll finish what we started. And Hilton is crazy if he thinks I won't read the letter. What if he's teaching my son how to commit crimes?

*[Dear ULRIC ALARICK*

*This is the law of our family: As old and as true as the sky, so will the Wolf that keeps the laws in the Creed.*

*The Wolf that keeps the Creed shall prosper, and the Wolf that breaks it shall die.*

*For the strength of the pack is the Wolf, and the strength of the Wolf is the pack.*

*The Alpha never follows the pack, but always leads the pack.*

*Always remember:*
*If they stand behind you, protect them.*
*If they stand beside you, respect them.*
*If they stand against you, defeat them.*
*And if they pledge their allegiance to you, their lives are yours.*

*I hereby pledge my allegiance to you.*

*Your Uncle,*

*HILTON*

*Lotus, why did you read this letter? Didn't I tell you not to open it?]*

Why am I crying and smiling at the same time? I keep reading it over and over again. These words read like they were plucked out of the Creed. Hilton lay down his life for my son, and he knew I would read it. Maybe he's right, I should trust him blindly.

Just as I put the letter away, Don walks in.

"Can I talk to you about something?" I jump at it before I get cold feet.

"Yeah?" He takes his T-shirt off and I'm immediately distracted. Goddamn, his body!

"I need to tell you something."

"What's up?"

"Please don't hate me. I did it for us. I swear, I never meant to betray you. To be honest, I wasn't going to tell you, but looking at Ricky and knowing what the future holds for him made me realise that I can't keep this a secret any longer."

He looks at me quizzically and my courage flies away.

"What are you on about?" He sits on the bed and takes off his shoes. "I'm tired. I want to sleep. I have an early morning."

He does look drained but it's now or never. Eyes closed, deep breath, here goes my life. "I went to see your father before I had Ricky."

"Go on," he says with an eerily calm demeanour.

"I asked him to convince you to be the leader of the Wolves." I brave it and tell him everything, with a seasoning of lies to leave Hilton out of it. Not to blow my own horn, but I sound like a bad-ass to have pulled that off all by myself.

"Is that all?"

I nod, careful to avoid his eye. I'm scared but at least the cat is out of the bag now.

"Cool then. I'm going to sleep."

"You have nothing to say? Are you not mad at me?"

"Mad at you for what?"

"Umm, for keeping this from you? For going behind your back?"

"Why would I be? I knew everything."

"You what? All this time you knew?" Why am I feeling betrayed?

"Of course. There's nothing I don't know. I thought you knew that by now." He tugs the covers back and gets into bed.

Secrets I have hidden from him race each other across my mind. What else does he know?

"But how? Who told you?"

"I'm not a snitch. Snitches get stitches and end up in ditches." He chuckles like it's all a joke.

"So you knew all along? And you said nothing because?" I'm

struggling to come to terms with all this. In fact, I'm getting worked up. I feel played.

"Because you also said nothing. Silence for silence, how is that not fair, my angel?" He adds that scoff that I hate.

Sigh. Double sigh. Triple sigh. All the sighs in the world actually!

"I didn't become an Alpha by chance, my *skat*, and I most certainly won't be becoming a General or The Alpha, or whatever you call it. Good going though. Please switch off the lights."

"What do you mean? You have to! It's the only way."

"No, thanks. Goodnight."

I feel defeated. What the hell? How was he okay with me going behind his back and scheming to rank him up? I thought I knew him. I thought betrayal was a deal-breaker for him. When did that change? What counts as betrayal to him? Because I'm no longer sure. If he won't be stepping up, then all my effort was for nothing. Does this man know the coals I had to walk on to make sure the Wolves become ours? All the conniving and bribing? I damn near sold my soul to the devil just to get him to the top! I walked through prison corridors and made crossroad deals, heavily pregnant *nogal!* I would be damned if I let him toss my hard work out of the window. He will lead the Wolves, by fire, by force!

I'm struggling to sleep. I need to have a serious talk with Hilton, but I'm not stupid, I won't call him so late at night. So I text him instead, asking him to meet with me as soon as he can.

I'm busy Googling things like *'How to lose weight after giving birth'* and *'How long should I wait after pregnancy before getting a tummy tuck?'* to stop myself from going crazy. I'm about to put my phone away when a message pops up.

*'Happy midnight,'* it reads.

I don't recognise the number so I roll my eyes and go back to Google. Happy midnight? Who says that?

Another message comes through. *'Is it a boy or girl?'*

Another one follows, *'When can I see you, pretty girl?'*

A chill runs down my spine and I'm sure my heart stops for several seconds. I honestly didn't need this right now. My hand is shaking and my breath is coming in gasps. I part my lips a little and allow my mouth to help me breathe. He disappeared for months. I thought he had finally left me alone. Does Don know about him? What exactly does he know? I'm so terrified, I'm numb. Now seems like a good time to start praying.

"Why aren't you sleeping?" Don's voice jolts me out of my struggling prayer.

"No reason."

"You should get some sleep." He rolls over and faces me. "You're not good. Are you still mad that I knew the secrets you were trying to keep from me?" He opens his eyes, lifts his head, double folds the pillow and looks at me.

Deep inside I'm petrified but I can't let him see that. I have to keep my head up, like his favourite Tupac song says. Can he go back to sleep so I can continue going crazy in peace?

"If it's any consolation, you tried... Fine, you outdid yourself, and I've never been more proud to call you mine. But it was very reckless of you and you should have never done it. This is my life, not yours."

Did he just compliment me and then take it back?

"I hate that you put our son's life in danger, but I appreciate everything you did. Are you happy now? Can we sleep?"

"No, I'm not happy."

"Okay, fine. I'll think about it. Happy now?"

"You don't have to be The Alpha if you don't want. No one needs to die. You can be the General like the original plan."

"I don't want to be a General. I'm not in the military or the Salvation Army. I'm an Alpha. Why change a good title? People will call me what? General Alpha?"

I wish he could take this seriously.

"Well, dead people don't have titles," I mumble.

"I don't know what you want from me. I said I'll think about it."

"But baby..."

"Let's sleep, please, my angel. We can talk tomorrow."

I sigh and turn off my bedside lamp. I curl up in his arms, facing away from him and making a silent plea for sleep to take over and stay with me all night. The position hurts my hand, so I untangle myself from his hold and lie on my back, looking at the dark ceiling. No matter how hard I try to remember how terrible Dalu was to me, I keep seeing a gentle guy who wanted to give me the world. All the times he called me 'pretty girl' and topped it off with that smile of his replay in my head. Did his sister have a point? Did I trigger the monster he became? I guess my ex was right after all; I do induce psychos. I know what Elik said after going through the flash drive, and all the cruel things Dalu planned for me even before he met me, but I can't help the thoughts.

'Hey, pretty girl, it's your world, conquer it', he said to me at the airport that time. He had forgiven me already and had offered me a life-changing job in his company. I'd stood him up the previous night, which was his birthday, and went to Don instead.

I remember this one clearly. We were cuddling in the dark on the steps of Rhodes Memorial. He held me and professed his undying love for me. 'No one has ever made me feel the way you do. I just want to be with you, travel the world with you, play with you, build an empire with you. I just want you, Lotus.'

Am I supposed to believe that he was lying? I know, I know, but I don't know *mann*.

The memories roll out, picking up pace and accusing me of hurting someone whose only crime was loving me. He hurt me. He drugged me. He almost killed my child. He stalked me for months. He turned my friends against me. He lied to me. He tried to have me killed. Why are those memories not coming forward?

Don reaches for me. I hate how I can't tell him how I messed up, but I need to be held, so I move closer and let his arms envelop me. Where do I begin explaining how guilty I am for hurting another guy, or how scared I am that he's back again?

# THIRTY TWO

Don's father held his end of the stick, so Don is going to be The Alpha, or die trying, and he *allowed* us to help him. It's been a hectic couple of days, but I'm not complaining; it's actually helped to keep my mind off Dalubuhle. We can't afford any mistakes with this. We are having the final meeting today. We are just waiting for Caleb and Tristan to arrive so we can get started. I'm going to feed Ricky so long and leave him with the nanny. Hopefully, by the time I get back, they will be here.

Ricky just wouldn't settle down so I took longer than expected. But at least everyone is here now. Hilton is sitting alone, looking ever so murderous. Tristan is on his phone, looking ever so bored. Don is staring at me, looking ever so irresistible. Caleb is sitting next to Don, looking ever so refined. Caleb looks like he doesn't belong here. He would dominate the runway and model for brands if he put his mind to it. Even the few tattoos in sight are neatly done and alluring. They are not graves, coffins, broken fingers, swords or ex's names like other people's.

"That's my hoodie," Hilton greets me, jolting me out of my inappropriate thoughts of Don.

I stick my tongue out at him, and he looks at me blankly. That's between him and Don, he should leave me out of it.

I make sure all the doors and windows are closed before taking a seat. This meeting is highly classified; we can't afford eavesdroppers. When I'm satisfied, I turn to them. Tristan looks like he would rather be elsewhere, I don't even think he's paying attention.

"We're having the party tonight. Everything is in place. I just need you guys to get more beers and to man the braai stands. I have everything else covered. And Caleb, you will not tell Chelsea any of what we'll discuss here." I know how pillow talk goes. Don used to let me in on deep secrets in between rounds. I can't have Chelsea deeply involved in this; I know how her mouth runs. If we ever pissed her off, we'd all end up in prison. Maybe Don and his crew wouldn't mind, but I most certainly would.

"I know you guys can't get rid of the other Alphas because you're bound by a code in the Creed. So you won't have a direct hand in it. I'll make sure Skinner and Dust take the laced drinks. They won't make it through the night and none of it will point back to us. Doc cleared everything."

"Not happening. Do you know how dangerous those guys are? Do you know who we're dealing with? This is not child's play! I don't want you involved in any of it," Don says.

Isn't it a bit too late to start playing the concerned Baby Daddy? I know exactly what those guys are capable of. They are Alphas, and unlike Don who prefers talking things through first, they kill first and ask questions later. Skinner earned that name because he skins his victims alive for fun. Dust, well, you know the expression 'Dust to Dust'. He's quick to turn enemies into dust. I don't like them at all. They don't deserve to be alive. They are 28s, so they kill brutally, sell drugs to school kids, have no respect for women and they pride themselves on being rapists. Such people shouldn't be allowed to exist among us. Don is the only Alpha who isn't a 28. I wouldn't be with him if he was.

"Listen." I raise my hand and Don shakes his head, looking ready to protest. What exactly did he think was going to happen? Did he think we would just ask the other Alphas to step down and call it a day? That's why he should have been more involved in the planning.

Hilton looks unfazed and almost bored. Maybe because he's the one who helped me hatch this brilliant plan and still let me take all the credit.

"So Skinner and Dust will take the drinks. But to make it look legit, Don, we have to poison you too. That way it won't look suspicious. You'll consume just enough to make you sick but not to kill you. The doctor will give you an antidote or something to make you better and give the other Alphas something to accelerate their deaths. He knows best."

The Wolves' doctor is the best thing that ever happened to us. His attitude and how he isn't scared of Don, or even Hilton, cracks me up every time. He was reluctant to work with us on this one but he's dead loyal to Don, like the rest of us, so he came on board and trained me on *How To Get Away With Murder.*

Don looks unsure and he turns to Hilton for direction.

"It's the only way," Hilton says.

Caleb is dead quiet, I wonder if he's alive. Is he offended that I brought up Chelsea? I had to say what I said.

"Okay fine. Let's say we do all that. How about Ghost? He doesn't drink or eat at parties, and he's the most vicious."

Impatient much? I was getting there. Ghost is a walking nightmare. He's also known as Diablo because he makes his victims' lives hell before sending them to the next life. He's cruel, to put it bluntly. I used to dislike him, but I loathed him when Don told me how he abducted a girl and made her his sex slave. After months of enduring him, while her family was searching for her, she tried to escape and he mutilated her genitals and cut off her head, put everything in a coffin and had it delivered to her family. It's only Don's pack that seems to be human. That's more reason why Don needs to take over and make the Wolves great again.

"Well, everyone knows how much Ghost hates you and how he basically wants to be you." Even saying his name makes my skin crawl.

"Go on," Don says.

"I'll personally take care of Ghost. I'll seduce him. What better way for him to hurt you than sleeping with your bitch?"

"The fuck? You're not sleeping with anyone! I'll kill both of you!" Don goes from zero to hundred.

Hilton looks amused.

"Relax. I'll just lead him on, drug him and take him to the spare room. Then you guys will walk in on him trying to 'force himself on me'. Everyone knows how he is but they turn a blind eye. But by trying to force himself on another Alpha's woman, he would have broken several rules in the Creed. Grounds to take him out, fair and square." I feel so smart right now, I even have a satisfied grin.

Hilton subtly nods his approval, and I might be imagining it but he looks like he's proud of me. Caleb says it's an excellent idea and Tristan says it's alright. Don is not convinced. He hates the thought of Ghost's dirty hands on me but he agrees that the death of Ghost would be a service to the public.

"Go over the plan from the beginning, in detail. Tell us what each of us have to do, how to do it and when to do it," Don says.

"Wait, baby. The doctor is almost here. Let's wait for him to arrive so we can go through the preps together."

I'm looking at them looking at me, and I love it. I feel like the matriarch of the Wolves. They are the muscle and I'm the brains of the family.

The doctor graces us with his medical presence. Impatient, sassy and with an unmatched attitude. After exchanging pleasantries, he reminds us that time is money and he charges by the hour.

# *THIRTY THREE*

All is set and it's all systems go. Drinks of all strengths, weed of all types, meat of all kinds, snacks of all sorts - everything is here and it's about to go down. It's going to be epic! I made sure all the important rooms were locked. I won't have any funny business in my house.

I organise the glasses and smile triumphantly. I make party planning look easy. I have Chelsea on board, which is risky because I asked her to trust me blindly and go with the flow. It's shocking that she agreed. Anything to be around Caleb, I guess.

Go ahead and judge me for downing a shot of tequila, but I need the courage to see this through. If I mess this up, my entire family is screwed, and I'll die first before that happens. Chelsea and I are playing the perfect hostesses; greeting people with smiles and handing out welcome drinks. I hate that the girls who have arrived are not giving us a hand. The Wolves are smoking in the living room and two people have already spilt beer on the carpet!

Dust and Skinner arrive with their entourages and immediately start acting like they own the place. I need another shot to maintain my composure. I emphasise to Chelsea how important it is that Dust and Skinner drink their designated drinks without fail. She's a certified temptress so it shouldn't be that hard.

My heart settles when I see them downing the contents of their glasses. I give Don a glass and he looks at me as if asking if he should really drink. I nod. As much as I hate it, he has to.

Ghost finally arrives. Clearly, he likes making an entrance. I'm relieved; I was beginning to think he wouldn't show up, but I also want to vomit at the thought of his crimes against humanity.

"Hi, Ghost, welcome. Looking good as always." I smile graciously at him and give him a hug that pushes my boobs into his chest.

He looks at me suspiciously and I fake-blush.

"I'm sorry for that. It's just... never mind. Welcome. Let me get you a drink."

"I don't want a drink," he says firmly.

"You sure? Drinks are nice. Whatever you want, I'll get it for you, Ghost. What... ever... you... want."

"I said no drinks, bitch! Get out of my way."

Ouch! I cringe inside but I maintain the smile and let him walk through. I need another shot.

"Were you flirting with that creep?" Chelsea pulls me to the kitchen.

"Of course not."

"Yes, you were! Why would you do that?"

"I wasn't."

She gives me a disapproving look but thankfully, she drops it.

"Should you be drinking? Aren't you like breastfeeding or something? You were even drinking when you were heavily pregnant. You shouldn't be drinking, Lotus."

"The doctor said I can have up to three shots a day as long as I wait a bit before feeding Ricky," I lie with a straight face. The doctor actually said I should lay off alcohol. But it's just a few shots, it doesn't count.

She lets it go with a disgruntled mumble.

"Nice dress by the way. You look like a goddess," I compliment her to distract her thought process. But she does look good, no lie. I lean over and kiss her on the cheek before embracing her in a warm hug. I don't hate her. I actually hope we get back together one day.

A girl asking if we have tonic disturbs our moment. She looks as high as a kite. I leave Chelsea to deal with her and return to my hostess duties. I walk around asking people if they are still fine, offering them food and drinks, and just being the nice person that I am. I'm avoiding Don and I'm carefully watching Ghost's every move. I have no idea how I'll get through to him. He picks up a spliff and a girl. He just randomly picked up a girl from his squad and dragged her by the arm like a piece of something he owns. And no one did anything.

I take a deep breath and follow them outside. My heart picks up pace with every step but I thug it out. He opens a car door, shoves the girl inside and she squeals loudly.

"Ghost, is that you?" I call out as if I'm shocked to see him.

I clear my throat and call again. My voice sounded shaky the first time.

"You again! You're like a mosquito. What do you want?"

"I was going to get something in my friend's car and I saw you and thought I should talk to you."

"I'm busy. Go and find someone else to talk to."

I walk towards him until I'm so close, we are touching. I take his hand and look around as if I don't want to be seen. I'm relieved when he doesn't shake me off. I lead him to the back of his car and pin him against it.

"I'm sorry, I've been a terrible host. You didn't eat or drink anything. Allow me to make it up to you."

Although it's dimly lit, I can see his face clearly. I don't know how

I'm not throwing up right now. His breath stinks and the scars on his face make him look like the bride of Chucky. Yuck!

I stand on my toes and quickly kiss him before he can stop me.

"What are you doing?" He pushes me away.

"Oh, I'm sorry, I guess I misread the chemistry between us. My bad."

He looks confused so I take another chance and step towards him. "So is it true?"

"Is what true?" He barks but doesn't push me away.

"That you fuck like a stallion."

His face semi-relaxes. I can tell he liked that.

"Can you keep a secret?" I continue treading the dangerous path.

"It depends," he says, less harshly.

"I want you to fuck me, but Donavan can never find out. Girls talk and everyone raves about how you handle your business. No strings attached and it stays between us."

Without warning, he leans down and kisses me roughly. His breath on my face is like poisonous fumes and I throw up at the back of my throat. He grabs my ass so hard it's as if he will rip it off my body. His other hand cups my breast and squeezes like he's trying to get milk out of it. Now that really hurt! I'm thankful for the padded bra or else I would be on the ground writhing in excruciating pain with milk oozing all over the place. I grit my teeth to stop from screaming.

"Let's take it to the house. We'll use the back door. No one has to know," I whisper.

He laughs; I'm confused. His breath attacks my nose and droplets from the gap left by his missing teeth spray my face.

"So it is true!"

"What's true?"

He laughs in my face again and now I'm unsettled.

"What's true?" I ask again, still trying to sound cheerful and alluring.

"That Alpha Donavan wifed a whore." He pushes me away, disappears into his car, starts the engine and drives off.

I lean on the next car to remain on my feet. I feel sick, literally and figuratively. I threw myself at that disgusting pig only to be called a whore. My ego has never been more bruised. I desperately need to brush my teeth, and a shot of something stronger than tequila will be nice right now. His stench is stuck in my lungs, suffocating me and making me feel worse. I can't believe I kissed those dagga-burnt lips and had that shit-stinking breath in my mouth.

*So it's true that Alpha Donavan wifed a whore,* Ghost's mocking voice echoes in my head. I don't know why that hurts. Do all Wolves from the other packs think I'm a whore? Why would anyone think that of me? How does that make Don feel? Hilton told me how Don once lost his mind and went on a hunting spree, hurting anyone who dared call me a whore. I thought he was exaggerating. When he told me that, I asked him if he thought I was a whore and he asked me what that was. I said, "Someone who sleeps around, you know, who sleeps with many people." And he said, "How many people have you slept with in your life? More than one?" I nodded and he said, "So you're a whore. Everyone's a whore." He made me feel okay without even trying to.

"Well, that went great." Hilton emerges from the shadows.

Think about the devil and it appears.

"Hilton?"

"Who were you expecting?"

"Certainly not you!" I snap. I'm not in the mood right now and I hate the thought that he was watching me making a fool out of myself.

"I told you seducing Ghost wouldn't work but you thought you were clever."

He actually told me that, and he's right, I thought I was smart. But do you think I'll admit it? Not in a million years!

"Why wouldn't he want me? I practically handed myself to him on a silver platter."

"That's why he didn't want you."

I'm confused. My inner goddess is so crushed, I want to punch the car next to him.

"I look good, don't I?" I adjust my cleavage. My self-esteem really took a knock tonight.

"You forced yourself on him. You went on too strong. It was pitiful to watch."

"Ouch!"

"Truth. You made a complete fool of yourself."

Okay, now he's just trying to hurt me. I'm hurt enough as it is. I won't entertain him.

"Men like Ghost get off other people's pain. Watching their victims suffer makes them feel powerful. He didn't want you because he knew you would enjoy it. He doesn't want his victims to enjoy. He hurts and humiliates. He wants them powerless as he takes what he wants. That gets him off, not an overexcited girl practically begging for his attention."

"I thought men found pleasure in pleasuring women."

"Which part of what I said didn't you understand?"

Mxm. Why was he even following me? I'm not surprised that he was but I don't like it.

He moves closer, then he turns his face away with his nose turned up. "*Sies*. You stink. Brush your teeth."

"Hilton..."

"What?"

"It's time for plan B." I step closer to him just so Ghost's stench can fill his face.

"I didn't know there was a plan B." He steps back.

"There wasn't. But there is now." I step to him.

"Which is?" He takes two steps back and bumps into a car.

I step to him, and now that he can't run away, I keep him pinned to the car. I grab his hoodie close to the shoulders and stand on my toes so I can reach his ear. I have to whisper; walls have ears.

"Ghost has made everything easier. I have the perfect plan B. I need you to trust me."

"Trust you?"

"You have no option, partner. We're in this together and we'll see it through, together. Now punch me in the face as hard as you can." It hurts even thinking about it. One punch from Hilton and I could die.

He moves his head back and looks at me with 'explain' eyes.

"Here's what happened. Ghost wants to be The Alpha, so he poisoned the other Alphas and left the party so that he wouldn't be a suspect. He's not very smart, you see. Him leaving actually proves his guilt. Anyway, I saw him slipping something into the drinks he sent to the Alphas and I confronted him, which some people might have mistaken for flirting."

"Go on." He turns his nose up to avoid breathing in Ghost's stench. He's such a drama queen, but time is of the essence, I'll play games another time.

"I confronted him a second time and he left the house. I followed him and asked him what he put in the Alphas' drinks. That's when he hit me and said he would cut off my tongue if I kept accusing him. Actually, I think he wanted to kill me. That's spicier, let's go with that. Okay, then he pushed me against the car and strangled me like this." I wrap my hand around Hilton's unsuspecting neck and close it around his throat. I push my body closer to him to trap him against the car. Luckily, I don't mean to kill him, so I drop my hand and step back.

"Just like that, but harder because he's a seasoned killer and I'm not. So I punched him in the stomach, and he punched me in the face, and I kicked him in the nuts, and he fell down, and I ran away."

"Whoa, slow down, superhero! No one would escape Ghost that easily, so change that last part," he says, still rubbing his neck.

"Okay fine. I followed him and he punched me. A group of girls was approaching, so he had no option but to let me go."

"Much better. The girls won't be there to testify. It will be your word against his." He sounds satisfied.

"Exactly. I probably should add that he tried to force himself on me. Now punch me. We don't have all night."

"I won't punch you. Punch yourself."

"Come on. I have to make it believable. Just don't break my nose or knock my teeth out."

"Not happening. Now get back into the house and I'll check on Alpha. If he dies, I promise I'll kill you."

I do not doubt that he would actually kill me if Don died.

I guess I need another plan then. Maybe I can bang my face against a tree or run straight into a wall. That sounds painful. I'm so pissed at Ghost, I'm going to enjoy doing this to him. How dare he turn me down like that! In front of Hilton *nogal!*

I don't know what's gotten over me. It's probably the fact that I have been stuck on Hilton this entire conversation. I let go of his hoodie and wrap my arms around him. I lay my forehead on his chest and hold him close. He doesn't hold me back and that's alright with me. I just want him to know that I'm grateful for everything, but since I don't have the right words to express it, this hug will have to do.

After a little while, he pushes me back, not as roughly as Ghost did, but still enough to make me stagger. A hot slap lands across my face and I make a 180-degree turn before falling to the ground.

"Fuck!" I screech at him.

I'm seeing stars and I think I just went deaf. I spit out what I think is blood and curse at him again. By the time I get back on my feet, he's gone. Damn him! Did he have to hit me that hard? My jaw is burning and the clap is still ringing in my ears. I can't feel my face.

I reach for the small blade in my pocket that I carried in case things got out of control with Ghost and I had to defend myself. I grit my teeth and cut my arm with a shaky hand, just enough to draw some blood. I let it well up and then smear some on my clothes and let a few drops fall on my cheek for good measure. I also wipe my mouth with a bit of blood so it looks like there's a lot coming from inside.

I burst into the living room, wailing like a fresh widow. My face is throbbing, and I can taste the metallic tang of blood in my mouth. Chelsea rushes over. When she tries to hold me, I scream even louder.

"What happened?"

"He tried to kill me."

The room goes completely silent, as if everyone is frozen in shock. Chelsea looks horrified and keeps trying to calm me down, but her efforts only make me scream louder.

Caleb pushes through the small group of Wolves that has gathered around me. He places a hand on my shoulder, trying to steady me. "Who did this to you?"

"Gho...o...st," I manage to say through sobs, the name coming out in broken hiccups.

"Alpha Ghost?" someone asks.

I nod vigorously. "He... he tried... to... to kill me!"

"Come, sit down." Chelsea guides me.

I walk slowly as if my legs will give out if I lift them higher. I collapse onto the couch and bury my face in my hands. I sob loudly, feeling every pair of eyes in the room boring through me.

After a while, I calm down enough to speak. "I saw Ghost putting something in the other Alpha's drinks. I confronted him but he told me off. I confronted him again and he got upset, pulled a girl from his pack and left. I followed him and he punched me and said he would cut off my tongue if I kept asking him questions. When I tried to run, he pushed me against the car and strangled me." I clutch my neck with both hands and resume sobbing.

Chelsea comforts me until I calm down enough to speak.

"Then he tried to force himself on me. When I fought back, he punched me again and kicked me. He was going to do it but a small group of girls was approaching so he let me go and drove off."

I hear gasps and murmurs.

"He's a monster!" I scream, my voice breaking all over again.

"Chelsea, get her some water and take her to her bedroom," Caleb says.

I catch Hilton's eye across the room when I stand up. He subtly shakes his head like he can't believe it.

We get into the guest bathroom and I look at my face in the mirror. It's already looking bad so I know I'll wake up looking awful. I gently rinse my mouth with mouthwash. It stings like a mother! But between pain and bad breath, I'll choose pain any day.

"I need to find, Don. I'll be fine," I say to Chelsea.

She looks worried but nods.

"Shout if you need me. I'm here for you. It's going to be okay."

I pull her into a tight hug. Something wells up inside me and I blurt out, "I love you so much, Chelsea".

She holds me tighter. "I love you too. We'll get through this together, okay?"

I know all this might trigger her so I need her to leave soon, but first, I have to find Don.

I find him in our ensuite bathroom, on his knees, clutching his stomach. I forget my own pain and dart out to find the doctor.

I freeze by the door of the living room. I did not notice the Alphas before as I was caught in my own distress. I know I wanted this but not like this. I stand there, heaving but barely making a sound.

"Let's call an ambulance," Chelsea says.

"No ambulances, no police," Hilton says, looking unbothered.

"They're dying! We need to do something," Chelsea sounds desperate.

I hate that we roped her into this but didn't give her the details. Now she's in the dark and is genuinely panicking.

"Caleb, control your woman," Hilton says before going down on his knees and helping Dust sit up.

"Why is it only the Alphas falling sick? Where are Alpha Donavan and Alpha Ghost? What did Alpha Ghost put in their drinks?" Dust's Protector asks.

I'm glad he asked. Now that the seed has been planted in everyone's brain, carrying on the theory will be easier.

I rush back to the bedroom and find Don on the floor, writhing like a snake. A sweat has broken on his brow and his temperature is rising.

"My stomach is burning. Go and get me more milk."

"I will, but we need to get you to the living room. They must see you with their own eyes."

"I'm in pain."

"I know, my love, but you have to do this." My eyes water. He must be in serious pain for him to admit it. He gets up anyway and balances on my shoulder.

Hilton takes over as soon as we make it to the living room.

"Alright, party is over. Everyone out." Hilton claps his hands and people don't need to be told twice.

Everyone leaves except for Chelsea, Caleb, Dust, Skinner, their Protectors, the doctor and me.

"You too, women, disappear," Hilton dismisses us.

"Are you crazy? I'm not going anywhere. My man is dying and you're telling me to leave?" I feel like I'm going mad. Maybe I am going mad.

I rush to the kitchen, fill three glasses with fresh milk and bring them to the Alphas. Dust is convulsing and it's looking really bad for him. There isn't much sand left in his hourglass. Skinner looks flushed, but being an

Alpha comes with its consequences. He has to be strong even at his weakest. He looks like death, but he's handling it like a pro. Don doesn't look too good either. He must pull through. He has to. I start sobbing uncontrollably, much to Hilton's annoyance. Chelsea is getting worked up and she looks like she will break down any moment, which further annoys Hilton.

Caleb says he'll take her home, and Hilton rudely expresses how that's an excellent idea because she was beginning to give him a headache.

I pull myself together just enough to pull her to the side. "Please go with the nanny and Ricky. They can use my old room. I'll feel much better with him out of the way."

"Of course, babe."

I packed and briefed the nanny earlier so that doesn't take long. We use the back door because I know Don will not approve and I don't want to fight with him.

"Will he be alright, Doc?" I feel Dust's face with the back of my hand when I rejoin them. His temperature is through the roof.

"He should be alright. I've given him something to settle his stomach. Maybe he drank too much... Anyone else feeling a bit offish or can I leave now?" The doctor asks in his usual tone.

"You're not going anywhere! Fix them!" I scream at him. I'm overwhelmed with so many emotions, I can't even tell which ones are real anymore.

"Fix them? What exactly do you think I studied? Fixology? Why don't I go home and sleep and you fix them yourself?"

"Fixology? Seriously? You're the doctor! I don't care what you studied, just fix them."

He looks at me up and down. "I don't have time for this. I'm done here. I'll send my invoice. Call me only if someone's dying." He tries to leave but I block his way.

"You're not going anywhere. You heard me. Fix them!"

He looks confused for a moment, but I don't give him the chance to respond. Skinner groans and sits back on the couch clutching his stomach, agony written all over his face. I rush to his side, nearly bumping heads with his Protector.

"Alpha Skinner, please, you have to be okay."

He tries to say he's fine but the cramps are obviously getting stronger than his ego.

"*Skat*", Don murmurs in a weak voice.

I abandon Skinner, stumble over to Don, and fall on my knees next to him.

"Baby, please be okay." My tears soak into his hoodie as I bury my face on his shoulder. My face hurts and I'm feeling pain in places I don't know but I don't care about any of it. I pull my hair and scream, then quickly pull myself together.

Someone pulls me back. I shrug them off roughly and end up sitting on my heels. This can't be happening. I lift my hands up like I'm in church and pray out loud. "Please, God, the Source, the universe, ancestors, anyone listening, please help!" I shut my eyes tightly, press my hands together on my chest and pray violently. I don't care how crazy I look right now, I just need this prayer to get to heaven urgently.

"This is madness. Take me home," Skinner says and his Protector agrees.

Actually, yes. I don't want people dying in this house and becoming ghosts here. They should all go. I won't say it out loud though and risk sounding heartless.

"Stay with your Alphas," Hilton says to the other Protectors.

"The Source will protect you," Don says weakly.

Many Wolves believe in the Source, and today more than ever, I hope the Source protects my man.

When everyone is gone, Hilton, the doctor and I gather around Don and fuss over him. He's getting worse and the doctor is beginning to look unsure, which is making me frantic.

\* \* \* \* \*

It's 3 am and I haven't slept a wink. Don is getting worse. His fever is high and his face looks deathly pale. He's groaning from cramps and clinging to my hand. I'm scared, and so is everyone else. The doctor says he will be fine but there is no trace of assurance or the usual nonchalance in his voice. Things are not looking good.

My face is swollen but I stopped the doctor from 'looking at it'. I need to look as bad as possible, come morning. I don't think Hilton feels bad for slapping me. He just carried on with his life as if nothing happened. Maybe it's because I told him that all that blood wasn't because of him. To be honest, I have been out of my senses all night so I can't blame him. Don was upset when I told him but he didn't have the energy to fight. His priority is staying alive. My face will heal, but if he dies, my heart never will.

Hilton's phone rings and he steps outside without excusing himself. Manners don't come naturally to him.

He returns a few moments later.

"Dust has turned to dust."

It takes me longer than the others to understand what he means. It's because he said it like it was nothing, so my brain didn't process it urgently. Caleb is relieved, Hilton is indifferent, Tristan is traumatised, the doctor looks worried and Don doesn't react. I feel terrible. I thought their death was what I wanted but a small voice in my head keeps asking, *'When did you become this person, a MURDERER?'*

Not long after, Hilton's phone rings again and this time he answers it without going outside. After a few unpleasant pleasantries, he hangs up.

"Skinner is gone."

Dead silence follows. I should be happy, right? Well, I'm not. Not by a long shot.

"Tristan, take Alpha to the bedroom. Caleb, round up everyone for a meeting at 8 am on the dot. Doc, make sure my cousin stays breathing if you know what's good for you. Lotus, follow me," Hilton gives us orders.

He doesn't wait for me to catch up.

The cold air hits hard on my swollen face and my eyes struggle to adjust to the sudden darkness. The distant sound of ocean waves crashing against rocks in the stillness of dawn lends me fleeting solace.

I find him waiting by the corner. He's just a tall silhouette before me in the dark.

"Come closer. You never know who's listening."

I accidentally step on his foot and he doesn't complain.

"I need you sharp, Lotus. I need you focused. Put on your best performance, like you did earlier. No screw-ups, do you understand?"

I nod, not sure if he can see me. I don't know if I can do it but I have to faith it till I make it. We are in too deep; there is no turning back now. Lives are being lost, and if we are not careful, we might join them on the other side.

"6 am sharp... Stop stressing about Alpha; he'll pull through this." I don't know if he's trying to convince himself or me but I agree.

He takes his phone out of his pocket, turns the flashlight on and shines it on my face. I close my eyes and block the light with my arm.

"Take your hand off."

I find myself obeying but I keep my eyes closed to avoid being blinded.

"Does it hurt?"

"Yes."

"Will it heal? Will your face go back to normal without leaving a scar?"

"It will heal just fine. Give it a few days."

"Good."

A moment of silence follows until the light leaves my face. Only then do I open my eyes. He walks away without saying goodbye, leaving me standing in the dark.

# *THIRTY FOUR*

The road is pretty empty, save for a few cars driving in the opposite direction. Hilton hasn't said a word since we left. I appreciate the silence because I can safely sit with my nerves and be the judge of my own conscience. I hold my coat tighter and keep looking out the window at the rockface following the road. My mind is not a very good place to be in right now. Two men are dead.

The rhythmic swish of the wipers is soothing, and watching the trees gliding in the opposite direction is strangely calming. I blow into the window and draw a circle with my finger. I keep running my finger over the outline and following the tiny raindrops falling on the outside of the glass. It feels like the day I left Cape Town. I sat in that bus, wailing and screaming in agony on the inside, but silently crying on the outside. I followed a raindrop with my eyes until it joined a stream of water at the bottom, then I followed another, and another.

"Are you alright?" Hilton's voice pulls me out of my head.

"Yes." My voice comes out soft but steady, the exact opposite of what I'm feeling inside.

He gives me a quick glance before focusing back on the road. "Are you sure?"

I rub my hands together. "I'm scared."

"Pull yourself together."

"And if I fail?"

"Don't even let the thought cross your mind."

He gives me another side look and our eyes meet for a brief second before he looks away. I couldn't guess what he was thinking even if I tried. I need reassurance but it's like looking at a mountain for answers. I look away, wishing I hadn't admitted out loud how scared I am. So much is at stake. There will be many Wolves in there. So much testosterone, I don't know how I'll survive.

It's 7:27 am when we park outside the safehouse. There are all kinds of cars; from high-end German machines to *skorokoros*, from gold-plated to barely-any-paint-left. Most have a few things in common - tinted windows and suspension dropped too low for their own good.

"Are you good?" Hilton asks as I step out of the car.

I nod, not trusting myself to speak. I part my lips to sigh and I watch my breath turning into a thin cloud of mist.

"Focus!" He snaps his fingers so close to my face, he almost hits my nose.

I hold his arm with both hands. I got this. I can't speak right now but I promise, I really got this.

"Remember, I can't be throwing lies around in there. I'm bound by laws you don't understand. So keep me out of your mouth as much as possible."

"I know. I'm not stupid."

"Are you sure?" He raises an eyebrow, amusement playing on his face.

"Of course, I'm sure. I'm not stupid."

"I was just checking."

I want to make a face at him but my frayed nerves make it impossible.

"Lotus, our future rests on your shoulders. I get it, I'm nothing to you, so you won't do it for me. So please do it for my cousin and my nephew, at least."

Did he just use my usual tactic on me?

"It's not true."

"What's not true?"

"That you don't mean anything to me. Hilton, you mean a lot to me. More than you'll ever know in fact. So as much as I'm doing this for my boys, I'm doing it for you too."

His eye twitches and I know that's all the thanks I'll get.

Our eyes lock. He has frightening eyes that speak of darkness and sin, yet somehow I can't bring myself to peel my eyes away. Behind those piercing eyes lies a silent cry for help, a vulnerable little boy yearning for a hug. I see warmth and unconditional love behind the bloodlust, and all I want to do right now is hold him in my arms and tell him that everything will be okay.

"Let me round everyone up, get them on their best behaviour, and you can follow in five minutes. Don't count on a welcome drink; no one's expecting you."

I'm about to say I understand when he walks away. In his own special way, I know he cares a lot about me. I know that he'll be there for me no matter what. This is a man who killed for me.

I get back in the car and lock the doors. Looking at myself in the mirror cheers me up a little. Even with one side of my face swollen, I still look gorgeous. Not to sound vain or anything but I look so good in this dress it might be illegal. Black is definitely my colour. Give me a fascinator and I'll get out of this car looking like a mistress going to a rich philanderer's funeral.

Reality rains on my parade and I'm back to being nervous. I walk towards the house, giving myself a pep-talk. I take a deep breath before opening the door. Two ruthless-looking guys are standing guard inside. From the look of things, they were expecting me after all, so they might as well get me a welcome drink!

They make me remove my coat and pat me up and down, searching for hidden weapons. It's uncomfortable but I let them have their way. When they are satisfied, they usher me into the next room and point me to the hidden door in the closet. I find my way down the steps, my lungs flapping uncontrollably. I hesitate on the last step, memories of my father racing each other across my head.

I take a deep breath, then stride into a hall full of Wolves. I'm not sure whether to smile so I can charm them, to be stoic so I can blend in, or to follow my heart and run back up the steps. I can feel their curious stares and judgemental thoughts. Six, twelve, eighteen, twenty four and Ghost. Twenty five pairs of eyes on me. If looks could kill, I would drop dead right now.

I know all the Wolves from Don's pack and that's giving me a bit of confidence. Hilton, Caleb, Tristan, Chucky-face and two others who usually guard the house. I recognise some faces from other packs as well, from my father's funeral and from the party last night. I catch Hilton's eye and he nods so subtly, I would have missed it if I wasn't used to him. I'm shivering inside but I'm doing my best to remain composed. It would be nice if someone said something or told me what to do.

My father died right there where Ghost is sitting. I close my fist so no one realises I'm shaking.

"Why is this bitch here?" Ghost goes off like the vile thing that he is. Looking at his lips makes me internally gag.

"Why is there a female here?" another asks.

"Are we getting free sex today?" another Wolf sneers.

"Why is she here?" another one adds.

Woodstockers are so uncouth like their Alpha, Ghost!

"Let her talk," Ghost eventually says, and the room falls silent.

Phew! "Hello, hi. I umm..." I wave a little and immediately regret it.

"Why are you here?" a rude voice interrupts and I turn towards it.

"Me?" I point at myself.

"Of course, you! Who are you?"

"Oh, I'm sorry. My name is Lotus Janse van Rensburg. I'm Alpha Donavan's woman."

Mocking, chuckling and laughing ensue. It's annoying but I didn't expect any better, even though I'm not sure what's funny.

*'Pull yourself together!'* Hilton's voice echoes in my head. *'Don't*

*mind them. Keep your eyes on the ball.'*

I clear my throat and try to readjust my posture but fail miserably.

"Why the hell is this bitch here? Someone throw her out!" Ghost barks.

His lapdog approaches me. It must suck taking orders from someone like Ghost. What a sad life. I believe Protectors and Alphas should have a Don and Hilton relationship, not a master-slave one like these two.

I hold my hands up in surrender. He shouldn't touch me.

"I was called here to testify. If I'm not welcome, I'll leave. Forgive me, I don't know how you guys operate. I was told to be here, that's why I'm here."

"Lotus, take a seat." Hilton shows me to an unnecessarily large chair positioned directly across Ghost. "Apologies for not informing you earlier, Alpha Ghost. There was no time. The Adjudicator will be here soon."

"What is this? The Adjudicator has been summoned?" Ghost's eyes widen and a flicker of fear crosses his eyes.

"Yes, Alpha." Hilton bows.

I find my way to the seat and keep playing with my fingers. Hilton prepped me but this is too much anxiety for me. The Adjudicator, or The Book as they sometimes call him, is rarely seen by the Wolves. He is only summoned for serious disputes, the kind that often end with someone dead. He is called *The Book* because he is tattooed all over. Every piece of skin on his body that can be tattooed is tattooed with the laws of the Wolves. Rumour has it he's all-seeing and can sniff out lies from a mile away. A shiver runs down my spine and I grit my teeth. If I wasn't scared before, now I am.

*The Adjudicator is the living embodiment of the Creed, neutral and impartial, enforcing the gang's laws with unwavering authority.*

Heavy footsteps echo down the stairs and the Wolves fall silent. The air is suddenly thick with tension. The door creaks open and an imposing man in a long black coat, black boots and a wide-brimmed black hat walks in. He is walking with a black cane, which I think is more of a fashion statement than for support. His presence is so commanding, it feels like even the air itself is parting to make way for him. He walks slowly, with a rhythm, his boots thudding with each step. He goes from Wolf to Wolf, stopping briefly in front of each one. When he stops in front of me, his eyes lock onto mine, piercing through me as if he can see right into my soul. He doesn't blink, doesn't move, and I don't either. He has tattoos all over his face, making him look like a newspaper.

He eventually turns away and I exhale a long, silent breath, surprised to realise I'd been holding it the whole time.

He walks to the centre of the room and stops.

"I will not waste your time or mine." His voice is smooth and measured, with a hint of melancholy.

"I see that representatives from all four packs are present. Fairness, truth and integrity will guide these proceedings. The Creed shall be upheld, for it is the foundation of our laws and the core of our honour." He pauses and looks around, his gaze sweeping everyone in the room.

"We are here for the trial of Alpha Ghost of the Woodstock Turf. He stands accused of treachery, murder and poisoning his fellow Alphas. Additionally, he is charged with attempting to force himself on another Alpha's bitch and assaulting her. Let the proceedings begin."

Ghost looks like he just saw a ghost. I'm suspecting it's the first time he's hearing these charges. I think it will be best if I look away from him.

"The Creed says, *'A Wolf doesn't love because love makes it weak, distracted and vulnerable. A Wolf that falls in love for the first time should kill his lover so he can learn never to love again. Let his heart die. The Wolf shall heal and never endure pain again. To love, kill and die - the three phases of a Wolf.'*" He sounds like an overconfident primary school pupil reciting a poem crammed for a talent show.

I'm not sure where he's going with this, but everyone else is nodding, so maybe they understand something I don't.

"It then says, *'An Alpha is above the ordinary Wolf, and with a step up the hierarchy comes certain privileges. An Alpha is strong, powerful and in control of his emotions. Unlike a regular Wolf, an Alpha has the ability to bond with a bitch without being consumed by love.'*"

What's happening here? I hope he's not marrying me to Ghost in a touch-is-a-move twisted way.

"The Creed goes on to say, *'When an Alpha fathers a child with a bitch to whom he's bonded, their bond becomes akin to a marriage. The Alpha must turn his bitch into a Wolf to ensure her allegiance to the pack, so she never betrays the secrets of the pack. For 'till death do us part' is an idea to humans, but a fact to Wolves.'*"

I'm officially confused.

"If it's true that Alpha Ghost assaulted Alpha Donavan's bitch, it's as good as he assaulted Alpha Donavan himself and will be judged accordingly."

He turns to me and holds my gaze for what feels like an eternity.

"Are you truly Alpha Donavan's bitch?"

"Yes, I am."

"Do you stand by that claim?"

"Yes, I do." I look him straight in the eye.

"Does anyone here vouch for her? Can anyone confirm that she is truly Alpha Donavan's chosen? Is she recognised as his bonded? Did Alpha Donavan complete the ritual required by the Creed? Has anyone witnessed the sacred ceremony?" He turns to the Wolves.

I think I'll pee myself. We didn't do any ceremony and the Wolves can't lie in here. I tap my foot and only stop after I catch Tristan watching me.

Hilton's hand is the first to go up, followed by Caleb's. My heart settles a little when I realise the Adjudicator's mistake - he asked many questions at once. Tristan's hand goes up next, and the hands of the remaining Wolves from Don's pack follow. Six votes! I'm smiling but trying to keep my composure.

He turns back to me. "The Creed says, *'When an Alpha claims a bitch, he must brand her with his mark.'* Do you bear his name or symbol?"

"I do."

"Show us."

I pull back the sleeve of my coat and extend my wrist.

"D. O. N... Don," the Adjudicator reads aloud.

"Is it real?" Ghosts says.

"It is, Alpha Ghost. She has his name on her body."

To think that when I got this tattoo on my birthday, it had nothing to do with the Creed or Wolves. I was just drunk and wanted to show Don my appreciation.

"You pass once more. However, to truly be claimed by an Alpha, you must bear the mark of the Wolf. Do you have it?"

I look unsure just for show. I low-key wish Don was here. I think he would be proud of me. There are a few mumblings as time passes but I keep looking down.

"This bitch is a liar! Throw her out! We don't need skirts here; it's a business that requires testicles!" Ghost howls.

A few voices from his pack agree, and he goes off at me like a train without brakes. He calls me every name in the book and promises to destroy me and everyone who has ever said my name. He calls Don all types of foul things and says he hopes he dies. He promises to kill me and send me off to join Dust, Skinner and my father in hell."

The Adjudicator keeps his eyes cast down and does not interfere. His hat is making it hard to read his expression.

Eventually, he taps his cane against the floor and calls for silence. Ghost continues ranting.

"Silence!" the Adjudicator says sharply, and the room falls quiet.

He turns to me. "Do you bear the mark of the Wolf or not?"

"I do."

"Show us."

I stand up slowly and open my coat, my hands trembling as I undo one button at a time. The Wolves gather around, their eyes fixed on me. I can't believe I'm doing this, but hey, many women have done worse for love. Some, like Juliet, even died for it, so judge me not.

I lift my dress carefully until the wolf on my hip is exposed. I'm sure it's the most beautiful tattoo they have ever seen. It's a replica of Don's.

"She's got the wolf!" someone exclaims.

"She has the mark! Alpha Donavan branded her," another says.

The look on Ghost's face is priceless. I've never seen life drain from someone's eyes so fast. I wish I had a camera to capture it.

Goodness gracious, is that a boner on that Wolf? Wow! That's my cue; showtime's over.

It takes a while for the Wolves to settle down this time. When they eventually do, the Adjudicator resumes.

"Now that we're past the vetting process, let's move on to the trial."

There is a lot of nodding and murmurs of anticipation.

"Two days back, we had four Alphas. Today, we have two. Who would want to take out Alphas?"

"Someone eliminating competition," one suggests.

"Maybe it's the Hard Livings," another says.

"Or someone within the family wanting to become General," another proposes.

"Think about it. We have two cold bodies and we have one standing at death's door. I think Alpha Ghost did it. I think he decided to eliminate his co-Alphas," another Wolf concludes.

The Adjudicator nods at every suggestion, encouraging more.

"The charges are serious, and the implications even more so. We must deliberate with care lest we spill a brother's blood in vain."

I raise my hand and the Adjudicator nods at me.

"I saw Alpha Ghost put something in the drinks that he passed to the other Alphas. I didn't think much of it at the time. I thought it was just a happy pill or something," my voice trembles and I bite my nails.

The room erupts in shock, but the Adjudicator remains composed. Ghost hurls a string of insults and charges at me. His face is so close to mine, I'm afraid he will bite me. I try to push back into the chair, but there isn't much space to work with. He smells like something crawled inside him and died. I can't believe I had his tongue in my mouth.

"Lying whore!" He draws phlegm and spits it on my face.

I can't stop the tears as I wipe it off with the sleeve of my coat. Why are they not holding him back?

"Lying cunt! It makes sense why Donavan scraped you out of Ryan's rotten ball sack! He's a pussy-whipped sissy who takes orders from a General's daughter that fucks everything with a cock. Hilton is the real Alpha of the Cape Flats! Donavan is not a man! He's as useless as Dust and Skinner were! Pathetic weaklings who never deserved to be Alphas! Stop lying on my name!" He raises a fist, but Hilton steps in, saving me from a punch to the face.

"Alpha Ghost, return to your seat," the Adjudicator says.

"She is a..."

"Silence!"

Ghost sits down, still fuming, his nostrils flaring. I'm sniffling softly, trying to pull myself together. The room is tense. The Wolves are looking from Ghost to me and back again. The Adjudicator takes a moment before resuming.

"Alpha Ghost mentioned that Donavan's bitch is General Ryan's daughter. Is that so?"

"Yes. She is the daughter of Ryan, the last General," Hilton says.

Gasps spread through the room, and the Wolves exchange surprised looks. It seems most of them didn't know that the General was my father.

The Adjudicator resumes. "The Creed says, *'The accused must be brought to trial. A unanimous decision must be made. The brother who spilt his brother's blood must die.'* If Alpha Ghost is indeed guilty, the Creed is clear. *'If a brother harms another brother, he should be eliminated before he poisons the entire pack'.* But he is not an ordinary Wolf. He's an Alpha. As such, *'If an Alpha is accused of a horrendous crime, the decision to punish should be collective. If seven or more Wolves declare him guilty, then guilty he is.'*"

He looks around the room and I sniff when his eyes fall on me.

"Those in favour of proceeding with the trial of Alpha Ghost, raise your hand. If he's innocent, he walks. If he's guilty, he dies."

Hands start rising, one by one, until the only hands remaining down are Ghost's, his Protector's, the Adjudicator's, Hilton's and mine. Even members of his pack have their hands raised high. It's both concerning and fascinating how fast loyalty fell off.

"Very well then. The Creed says, *'When an Alpha is unable to represent himself, his Protector can and may represent him.'* As such, Hilton will represent Alpha Donavan. The trial starts in two hours."

# THIRTY FIVE

Ghost is seated on the Trial Chair in the centre of the room. It's an antique wooden chair that belonged to the father of the founding brothers of the Wolves, the first General. How it became a symbol of torture, I can only wonder. Under the chair is a large sheet of heavy-duty plastic to prevent any mess in the event of bloodshed. He was forced to take off his pimp-style leather jacket, un-ironed shirt and once-white wife beater. The Wolves believe that someone on trial should be topless so that his heart is visible, as if they have X-ray vision!

Ghost is sickly thin; his ribs are practically sticking out. His skin is shrivelled and his tattoos look like a bucket of ink fell from the sky and splattered all over him. His wolf looks like a dog with rabies; I'm not even exaggerating. He looks so weathered, I can smell his fear. Such a display of weakness is going to be used against him. Many will see it as guilt, because what could an innocent person be afraid of? I hope they make his death slow and excruciating as a tribute to all the innocent people he terrorised.

His wrists are handcuffed to each of the chair's arms and his ankles are tied to its legs. The four Protectors are standing around him: East, South, West and North, as the Creed prescribes. They are not just protectors of their Alphas, they are protectors of the Creed. They make sure the rules and laws are upheld. Right now, they are protecting the truth and guarding the integrity of an Alpha, whatever that means. They are still and upright like toy soldiers. It's a bit unsettling, but what isn't in this world of theirs? Hilton is on Ghost's right hand. Our eyes keep catching each other, but we are careful not to hold the gaze. It's hard to focus in the midst of this organised mayhem. Everyone seems to know what to do while I have to remain composed and dodge memories of my father at the same time.

The rest of the Wolves are standing in a semicircle, in two rows, facing Ghost. They are far enough to give him space to breathe but close enough to see his face so they can 'read' the truth when he answers questions. I know! They are very weird. They are all waiting for the trial to begin, but since silence during a trial is their order, they can't say anything. There is an eerie silence in the room. The only sound is the thudding of the Adjudicator's boots as he walks around.

I'm standing at the far end, next to Caleb. An image of Don flashes through my mind. I don't know how he'll feel about all this. He knew I would be doing it, but he didn't know the extent to which it would go. He thought I would be in and out, not stay for the duration of the trial. He never wanted me to be a part of this life, but let's be honest, it was inevitable. No one dances with the devil and leaves hell unburnt. An image of my son replaces Don's, looking at me with his gorgeous, toothless smile and those big blue eyes. I quickly swat the thoughts away. I have the future of everyone I care about in my hands. It all boils down to what I will say; how I'll testify. I have the fate of a man in my hands and I'm going to throw him into the deepest pit of hell and pray he burns for all eternity. If Ghost walks free, we are all dead. His vengeful reputation precedes him. I don't want to experience his wrath first-hand.

The Adjudicator finally begins the case of The Wolves vs Alpha Ghost. He recites the laws and rules of a trial according to the Creed before passing things over to Hilton. I hope justice will be served, for every woman who suffered under Ghost's stinking body, every innocent life he destroyed, every family he broke and all the girls and boys who live with eternal trauma because of what he did to them.

"Alpha Ghost, do you swear to tell the truth, the whole truth, and nothing but the truth?" Hilton begins.

"I swear," Ghost responds, the contempt in his voice very clear.

"Swear on the Source."

"I don't believe in so-called special spirits that linger around all day watching us. I'm not foolish."

*Yes, you're foolish, and I like it,* I think to myself.

"Alpha Ghost, do you want to be the next General?"

"All Alphas want to be the next General."

"Fair enough. But how badly do you want it?"

"As badly as anyone in my position."

"Are you aware that Alpha Skinner and Alpha Dust are dead?"

"Yes." He looks at Hilton like he's incompetent.

"Do you know that Alpha Donavan is lying at death's door?"

"Everyone has heard the news."

Still full of sass, I see. He is putting up a brave front. If I were him, I would be sucking up to everyone and grovelling.

"Did you have anything to do with their poisoning?"

"Of course not!"

"Are you sad that Alpha Donavan is dying?"

"Why would I be sad? I'm not the one dying."

*...yet.* I silently add for him.

"Did you have anything at all to do with the deaths of Alpha Skinner and Alpha Dust?"

"Of course not!"

"Alpha Ghost, why did you leave the party early last night?"

I watch his Adam's apple bob. I know he won't openly confess to abducting that girl. A part of me hopes he didn't hurt her, but who am I kidding?

"Everyone knows I don't like parties. I showed my face and left. I do what I want. When did leaving a *kak* party become a sin?" He feigns a laugh and looks around for support but ends up looking stupid.

"It became a sin the moment you walked out and suddenly all the Alphas started dying. So the question is, were you leaving the party or were you running away?"

"Running away from what?"

"From your sins, Alpha Ghost. Running away from the crime scene."

"My sins? The sins this whore says I'm guilty of? Who is she to accuse me?! Is she the Source's new wife?"

I see a few fists clench and brows furrow at the blasphemy.

"Did you run away so that you wouldn't get caught? You came, poisoned them and left."

"I did no such thing!" He looks around for help, I suppose, but the Wolves are like statues. No one is moving or reacting.

"Didn't you say Alpha Skinner and Alpha Dust were not worthy of their titles and deserved to die like the strays they were?"

"Yes, but that doesn't mean I killed them."

"Didn't you say Alpha Donavan is weak and doesn't deserve to be an Alpha?"

"He is weak! That's a fact! But he leads his pack, not mine, so it has nothing to do with me."

"Doesn't it? You believe you're the only one who deserves to be an Alpha, so naturally, you think you should be the leader of the Wolves. But there were three other contenders, so you had to take them out."

"No!"

"Yes!"

"No!" he protests, trying to break free.

His eyes dart around the room frantically, begging for sympathy, but no one moves.

"Why are you doing this, Lotus?" He turns to me and I look down. *He knows my name? Nice!*

"Why don't you tell everyone how you came onto me and were begging me to fuck you after I left the party? Is that why you're upset? I can fuck you if that's what you want and we let all this nonsense go."

"You're sick! ... Leave me alone." I sniff back tears and hug myself.

"Lotus, tell us what happened."

"Tell them! You're doing all this because I rejected you!"

"Alpha Ghost, let her speak."

I sniff back loudly and wipe my tears with the back of my hand. "I followed Alpha Ghost after he left the house. I wanted to confront him about what he put in the Alphas' drinks. He was dragging a girl behind him. The girl kept begging him to let her go but he pushed her into his car and locked her inside. I tried talking to him but he pushed me against the car, groped me... and...and..." I break down and cry.

"I didn't grope you! You asked for it! You begged me to!"

"He wanted to force himself on me. He grabbed me, and when I tried to fight him off, he punched me. Look what he did to me." I point to my face.

"I didn't want to fuck you. You're not my type."

*Ouch! What the hell?! I'm everyone's type!*

"Hilton saw us. Hilton, tell the truth. That's a binding command! Tell everyone what you saw. She came onto me! Tell them, Hilton." Ghost half commands-half pleads. He has no cards left to play. It takes desperation for a man to ask for help from his enemy.

"Hilton, what did you see?" The Adjudicator says.

I know he can't lie because an Alpha commanded him to tell the truth. These binding laws of theirs are exhausting.

"I saw Alpha Ghost kissing Alpha Donavan's woman. He had one hand on her breast and another on her behind. That's what I saw. She also came into the house bleeding and hysterical. Alpha Dust and Alpha Skinner's Protectors can testify to that."

Ghost looks like his eyes will roll out of their sockets and fall onto the floor as the other Protectors back Hilton up. He knows Hilton didn't exactly lie. What was he expecting? Hilton to take his side? He's even more daft than I thought.

"Hilton, proceed," the Adjudicator says.

I almost feel sorry for Ghost *shame.*

When Hilton is done, the Adjudicator takes over.

"Alpha Ghost, Do you have any closing words before a decision is made?"

"Brothers, you know me. I have run with the family since I was ten. I worked my way up the ranks to become an Alpha. I earned my place. I treat my brothers with respect. I joke around sometimes, what brothers don't? I did not kill Skinner and Dust, and I'm not responsible for Donavan's sickness. Poisoning is not my style... Lady, please, I apologise for the way I spoke to you yesterday. I didn't do any of this. You know I didn't." He babbles on about family, blood ties, loyalty, justice and how much he loves the Wolves.

When he's done, it's time for a verdict.

"We have come to the end of the trial. Alpha Ghost has answered all the questions. His heart was bare, so you saw the truth and you saw the lies. His eyes were open, so you read the truth and you read the lies. Trust your instincts and don't doubt your judgement. If you have searched your heart and found him guilty, you will raise your hand. If you find him innocent, you will keep your hand down. Now close your eyes and cast your vote at the count of three," the Adjudicator says.

They must close their eyes when they vote so that they make individual decisions without being influenced by others. Avoiding peer pressure and such. I don't get to vote, so my eyes remain open.

He starts counting. When he gets to three, hands start rising.

Ghost is gasping like a fish out of water.

"You may now open your eyes."

They look around and there is no need to count.

Ghost is begging for mercy and asking the Wolves to reconsider. Why is it always the cowards that terrorise people?

"Alpha Ghost, by the laws in the Creed, I find you guilty on all counts. Your sentence is death," the Adjudicator says coldly before turning towards the door leading to the staircase, his cane tapping on the floor as he disappears.

I want Ghost's death to happen, obviously, but I don't want to stick around for the gory show. I turn to leave but one of Ghost's guys stands in my way and hands me a knife. I don't want gifts right now, and even if I did, this knife isn't something I would accept.

"You must do the honours. Cut off his tongue first so that he doesn't talk back when you carve him."

"What? Hell no!" Why am I in it now?

I can't believe how seriously they take their Wolf Dynasty. A silver knife because werewolves are allergic to silver?

"He tried to sleep with you. The Creed says, *'When a man sleeps with an Alpha's woman, his stomach should be ripped open and a rat put inside to nibble on his insides. At the count of 50, his balls should be chopped off and stuffed into his mouth.'* So while we go and find a rat, you carve him."

"What?" I could never do that!

"The Creed dictates it. You are the witness. Get your revenge."

"I don't want to."

"Take the knife and do it." He has a smug look; I don't understand what's amusing.

He's not budging. I feel my stomach tying itself into knots and air crowding my lungs.

"Can't someone else do it? I don't want to do it. Can't I like, you know, command you to do it for me?"

"Command me?" He laughs like it's the most ridiculous thing he's ever heard.

I take the knife with a shaking hand. I'm searching my head, trying to remember what exactly the Creed says about situations like these. If it was shooting him once, maybe I would try, but he's guilty of so many things, I have to completely dismember him. I have to cut off his tongue, carve out his wolf tattoo, rip his stomach open - it's way above my paygrade. If I don't do it, then what? Will he walk free? But the Adjudicator passed the death sentence so he has to die. I turn to Hilton. He has to help me. I'm clutching the knife so tight, I might crush it. I have seen people die before. Heck, I watched my own father die right here, but it was different.

"I'm sorry, I can't."

"Can't is not an option."

"You don't understand. I really can't."

"Not an option."

This guy doesn't know me from Adam, so I don't know what his problem is. He's enjoying this, and for the life of me, I don't understand why. My best bet is that he's the smart one in the pack, the go-to guy for all Creed consultations, the Albert Einstein everyone treasures for his high IQ. Probably Ghost's little bitch too. So he wants me to kill Ghost just to get back at me. Men are so petty!

"Please go ahead. We're all waiting."

I start crying, unashamedly. I need him to leave me alone. Why isn't anyone helping me?

"Rules are rules. Alpha Ghost is waiting for you to put him out of his misery. He's not a very patient man."

"He's right. You have to do it," another Wolf says.

Who asked him? Mxm!

I don't think I have much of a choice. I have been thinking fast but obviously not fast enough because I still don't have a way out. How will I live with myself?

*'Only an Alpha or a General can execute an Alpha,'* I keep repeating that statement in my head, looking for a loophole. But there's no Alpha or General here, so what does the Creed say about situations like this?

"I'll do it on her behalf," Hilton says.

Before I can even breathe a sigh of relief, Smarty Pants ruins it. "You know you can't do that, Hilton. Rules are rules."

"Come on, man. She's just... she... let me do it."

I know he means well but I don't think he can help me this time. Rules are rules, and it doesn't look like I can break this one. I just need a way to bend it but I'm blank.

Yes! *Light bulb moment* That's it! I always knew I was smart. This better work. I don't know if anyone here believes in ancestors. I also usually don't but I think this idea came from them.

"But the Creed mentions something about culture and origins, and um, Hilton?"

"'*A Wolf remains a man, and the origins from which he arises should be held in reverence,*'" Hilton says.

"Yes, that! I believe in my ancestors as much as some of you believe in the Source. The thing is, I had a baby not too long ago, and because of that, I'm breastfeeding and stuff. If I get blood on my hands, my child will die. Alpha Donavan's child will die. In my culture, a breastfeeding woman cannot have blood on her hands, not even a chicken's."

They remain quiet and I know I need to say more before I can ask for votes.

"I'm just asking you to show a bit of empathy. You know, to respect my roots, my origins. Is it fair to sacrifice the innocent child of an Alpha because of a guilty man who has no regard whatsoever for our family?" Nothing like a leader without principles, right?

"With a show of hands, how many of you are releasing her from this duty? Close your eyes and cast your vote at the count of three," Hilton says.

He starts counting down and I keep my fingers crossed. When he gets to three, hands start rising, one by one, and I quickly count in my head. I feel like screaming 'Hallelujah' when I get to eighteen. Majority rules. As expected, Smarty Pants' hand remained as low as his self-esteem. I'm so excited, I forget to stay in character. I smile stupidly at Hilton. He doesn't smile back but the twitch in his eye tells me that he's proud of me.

"Alright. All settled then. She must pick someone to do it for her," Smarty Pants says begrudgingly.

"I'll do it," Hilton volunteers.

"No, not you. When you get involved, things get messy." I wink at him.

I think he just rolled his eyes at me but I can't be too sure because they didn't move at all.

I place the knife in Smarty Pants' hand. The smart ones usually hate blood; take Caleb for example.

"Hilton, please take me home."

"Yes, ma'am." He's so impressed with me, he can't even hide it.

"Caleb, please come with us." I need to get him out. He hates blood and everything associated with it. I have no idea how he's a Cleaner. Tristan and the others will remain behind to witness everything.

I would like to say that was a great experience, but if I'm being completely honest, it wasn't. Don better not die on me after all this. Caleb will drive his car and I'll ride with Hilton. It's still drizzling outside, so I pick up pace and wait by the car, covering my head with my hands. Why did I even bother? Hilton is strolling towards me with zero urgency.

"You have grown," he says as he opens my door.

I grin at him and almost fling my arms around him.

I'm chatty all the way home, reminding him how awesome I was as if he wasn't there. I was the perfect victim. He doesn't say much, and when I ask him what he meant when he said I have grown, he says, "Don't push it."

I slap his arm and laugh before chatting his ears off some more.

He opens my door, and as I step outside, he wraps his arms around me. That caught me off guard. He's holding me so tight, I can't breathe or move my arms, but I don't complain. His hugs come once in a season, so I would rather suffocate than ask him to loosen the hold. He squeezes me like a pillow before letting me go.

"You did great, but that was your last stint. Alpha and I will take it from here. He never wanted this life for you, and frankly, neither do I. He loves you because you're pure, something we're not. So if you become the female version of him, he won't continue seeing you the same way. You're his angel, whatever that means, because everyone with half a brain knows angels are male. It's been fun and games, but this is the end."

I also don't want this anymore. It wasn't supposed to go this far. We had to improvise when Don fell sicker than intended.

"I agree."

"You do?" He looks shocked that I didn't put up a fight.

"Yes, you're right."

"I am?"

"Yes, Hilton." I chuckle and hang on to his arm as we walk into the house.

"Shouldn't we take Don to the hospital if he's still dying?"

"Didn't he teach you anything about hospitals and the police?"

"He did."

"What did he say?"

"He said we only call the police when we're ready to go to jail, and we only go to the hospital when we're ready to die."

"Good. Now go on in and make sure Alpha is dressed. I'll join you in a minute."

Why would Don be naked? You know what, never mind.

I'm relieved to find the doctor by Don's bedside. Don's getting better, thankfully. I can't wait to update him about everything that happened. The doctor more or less tells him that he's weak, that's why he almost died. He tells him to eat more fruits and drink more water so he can be as healthy inside as he is outside. I don't know why Don is offended by that.

"Where's Ulric?" he says after I have settled next to him.

"Who?"

"Our son, Lotus, damn it! Where is he?"

"Oh, Ricky! Don't worry about him, I'm sure he's fine."

"Where is he?"

"He's with Chelsea."

"Chelsea? Since yesterday? You haven't seen him ever since?"

"I'm sure he's fine. Relax, I'll call Chelsea right away."

"Relax? Relax, Lotus? What did he eat? Did he bath? Did he change clothes? Did he sleep well? How could you?!"

Why is he mad at me? I did what any responsible mother would do; get the baby out of harm's way. I meant to pick him up on our way from Ghost's trial but it slipped my mind.

"He's with the nanny. Why are you making a big deal out of this?"

"I'm going to get my son. I can't believe you right now. What kind of mother are you? You're so careless! You're a mother now, act like it!"

"But I was busy taking care of you! I was up all night taking care of you! I was out there this morning taking care of you!" What the hell is wrong with him?

"I can take care of myself. But can my son take care of himself? You really care that little about my child?"

*My son, my child.* Did he make him alone? I can't believe he thinks I don't love my son and is calling me a bad mother.

A knock interrupts our heated back and forth.

"Go away!" we say at the same time.

"Why are you fighting?" Hilton walks in.

"Your Alpha is saying I'm a bad mother. Can you believe it?"

"It's not a lie. What kind of mother leaves her child alone for days without food?" Don says.

"Wow!" He was so much better when he was dying and unable to speak.

"The pot calling the kettle black?" Hilton raises an eyebrow.

"Are you saying what she did is right?" Don says.

"Ey, this has nothing to do with me. Alpha, get some rest. Lotus, go and get your child. Problem solved."

Let me get out of here before I feature in the *Husband Killer.* I had a hectic morning; he doesn't know the half of it.

# *THIRTY SIX*

Don is the last Alpha standing, and so he runs the Wolves now. It's not official yet because they love complicating things. There is a whole ceremony planned on the full moon. Sometimes I wonder if they are aware that they are not actual wolves.

We haven't discussed the death of Dust and Skinner, Ghost's trial, and everything that happened. It's as if we all somehow ended up believing that Ghost killed the other Alphas and was unalived for it. I wish I could say things are back to normal, but not everyone has accepted that their Alpha is dead, meaning they now have to bow down to Don. There have been fights between packs and talks of rebellion. Don just has to survive until the full moon. Once he's crowned The Alpha, all Wolves will bow down and none of them will even think of touching him. Hilton told me all that, of course.

Dalu hasn't texted me since that day but I'm still on edge. Every time my phone chimes, or anyone's phone for that matter, my heart skips a beat. I can't live like this, that's why I asked Hilton to come over.

I stand by the doorway, watching Hilton watching Ricky. It's more like how Don watches him - with fascination and awe.

"You have five minutes. Start talking," he says without looking up.

"Do you have eyes at the back of your head?" I walk in.

He stands up straight and turns to face me. "You said it was important."

I close the door and move closer to him to avoid anyone overhearing our conversation. I hate that I tell Hilton things I have never told Don, or anyone else for that matter. Hilton makes it easy. Half the time he stares at me blankly as if he doesn't hear a word I say. The other half, he tells me that I talk too much and I should learn to keep things to myself. I don't know how to explain it but I always find a sense of safety in him. If I was in danger, he would be the first person I would call. When I need him, he shows up, like he did today.

"Dalubuhle is back in the picture. He texted me."

"So? What has that got to do with me?"

"Why are you not surprised?"

"Why should I be surprised?"

"Hilton!" I'm scared out of my mind and he doesn't care.

"Like I told Caleb then, I'll tell you now. Leave me out of that stinky mess."

"What if he comes for Ricky?"

An emotion I can't decode crosses his eyes.

"I knew this would come back to bite all of you, but Caleb being the self-appointed crusader of non-violence said that the boy didn't deserve to go to the graveyard but to a loony bin. He said the enemy was Viper, not his son."

I will never understand why Caleb helped Dalu. I feel like telling Hilton my suspicions about Caleb being a mole but it doesn't feel like the right time.

"Why didn't Caleb take care of him? He was working with the General. He's Viper's son! Wasn't that enough to take him out?"

"Probably because of Tristan. You know what, I don't want to be involved."

"Tristan? What does he have to do with Dalu?"

He shrugs.

"Who else knew where Dalu was? Why didn't you tell me?" I square with him. I can't deal with the lies and secrets in this family!

"What is this? An interrogation? You have one minute left. Use it wisely."

Deep sigh. "I need your help."

When he sighs and relaxes, I say a silent prayer of gratitude.

"What did the message say?" His voice sounds a little less brassy.

"He said he wants to see me."

"Is that why you called me here? You said it was important."

"How is this not important? Anyway, we need to go and see him and put an end to it. It has gone on for far too long."

"We?" He raises an eyebrow.

"Well, yes!"

"No. I'm not getting involved."

"If you won't help then I'll handle it myself."

"How exactly do you plan to do that?"

"I have a gun. It's about time I used it."

I don't think I have it in me to look a man I used to sleep with in the eye and kill him in cold blood. But as they say, if you want something done right, do it yourself.

"And if you get caught?"

"I'll claim self-defence."

He looks at me as if studying my face. "You're getting addicted to this life. You enjoy it."

"What? No, I don't!"

"You do. Stop before it's too late."

"This is the very last time. I swear on my father's name." I cross my fingers to emphasise my point.

"You need to stop swearing on your father's name."

"He meant nothing to me, that's why it's easy to throw his name around like a ball and not feel bad about it."

He gives me a knowing look and I'm glad he doesn't say anything. He knows how I truly felt about the General.

"You're the one who told me that people like Dalu don't stop unless you stop them. So will you help me or what?"

He lets out a resigned huff. "You don't understand, do you? If you go there, Alpha will find out. Do you honestly think he doesn't know the whereabouts of Viper's son? There are very few things Alpha doesn't know. It will help you not to forget that."

My blood runs cold for a moment. How much exactly does Don know?

"Let it go. Caleb will clean up his mess when the time is right. If you go there, Alpha will bury your body in a shallow grave. So if you're interested in staying alive, you will not go to that boy."

I feel icy shivers in my bones. "But..."

"But suit yourself. You'll have plenty of time to introspect in the grave."

"Maybe I should just tell Don everything, you know? I'm tired of this secret." Of course I don't mean that.

"And you'll die. Is that what you want? Should I help you with that?" He pulls out his gun and points it at me with a blank stare. A memory of Don holding a gun to my head in the car when Dalu dropped me off crosses my mind and I screech.

"What the hell is wrong with you? Put that thing away! Are you crazy?" I cover my face with my arms as if they are bulletproof.

"You want to die but you don't want to be killed," he mumbles.

"Fine, I won't do it. But tell me, why is Dalu alive if Don knows where he is?"

"Living people talk. Dead people don't."

"Huh?"

He steps closer and his mint breath fans my face. "I know what you're thinking. Don't do it," his baritone voice comes out low and gruff. Then he walks towards the door, leaving me standing there.

Ricky starts crying and I walk out as fast as I can. He probably needs a diaper change and nope, I can't deal with poop smell right now. I settle on the couch, put on my favourite show and increase the volume to drown Ricky's cries.

I'm halfway through the episode when the nanny disturbs me.

"Madam, he's sleeping now. Should I go and put him to sleep?"

I thought she said he's sleeping, so what does she mean *'put him to sleep'*?

"No, bring him here. I'll put him to sleep myself." I stretch my arms to receive Ricky.

"Are you sure?" She looks concerned.

"Yes, I'm sure. Give me my son."

She thinks I can't do something as simple as laying my own child in a cot? People are seriously getting on my nerves these days.

I dismiss her because I need some alone time. I watch Ricky sleeping in my arms. A few beads of sweat dot his forehead, looking like they belong there. He's so beautiful and pure, I can't stop staring. A tear falls out of my eye and drops on his cheek. I'm trying not to sniff too loudly; I would hate for him to wake up and spoil the mood. The pain in my heart intensifies and the lump in my throat keeps growing. The emotions came from nowhere.

I only notice Don when he sits next to me and puts his arm over my shoulder. For the first time, he doesn't take Ricky away from me. When he squeezes my shoulder and leans in, I cry harder. I'm failing at parenting. I feel so useless.

"I'll be right back." He takes Ricky to the nursery.

I bury my face in my hands and completely break down. Why does it hurt so much?

I'm still weeping when he returns. He rubs my back as I convulse in his arms. Him being here is the reason I'm crying so much now.

"It's okay, my angel. Do you want to talk about it?"

I shake my head. I wouldn't even know where to begin.

"What's wrong? What happened?"

How do I explain something that I don't understand myself? One moment I was holding my son and admiring his looks, the next I was a wreck.

"Talk to me, *skat*. What's wrong?"

Something in his voice makes me want to break down all over again.

"Ricky hates me."

"Why would you think that?"

"He always cries when he's with me but he's happy with everyone else. It's just... I've just been feeling so overwhelmed about everything and it hurts that I'm not close to my own child. It hurts that everyone else makes him laugh but all he does with me is cry. I get jealous every time I see you with him. You guys are always laughing and happy. How come he never reacts that way to me? Why can't he ever be happy with me? He loves you, he doesn't love me." It stings hearing it even in my own voice.

"You know that's not true," he drops his voice, probably because he knows it's true.

"You don't even trust me with him because of that one time. I didn't mean to abandon him. I had to make sure he had a family to grow up in. I needed him to grow up with his father around, unlike me. The other Alphas were going to kill you, it was only a matter of time. I didn't want my son asking me one day what happened to his father and having to tell him he died, yet I could have prevented it. I know it was wrong of me to send him away with Chelsea, but I did it for you and him. I did it for us. Why can't you see that?"

He takes my hands and looks into my eyes. "I'm sorry for the way I've been with you lately. I felt weak for having my woman fight my battles. I hated myself for putting you in that position, and I guess I started taking it out on you. I'm sorry that I always take Ulric away from you. I always assume that you have plenty of time to bond when I'm not at home."

Is he trying to make me cry again? Because it's working.

"Let's talk, my angel." He sits more comfortably.

I thought we were already talking but okay.

"I love you. I know I don't say it as often as you want me to, but I do. You're my woman. You're the mother of my child. I love you and Ulric with my life. Nothing else matters."

He's baring his soul, and I love it so much, I don't want it to end.

"I love you too, baby, so so much." I completely break down.

When I eventually calm down, he takes my hand and leads me to our bedroom.

He pulls me closer and his hands move to the hem of my blouse. He lifts it slowly, exposing my skin to his warm touch.

"You're beautiful," he says, his fingers grazing over my curves as if committing every detail to memory. He takes his time undressing me. I want him to touch me everywhere and kiss me some more.

"You're so beautiful, my *skat*." He peels my hands away when I instinctively cover my stomach.

As my blouse falls away, he leans in and his lips brush against my collarbone, trailing kisses up my neck. His mouth is hot against my skin, awakening feelings I haven't experienced in a long time. I let out a soft moan, arching my back as his hand finds my breast. My fingers weave into his hair. "Please," I whisper desperately.

"Today, more than ever, I wish I could make love to you. I just want to hold you and feel you wrapped around me. I miss being inside you, showing you how much I love you."

That's so hot, damn!

"You can."

"What do you mean I can?"

"I mean you can make love to me." It's been forever; I'm getting nervous just thinking about it.

"Are you sure? Because really, I can wait. If you need more time, I can wait."

"Yes baby, I'm sure. It's been months. I'm ready."

I guide his hand back to my breast and his eyes darken with lust. His lips crash on mine hungrily, each kiss feeling like raindrops on a desert: wet, quenching and reassuring. He guides me backwards until I feel our bed against the back of my legs. He lays me down gently and joins me on the bed. It's been too long since we've been this close.

"I've missed you," he whispers, pressing his body against mine.

"I've missed you too," I breathe more than I say.

He grips my hips and grinds against me. The friction sends shockwaves through my body, and I writhe under him, begging him to take me.

"Don," I gasp.

He kisses me again, his tongue sliding against mine, his body heavy on top of me. I can feel his hardness pressing against me and it's driving me wild with need.

He pulls back just enough to meet my eyes. "Are you sure?"

"Yes, baby." The words tumble from my lips.

He positions himself between my legs, teasing me with the promise of what's to come. I can feel his breath against my skin, each exhale sending shivers through my body. Then finally he pushes inside, and I gasp at the sensation. It feels so good, I can't stop the loud moan that escapes my lips.

"Fuck," he moans, moving slowly. Each thrust is deliberate, making me cling to him harder, pulling him deeper, wanting to feel every inch of him.

"I love you," he whispers in my ear, going deeper with each stroke.

"I love you too."

He picks up the pace, and before long, our bodies are moving in perfect harmony. It's not long before I begin to quiver and my walls tighten around him as waves of pleasure crash over me.

"Baby, I'm..."

"Let go, my angel."

I scream his name and my nails dig deeper into his back as pleasure explodes through me like a million stars. His hand tightens on my thigh, holding me in place as he keeps at it, hitting the right spot until I feel like I'm floating. With one final thrust, his body tenses, his grip tightens and I feel him pulsing inside me, filling me with warmth. We stay there for a moment, holding on to each other, feeling like the world around us has stopped.

I already know from the look in his eyes that it's going to be a long night.

# *THIRTY SEVEN*

Tonight is the Rite of Ascension. Don will officially be crowned The Alpha, the leader of all Wolves. It has never happened before, so it's a big deal, and I'm happy to be a part of it. All the hard work and sacrifices are finally paying off.

I'm sitting with Don at the back. Hilton is annoyed with us because I can't stop giggling and Don is indulging me. The off-road is bumpy and unkind to the small car, but I'm too excited to care about a little discomfort. Although it's a full moon, it's pretty dark. We drive until we see lights twinkling in the distance. They look like tiny fireflies dancing in the dark. They grow larger as we get closer, until we park between two cars, joining the circle. There is a large clearing in front of us that looks like an empty field. Cars are arranged around the perimeter, with their headlights switched on but dimmed.

It's insane how big the Wolves' family is! There are people everywhere, standing in small groups, chit-chatting and laughing into the night. Not all the Wolves will be attending, but the turn up is impressive. Only now do I realise where we are.

"No way!"

"What?" Hilton asks.

"Don once brought me here. This is where we made Ricky."

"On our sacred ground?"

"Well..."

He raises his hand and stops me before I can tell him that I didn't know it was sacred ground when Don bent me over the hood of his car. And no, we didn't make Ricky here, but we sure as hell practised, just after Don told me about Candice and shattered my heart. I smile to myself, the beautiful parts of the memory playing in my head. I can't believe how far Don and I have come.

"Alpha!" Hilton says sternly.

"No comment." Don laughs. "I need to talk to Caleb. I'll be right back."

He disappears between cars, leaving Hilton and me leaning against his car.

"It's a beautiful night," Hilton breaks the silence.

"Since when are you sentimental?" I elbow him.

"Am I not allowed to appreciate a good night?" He side-eyes me.

"It's a free world, my guy. Just don't go writing poetry about it."

He scoffs this time as he pulls out a packet of cigarettes from his pocket.

"Want one?" He offers and I roll my eyes. He knows I don't smoke.

It is a beautiful night and I'm happy to be here with Hilton by my side. He's my only friend; the brother I never had. He's the only person on earth who knows everything about me. I tell him things I have never told anyone, not even Don.

He places his hand on my shoulder and leans in. "We did it."

I break into a huge grin. "We did it, Hilly!"

I want to throw my arms around him but I wrap my arm around his instead and rest my head on his shoulder. Everyone is gathered here today because of us. The Wolves belong to our family now because of us. All this wouldn't be happening if it wasn't for us. We did it!

"My brothers and I owe you a lot."

"Yes, you do." I detangle our arms and stand in front of him. "But first, you owe me a hug."

He laughs a little and opens his arms. I expected him to tell me to forget about it or to just give me a blank stare. I walk into his arms and he envelops me. He smells divine! That perfume I gifted him smells like heaven.

He lets me go and we lean back against the car. I start telling him a story and he continues smoking his cigarette. The moon is creeping up the sky and there is something magical in the air. I'm bubbling with excitement, I can't contain it.

It must be half an hour later when Hilton says it's almost time. When I ask how he knows, he points at the moon.

Okay, got it.

"Go and find Alpha. I'll round up the Guardians."

I find Don laughing and smoking weed with Caleb and Tristan. They smoke so much, it's concerning. Tristan and Caleb walk towards the large group and I remain behind with Don.

"Are you ready?" I fix his collar and smooth out his jacket.

"As ready as I'll ever be."

"You'll be alright. You were made for this. The Wolves couldn't ask for a better leader."

"And I couldn't ask for a better woman." The blue of his eyes shines brighter in the moonlight. It's the most beautiful thing I've ever seen.

"You look good. I wish I could take your clothes off right now," I unintentionally voice my thoughts.

He blushes and kisses me on the cheek. "I love you."

Now he's just trying to make me emotional. "I love you too."

We walk slowly towards the crowd, hand in hand, until he has to break away from me.

"Let me find Hilton. Stay with Caleb and Tris, okay?"

"Okay, Alpha."

His silver tooth gleams in the bright light as he smiles. He kisses me before letting me go; I can't stop smiling.

Hilton calls for attention by shooting a gun into the air. Each Wolf joins their pack until there are four distinct groups - east, south, west and north. We are witnessing history being made in real time. Everyone is wearing black, to blend into the night with the shadows. I'm wearing boots, jeans and a leather jacket. All I'm missing is a motorbike to complete the look.

The ceremony begins with a procession of the Guardians from every pack and the four Protectors. The Adjudicator leads the parade, carrying the Creed in his hands. When they come to a standstill, in a straight line, Don walks to the middle and Hilton stands on his right hand. Dead silence follows and I accidentally crunch leaves under my boot, earning a sharp eye from Tristan.

When the moon reaches its zenith, the Adjudicator begins the ceremony. His voice is deep but steady, and he's dressed exactly like he was at Ghost's trial.

"Under the moon, we pledge our loyalty to each other and to the pack. As we stand on the ground on which our founding brothers rest, we vow to protect our territory and each other. We swear to uphold the values of our code; loyalty, respect and strength. Tonight, under the moon, Alpha Donavan will ascend to the highest level of our ranks, assuming his role as the undisputed leader of our family, The Alpha of the Wolves."

He recites some rules and laws from the Creed and I recite with him, just in my head, feeling like I belong here. He then asks Don to get on his knees and be sworn in. It's like the inauguration of a president, except the choice of words makes it sound like someone joining an underworld cult. With each vow, I feel a swell of pride in my chest knowing that my man is the chosen one and I got him there.

"All hail Donavan, The Alpha of the Wolves!"

The Wolves erupt in a collective howl and I find myself howling with them.

When we eventually quiet down, Don rises to his feet and salutes the moon as the Creed prescribes, before addressing us. He promises justice, wealth, growth, strength, expansion, an unwavering brotherhood and a whole lot of political-sounding things. When he's done talking, he steps back, leaving Hilton standing alone in front of the row of Guardians.

Hilton is looking in my direction and I hope he saw my wink.

The Protectors of the fallen Alphas, Dust, Skinner and Ghost, step forward and kneel before Hilton with their heads bowed. They are passing on their power, or 'passing the fang' as they call it. With their Alphas dead, they are ranking down to Guardians and giving up their authority to Hilton, the ultimate Protector. One by one, they remove their jackets and T-shirts and stand tall as Hilton carves one star off their shoulders with a knife. None of them flinch or make a sound. There is dead silence all around as we watch Hilton skilfully un-tattooing the Protectors. I can't imagine the pain.

When that is done, and the Adjudicator has sealed the ritual with a quote from the Creed, Don takes over for the final part of the ceremony. He gives a brief speech full of assurances and more promises. When he's done, he raises his fingers in their signature salute, the thumb and first two fingers raised, and says in a loud voice, "We are GIFTED!"

"And Gifted I Fight Till Eternal Death," I chant with the chorus of voices.

"And four shall become one under the moon and on the bones of our founding brothers," the Adjudicator says.

The Wolves start moving. They change positions until the four groups have merged into one big group. They are howling and making happy noises as they go. They really take being wolves way too seriously!

*'We did it.'* I throw a peace sign to the moon. I feel like screaming out loud.

It's a celebration all around; the guys are whistling, high-fiving, laughing and howling - it takes a while for everyone to calm down.

The Guardians pledge their allegiance to Don, one by one, and walk away. When Don, Hilton and the Adjudicator are the only ones left in the centre, the Adjudicator blesses Don and disappears into the night.

Then one by one, each Wolf takes a knee before Don before walking away. It takes a while before only Caleb, Tristan and I are left. Caleb nods at Don before taking the knee, and Tristan follows suit.

I'm smiling from ear to ear as Don walks towards me with a pleased look on his face. He kisses me so passionately, I feel my kitty purring. His hands go around my waist when our lips break apart and I look up at him, mirroring his happiness.

"I love you, my *skat.*"

"I love you too, my Alpha."

He pulls me in for another kiss as we stroll towards his car, his arm draped around my shoulders and mine around his waist. Most of the Wolves have left and the rest are leaving, making noise as they go.

"You're killing me in that outfit. I couldn't focus every time I looked in your direction. Do you know how hard it is to concentrate when you look like that?"

"What can I say? I wanted to look good for my man."

"That outfit is gonna get you in trouble, my angel." He smirks, leaning in closer. "What do you say we stay behind? Just me and you."

"And Hilton?"

"He'll go with Caleb and Tris."

"Mmm, what do you have in mind?"

"I don't know, maybe we can recreate that memory on my car," he whispers in my ear.

Heat rushes to my cheeks and I bury my face in his arm. I can't think of a better way to celebrate my man's ascension. Watching him rank up tonight and seeing everyone bowing to him was all the foreplay I needed. More than once, I wanted to shout, "That's my man, y'all!"

As the last of the Wolves drive off, I notice our car has been moved to the other side of the clearing, to the spot where we did it that time. The flashbacks get me giddy, never mind how heartbroken I was that day.

"*Skat.*" Don's eyes sparkle with mischief as he steps closer. So close a paper would hardly fit between us.

"What's that you told Hilton I did to you right here?"

"Well, I didn't tell him how you bent me over the car and owned me."

"You're killing me, you know that?" He holds my waist, his lips just inches from mine. "Do you have any idea how much I want you right now?" His voice drops to a deeper pitch.

I bury my face in his chest, suddenly feeling shy.

He gently pushes my head back so I can look at him. "You have no idea how much I love this. Just being close to you like this, with nothing else around us. Just you and me. I want you so bad right now." He kisses me softly, then stops and pulls back a bit. "Lotus, what are you doing to me?"

I blush hard and hold on to him. I feel so powerful, so desired, so wanted.

He peels my jacket off, then crouches to remove my boots and jeans. He positions me against the car, and it's not long before I'm screaming his name into the night. We keep at it until we reach the climax together and collapse against the car, breathless and spent. We stay there for a moment, just breathing in the night air. Tonight feels even more special now, as if the earth itself is holding onto this moment with us. I wish we could stay here forever, but the wind is starting to bite.

"It's getting chilly." I rub my arms.

He reluctantly lets me go and helps me into my clothes. He opens the door for me and I slide in before he walks around to the driver's side. His hand finds mine as soon as he sits down. The way he's looking at me with lust, love and adoration has me getting wet all over again.

# *THIRTY EIGHT*

Chelsea walks in dressed like the advocate she will be one day. She is pretending very well without knowing all the facts. Well, she does that a lot lately and I'm not complaining. We are both just coasting through this friendship, using each other shamelessly.

"Donavan."

"Chelsea." He smirks, I don't even know what for.

Their hatred for each other runs too deep.

"I'll bring your woman back in one piece. Thank you for sharing her with me. You're so kind, Alpha Donavan. The world really doesn't deserve you."

"Cut the sarcasm, darling. It doesn't suit you... You girls drive safely. Let me know when you get there."

Before I follow Chelsea out, he reaches for my arm and stops me. "Be okay for me, my angel. Ulric and I will be fine."

I feel a sting at the back of my eyes as he lowers his head and kisses me.

"I love you, baby."

"I know you do, my angel."

Ulric starts crying and that's my signal to leave. I can't stand his tantrums sometimes.

We are using Chelsea's car because I highly suspect that my car has a tracker I don't know about. Chelsea can't stop raving about Caleb and how good he is to her. They finally got it right. She has it really good; flowers, chocolates, picnics, movies, UberEats - the girl is spoiled rotten. Who said there are no rewards for cheating? Caleb is probably doing the most trying to prove he's better than Elik. *Shame.*

"So, spill. Why exactly are we driving in the opposite direction to what we told them? Why are we visiting that psycho again? You and Don are happy and everything is going great. Why would you jeopardise that?"

I can't tell her the whole truth.

"It's complicated. Caleb was supposed to get rid of him but your man being your man got him institutionalised instead. He's supposedly better now and needs closure, and in exchange, he'll leave me alone."

"That's exactly what manipulators do. They abuse you, then turn around and play the victim so you can feel sorry for them. It works like a charm every single time. Exhibit A - us driving cross country to see a guy who wanted to steal your child and get you killed."

"I'm pretty sure he doesn't want me dead... anymore."

"I just think it's a bad idea, that's all."

"What other option do I have?"

"Well, for a start you could tell Donavan everything and let him handle it. You're the victim here."

"Oh, hell no!"

"Fine, do it your way... Anyway, you never told me. How was it with Dalu?" She makes a 180 change of topic.

She is very interested in Dalu in a disturbing, fetishy kind of way. She says making out with someone who has split personalities must be like having an orgy. I know the conversation has stopped being serious when she asks if I ever did it with his evil version because she thinks the sex would have been crazy.

I change the subject and steer the conversation back to her love life. She's so sprung, it's super cute, and she's more than generous with the details. I honestly didn't need to know all that. I'll never look at Caleb the same.

"Babe, can I ask you a question? Don's father was given a life sentence in prison. How is he getting out? I thought a life sentence meant someone spending the rest of their life in prison."

"Well, lifers who received a life sentence before 2004 are eligible for parole after serving at least 13 years of their sentence, and those after 2004 need to serve a minimum of 25 years. But with Don's dad, I really don't know. No one defeats the law more than the Wolves. Anything is possible with them."

"I see."

We end up talking about nothing and everything. With snacks, a fire playlist and endless stories, this road trip is turning out even better than expected.

The check-in to the hotel is smooth. I'm getting nervous by the minute but I'm handling it very well.

"Let me go and get it over with. I'll be right back." I take the car keys.

"Do you want me to come with you?"

"This is something I have to do on my own."

I can tell she wants to protest but I'm glad she doesn't.

"Call me if you need me."

"I'll be fine. I'll be right back, I promise."

She doesn't look convinced, but I don't stay long enough to go back and forth with her.

The GPS guides me, and before long, I pull into the institution and park at the far end. I tap the steering wheel with my thumbs, fighting off the cold feet. There will be no turning back once I walk through those doors. My palms are sweating and I'm trying to ignore the voice telling me to reverse and drive away. I remind myself what's at stake if I don't get in there. I take a deep breath and get out of the car. I didn't drive this far just to come and look at buildings.

The receptionist ushers me to a waiting lounge. Everything looks clinical, with crispy Mental Health magazines on a glass table, minimal decor, a neutral palette and low-volume spa-type music pouring out of the ceiling.

"Lotus," a rounded voice disturbs my concentration.

"Yes." I look up and I'm met by a serene face.

"Can I chat with you for a minute? I know Dalu is waiting for you, but can I talk to you for two minutes."

"Sure."

I follow the lady down a short corridor, admiring her small frame in a fitted black suit and stilettos. She leads me into an office that's as elegant as her outfit. The floors are perfectly carpeted and the paint has a rich feel. A beautiful portrait of a yogi in a headstand hangs on the wall. When I start thinking the woman in the picture looks like me, I realise I might need to be admitted right here to deal with my narcissistic personality disorder. Although I don't see how it's a disorder if it's true.

"Water?" She offers, already filling a glass with lemon and cucumber-infused water. I accept, even though I'm not thirsty.

She's over-smiling and it's making me wonder what's making her uneasy. People don't normally smile with all their teeth like that. She reminds me of a puppy I saw on TikTok this morning.

"I'm sorry for hijacking you. I won't take long, I promise. I've been helping Dalu for the time he has been here, and I feel like I know you because you're all he ever talked about, in the beginning that is. Then he forgot all about you, so I don't know if showing up out of nowhere is a good idea."

"Excuse me?" I don't want to be rude but what is she trying to say?

"You look like a good person, Lotus, so I'll go ahead and tell you. Dalu was broken when he first checked in. You're aware of his condition, aren't you?"

I stare at her Hilton style. What is she talking about?

"You know, after everything that happened with his uncle, his father and your people, he doesn't need this."

I fold my arms and sit back.

"Dalu loved you in his own way. When you betrayed him, his protective alter ego was activated. He had buried that part of himself away, and the pain he felt when you left set him off. You did that to him, Lotus. It's not my place to ask but why are you here?"

"You're right, it's not your place." I don't flinch.

"I'm sorry if this is coming off the wrong way, but Dalu is healing. It took a lot for him to get to where he is today. So I don't understand why you would want to undo that."

"To be honest, I'm so over this conversation. Can I see Dalu now?"

"Don't you think leaving, as in like going home, might be the best thing you can do for D? You already damaged him once. Why would you want to do it again?"

D? Oh my goodness! She's sleeping with him! This is jealousy talking.

"Don't worry. I have no interest in him anymore. I'll always be the love of his life and there'll never be another me. I'll always be the one that got away, and I completely understand why that's coming off as a threat to you, but you can relax. I don't want him like that anymore. I'm just here to give him the closure he deserves." *Shame mann*, she's threatened by me. Who can blame her though?

"Are you even allowed to fall in love with your patients?"

Her face twitches and I know I'm on to her.

"No, no, it's nothing like that at all. I'm just looking out for a patient," she tries denying it but she's doing a bad job at it. Her hands and face have confirmed my suspicions.

"Lotus..."

"Look, I'm not a medical expert, but are you allowed to talk to me about Dalu's condition and all? Doesn't patient confidentiality apply in this case? I can't wait to post about this on social media."

"I'm sorry, Lotus, I didn't mean any harm. I'm sorry. Like I said, I was looking out for my patient, that's all."

"Well, can I see your patient now?"

"Of course! Come with me."

I almost feel bad as I walk out of her office because I have decided to make her the scapegoat. In every war, there are casualties, and sometimes volunteers, like in this case.

She leads me down a sterile corridor. I know it doesn't look like it but it hurts me to be doing this. But like I said, if you want something done right, you have to do it yourself. The therapist, or whatever she is, hesitates at the door as if she wants to follow in, but I shut her down with my eye and she scurries away.

Dalu is sitting on a two-seater couch, his eyes vacant yet fixed, probably trapped in the chaos of his own mind. I fail to marry the sweet auditor I shamelessly flirted with that fateful day to the guy in front of me right now. He looks unkempt but healthy. I don't know why I thought he would look sickly, bony and like a junkie. It takes an awkward moment for him to register my presence, and when he does, he gets up and opens his arms with a big smile. I hug him back and he squeezes me a little too tight. I'm getting cold feet all over again.

"Hey, pretty girl."

That *'pretty girl'* has me feeling like shit.

"Sit."

I join him on the couch. He takes my hands in his and our eyes meet. He loved doing this back then. It's so awkward, I can't wait for it to be over.

"Thank you for coming... You still look as pretty as the first time I saw you."

I fake blush and return the compliment.

We talk about the weather, my trip and climate change. We are really forcing the conversation.

"Want a wine gum?" I take a packet out of my bag and throw one in my mouth.

I know how much he loves wine gums. He takes the packet and starts eating them like he's eating popcorn, just like I hoped he would. They are edibles. I wish I could be around to watch the good plant kick in and paranoia drive him crazy.

"I appreciate that you drove all the way here. I'm hoping for once we will have an honest conversation and go our separate ways in peace."

I nod in agreement.

"Did you ever love me, Lotus?"

I laugh awkwardly before mustering the courage not to lie. The objective is not to hurt him, but I want to tell the truth for once. He deserves that much, and so do I.

"I did. I was willing to learn how to, at least. With time I would have loved you the way you deserved. The truth is, in the beginning, you were an escape because Don had ghosted me. Remember that day, on your birthday? I didn't come to you as promised because Don showed up and I went with him."

He doesn't react the way I expected. It's almost as if he already knew.

"So you loved me?"

I'm confused because I thought my explanation was clear.

"Yes, Dalu, I loved you." Let me just humour him.

"Why?"

What does he mean why?

"You were what I thought I wanted in a man. You were packaged right: educated, well-mannered, from a good family, kind, stable and you looked good. I wanted to want you badly, but I guess the heart wants what it wants."

"I see. I kinda knew that," he says in a low voice.

"You did?"

"Yes. Well, the first time I didn't know. But when you came over to Joburg and had all those tattoos, I knew you would never be mine."

I don't know what to say.

"As much as you say I was the ideal package, you were my ideal package too. You were the perfect girl. So I was willing to be second best as long as I got to keep you," he says, oblivious to my wandering attention.

I look around and it finally registers where I know that plant from. It can't be! I really hope I'm wrong.

"Tell me the truth. Did you ever enjoy the sex at least or was that an act too? I know you faked the orgasms, but was it any good or you were doing it just for the sake of it?"

I swallow hard. My phone vibrates and I turn it upside down.

"It wasn't an act. It was beautiful and all my feelings around it were real. I didn't fake everything. Like many women, I don't always get there, but that doesn't mean I don't enjoy the ride. Like I said, I loved you. I know it wasn't enough but I cared about you."

"So did you enjoy it or not?"

Awkward but okay. "Yes, Dalu, I enjoyed the sex, happy?"

"Very."

An awkward silence follows and my phone vibrates again.

"You know what really got to me? I was on the right track and then you came along and messed it all up. My father thinks I'm weak. Nothing I do is ever good enough for him. I found the General of the Wolves and won him over. I did that! Me! Do you know what my father did? He took over and messed up everything. The General died. I had it all under control but he just couldn't trust me. I would have won us the war if he had let me. After all my sacrifices, he still doesn't trust me. He thinks my brain is broken."

"The General?" I'm still stuck on that. I form a fist and clench my teeth.

"Your father, Lotus, catch up! He wanted Donavan dead and I wanted Donavan dead. He wanted power and I wanted power. The funny thing is he promised to give you to me if I helped him get rid of Donavan." He laughs and I cringe. How was he going to give me to Dalu? I don't understand.

"But my father is mad at me, and your father is probably having an orgy with my uncle and Beelzebub in hell. You see what I did to my uncle? I'm going to do that to everyone who has ever crossed me."

I can feel my hand shaking as I turn my phone up.

"You know, I was so focused on winning that I didn't see I was losing until it was too late. When I lost sight of my real goals, that's when everything went downhill."

I open my phone and see three missed calls from Hilton. That's not good. Dalu's voice fades away as I scroll to my chat with Hilton.

"... don't you agree?"

"What are you even talking about?" I stopped hearing him the moment I saw Hilton's name.

"I'm talking about the love of my life."

"Me?"

"No."

"What? I thought I was the love of your life."

He chuckles. "You overestimate yourself, pretty girl. You give yourself way too much credit."

"You're insane."

"I know. You all think that. Zoe thinks I'm mentally disturbed. My mother treats me like a broken toy. My father treats me like I can't think on my own. You call me all sorts of names. The problem is that you're too predictable. You think I don't know you have a gun in your handbag? You're just not going to use it because, come on, Lotus, be realistic."

*'Get out of that place right now!'* a message from Hilton reads.

My phone rings before I can text back. It's Hilton again. I have to go.

"Leaving already? Thanks for dropping by. I'll edit the video and make sure Donavan hears the parts where you confess your undying love for me and how much you enjoyed me fucking you."

"You bastard!" I lift my hand to strike him but he's faster.

"I know everything about you. It pays having people in the right places. I'm always up to date with your sad little life. Making you pay is going to be fun. If you think what Roland did to you was bad, wait until you see what I have in store for you."

It's not even the threats on my life that hit me the hardest, it's the fact that the mole in the Wolves is still snitching.

"Who's your inside person in the Wolves?"

"Wouldn't you like to know?" He laughs in my face. "You have no idea how much you helped us. We would have never known about Gordon's Bay, or how to get your father on our side, or the whole operation in Pretoria, if it wasn't for you. The Hard Livings thank you for your service, my lady." He pushes me without warning and I fall on the couch. I quickly get up, grab my bag and phone, and rush towards the door.

I look back as I turn the corner and I see Dalu standing in the corridor, laughing at me. I can't get to the car fast enough. I drive away, yelling at myself for being stupid.

I answer my phone when it rings this time and Hilton doesn't wait for me to greet. "I told you not to go there. Get the hell away from that place now!" He hangs up.

I park at the darkest end of the parking lot outside the hotel. I'm drowning in my emotions. I feel so stupid. I don't know what I expected. I couldn't just whip out a gun and shoot Dalu dead, even though I wish I had.

I try Hilton's phone but it goes unanswered. Fuck! I bury my face in the steering wheel and scream.

Wait a minute. That plant! What are the odds that Dalu would have the same plant we were gifted at Ricky's zeroeth birthday party? No way! I grab my phone from the passenger seat and dial.

"Hello," the voice answers on the other end.

"I know about you and Dalubuhle."

Silence follows but I can hear him breathing.

"Are you at the hotel now?" he finally says.

"How did you... you know what, yes I'm at the fucken hotel!"

"Meet me outside in twenty minutes." The line goes dead before I can say I'm outside.

I can't believe it. I should have known. It all makes sense now. How he always *understood* my situation with Dalu, and how Dalu knew my every move and got my phone number every time I changed it. I just don't understand why he did it. How could he betray his brothers like that?

It feels like forever before a car drives into the parking lot. I walk across, looking over my shoulder to make sure no one is watching me. I slide into the passenger seat. The fact that he doesn't look rattled shocks me even more.

"You and Dalu?"

"You and Dalu?" he mimics.

"It was you all along!"

He looks at me and smirks, looking irritated more than anything.

"How could you?"

"How could I what, Lotus? The whole world revolves around you! All our lives have to stop for you! Do you ever care about anyone at all?"

What is he mad about? If anyone should be mad here, it's me.

"Do not turn this on me! You betrayed your family, not me!"

"You're one to talk. Get off your moral high horse. Because of you, I lost a lot!"

"You've been spying for Dalubuhle. How could you betray your brothers like that? They trusted you with their lives! I trusted you! Don is going to be so shattered when he hears this."

"Well, thankfully he's never going to hear anything," he says, his voice dripping with unconcern.

"You think I'm going to keep this from him?"

"I don't know. But if you decide to tell him, make sure to dig two graves because I'm not going down alone." He scoffs.

"You wouldn't!"

"Try me."

This is so messed up. I don't know how I'm feeling. Hurt, a little. Angry, maybe. Shocked, definitely.

"How long?"

He shoots me an unfriendly look, so I raise my hands and withdraw my question.

"Okay, why?"

"That's none of your business."

"Why didn't you just..."

"What do you think would have happened if it came out that I was feeding the son of the General of the Hard Livings information? Huh?"

"I don't know, but I know you would have deserved whatever would have been done to you. I just don't understand why you did it. I'm sorry but I can't keep this from Don."

"We're in the same boat, so my secret is safe with you. You throw me under the bus, I drag you to hell with me."

"People died because of you!"

"Oh, you want us to compare body counts now? How many people have died because of you?"

That stings and I have no solid comeback. "How could you..."

"I don't owe you any explanation, so stop interrogating me."

"Fine! Why are you even here? Were you following me?" A dumb question considering he's my tail.

"Hilton knew you wouldn't listen to him. And once again, I had to drop everything and follow your highness out of the province. So no, you're not going to sit there and judge me."

I'm getting a headache from all the mess in my head.

"What happened in there? What did Dalu say?"

"He tricked me into saying I loved him and confessing that we had sex. He's going to send the video to Don."

"Why don't you ever listen? Hilton told you to leave it alone. But no, you had to go and fuck up as usual. Why do you always mess things up? Why can't you just stay out of the way and play happy families with your son? Why can't you learn from Caleb and Elik's girls and stay out of the way?"

I cover my face with my hands. I can hear my heart beating in the silence that follows.

"Lotus, are you sleeping with Hilton?" he asks as if it just dawned on him.

"What? Hell no! Why would you even ask that?" I sit up. WTF!

"Can never be too sure with you."

"What's that supposed to mean?"

He scoffs.

I take a deep breath so I don't end up in jail. He takes a deep breath too and meets my eye with something that looks like disgust.

"This is the very last time, Lotus. We deal with this and then we're done. I don't want anything to do with you. Do you understand me? You will tell Alpha that you don't want me to be your tail anymore. Do you understand?"

"Yes."

"Good. Just to be clear, I'm doing this for Hilton and not you. Now go pack your bags and go back to Cape Town tomorrow. Stop at as many fuel stations as you can along the way, collecting alibis."

"Alibis for what?"

"Come on. You think I'm going to give Dalu a hug?"

"No, I..."

"Then do as I said. And word of advice: if you really love your friend, then leave her alone."

"I can't break up with Chelsea. She's my friend."

"And there it is, the selfishness. You don't even like her but you won't let go because everything is about you, regardless of who gets hurt along the way."

"Wow! You know what, fuck you, Tristan!"

"Fuck you too, Lotus!"

*Yerrr!* I bang the car door hard. How dare he judge me yet he is ten times worse!

# THIRTY NINE

The house is too silent. Where is everyone? I thought I would come back to the Wolves having a party at my house and my son puffing on some weed. I'm kidding about the weed part, geez! Don is nothing if not the world's most perfect dad. He took up the fatherly role so naturally, I still can't believe it. At the rate our parenting skills are going, I foresee Ricky's first word being Dada.

It's too quiet; something is not right.

"Anybody home?" My voice echoes, giving me chills.

Maybe Don is on the other side with Ricky, getting him to sleep. It should be time for his nap, right? What time does he even go to bed? I promise I'll do better now that all my demons are put to rest. I quickly walk through the corridor and only the clicking of my shoe can be heard. I try to calm my beating heart; I'm probably just jumpy because I saw Dalu. I had to tie up all the loose ends. Now I can go back to being the perfect mother and perfect girlfriend to my Alpha. I will go to the nursery first, to check on Ricky.

"Lotus."

My heart almost drops to my shoes and I place my hand over my thudding chest. What is he doing in the darkened office? Since when am I Lotus? What happened to *skat*? I have been gone for two days. Shouldn't he be excited to see me?

He has his back to me and is staring out the window. Even though his aura is heavy, the eyes of the wolf around his neck gleaming in the dark, have my clit twitching.

"Baby, you scared me! Why are you standing in a dark room? Where is Ricky? Where are Caleb and Hilton? I thought you guys would throw me a welcome home party or something." I can't seem to stop myself from prattling on.

I turn up the light in the office. I don't usually come in here; it's sort of an uncommunicated understanding that his office is off-limits. Any other day I'd be running my eyes around the desk and walls in curiosity, but right now I'm jumpy and worried by the fact that my man hasn't even turned to face me. I mean, I had gone out of State. A little 'welcome home, honey' wouldn't hurt.

"Baby?" I prompt, putting my hand over his tattooed bicep.

I feel him tense at my touch and he looks at my hand.

"Is that the same hand that was busy holding that fucker?"

I try to snatch my hand away but I'm not fast enough. He has ensnared it in his huge palm. He's holding it so tight, I can almost feel my bones breaking.

"Answer me. Is this the hand you used to stroke his shrivelled little dick?"

Well, not that Dalu had the same impressive penis as Don, but I wouldn't call it shrivelled, and neither was it little. I'm facing my possible execution here, I can't afford to piss off my executioner more than he is right now.

"Baby, what are you talking about? Will you at least look at me and tell me what all this is about?" I'm trying hard to steady my voice and free my hand, but I'm failing miserably.

"Why should I look at you? So that you can look me in the eye and lie to me again like you have been doing all this time? I gave you my heart, Lotus. I made you the queen of my empire, and you do me dirty like this?"

The more agitated he gets with his speech, the more he crushes my hand. I can't feel my fingers anymore. Did Hilton or Caleb rat me out? It was probably Elik or his haughty woman, Fierce! Could it be Tristan or Chelsea? What should I do?

*'Deny!'* my subconscious urges me, but isn't it too late to deny now? Maybe I should plead with him and cry, that sometimes works.

"I'm sorry, Don. In the beginning, my heart was torn in two. I didn't know what to make of your advances. You always disappeared on me. I didn't mean to sleep with Dalu, I swear! It was a long time ago. He forced me to, or his alter ego, I don't know, after I told him I was pregnant with your baby, I..."

"Enough!" His roar cuts in and I feel warm wetness spread through my legs. "Enough with the lies, Lotus! Enough already! I know everything. Every kiss, every touch, every lie, I know."

*Oh God! I know I haven't been a very good Christian lately, but please, for old times' sake, please don't let him kill me. My son still needs me. Please Lord, spare my life,* I'm praying hard and I have given up trying to get my hand out of his deathly grip.

"I'm sorry. I can explain. Baby, please let me explain. For Ricky, please let me explain."

"Don't you dare mention my son with those filthy lie-infested lips. He's barely attached to you and that makes what I'm about to do so much easier."

The finality in his voice has my heart thudding so loudly, the sound is drowning my ears. I want to beg and plead for my life, but my voice is stuck in my throat. It feels like my tongue is glued to the roof of my mouth.

"What? You have no more lies to defend yourself with? Any last words for our son?"

I shake my head and try unsuccessfully to wipe away all the tears falling from my eyes. I try again to clear my throat but my attempts are futile. Don is looming over me menacingly and I see nothing but hatred and a thirst for vengeance in his eyes. He chuckles and the sound sends chills down my spine. It's the laugh of Death.

"Just as well. I don't want my son to hear anything that spews from your vile mouth. I gave you everything! My life and my pride. I gave you my heart, Lotus, but all along you've been stomping on it. Do you know how many people I've punished for calling you a whore? Turns out I was the clown all along. You don't take someone who belongs to the streets and make her the mother of your children. Tell the devil and your father I said fuck their cunts."

I'm holding onto his chest, that's how close he is to me, yet I can't seem to reach the man I love so much, I changed a lot about myself to protect and accommodate his lifestyle. I kind of knew this day would come if he ever found out, but I had successfully fooled myself into thinking the love he had for me would be enough to make him forgive me, and at least spare my life for the sake of our son.

I feel the cold steel of a gun pressed to my temple. All the faces of people whose deaths I had a hand in flash before my eyes. My father. Dust. Skinner. Ghost. Dalu. The repulsive face of Ghost as he pleads for his life lingers the longest. I open my eyes to rid myself of the faces that keep haunting and mocking me. The gorgeous blue eyes I love so much are stained with blood. It's like I'm looking into my father's eyes.

"My son won't miss you. It's not like you were any kind of mother to him. I'm actually helping him, otherwise you would have found a way to destroy him, the same way you have destroyed the life of every man who has ever had the misfortune of coming into your life. You killed your own father. Your ex is rotting in prison because of you. Your other ex is in a mortuary because of you. And now you have destroyed me." Each word is like a stab in my gut and he keeps twisting the knife.

I want to beg him to just pull the trigger already. He's right. I'm a useless mother and Ricky will be better off without me. He hates me. I just pray that Don allows him to visit my family. *Shame*, my poor grandmother; she tried to raise me to be a decent girl, but this is where I ended up. I pray that my mother will find love one day and be happy. At least one of us deserves a happily ever after.

The gun is so close and everything is so silent I can hear all the internal mechanisms working when he pulls the hammer back. I shut my eyes again.

"I just want you to know that I love you. It's always been you that I've loved. You and Ricky are my whole world and I pray that you don't take out my sins on him. I love you, Donavan. Please tell Ulric I love him when he's old enough to understand."

"Your love is worthless, Lotus. And it's Ulric. Say it right, dammit!"

The gun goes off and I jump.

I touch my head expecting to feel a bloody hole but only sweat is plastering my hair to my face. My senses take forever to return. I'm still in the hotel room and Chelsea is sleeping peacefully in her bed. The warm wetness in the sheets tells me that I pissed on myself. With shaking hands, I pull my phone from under the pillow.

"Why are you calling me this late? Are you in any trouble? Where's Chelsea?" The concern in his voice makes me sob.

"I'm sorry baby, I'm so sorry," I apologise in between sobs.

"What's wrong? Should I come over there? How many hours will it take?"

"No, don't come. One of us has to be there for Ricky. I just had a horrible dream and I realise I've been a horrible girlfriend to you and an even more horrible mother to our son. I don't deserve you both. I'm so sorry."

"Stop talking like that. You're the best girlfriend and mother in the whole world. You just need a little help, that's all. I talked to Elik yesterday. He believes you might be suffering from postnatal depression or something like that, and everything that happened made it worse. I was waiting for you to come back home so I could talk to you about seeing someone."

I sigh deeply, blowing the air out of my mouth loudly. I'll do anything at this point. My family deserves a better version of me, not this wreck. I can't even recognise myself.

"Now get some rest, my *skat*. We need you back home tomorrow. We both miss you, but I miss you the most." The love in his voice has tears spilling out of my eyes.

I nod repeatedly like he can see me. After saying a thousand I love yous, I end the call.

There is no way I can sleep in a pool of my own urine, so I go and bath first before putting the bedding in the tub. I improvise by pouring bathing foam since I don't have any washing powder or soap.

Chelsea sleeps like the dead. She doesn't even move when I slip into her bed. I listen to her soft snores as I clutch the hotel gown to my body.

# *FORTY*

I skim through a magazine, the glossy pages reflecting the soft overhead lighting. I'm not really paying attention to what's written on them, I'm just staring at the pictures, daydreaming about being somewhere on another continent. There is a hush calmness in the room, probably because of the neutral colours and the fancy but minimal furnishings. The antiseptic stench and the scent of the fresh flowers on the little coffee table are not blending very well; it's making me want to gag. An interesting abstract painting is hanging pretty on one wall, its vibrant swirls trying their best to liven up the otherwise boring room.

Across from me is a teenager who looks like she's been through a lot; you don't need a psychology degree to figure that out. You can just tell she has had a hard life. I can't help but wonder what happened to her. Can I ask her 'What are you in for?' I shake off the thoughts and go back to the pages of the magazine.

My therapy session should be starting soon. It's been a long two weeks. I didn't expect that coming face-to-face with myself would be that difficult. I got to meet versions of myself I had created along the way to keep dealing with life. I guess I'm like Dalu in a way. But I'm normal, I didn't create psycho-killer alter egos.

I was forced to face my demons and all that deep stuff, and I think I'm finally getting it right. Dalu's face is quickly fading from my mind and that's exactly what my soul needs. I specifically asked Tristan not to tell me the details. Knowing he was gone was enough. At least now I don't have to go through my fabulous life looking over my shoulder. I'm not vain; it's called self-love!

I'm a bit nervous because no matter how many times I do this, it doesn't get easier. Remember that thing I said about meeting versions of myself? It's really not fun, but I committed to these sessions, and in a strange way, I have grown to love them.

The therapist asked me a few questions during our first session and I was as vague as I could be. She surprised me by not pushing for details. Shouldn't shrinks dig out all the dirt in you and make you say things you don't want to say? Let's go with therapist; shrink makes me sound mentally disturbed. Doctor maybe, or psychiatrist? Nah, makes me sound sick in the head like someone we used to know. So therapist it is. I told her about the horrible dreams that kept me up at night but I refused to tell her exactly what they were about. Like Hilton said I should, I'll take my secrets to the grave. For all I knew, she could have been on Don's payroll. I didn't want her ratting me out. After I was done narrating my night terrors, she gave me tissues and calmly read me like a book.

"You seem shocked, Lotus. This is not my first year in practice. I've been doing this for over twenty years now in a city crawling with drug lords, gangs and troubled teens who turn to drugs. The weave on your head and the handbags you carry suggest you're the pampered girlfriend of someone well-off. I'm guessing from all the hush-hush that he doesn't make his money selling Herbalife. The way you're terrified of his reaction to your betrayal signifies that he's either a ruthless gang leader or a narcissistic killer, but most likely both. You know his ruthless side and you have experienced or seen him do things that you can't tell anyone about because you want to protect him. But you're also scared of him. At least on a subconscious level."

She had my jaw on the floor on that very first session and earned my grudging respect. So I can be as open as I can with her without revealing incriminating stuff, and she gets most of it without prying or asking me to spell it out for her. That has made me relax and be a more cooperative patient. But the more I open up, the more vulnerable I become. I hate being weak and vulnerable. I'm just glad she hasn't said anything lame like forgive yourself blah-blah, I mean have you seen me? What is there to forgive? I'm not the first woman to be unsure about a guy during their first year together and try to choose what looks like a better option at the time. And I won't be the last to do a guy dirty either. It's the circle of life.

"Lotus," the friendly secretary says with a smile.

And I'm up! I dump the magazine on the coffee table and find my way in. I settle into the comfortable chair and get ready to face myself.

"How are you feeling today?" Dr. Brown starts.

Every day for the past two weeks she has asked me this question in the same calm voice. If I were to liken it to anything, I would say her voice reminds me of the sound of the ocean just before dawn. You know that calmness of waves washing over rocks and flowing back into the ocean?

I take time to assess all my feelings, not really to process or organise them, but just to acknowledge them as she has taught me.

"I feel exhausted. Frustrated that I haven't fixed myself yet. Angry at myself. Despaired. The pain of failing my man and my son. Lost. It feels like ever since I put a label on how I feel, it has only exacerbated whatever this depression is. I keep on having the same dreams. It's either my man shoots me in the head or I find him with a gunshot wound on his head and a letter splattered with his blood. These dreams are draining me because I can't tell them to anyone else, especially my man, because if he knew the reason behind them then they might just come true. What makes it worse is that he has been so understanding about it and that makes me feel like a shitty, shitty person."

She hands me a box of tissues and waits as I blow my nose and dry my eyes. At least she doesn't have a notepad, so it feels like I'm just offloading to a friend. Chelsea has made it obvious that she doesn't like Don. She's never objective when it comes to him, which is funny because apparently Caleb poops candy floss. Also, I don't know what she'll tell Caleb when she's deep in pillow talk. Caleb and I are cool, but not back to the way we were before Chelsea fucked up and threw herself at Elik. Again, I got blamed and Chelsea got the romantic getaways.

I was so desperate, I told Hilton about the recurring dreams. I had to tell someone before they drove me crazy. And in true Hilton fashion, he just shrugged and said, "Then don't sleep". My life feels like a low-budget horror-thriller movie sometimes. After shouting at Hilton and telling him how insensitive he was, he shrugged again like it was nothing and said I should go and be soapy to my shrink but take my secrets to the grave. How is it even possible to be as disconnected as Hilton is?

"Let's start with your dreams then. When you wake up from them, what do you tell your man you were dreaming about?"

The truth is, I tell him I'm having nightmares about Ghost, Dust and Skinner, which isn't entirely untrue, but I have made peace with the fact that this is one secret I'm taking to the grave. I feel bad though when Don starts blaming himself. He feels terrible for allowing me into his world. He feels like he tainted me, and I'm running out of reassurances to give him. I didn't mean for things to escalate to this point. I want to make things right. But how do I do that without incriminating myself? My paranoia is on steroids these days. Don can never know about me and Dalu. Not even in the next life. I want my son to grow up in a happy home. If it means dealing with these nightmares for the rest of my life, then so be it. See, I'm selfless. I'm taking one for the team!

"Lotus," her voice draws me out of my head and I realise I didn't answer her question. "I'm beginning to think there's more to these dreams, bear with me for a minute. Don't you think these nightmares are a result of the things you went through? The dark side of your partner that you can't speak about? I feel like these nightmares are a result of things you've seen and witnessed as opposed to things you fear, that's why they are so vivid."

She has no idea! If only she knew half the things I have seen. But silence is golden so I keep my mouth shut and let her do the talking.

"Somehow you have associated all this trauma with your son." Her voice hasn't changed its calm monotone.

Could it be that she's right? I really thought I had everything under control. That I had grown badass. I had people killed without thinking too much of it. The implication of what I did hits me and I'm suddenly shivering and feeling hot flashes. My heart is picking up pace and I'm feeling a bit dizzy. It's like I'm watching it all over again. My father's face with his eyes open as if he can see me. The two alphas groaning in pain as the poison takes its toll. Ghost begging me to spare him. Dalu asking me why. Don almost dying. How would I have been able to look my son in the eye had I killed his father? How do I look at him now knowing that I'm a killer, a liar and a cheat? I don't deserve to be a mother.

"Breathe, Lotus, breathe. There you go. Drag more air into your lungs. Just like that, deeper, exhale. Breathe in deeply, exhale."

We go through breathing exercises until I feel better.

"What is it that you fear the most?"

The abrupt shift from the dreams has my thoughts scrambled up and I reply with the first thing that comes to mind.

"Losing myself."

She nods, signifying that I must carry on. I gulp down a whole glass of water and pour some more before my throat opens up. I told you meeting myself is not fun.

"Losing myself in my man's world. He consumes me and I love him so much, I'd do anything for him. But he comes with a lot of baggage. Sure, there are the luxuries and the readily available funds, but they come at such a cost. Don't get me wrong, I don't want him to change. I accepted that his life is part of who he is and I learned to love that side of him too. Besides, I get to see the soft side of him that no one else gets to see. But I grew up mostly in the straight and narrow, my grandmother made sure of that, and I fear I'm losing that part of myself. I've lied so much, I have even tricked myself into believing my own lies. I haven't set foot inside a church in forever now. That's why for a while I strung the other guy along. He was safe, and with him I got to be fully alive. I didn't have to have my guard up and look over my shoulder all the time. Well, that is until I made him psycho. Now I'm a mother and I feel like I'm losing myself even more. I tried to hold on to the old me when I was pregnant. I drank, but that only made me feel guilty and like the world's worst mother. Everyone else seems to think so anyway, even my son. I just want to go back to being me again." My voice cracks and I pause. I sip on water while she waits patiently.

"Along the way, I've discovered things about myself. Like, all my life I wanted to know who my father was and maybe have a relationship with him. I finally got to meet him and he turned out to be a nightmare. I wish I never met him. I kept digging and pushing and I lost my mother in the process. I lost my grandmother too. Chelsea wasn't speaking to me either. Fierce too. All the important women in my life missed out on the better part of my pregnancy. I was all alone. When I needed them the most, they deserted me. I just want to go back to being the girl earning peanuts, living above her means and smooching off her best friend. Life was so much simpler then. My mother skipped my birthday for the first time since I was born. Not even a text message from her." Admitting all this and saying it out loud feels like a huge boulder has been displaced from my chest. I feel lighter.

I don't want it to seem like I don't appreciate all the blessings that are in my life. I do, I really do. I'm grateful for Don; his love, his generosity and for giving me Ricky. I'm grateful for the way he loves me. I mean, I took a rock and made it human. I'm a miracle worker. It's just that every time he closes himself off with his brothers or goes away for days on end without communication, I get very worried. I worry even more about how easily I have accepted parts of his life, you know, the drugs, the guns and the blood. But I don't know how to separate my love for him from the life he leads, and unfortunately, I'm bound to live that life with him by virtue of association.

I'm also grateful for Hilton. I know he would protect me with his life. He's always there for me. He saves me at every turn and never mentions it or asks for anything in return.

"It seems like you're struggling to bond with your child because you're afraid of repeating the mistakes your mother made with you. You're scared of being like her. It's understandable, especially since the women you care about and whose attention you crave weren't there during your pregnancy. Their absence might have influenced how you view your son. You might have spent more time seeking attention from others rather than giving it to him. And it sounds like there's some resentment towards him, possibly because you feel he damaged your perfect body.

There's also the guilt about drinking during your pregnancy. Your father's absence and the pain it caused you, and continues to cause, are significant too. Until you acknowledge and address these feelings, they won't go away. It's important to work through these emotions to start healing. We'll take it one step at a time."

I feel another panic attack approaching and we go through breathing exercises again.

"Last time you said sometimes you feel like you have no one to talk to. How is that possible when you say your best friend and you are practically sisters?"

My Chelsea bun. I find myself narrating what my ex and his friends did to her. I don't know how I got there. One moment I was talking about how grateful I am for her, and the next I went deep. Dr. Brown keeps asking questions about our relationship and I'm as honest as I can be. Chelsea and I used to be tight. We are trying now. It hasn't been the same since we reunited, but I think we are getting there.

"I see. You need to realise that you don't owe Chelsea anything. You're not responsible for what your ex did. You're not indebted to Chelsea. You don't need to apologise for her behaviour or how she treated you when you decided to leave Cape Town. Love her from a place of love not from a place of paying back a debt. You also need to stand up to your friend some more. Friends shouldn't make you feel small or bad about your choices. Take charge of your relationship with her and build a friendship where both of you are equals."

We talk more about my friendship with Chelsea and how her actions affected my relationships with Elik, Fierce and Caleb. It's depressing, and I'm relieved when we move on from the topic. I like Chelsea, so I don't want to awaken any thoughts that might make me like her less.

"What are the things you loved to do before meeting your partner?"

I smile for the first time since this session began.

"Running. Church. Clubbing. Especially clubbing. That's actually how I met him." I smile to myself, remembering that night. Don kept sending drinks to our table, and a few hours later, I was under him in his bed. He named my favourite spot, his club, after me before I even met him. I wish I could go back to that time in my life.

"Why don't you go clubbing anymore?" The same calm voice hasn't been tainted by any judgement yet.

"Because that makes me a bad mother. My child is only months old. Shouldn't I be at that stage where all I want to do is stare at his gorgeous face all day? Shouldn't I be constantly updating the world about how he's growing instead of being out at a club?"

Dr. Brown sighs before taking her glasses off and pinching the bridge of her nose bridge of her nose before putting the glasses back on.

"Lotus, just because you have become a mother doesn't mean you should stop being Lotus. There's no formula to being a mother, and there's really no such thing as a good mother or a super mum. It's just women trying to model their children's lives. Your son won't know about clubbing until he's older, but what he will know is the energy you carry around him. The slight resentment that you harbour against him. He needs you to be a happy mother more than he needs you to be a perfect mother. So if clubbing makes you happy then by all means put on your dancing shoes and go clubbing. You can't pour from an empty cup. Just find a way to incorporate clubbing into your life. Maybe wait for him to sleep and tuck him in before taking off to have time to yourself. You have help. Don't feel like leaving Ulric with someone else makes you any less of a mother or a bad one."

Even she pronounces my son's name better than I do. Yeah, I really need to take lessons now. UL-RIC - I need to practise that.

"What if even the help gives me judgemental looks?" That woman is something else. She makes me uncomfortable sometimes. She can say everything with just a look and turning the corners of her mouth down.

"Then fire her, or sit her down and talk to her. Simple."

Simple, she says. What's simple about that?

"Our time is almost up now. Your assignment this week is for you to go for a run at least once and hang out in your favourite spot with friends. Drink and go wild after tucking your son in. Let loose and have some crazy drunken sex."

My cheeks burn at the thought of having crazy drunken sex with Don. Going at it like animals is my favourite thing to do. Maybe even throw in some weed, you know, and completely unleash the freak.

I feel like myself again. Who knew therapy could be this helpful? I used to think it was pointless to pay someone just to talk, but now I get it.

# *FORTY ONE*

I had the best weekend ever! I hadn't realised how much of myself I had put on hold trying to fit into Don's world. But I'm back now.

Friday night, Chelsea and I set Longstreet on fire. I'm so rusted, I was tipsy after two Long Islands, but I winged it and downed a third. I downed four blowjobs after that, and by midnight I was seeing double and laughing too much, so I called time out. Caleb picked Chelsea up, and Don and I had shots in his office before hitting the road. We had our first round in the car, on the side of the highway. It was insane!

We got home and Don lit a blunt. We were laughing and chilling, back to old us. I got higher than a kite and Don fucked my brains out right on the couch. Quite risky because the nanny could have decided to come and check why there was all that noise, or the Wolves guarding the house could have walked in. I swear my eyes rolled in when I had the most explosive orgasm of my life. I didn't even make a sound. I just lay there shaking with my mouth open. I think even Don missed our uninhibited sex because damn boy!

I was on a roll on '*Bringing Back Lotus*'. I sat the nanny down and told her that I didn't appreciate her attitude. It's either she shapes up or I'm kicking her out to the curb. It worked like magic. She has been such a darling ever since. She even made me a yucky concoction for my hangover the other day.

On Monday morning, I went for a run. I felt alive as I ran against the wind. In the afternoon, I was back in therapy. The next homework Dr. Brown gave me was to involve Ricky in the kid-friendly activities that I love to do. The way she emphasised 'kid-friendly' was as if I would take him to a club. Like seriously, not even I would do that. Clubs are No Under 21. Not that I would take him if they weren't. Anyway, on Saturday I did exactly what the doctor ordered. I took my family out. Don being Don put up a fight, but my emotional blackmailing and tantrums got his grumpy self in line. So with Ricky looking cuter than a button in his bespoke Silver Cross Balmoral pram, we made our way to Polkadraai Farm in Stellenbosch. We had comfortable shoes on, a cap and a big hat as his and hers because hey, the Cape Town sun was shining directly from hell, and a big smile on my face.

We started off with strawberry picking. We both got the big buckets so we could spend more time in the fields - my idea. We had to walk all the way to the end, and never has harvesting been so fun! When Ricky started crying, Don became dad of the year. He's so good with our boy, it makes me want to cry every time.

After filling up our buckets and me vowing to go on a strawberry-only diet, we settled for burgers and chips. So much for discipline. We had so much fun, I can't wait to do it again. Even Don enjoyed himself, even though he will never admit it.

After stuffing our faces, I wanted us to go on the tractor ride but the stroller was a problem, so we ended up settling for face painting instead. Don wasn't having it and I was forced to force him to do that too. I mean, hello! I have a huge ass wolf on my thigh; a little face painting wasn't going to kill him. Predictably, he wanted to get a wolf painting and we were assured the paint wouldn't hurt Ricky. My baby looked so adorable as a little wolf. I chose angel wings for obvious reasons. I am the angel in this family; always looking out for them and keeping everyone grounded.

I posted a side profile of Ricky's face and a small part of Don's on my WhatsApp status. Their faces were basically incognito. Everyone was making a fuss over my gorgeous family and Ricky's stroller. The bar has been set. I wish I was still active on Instagram.

On Sunday, we went to visit the children from the Cape Flats that Don and Merishka take care of. Remember they used to meet at our house in Gordon's Bay? They have a different venue now. They were thrilled to see me and Merishka was extra nice, I don't know why. I totally loved the way Don was showing off our son. I know I have said this a million times but we made the most gorgeous little human being ever and everyone loves him. What's there not to love on that blue-eyed, toothless, smiley face?

So yeah, I have been stepping up in the mothering field. I'm not quite there yet but I'm working on it. I have been taking Ricky out on dates when it's just the two of us. I hate that we always have guards but it's the life I chose so I have stopped fighting it. They know to keep their distance from us, so all is well. I took him to watch *Madagascar* in theatre, then *The Lion King* movie with the realistic animals. I doubt he knew what was going on and I'm just grateful that he didn't cry. I had to apologise profusely to him for how they ruined Mufasa's death. And what was up with the malnourished-looking Scar? They messed up *shame*. I promised to get Ricky the original version because wow!

Ricky now loves basking in my attention. You have no idea how fulfilling it is. He doesn't hate me anymore and he cries when I leave. We now have that relationship he had with Don from the get-go, although he still chooses Don over me when he has to pick. Now he laughs with me and clings to me. And best of all, he falls asleep in my arms almost every night. I think our one-on-one dates have been a success. We have the best conversations, with him in his high chair and me doing all the talking while he gurgles. I discovered that he loves music, so whenever I'm holding him, I make sure my phone is nowhere in sight because I'm that replaceable. He will cry for my phone until I give him just for him to drop it.

Dr. Brown was right. I feel like myself again. Everything is perfect except for one thing. I haven't managed to get through to Don's grandparents. Don's grandmother is impossible. Hilton is covering up for me with Don's father but I don't know how long that's going to hold. When I last called their house, she threatened to call the police. Talk about being dramatic. Hilton said my best bet would be talking to Don's grandfather instead, so we will be going there on Sunday. The plan is to camp outside their house and wait until the grumpy grandmother leaves for church, then I go in and try to win the grandfather over. I'm not holding my breath.

\* \* \* \* \*

"Hey, wake up. Chelsea is here." Don shakes me, and I groggily open my eyes.

"Oh, shit! I forgot that she was coming to sleep over today."

"It might be good for you. I won't be back till after midnight, so at least she'll keep you company." He gives me a quick kiss before walking out.

I drag myself out of bed and crawl my feet into slippers. I don't do much to fix my face.

"Where's Ricky? Aunty wants to see him." Chelsea hugs me.

"In the nursery. I'm sure he's sleeping."

"You okay? You look like hell." She studies my face like a concerned parent.

"I'm fine. I just woke up. I had a long day with Ricky. He wasn't feeling too well." I force a smile, avoiding eye contact to hide my lies.

"I see. Well, I brought ice cream. Maybe we can watch a movie or something."

That sounds like a plan. I would love to sit in the dark, in silence, and pretend to focus on the screen. I take her bag to the guest room and she goes to the kitchen to prepare snacks.

"Are you sure you're okay? We don't have to do anything. We can watch the movie tomorrow," she says when I join her in the kitchen.

"No, I'm good. I'm still waking up, that's all."

"Alrighty then. You make popcorn and I'll take these to the lounge."

She returns and thankfully, my mood is brightening. I find myself telling her about the sex I had earlier with Don in the study. It was insane! I feel myself twitching at the memory.

"Whatever the Wolves are taking lately, please let them continue because Caleb is on it too, and I'm not complaining." She blushes all on her own.

"No details, please. I'm too young." I take juice and grapes from the fridge.

"But you just gave me all the details of your sexcapade! Why can't I tell you mine? Don't you want to know what he did to me outside his car last night?" She proceeds to pollute my ears.

Every day I'm made to see Caleb in a different light. Where did he learn to do all that?! Chelsea is going on and on about Caleb and I love it for her. It warms my heart to see her like this. She doesn't deserve him but she deserves happiness like the rest of us.

We end up talking about her work and life in general. The conversation is flowing and the movie is long forgotten.

"Are you really okay? You know you can talk to me. What happened when you met Dalu?"

I asked not to talk about it when it happened. I'd hoped never to talk about it, but I guess I'm not very good at setting boundaries.

"You were right. He manipulated me to come so he could collect evidence that I visited him. He never changed; I was stupid to think otherwise."

"I'm so sorry. You never have to see him again."

Even if I wanted to see him again, I could never. No one will ever see him again.

"How's the counselling going?"

"It's good. I'm enjoying it. How are your sessions going?"

She resumed therapy when I started mine. It felt a bit weird because she made it look like a competition of some sort.

"It's been good. You know, it has put a lot of things into perspective for me." She shifts to face me more. "I'm sorry for abandoning you all those months. I'm sorry I wasn't there when you needed me the most. I'm sorry I ignored your messages. I don't have a good reason why I did it. The longer I went without talking to you, the more I didn't know what to say to you. I was wrong, and I'm truly sorry."

She shouldn't make me emotional now. I'm already on the edge as we speak. One light push and I'll break down.

"What happened to us, Chels? How did we end up here? Remember how excited we were about life after graduation? We were going to travel the world and live our best lives. We were never going to allow any man to come between us. How did we get here?"

"I don't know. I ask myself that question a lot."

"But your life is perfect. You still have it all. The man, the job, family, new friends, the life. You have it all." I hate how jealous I sound. I go through her Instagram profile an unhealthy number of times. She even has my mother in her collection of good things.

"Do I?" She looks away.

"What's wrong?" I hold her arm and she looks at me with glassy eyes.

"Everything. I'm a mess. I'm a functional alcoholic, Lotus."

"What? Since when? What happened?" She drinks a lot, we all do, but calling herself an alcoholic is a bit extreme.

"I guess all the years of bottled-up emotions finally caught up with me. You know, I had my life planned out, then those guys happened and I crashed. Now my world keeps spinning, and no matter how hard I try, I often find myself on my knees picking up the pieces. It's been years now but I'm still messed up."

I don't know what to say. I don't know how not to blame myself for it.

"Before Donavan and Caleb and everything, my life was falling back into place. I was finally healing." She looks at me. "I had you, Lotus."

I swallow the lump in my throat.

"Then Donavan came into your life, but I still had you. Then Caleb came into mine and for a split second, everything I ever wanted existed at the same time. I had it all, but what those monsters did to me kept popping up. I didn't want to tell you because I knew you would blame yourself. So I started drinking more than usual. You know how much I love my alcohol. You just didn't see the flask I carried to work, or the shots I poured into my coffee in the morning, or the bottles in the box under my bed. I kept it together because you were always there for me. I loved you, maybe a little too much as my therapist says. He said I focused on you to avoid focusing on myself. Then you and Donavan became serious and you hardly had any time left for me. I started drinking more to fill the void. Then you chose him over me and my world shut down. You left me, Lotus." Her voice breaks and I look down. I don't know what to say.

"I didn't show up on the day you left because I was lying knocked out on the floor. I only woke up later that night. Hulk tried to be there for me but I pushed him away. He eventually got tired and left me. I wanted Caleb, and my therapist says it's because he was best friends with your man and I wanted what you had."

Poor Hulk. I genuinely wish he's happy wherever he is. He carried

Chelsea for a long time, and even though they were toxic, they worked.

"Then the Elik thing happened and Caleb left me, so I started drinking even more. Strangely, Caleb was the only one there for me. Even after what I'd done, he didn't stop caring about me. He wanted me to be okay. Every now and then I'd find a Runner parked outside my place to check if I was alright."

A tear rolls out of my eye and I catch it before it falls.

"I need to come clean to you, babe."

I'm not sure I want to hear what she has to say.

"I only revived our friendship because I wanted access to Caleb. And it worked. I have him back now and it's beautiful."

I wipe my tears. I'm so conflicted.

"I shouldn't have used you like that. You were the only constant in my life, and I'm sorry that I missed out on most of your pregnancy. I'm sorry I wasn't there for you when Dalu hurt you. I'm sorry that even when you took me back, I wasn't honest with you. I'm sorry that I took your mum from you and rubbed it in your face. I love you, and I miss us so much. I'm so sorry."

We hold on to each other and cry. I want to let her all in but I don't trust her not to hurt me again. The space in my heart that was reserved for her is not there anymore. My son, Don and Hilton are the only people that live in the core of my heart.

We stay there for a long while, wrapped in each other's arms. She was my entire world. I loved her with everything I was and everything I had. We went through hell and back, tackled therapy and vacations, walked through prisons and churches, went to weddings and funerals, cried together in graveyards and courthouses. We shared everything. My family loved her, and hers loved me. We knew each other inside out; our dreams, fears, relationships; we knew it all. I never thought anything could tear us apart, especially a man. Even when she stopped talking to me, I tried. I tried really hard because I believed she loved me as much as I loved her. I poured my heart out day after day, begged and grovelled, but she ignored me every time. I stalked her Instagram, liking every post, sometimes leaving comments I would later delete, hoping she would see me and remember what we used to be. Hoping she would come back to me. Then she showed up from nowhere, and even though I knew it wasn't real, I clung on because I desperately wanted it to be.

"I forgive you, Chels, and I'm sorry too."

Her body trembles as she sobs hard in my arms, and I hold her closer. I love her, I do; I just have to figure out how to love her like I used to.

When we eventually calm down, we go to the kitchen and dish out ice cream, all the while trying to cheer each other up. We eventually pick a movie and turn off the lights.

Don walks in halfway into the movie, with two plastic bags.

"You're back early." I eye the bags curiously.

"Change of plans. I'll go and watch football on the other side. I brought you something."

"Aww, thank you, baby." I receive my bag with a smile. He's so sweet. I already know what's inside - wings and sweet potato fries.

"This one's yours, Chelsea." He hands her the other bag.

"You got me something?"

I'm as shocked as she is.

She opens it and pulls out a box of bacon jalapeño cheese bombs, her favourite guilty pleasure from Club Lotus. There are four cans of Dr Pepper as well. Chelsea loves Dr Pepper, and since it's hard to find in Cape Town, Don must have really gone out of his way to get it.

"Donavan!" Chelsea squeals.

She gets up and hugs him. This is the sweetest make-up ever. I'm so proud of Don for being the bigger person. I never thought I would see the day.

Don leaves after a bit of chit-chat, and Chelsea and I dive into our treats. The conversation is flowing and we are in high spirits. We laugh about random things and reminisce about some funny situations we've found ourselves in. The movie is playing in the background, long forgotten. Before we know it, it's way past midnight. Even though we're both tired, and going to bed is a good idea, we don't want the night to end.

# *FORTY TWO*

I draw the curtains to let some light in while waiting for water to boil. It looks like it's going to be a beautiful day. The weather is perfect; it's not too cold or too hot, it's just right. I think we should go down to the ocean and have a picnic by the rocks, but coffee first. A coffee machine would be a welcome gift, if anyone was wondering what to get me for Christmas. I make a cup of hot chocolate for Chelsea and coffee for myself.

I find her in the guest room, all dressed up and looking like she's ready to go. She had agreed to spend the day with me so I'm a bit confused.

"Are you leaving?" I hand her the cup and sit on the bed.

"I need to go and get my laptop so I can do a bit of work later. I'll be back."

"Do you want me to come with you?"

"You don't have to."

"I don't mind. I'd love to get out of the house actually. Ricky can come with us."

"Well, the thing is, I'm meeting Caleb afterwards. I'll be back before dinner though, so start thinking of what to cook."

"You guys are like high school kids. It's adorable."

She blushes, and before we know it, we are talking about Caleb. I officially know too much about him. Everything that has Caleb in it brings out her playful side. I love to see it.

Speak of the devil! Her phone rings and it's him. I give her a small wave and head back to the kitchen. I'm going to cook up a feast tonight. Maybe I'll even bake a cake, you know, to celebrate the resurrection of our friendship. Maybe I should have a braai and invite the guys. But someone could say the wrong thing, and Caleb might end up taking all of Chelsea's attention and ruin everything. I also need to remember to hide all the alcohol in the house.

I need to text Don a grocery list so he can get Tristan or another Runner to pick everything up. I could text Tristan directly but we are not exactly on speaking terms. I asked Don to assign me a different tail, but when I couldn't give a clear reason why, he said Tristan was staying. And of course Tristan was mad at me for it. What was I supposed to do? I wish he knew how much I don't enjoy seeing his face either.

I wish everyone was like Hilton. He was furious at me for going to see Dalu after he specifically told me not to, but after I apologised and took accountability, he scoffed and we were good again. Maybe it was the apology gift basket that did the trick. I filled it with biltong, an eighteen-year-old Glenfiddich, rugby tickets, nuts and dried fruit. Whatever it was, he forgave me, and if anything, it brought us closer.

Chelsea joins me in the kitchen, smiling ear to ear. Love looks good on her, I must say. She is looking gorgeous in boyfriend jeans and a cropped white tee, with a Country Road bag slung across her shoulder.

"I need to run now so I can be back earlier than later."

"Please come back. Don't sleep over at Caleb's place."

"I won't," she chuckles.

"Promise?"

"I promise."

I walk her to her car, chatting and laughing about everything and nothing.

"I swear I put them in here." She digs through her bag for her keys. It's so cute. It takes me back to the old days when she would search for the car keys before we'd head out to Longstreet. I never understood why she would put them in her bag instead of carrying them in her hand out of the house.

"Got them," she says. Her smile softens and she looks at me. "I love you, Lotus." She pulls me into a tight hug.

*That was random. Why are we getting emotional now?*

"I love you too. Drive safely, okay?"

She settles into the driver's seat and I wait to wave her off.

"Seriously? You've got to be kidding me!"

"What?" I lean in to see what's wrong.

"The battery's dead!" She throws her hands up in frustration.

"Really? Oh, man. And Don's not around to sort it out. Let me see if one of the guys can help."

"Don't worry. I can call an Uber... but now getting to Caleb afterwards will be a hassle," she sulks.

"You know what, just take my car."

"Are you sure?"

"Of course. Come on, let's go and get my keys."

We go back into the house and I hand her my car keys.

"Thanks, babe. You're the best."

I wave as she drives off. I feel like I have finally repaid her for all those times I drove her car.

What should I do with my suddenly free afternoon? Maybe I'll take a walk and enjoy the sunshine, or maybe I should start preparing for tonight's dinner. But it's too early for that, so I might as well finish that movie we abandoned yesterday.

\* \* \* \* \*

Time flies! It's past 11 already. I'm about to start a new episode of *Selling Sunset* when my phone rings and Chelsea's name flashes on my screen. I hope she cancelled with Caleb and is on her way back.

"There are men outside my door," she whispers.

"What men?" I put the bowl with the grapes aside.

"I don't know. I saw them through the peephole. They look dodgy," she whispers with a shaky voice.

"Call the police! No, call the caretaker, let me call Don."

My heart races as I dial Don's number. I scramble off the couch and search the house for the keys to the car in the garage. I wish Don wasn't so disorganised. Where the hell are the keys?

I find them in the kitchen and rush out. I hope all this is a misunderstanding. It can't be what I think it is. Why would anyone want to attack Chelsea?

"Answer the damn phone!" I yell at the ringing tone as I drive out of the garage.

I dial Don again and thank goodness he answers this time.

"There are dodgy men at my old flat. Chelsea is there. Please do something."

"What? Where are you?"

"I'm on my way there. I just left home."

"Let me go there. Go back home."

"Please hurry. What if they hurt her?" My voice cracks.

"I'm leaving town right now. I'll call you. Go back home!"

He's crazy if he thinks I'll go home when Chelsea is in danger. My phone rings as soon as I hang up, and I answer immediately.

"The caretaker is not answering. I think they have guns," Chelsea sobs.

Oh no! I really hope it's not what it looks like. I hope they have the wrong door.

"Listen to me. Get into your room and lock the door. Don's on his way," my voice betrays my own fear.

"I think they're breaking down the door."

"They won't get through the door. It's broad daylight, people in the other apartments will help. Don will get there soon. Get into your room and lock the door," I talk fast, my anxiety approaching its peak.

"I'm in your room, under the bed. I hope he gets here now," her voice quivers.

"He'll be there just now. Put your phone on silent and text Caleb. Don't make a sound. It's going to be fine. I'm on my way."

Why is Gordon's Bay so far?! Can't people drive faster?! It's a matter of life and death!

It takes me forever to get to Retreat.

Two police vans are parked near the gate, an ambulance is on the pavement and onlookers are huddled in groups across the street. I blatantly ignore the policeman's orders to stop.

"Chelsea!" I shout as I take the stairs, two at a time.

The door has been kicked in. I try to push past the policeman at the door but he blocks me. My eyes land on a pool of blood on the floor and my knees give up.

"Chelsea!" I try to crawl past the policeman but he blocks me.

"Ma'am, you can't be here. Please go outside," he insists, not caring about my emotions.

Caleb pushes past the policeman, calling out for Chelsea, and Don pulls me up and drags me outside. Everything is happening so fast, I'm getting dizzy.

"Stop it, *skat!* Focus!"

"Is she... is she dead?"

"I don't know, I just got here, but I need you to get out of here right now."

"But..."

"Right now, Lotus!"

I follow him down the steps, feeling like I'm going mad. I'm walking the wrong direction. I should be running towards Chelsea. I hope no one is recording this tragedy for social media content. Don keeps his hand tight on my wrist and leads me to a VW Golf GTI parked around the corner. He opens the back seat, and I don't need to be told to jump in.

"Go with Tristan."

"Baby..."

"Please, *skat.* I need you to do this," he pleads with a tinge of hopelessness in his voice. "Remember what I told you that time? It's happening. I need you to go. Give me your phone... Tris, guard her with your life."

"Yes, Alpha."

I hand Don my phone and the keys to the car I drove to get here. The locks click and Tristan drives off. It's like a bad dream that I'm desperate to wake up from.

"Where are we going?"

"First, Newlands."

"Then?"

"Out of town."

"What?" I thought he was taking me back home. I don't want to go out of town! I need to go to Chelsea.

"We can't do that. My son is at home." This can't be happening right now. I screw my eyes shut and vigorously shake my head hoping to shake the hallucination away. I open my eyes only to find myself still in a speeding car with Tristan behind the wheel.

"Can we pass by the house first so I can get my son and pack a few things?"

"No."

"My son..."

"Please shut up! I'm trying to think here." There is not a single thread of compassion in his voice.

I sit back and close my eyes. I keep trying to convince myself that Chelsea isn't dead, but the amount of blood I saw on the floor was too much. I hug myself as I bounce on the seat when the car speeds over a hump.

"Shut up, Lotus! Shut up!"

I ignore him and continue whimpering.

He parks around the corner from Elik's house and tells me to wait in the car. He says it so firmly, I don't even think of disobeying him.

He returns moments later and starts the car.

"Not a word!" he says when I sit up.

I cry shamelessly, praying and cursing in my head. I ask for intervention from the underground gang and the heavens above, yelling at them for not doing their jobs in the first place.

When I have cried my heart out, I lie down on the seat, still sniffling, using my arm as a pillow.

# FORTY THREE

I must have fallen asleep or zoned out indefinitely; I'm having a hard time distinguishing between reality and illusion. I sit up in time to see signs for Matjiesfontein. Where the hell are we? There isn't much to work with outside and I can't exactly ask Tristan. We drive past an old fuel station and further down until we turn into a farm. The dirt road takes us past signs of a river and all the way down to a cabin. There isn't anything else in sight. I don't like the idea of being isolated with a guy that hates me.

"We're here." Tristan kills the engine.

"Here where?"

"Get out," he snaps.

I have many questions I can't ask. Could this be the place Don spoke about? It fits the description of off-the-grid and inconvenient.

"The car doesn't have a tracker and I'm positive we were not followed."

I didn't ask; he just volunteered the information. I wish he hadn't because now I think we were followed. I don't have bags to unpack or anything to take out of the car. It's just me and my demons wishing we could run back home. I'm trying to be strong but my heart is aching so painfully, my chest is burning.

The cabin has a rustic charm. Under different circumstances, this would be a perfect getaway. The door opens into a space that remains dimly lit even after Tristan switches on the lights. There is a fluffy couch, a small table with a lamp, a storage box next to the couch and a homely fireplace. I don't get to fully take in the space because Tristan rudely tells me to get out of his way. For the life of me, I can't figure out why this guy hates me. He was snitching for the enemy I slept with. The way I see it, we should be friends.

I dump myself on the couch as he disappears behind one of the doors. He's gone for a while. I'm about to go and look for him when he appears through the door.

"Get a bottle of vodka in the kitchen somewhere."

Is he asking or commanding me? You know what, let me shame him by actually going to get it. I almost make a joke about the hazards of drinking while on the run but I don't think he'll find it funny. I also don't have the correct energy to deliver it well.

I find a bottle of Grey Goose in the cabinet and return to Tristan. He grabs the bottle like a barbarian and I internally shake my head. Where I come from, we practise good manners. We also say thank you. He doesn't even offer me some, and he guzzles it unceremoniously. I brought him a glass but I guess savages prefer drinking straight from the bottle.

Awkward cannot even begin to describe the atmosphere. I'm just sitting on the couch going through the most, and he's drinking like he's in a competition. Doesn't he want to dash it?

"Please tell me where we are and what's going on. Please." I add the extra please to try and bring out some light to defuse the hatred exuding from his pores.

He looks at me, then away, and starts reading the label behind the bottle. I honestly don't understand why he's mad. I know he doesn't want to be here. I don't either. So can he bring me up to speed and tell me everything already! He should be showing me kindness. We worked pretty well together in the past, and there was a time or two when he smiled at me. I thought like Hilton, we were friends of some sort.

"Where's the bathroom?"

He points to a door.

"I'm not going to run away, so no need to follow me," I try to lighten up the mood.

He doesn't react. He just looks at me in a Hiltony way. *Ja ne!* It's going to be a long stay.

As the door shuts behind me, I get flashbacks of the blood on Chelsea's floor. The weight of it all crashes down on me without warning. The bathroom starts spinning and I feel crammed in the small space. I stumble to the sink and cling to it as if it's my only lifeline, gasping for air and struggling to get enough. When my hands start hurting, I slide down the wall until I'm sitting on the floor. I press my palms hard against my face, feeling the sting of tears as I crush my eyes. I try to pep-talk myself out of it and hang onto reality. I can almost hear Dr. Brown's voice saying '*Breathe, Lotus*', but it's so faint and distant, it fades as fast as I conjured it. What if they go after Ricky? What if they got Don too? What if they come after us? They killed Chelsea! My head begins spinning again until I'm breathing through my mouth and clutching my hair.

*Breathe, Lotus.*

After what feels like a lifetime, my heart rate starts slowing down. I sit there, still shaking, slowly piecing myself back together. I eventually force myself up and wash my face, avoiding my reflection in the mirror. I look like I survived a mental breakdown.

I find Tristan sitting on a chair, with his shoes on the couch. He's looking in my direction but it's like I'm invisible to him.

"I switched on the geyser in case you want to take a shower," he says, shaking his head as if to dismiss a stressful thought.

I don't understand the grudge in his voice. It's as if he wants to cook me in the water when it boils. I want to lie down and hide my head under a pillow but let me be the bigger person first. I'm too exhausted to fight. Since we'll be spending who knows how long under the same roof, it might be better to make peace.

"I'm sorry, Tristan."

"For what?"

Acting ignorant just to make it harder than it already is? What a dick!

"For putting you in this position. I know you don't want to be here."

I get a glimpse of the gun on his waist as he leans back and his shirt rises. Normally, I would be scared, but today I feel nothing. I have brushed skin with death so many times in the near past, the threat of it doesn't faze me anymore. Deep down it's probably because I still believe he wouldn't hurt me.

"I said I'm sorry. I also don't want to be here."

"Whatever, Lotus. You're full of shit. Go to the bedroom and sleep." He takes another gulp of the vodka.

"I'm full of shit?" Excuse me! Talk about audacity! If anyone is full of shit, it's him. And how dare he dismiss me like that!

He snots like the pig he is and sips on the vodka.

"I'm sorry, sir, but you don't get to talk to me like that." I'm ready to fight; let him bring it on so I can take out all my trauma on him. I'm done playing nice.

He humphs in a condescending fashion. "Or what, ma'am?" Pronouncing the 'ma'am' with undiluted mockery.

"I don't understand why I'm the one even apologising here. You people did this to me. You and your brothers and your stupid wars did this to me. I shouldn't be here! I should be with my son and my friend! You all did this!" I raise my voice, not even trying to keep my temper in check.

"I did this? You think I'm enjoying this? Being out here guarding your ungrateful ass when I have better things to do? Cleaning up your messes at every turn? Getting blood on my hands for you? You think I enjoy it?"

"You know what..."

He cuts me off. "You think I like being on the run? This is exactly why a Wolf shouldn't have a woman. Alpha should have known better."

"Fuck you, Tristan! My friend could be dead for all I know yet you're here being an asshole! Fuck you very much!"

"You fucked Dalu and started all this mess, so don't you dare!"

"Oh yeah? And you're a snitch! You were Dalu's little bitch so I guess we both fucked him. You're a bottom-barrel rat who sold his own pack. You got your brothers killed. Shame on you!"

I see hurt flash across his eyes and he fails to blink it away. I almost feel guilty for lashing out at him but I quickly remember that he deserves it. Traitors don't deserve anything less than contempt from me. How dare he! I'm the victim here, so fuck him to hell and back.

He parts his lips and closes them again. It's good to know he's human after all and has feelings too, but I won't backslide. I purse my lips and avoid eye contact. I won't allow myself to feel bad for anything I said. Screw him! He takes a long gulp of the vodka and I hurl obscenities at him in my head.

"Where will I sleep, Tristan?" I make sure to pronounce his name as harshly as possible so he knows there is no endearment from my end.

"Why? Are you done throwing tantrums?"

"Whatever!"

"Lotus," he calls after me as I walk away. "Not that one. The door to your right."

The door opens to a quaint room with a bed covered in a cream duvet. I draw back a heavy curtain and cough as the dust fills my nose. The window sill, like the curtain, is dusty. It looks like no one has been here in a while. We really are in the middle of nowhere. There is nothing but bushes, grass and muddy water in sight.

I wish I had my phone. I hope Ricky is okay. The nanny is very good with him but he should be with me. That guilt again; I'm supposed to be going insane for being separated from my child but I'm more worried about Chelsea if anything.

I lie down on the bed and pull the throw over my feet. I stay awake for a while until the gods of sleep eventually show me mercy. That grace doesn't last long as I go straight into a nightmare and wake up kicking.

I pass Tristan on the couch and I don't say a word. I step out of my clothes and stand with water running down my body. All this feels like a strange dream. There is a knock on the door and I turn down the water to listen. I'm showering. What is wrong with him?!

"I brought you towels. I'll open the door and throw them in. I won't look."

The door opens and only his arm shows as he places the towels on the washing basket. I open the water again and continue washing myself. I take my time, soaking every inch of my skin and allowing the water to wash away time. The trickling of the shower is like the sound of summer rain - soothing and gentle. I wish I could stand here forever. I remember the shower I took this morning; it feels like ages ago. I wish Don was here with me. He would find a way to make everything better. Tears run down my face and the water washes them away.

I dry myself, thankful for the towels, and walk to the bedroom. I find a toiletry bag with basics, a new toothbrush, a pair of sweatpants, a T-shirt, socks and a hoodie on the bed. They are oversized but they will do. When I'm done and smelling more macho than an Old Spice man, I go to find Tristan. I find him busy with the pots in the kitchen.

"Just trying to make us something to eat. Wanna help?"

"No, thanks." I'm not here to work. Besides, I'm sure he can handle noodles and tinned stuff. I don't even think what he's doing qualifies as cooking. Preparing sounds more appropriate.

"There's a bottle of wine in the fridge. I'm not sure if it's cold yet."

Someone is going out of his way to apologise. I bet he will do it all but say the words.

Cabernet Sauvignon... Perfect. He had no business putting it in the fridge but I appreciate the effort. I find a glass in the cupboard and fill it to the brim. Bad wine manners but I have a healthy appetite and a lot of emotions to drown.

I go through the kitchen cupboards looking for something to nibble on. "You seriously need to restock on food. There aren't enough snacks here."

"Tell that to Elik when you see him."

"Why Elik?"

"This is his place. He doesn't like people here, so be careful with everything."

I'm surprised. I know the guy is basically a walking bank but I always took him for the villa-by-the-sea type, not a cabin-in-the-woods guy.

"I thought it was Don's place."

"No, it's not. It's Elik's."

"Oh well. You'll find me on the couch."

I had a rough day so this feels good. I wish there was a TV or something to keep me distracted, but the trickling of the river outside is a good alternative. It sounds peaceful and almost reassuring. The wine is hitting all the right spots and slowly drowning my ugly thoughts.

"Need a refill?" Tristan disturbs my thoughts, sliding the side table closer.

I look at him blankly. I'm not ready to play happy families yet. I don't trust him.

"I can pour my own wine."

I'm not sure what he finds so amusing. "I know, but indulge me, please."

I extend my glass, shooting him a defiant look. We can't let our guard down at the first hint of kindness. He owes me an apology.

He goes back to the kitchen and returns with two plates. He really did the most with instant noodles and tinned fish. This is really good!

We eat in silence and I keep running away from my thoughts. I was supposed to have dinner with Chelsea tonight. I was going to make Mac & Cheese with bacon bits, just the way she likes it. The wine is going down well and I'm chugging it like water. My head is feeling lighter by the second, in a good way.

I clear the plates and Tristan is not there when I get back. I snuggle up and reach for my glass.

"Chelsea's in the ICU. It's still touch and go but there's hope," he says when he rejoins me.

"She's alive?" I sit up. The weight that has been on my chest all day lifts and a surge of overwhelming relief washes over me.

"She is. She's not out of the woods yet, and I don't have all the details, so don't ask me. Ulric is good too. Alpha said don't worry about him. He's fine."

This evening is getting better by the second. I can now kick back, relax and enjoy the wine. No more interval breakdowns I've been experiencing today.

"What else did Don say?"

"Nothing much. It was a quick call. He asked if you're alright and I said you are."

I wish I could talk to him, but it's okay. Chelsea is alive, my man is in one piece and my son is alright. I can't think of any better news.

The temperature is dropping, and although the hoodie is doing a decent job at keeping the cold out, I'm still a bit cold. Tristan must have noticed because he offers to make a fire. I would like to help but my princess status doesn't allow me to play in cinders.

He finally gets the fire going and looks very pleased with himself. He lays down a throw on the rug and grabs a cushion from the couch. This is how I imagine Don would look in front of a fireplace, in our holiday house.

"You can join me if you want. It's very warm down here."

"Rephrase that and I just might."

He smiles a little. "May you please come and join me."

I carefully hold my glass and sit close to him. I know I have to take it slow on the alcohol before I make a fool of myself, or worse, pass out. I have already drank too much as is.

"Think we can talk?"

I'm glad he suggested it. I could use a good chat. Anything to forget my troubles really. The wine and the good news have me open-minded and in a forgiving mood.

"Look, I know emotions have been running high and things have been hectic today, but I shouldn't have taken it out on you. I was frustrated with the entire situation. I didn't think things would get this messy. I'm sorry for being... an asshole."

I laugh at that last part, remembering how upset I was when I said that.

"I understand. I'm sorry too for the things I said. Also, thank you for bringing me here and for taking care of me. I'll do my best not to throw any more tantrums."

He chuckles with me and I feel much better. Now he is forgiven!

"So what happens now?" I assume he has been in hiding before so he has experience.

"We just have to wait it out."

"Until when? What exactly is happening?"

"It's complicated. It's a whole web of disaster and I don't know how to break it down for you... if I'm even allowed to."

Come on now. He watched me get rid of Alphas, break into Dalu's apartment and outsmart Dalu. He was with me when my father got shot and before Dalu left us. Surely he knows I can handle anything.

"Tell me something, anything. Help me understand what's going on. You know you can trust me."

"How about I make you a promise instead? How about we just chill tonight and talk about nothing serious, and then tomorrow I tell you everything? Can we do that?"

It sounds like a fair deal, so I take it.

"Can we gossip about people too? Because you know the people in our circles have interesting lives."

"Gossip is not my style but I'm a fast learner."

It's not long before we are laughing like old friends. He has the most hilarious stories in the world. It's refreshing to see this side of him. I didn't think he was capable of letting his hair down like this. He doesn't believe any of my stories although all of them are true. Me, I have lived guys!

"So Caleb and Chelsea, how's that going for real? She said they're very solid now but I would love to know if Caleb is on the same page. No one else will tell me. You know I would much sooner get water out of a rock than gossip out of Don."

"He's pretty serious about her actually. It's kinda hard dating your friend's ex but they're getting there. And Chelsea is very pretty, so I understand where my brother is coming from. He's thinking of his children; I respect that."

"How could you say that!"

"Well, dating for looks is justified in my opinion. Kids get bullied at school, you know?"

He's so stupid, I can't help but laugh.

"Personally, I wouldn't eat a friend's leftovers, but Caleb is a better man than me."

"Come on. Chelsea is not a bad person. She has a big heart and Elik is hardly her ex. You guys exaggerated everything. She slept with Elik way before Caleb!"

"I don't know. I mean, she kinda slept with him again, or tried to, while she was with Caleb. Does that sound like a good person to you?"

I can't exactly defend that so change of topic it is.

"How's Elik in this mess? He doesn't fit the Wolf profile at all."

"I guess we all dig holes until one day we realise we dug too deep and can't get out. He's not a Wolf, but he's Alpha's friend, so he's guilty by association."

"How did they even become friends? That part baffles me. They're worlds apart."

"It's a long story, but just like me, he's paying off his debt and trying to get out."

"What do you mean?"

"Let's leave that for tomorrow. We promised not to talk about serious stuff tonight. How about you tell me about you and Hilton? How are you tight with the most feared Wolf? You're the only person he likes."

I smile and sip my wine. My sweet Hilly. The fact that no one else is as close to him as I am makes me love him even more.

"Do you have any idea how much he has done for you? How did you manage that?" He continues probing.

"I annoyed him into submission. I understand Hilton and he understands me. We make a great team... and no, Tristan, I've never had sex with Hilton. Eww!" I know he was thinking it.

"I didn't say anything," he chuckles. "Your lucky charm is strong. Hilton? I'm scared of him. We all are!"

"He's a great guy once you get to know him."

"No, he's not!"

"He is though. He's like the big brother I never had. He's just amazing."

"You know what, I won't even try to understand it."

"He's not bad, come on. Hilton is a sweetheart." I laugh at myself because sweetheart is not a good word to describe Hilton.

"A sweetheart? What do you guys even talk about?"

"I do most of the talking. He's a great listener. Can you believe we once watched a movie together from start to finish, popcorn and all?"

"No way!"

"I promise you. I've never seen Don so surprised in my life."

"What? I don't believe it! ... And speaking of Alpha, you never thought it creepy how he asked you out? An average girl would have run for the hills, or to the police station, or left the country altogether. But you jumped into his car and made a baby with him."

"I guess I'm not average. I don't know why it didn't scare me off. It was quite romantic if anything."

"Romantic? Well, I guess you have a way of taming devils. Here's to you." He lifts his glass for a toast.

"And you? Do you have someone in your life?"

"Nope. Love is not exactly my thing. I'm not up for commitment or anything long-term."

I won't judge.

I'm feeling so warm, tipsy and happy. I take off the hoodie. I wish I could take off the sweatpants too, but that would be grossly inappropriate, especially considering that I don't have panties on. We talk about a lot of random things until we are right back to talking about Chelsea.

"I met Chelsea in varsity. We kind of dated the same guy and we became friends from there. We've been best friends for years now. How was varsity for you?"

"It was insane! The house parties were out of this world." He tells me about his years at the University of Cape Town. I think those were the happiest days of his life.

"So how did you meet Dalu? Was it at a house party?"

"We said tomorrow."

I lift my hands in surrender and we laugh as if a joke was told.

"But seriously, Tristan. Why is someone like you mixed up in this mess of a life?"

"I could ask you the same question."

"Touché." We toast to that.

I laugh so hard at something he says, I spill some wine on my lap. I try to wipe it away only to spill the rest on the floor.

"Elik is going to kill us." He goes to the kitchen and returns with a dishcloth, a mop and another bottle of wine.

* * * * *

I'm not sure when I dozed off, but when I wake up, I'm sweaty and covered in a throw. The fire is dying down so it's pretty dark in the room. Tristan is sleeping next to me, snoring softly. I put a cushion under his head, careful not to wake him up, and extend the throw to cover him up as well. I snuggle back into warmth and go back to sleep.

# *FORTY FOUR*

My bladder wakes me up. I'm surprised that it's already morning. I'm alone on the rug in front of the dead fire. I drag myself up and I find Tristan in the kitchen wearing the uniform of the Wolves - sweatpants, sneakers and a hoodie. Only now it registers that I'm wearing his clothes. I don't know who I thought they belonged to.

I lean against the door frame, watching him. He has his face buried in his hands, with his elbows on the kitchen counter. The sleeves of his hoodie are rolled up, exposing the faded ink of an old tattoo in Roman numerals. His hair is sitting in small curls on his head, and the tiny ink of a cross on his ring finger looks like a birthmark. He looks like art.

"Tristan."

He doesn't respond. I call again but he doesn't respond again. I peel his hands off and he sighs and lifts his head.

"What's wrong?"

"Everything." He gets up and fills the kettle with water and switches it on, keeping his face away from me the whole time.

"Slept alright?" he asks without looking back.

"I did. And you?"

"I didn't sleep much. I had to get up and read."

"Read?" I sit on the bar stool and dangle my feet.

"Yup." He turns around, takes out a small pack of weed, smoothly rolls a joint and lights it up.

"You want?" He offers it to me.

"No, thanks." I get off the chair when the water is boiling. I could use a strong cup of coffee. "How many sugars for you?"

"Coffee should never be taken with sugar."

Oh, he's one of those coffee extremists. I hand him a cup and sit back with mine.

"How long do you think we're going to be here?"

"Hopefully not long. I have an exam on Friday."

"This Friday?"

"Yup. I have a lot of studying to do and I'd be happy to be out of here by Thursday."

"I'll pray for you."

He gives me a suspicious look and takes a puff on his joint.

"You know your friend took a bullet for you," he says after a moment of silence.

"What do you mean?"

"She left Gordon's Bay in your car. To people who don't know the two of you, she fits your profile. They were targeting you."

I thought about it yesterday, but having it confirmed makes it too real. If Chelsea dies, I'll never forgive myself.

"There's no point in beating yourself up about it." He puts out the almost-finished joint in a glass and gestures for me to follow him to the living room.

He gets the fire going in no time while I sit on the couch.

"Can I ask you something?"

"Shoot."

"Am I the reason for this war?"

He looks at me as if he thinks the truth will hurt me. "Dalu was Viper's son."

"So yes?"

"Not entirely. The current chaos is because Viper is grieving his son and he's making a spectacle of it. He doesn't know who to blame, so he's blaming the Wolves... and you. He's got it in his head that you messed up his son's life. He believes you pushed him off the rails."

"Me? I didn't drive Dalubuhle mad."

"Well, Viper doesn't know that. Dalu's sister blamed you for everything."

"I didn't though! He was already a nut case." It's unfair how people keep blaming me for everything.

"In his heart, he probably knows it, but acknowledging it would force him to admit he messed up as a father. Men like Viper don't easily own up to their mistakes."

I feel goosebumps on my skin. Does this mean when they realise they got the wrong girl they will come after me?

"It's bigger than you. At the end of the day, it's all about survival. Everyone wants more turf, more shebeens and more clubs in Longstreet. Everyone wants to rule Cape Town. It's kill before you get killed. So it's way above you. You're collateral if anything."

"But still, I feel bad about Dalu."

"Don't. Dalubuhle wasn't going to stop until you were dead. He wanted Ulric with everything in him. So don't feel bad... The weak always pass away anyway." The way he said that last part was dark.

"He blamed me for everything that went wrong in his life, and he won't let me rest even in death. Now I have people after me."

"Unfairly so. I knew Dalu very well, and trust me, it was never you. He had deep-seated issues... Can we talk about this later?"

I drink my coffee and stop myself from asking more questions.

"You're with the Wolves. Dalu was with the Hard Livings. They're brutal. He was an enemy; you need to start seeing him that way."

He's right. I need to stop feeling bad.

"You never told me how you joined the Wolves," I steer the conversation in another direction. All the Wolves have a different origin story and they are all fascinating.

"I wanted to be like Caleb so bad that by the time I realised what I'd gotten myself into, it was too late. The General made me feel important, and despite everything Caleb said, I signed up."

That's exactly what the General did with Don. What a monster! Preying on innocent children. Yet the mention of his name shifts something in my spirit. I still wish we had been allowed a chance.

"I don't hate it though, if you're wondering. It's just an inconvenience sometimes. Taking orders infringes on my freedom, but I get by alright. I guess I found my balance."

"If you don't hate it, why do you want out?" I sit up straight and push away the thoughts of my father that were threatening to paralyse me.

"I've paid my dues. It's time for a new adventure. Can we talk about this later?"

Agh, so what are we supposed to talk about now?

"You know, for the longest time, I didn't know that Caleb was your brother. I'd have never guessed."

"Why? Because I'm so much cooler than him?"

"Well, about that, the jury is still out."

He smiles sweetly and I warm up inside.

"What do you need an MBA for?" I pick up the book he was reading. "No one needs a degree to sell drugs."

"Wow! You're so shady. I'm in business. It comes in handy."

"It doesn't make any sense... Anyway, you never told me how exactly you knew Dalu." I close the book and put it aside.

He looks away as if it's a sensitive topic. "We were good friends. We even stayed together at some point... We go way back."

*Went.* "No way!"

"Yup! Why do you think Caleb kept letting him off the hook? He saw him as my innocent friend macking on Alpha's girl. I hadn't told anyone who exactly he was. We were really tight at some point. I didn't know he was Viper's son then."

"So many things don't make sense to me. How was his father even the boss of the Hard Livings? I met him once, and nothing about him said gangster."

"Why not? Is it because he wore suits and lived in a mansion?"

"Exactly that."

"I suppose not everyone comes branded like Alpha."

"That's a good one." I'll give him that. "So when I was sneaking around with Dalu, you knew?"

"Every last detail. I knew way more than I wished to know. I shouldn't be telling you this but he actually loved you and saw a future with you. He was ready to propose to you and everything. He was obsessed with you in an unhealthy way. So when you two didn't work out, it hit him hard. He started defaulting on his meds and it was downhill from there."

"Meds were not a recent thing?"

"No. He always had a personality disorder because of some dark shit that happened in his childhood, so the meds kept him together."

"He never told me any of that."

"Did you ever give him the chance to?" I don't like his eye.

I wish he hadn't told me that Dalu loved me. Now guilt is feasting on me. I want to ask how much Dalu told him about me, but I don't think I want to know anymore. I sense that he's not telling me everything about him and Dalu. I'll wait till after alcohol has been served.

"Remember when Alpha came to see you in the Eastern Cape but had to quickly come back?"

"Yes."

"He had come to get you. The war was finally over. We had won. I don't think I've ever seen him that excited. But then you had told Dalu our secrets and they now knew where to strike. So Alpha had to turn around and leave you behind."

He shouldn't tell me these things. They are hurtful.

A moment of silence follows as I grapple with my thoughts.

"I was mad at you because everything was falling apart all over again because of you. You told Dalu too much and armed Viper with secrets he never should have known. We lost good guys because of you, yet all you did was complain about how everyone wasn't acting right around you."

Now I feel terrible. Also, he's being hypocritical, but for peace's sake, I won't point it out. He did the exact same thing. I'm better because it wasn't intentional.

"How did Don not find out?"

"I think he has always known, but I guess it's true that love is blind. He probably refused to believe it or he chose to turn a blind eye, I don't know. But there's no way Alpha didn't know anything. Maybe not all of it. But whatever he knows, he didn't hear it from me."

"I really messed up."

"That you did... My turn to ask questions. Why did you throw away your entire life for a life you had no business being a part of?"

"Just like you, when I realised what I had gotten myself into, it was too late. I was in love, and you know how stupid love makes us."

"No, I don't know. I think with my head."

"Mxm, you're so stupid." I want to throw a feather at him.

We both laugh and he maintains that falling in love is the worst thing anyone can ever do.

"Tell me, do you plan on going back to school or getting a job and having your own career?"

"I've thought about it but I don't think it will happen."

"Why not?"

"I don't see myself studying and stressing about deadlines. Those days are behind me. As for work, I'd love to go back to work. It gave me a purpose. But there are no jobs out there, and when I think of all the stress I went through job hunting, I give up. I don't have the strength to deal with rejections every day."

"Well, there's no shame in being a kept woman. Don't feel pressured."

"Not having anything going on in your life gets boring and leads you to trouble. Look at my past year. Too much free time is a bad thing."

"Trouble can find you at work as well. You met Dalu at work."

"Touché." He's silly but he's right.

"You know what you should do? Open a salon or something and be your own boss. Wash some of Alpha's money. Then have a bank account you don't tell Alpha about and stash away as much as possible for yourself. You never know when it will rain."

"I could do that? Where would I get the money to start up?"

"Come on. You're Alpha's woman. You can get anything you want. You need to start being smart and take care of yourself. There are no guarantees in this line of work, so cover yourself as much as possible."

Fierce once suggested something like that. I'll definitely work on it.

"Have you ever thought of leaving Cape Town?" My turn to ask.

"All the time. I'm moving to Europe soon. This right here is my last debt to Alpha and the pack, then I'm out. I'm done. I need a fresh start."

"What? Does Don know this?"

"Of course. It was his idea, to get out, that is. We all fought hard to have him as the one Alpha because he's a good guy. He can release anyone from the pack if he feels like they have paid their dues and served the family well. Only a General had that power. So with Alpha as our leader, the decision is his to make."

That makes me proud. Don really is a good leader. And you know what they say about the women behind every successful man.

"That's beautiful." I'm really happy for him but I don't have the right words to express it. "Where in Europe are you going? Do you have a plan?" We don't want him homeless on a foreign continent.

"Germany. I'll be staying with a friend there. You might know him. Elik's little brother, Kofi."

"I know Kofi! You boys are going to be a problem together."

He laughs but he knows I'm right. They look too good for their own good.

"I already have my visa, a job and all. Everything is set."

"What? How did you manage that with your criminal record?"

"Who said I have a criminal record?"

"Well..." Does he want me to spell out the obvious? We all know that they have to kill a member of a rival gang to join the Wolves, and they have to kill their first girlfriends to complete their initiation. And as a Runner, his portfolio is full of many petty crimes. If all that doesn't get someone a criminal record then I don't know what can.

"You only get a criminal record if you get caught. I've never been accused of anything in my life. I'm not a criminal. I'm as clean as they come." He laughs. Even he knows that's funny.

"This is also Elik's last service. After this, he's out," he volunteers the information.

"What does that mean exactly?"

"Elik was introduced to Alpha by his friend, Lumka. Alpha and Elik hit it off and became tight friends. Then they started trading skills. When Alpha wanted something clean done, Elik would handle it, and when Elik wanted something dirty done, Alpha would handle it. Then some guy hurt Elik's girl badly but she didn't open a case, so he was going to walk. Elik couldn't accept that. So Alpha had to pull a lot of strings to set the guy up and get him into Pollsmoor. So Elik now owed Alpha beyond the usual favours and he's been working it off. Do you see why I don't dabble in love and attachments? It comes with a lot of unnecessary baggage."

"Information overload." I'm shocked, but I'm really happy that they are getting out. "You deserve a break. Europe will be very good for you."

"My bags are already packed. That's how much I can't wait."

We spend the afternoon watching movies on his laptop, in the bedroom. We finish a bottle of wine and laugh at how much Elik will be upset with us. By the time we leave this cabin, his little cellar will be empty.

Tristan falls asleep and I cover him with a blanket before going to the kitchen. I put a bottle of chardonnay in the fridge then look around in the cupboards. I'm going to make us dinner today. There isn't much to work with, so I opt for pasta and make sauce with tinned meatballs and chilli sauce.

I take a long shower afterwards and change into one of Tristan's T-shirts. It sucks that he has a bag of clothes and I don't. He says he always keeps a bag in the car for situations like these.

I go through the small pile of books in the storage box and settle for a romantic novel. I lie down on the rug, using one of the cushions as a pillow, and get lost in the pages. I'm dozing badly but I struggle on because the story is good and the erotic scenes have me hot and bothered and missing Don.

Tristan joins me over an hour later, looking well-rested. We chat as he gets comfortable on the couch with his textbook. I continue reading my novel, sprawled out on the cosy rug, my eyes staying open at all cost because I need to know what happens next. He is engrossed in his textbook and is taking down notes and using highlighters, reminding me of high school. After a long time, he calls time out. I'm done for the day too. I'll finish the book tomorrow.

"I need a drink."

"Drinking on an empty stomach is never a good idea. I cooked. Should we eat first?"

"That's awesome. I'm starving."

"Cool. Make the fire, I'll get the food." We put out the fire when we went to the bedroom earlier. The last thing we wanted was to wake up to a burning cabin.

I head to the kitchen to warm up the food. When it's sizzling hot, I dish it out and pour the wine into glasses. I hand Tristan his plate and glass and return to the kitchen for mine. I perch on the couch with my glass, waiting for the fire to get hot and the food to cool down.

The food is really good, if I do say so myself, and the wine complements it perfectly. What can I say? Food-Alcohol pairings are my forte.

We are laughing easily, joking and sharing the wildest stories. He clears the plates when we are done and joins me on the couch when he returns.

He takes a dramatic sip of his wine before setting the glass down ."Do you really want to know about me and Dalu?"

"I do." I shift to face him.

"Swear that everything we'll talk about will stay between us."

"Cross my heart and hope to die." I draw an X over my heart.

"It's a long story."

"I have all night." I lean back, settling in.

"The first time I saw him, I was walking up the Jammie steps at UCT, and he was walking down. Ever get that feeling when someone stares at you like they know you from somewhere? I got that feeling when I passed him. An hour later, I came down the same route. Guess who I found at the bottom of the stairs? Dalubuhle. I played it cool, acted like I didn't notice, but I was low-key curious. I greeted him and asked his name. He told me and he said he was waiting for a friend. Fast forward, he popped up everywhere. I'm not saying he was stalking me, but let's just say he was conveniently where I was more often than normal."

"That's creepy!" I don't know how he saw it as a sign to start a friendship.

"That probably should have been a red flag. Anyway, it turned out we had a mutual friend, and we clicked. I get it, I get it, total rookie move on my part. I should've seen the signs, right?"

"Yes, but I'm not judging. Carry on."

"One day I was venting about how the cost of living was eating up my paycheque and Dalu offered me to crash at his place rent-free. It was tempting, I won't lie, but I don't accept handouts."

"Rent-free? I know I would have jumped on it."

"I don't accept handouts. Free things are expensive. Besides, he had a roommate at the time because his father was trying to teach him a lesson or something like that."

"You're a better human than me. Roommate or not, he wouldn't have had to ask me twice. Rent-free in a posh apartment?"

"Not me. I love my space. But I took him up on the offer during exam time."

"How was Dalu as a friend? What did you guys get up to?"

"We always had something happening. House parties, clubs, and his crew loved Brass Bell in Kalk Bay, so we were there often. Festivals, concerts, carnivals, you name it. Dalu always got VIP tickets and handled the alcohol bill. He showed me a whole new side of Cape Town. By third year, we were best friends."

He looks at the wall as if what happened next is too painful to handle. I wait patiently, sipping on my wine.

"Then out of nowhere, he asked if I was in a gang. He got mad that I hadn't told him about my life outside him, but I explained myself and he said he understood. We were back to partying the next week. Everything went back to normal."

He stops talking and looks into the fire.

"Fourth year, he was throwing a birthday party at his pad. I had to work that night. I was working at one of our clubs but I thought I could swing by the party, drop off the weed and ecstasy he ordered, and make a quick exit. I couldn't miss my best friend's celebration. I got there and he insisted I stay for a beer. I figured one drink wouldn't hurt. We ended up on the balcony, chatting about our post-graduation plans."

He looks like he's fighting back bad memories. I don't rush him.

"Then he said he was going to open the whiskey he'd saved for his birthday. I was smoking a joint so I remained outside. He went in, and after a while, he came back with a glass for me. Soon after, I started feeling weird. I drank water but it didn't get better. He suggested I sleep it off. He left me in his room and returned to the party."

He did the same to me in Port Elizabeth. That bastard! I don't say it out loud to avoid derailing the story.

"Then what happened?" I ask when he has been quiet for too long.

"I woke up naked." He looks at me with glassy eyes and I wipe away the lone tear that escaped my eye. He took me back to that hotel room in Port Elizabeth. I was helpless and terrified. An image of Dalu smiling down at me crosses my mind and I reach for Tristan's hand and squeeze it.

"I was confused and had a headache from hell. I quickly dressed up and left for my place. I felt sick all day. I couldn't remember anything. Dalu wasn't answering his phone, and not knowing what had happened was driving me crazy. I finally saw him on campus days later, and he tried to act like he didn't know what I was talking about. That's when I met the real Dalubuhle for the first time. He had drugged me, shut down his party, undressed both of us and got into bed with me. He took pictures of us naked in all sorts of positions, including one with my dick in his mouth. I've never felt more violated. I couldn't understand why he did all that. I threatened to kill him but he said the Wolves would have those pictures before his body went cold. I couldn't afford that. The Creed explicitly forbids same-sex relationships. Only the 28s can sodomise, but even then, it's not a consensual relationship. I was screwed. The pictures looked like we were a couple. Then he dropped the bomb - he was with the Hard Livings. He also threatened to get me expelled for selling drugs. I couldn't afford that either. I needed that degree. To stop him from exposing me, I had to feed him information about the Wolves."

I move closer and rest my head on his shoulder. We sit in silence, watching the fire crackling.

"The first time I snitched, he recorded me. Now he had more evidence to blackmail me with. If, by whatever miracle, I survived the pictures, my brothers would execute me for being a rat."

"What a prick!"

"I had you break into his place that time not because I cared about what he had on the Wolves. I didn't give a damn about that. I just needed to make sure my pictures weren't part of his evidence."

Makes sense now. I'm glad I could help.

"So you never told anyone?"

"Not for years. I only told someone when things got out of control."

"Caleb?"

"Hilton."

"What? No!" I lift my head and look at him.

"Yes. I didn't know what else to do. My brothers were dying; I couldn't stomach it anymore. So I went to Hilton and asked for his protection and pledged my life in exchange. I was ready for the worst. Surprisingly, he understood. He said we had to work together to use Dalu to reel in the big fish. Offing him wouldn't cut it. We needed to reach the higher-ups. And it worked because he led us to the big dogs of the Hard Livings, and eventually, he led us to Viper and the General. All Hilton wanted in exchange was one favour down the line, no questions asked."

"What favour?"

"He cashed in that favour to save you and me. He used it to save us. That's why I followed you that day and took care of Dalu. With Dalu gone, we would both be free at last. That's what Hilton called in his favour for."

Wow, Hilly. I wish he was here so I could give him a big hug. I'm so touched, I can't help the tears. I hug Tristan because I need to hide my face and I don't know how to comfort him without making it all about me. He holds on to me and breaks down. That sends me over the edge because I have never seen him this human before.

# *FORTY FIVE*

Tristan wakes me up in the morning, all dressed up and looking dapper.

"I need to get going. I'll be back as soon as I finish writing. Please don't go outside."

"I wasn't planning to."

"Cool then. We'll talk when I get back. Don't panic if I'm late."

I wasn't going to panic but now he has planted the thought.

"Do you need me to bring anything?"

"Yes, please. Panties. Just grab a pack in any shop, medium, don't mind the style."

He raises an eyebrow. I will not explain how I have been surviving on one underwear the whole time, alternating between wearing it and going commando when it's washed.

"Get us food too. Bring pizza, burgers, wings and a lot of snacks. Maybe get gin and tonic too. That should last longer than wine."

"Alright. Anything else?"

"Will you be going past the house?"

"Unfortunately not."

"I thought as much but just had to ask."

"If there's nothing else, I'll see you later."

"Good luck. Remember 50% is a pass."

"50% is never good enough."

"Nerd!"

He locks the door from the outside and I hear the car kicking off.

We have grown pretty close. He sleeps on the couch and I sleep in the bedroom but we spend most of the time on the couch or on the floor. We watch movies on his laptop and we laugh a lot and dream big together. We wake up nursing hangovers every morning only to drink ourselves stupid again.

I need to take a nap, shower and eat, in that order.

I lie down with the novel I was reading until I doze off. I wake up around noon and I'm so bored. It's lonely without Tristan around.

By 4 pm, I have finished the novel and now I don't know what to do with my life. Seriously, why do writers leave us hanging like this? Why do they write series? Where the hell am I supposed to find book two now? Agh! I'm so annoyed! I might as well take another nap.

"Hey, sleepyhead," Tristan wakes me up.

"Hey. You're back early."

"It's 6 pm."

"I expected you later. How was the exam?" I push the blanket back and try to fully wake up.

"Not bad. How was the rest of your day?"

"It was alright... Gosh, I'm starving."

"Good, because then the food won't go to waste."

"Give me a minute. I'll be with you just now."

He closes the door and I get out of bed and put on a hoodie before joining him in the living room.

I want to eat everything all at once. I haven't had good food in days.

"I have good news and bad news. Which one do you want first?"

"Good first."

"We're going home in two days."

"What? Are you serious?"

"Why would I randomly lie like that?"

"Yes! Finally, I'm going to see Ricky! That's so exciting. Although I was getting used to this place."

"I'm sure you and Alpha can always come back. Elik is cool people."

"You said he doesn't like people here."

"Yet we're here, so clearly he has exceptions."

"Fair enough. What's the bad news?"

"Alpha won't be around when you get home."

"Where will he be?"

"Out of town."

"Oh." I won't let that spoil my mood. I'm going to see my son.

"Oh, and Chelsea is doing great. They said she's going to make a full recovery."

Now that is good news! I look to heaven and say thank you.

"So what changed? Why are we going home?"

"Viper was found dead in his cell. No one knows what happened." He looks at me and I understand. We all know what happened.

"That's good."

"With him gone, there can finally be peace. Too much has been lost in the war."

"Does that mean no more gang wars whatsoever?"

"There might be occasional scuffles, but nothing on the scale of the chaos we've seen this year. Alpha is going out of town for a sit-down with the Peacemakers. All the big shots from all gangs will be there. They need to declare a truce and lay down some ground rules to prevent another all-out war like what we've been through."

I wish he could see how happy this news is making me. Even the food is tasting nicer.

"Why are they meeting out of town though? Isn't Cape Town better?"

"They all need to be away from home ground. It's more peaceful that way."

"I see... Tris, I need a favour."

"No, I'm not killing any more for you." His attempt at a serious face crumbles quickly.

"Wow! It's not that."

"Then what is it?"

"I have crystal meth worth about fifty thousand rands. Can you please push it for me before you, uhm, resign?"

"Where did you get it? I don't want any trouble."

"Don gave it to me before I left Cape Town. I'll never be able to push it myself and I don't want Don knowing about the money I'll get from it."

"No promises but I'll see what I can do."

"Thank you. You'll get a decent cut."

Now he's seriously considering it. Men and money!

We resume talking about everything and nothing, stuffing our faces, and laughing late into the night.

# FORTY SIX

It's trauma upon trauma with me. Dr. Brown has her work cut out for her with me *shame*. I got back home on Sunday afternoon and spent the day with my son. The next morning, I went to the hospital to see Chelsea. Imagine my surprise when I saw my name on a no-entry list, complete with a picture! I wasn't allowed anywhere near Chelsea.

I'm gutted. I'm physically, emotionally and spiritually gutted. Chelsea's number hasn't been going through so I haven't spoken to her since the shooting. Caleb said he couldn't help me. I don't know if that meant he didn't want to or he wasn't able to. I didn't push him because he's not handling Chelsea's hospitalisation very well. I left her a thousand messages on Instagram but none of them have been read and my WhatsApp messages to her only have one tick. I just need to know how she's doing, that's all. I don't think she's the one who put me on the no-entry list. It must be her father.

I'm not sure what to do. Should I call her mother or should I wait it out? I keep opening her mother's number and closing my phone. I'm scared of the questions she might ask me. Chelsea would have easily called my mother if roles were reversed. Her mother likes me though, so you know what, let me just call her.

"Hello, mum. It's Lotus."

A brief silence follows and I silently breathe through my mouth.

"I know. How can I help you?"

"May I please speak to Chelsea."

"No, Lotus, you cannot."

"Mum?"

"I need you to leave my daughter alone. How much must she go through because of her friendship with you? If she stays friends with you, she will die. Is that what you want?"

The words hit me like a punch to the gut. I close my fist and fight to find my voice. "No."

"Good. Then leave her alone."

I don't know what to say, so I just swallow the lump in my throat. "Please let me speak to her."

"No, Lotus! If you really care about Chelsea, you'll never contact her again. Stay away from my daughter and my family."

"Mum, please."

"Goodbye, Lotus."

I slump back on the bed and close my eyes to process the pain. I thought she would ask me what happened and why I haven't visited yet. I didn't expect her to slam the door in my face like that. I want to respect her wishes but it feels like tearing away a piece of my own soul. Maybe I should put on a wig, hat and shades, and sneak into the hospital. Chelsea's face flashes in my mind. I wish she had stayed away forever. I was finally over her. I need to distract myself before I drown in my thoughts. I think I will go for a run.

\* \* \* \* \*

I needed that long shower after the run. I feel so much better now. I get comfortable on the bed and journal my thoughts. I'm so lost in my own world, I don't hear the door open.

"*Skat.*"

"Hey, baby. You got me flowers?" Don has a colourful bouquet in his hands and a smile to match it.

"Elik bought them and gave them to me to give to you."

He knows he could have lied, right? But that just made me smile even more. He's so innocently honest, it makes me mushy every time. I get up and hug him.

"Thank you. Tell Elik I said thank you."

He loosens the hold but doesn't let me go. "What's wrong?"

"Nothing." How did he see past my smile?

"It's me you're talking to. What's wrong?"

"Let me get a vase for the flowers then we can talk."

He walks behind me, whistling and goofing around, and today more than ever, I'm grateful for his silly remarks and over-exaggerated compliments.

He talks my ears off as I cut the stems and arrange the flowers in a vase. I don't know why he's so excited today. When I'm done, I grab a bottle of juice for myself and a beer for him and we go outside.

I don't think I appreciate this house enough. It's more than I could have ever asked for. The size, the architecture, the view of the ocean - it's gorgeous. I just haven't really made it my own. I was too consumed in Don's world to take care of things. I need to do better with the decor and art pieces. I also need to do something about the braai area outside.

We sit in silence for a bit, just taking it all in. The sound of the waves, the warm colours of the sky, the seagulls gliding overhead, the whisper of the breeze - it's perfect.

"So what's wrong?"

I thought he had forgotten.

I take a sip of my juice and organise my words.

"It's Chelsea. I called her mother to check on her but she told me to never contact her or Chelsea again. She was very harsh."

His face softens and he wraps his arm around me. I'm glad he doesn't say anything. He has a way of making things worse with his poor choice of words.

"I want to be there for her, but they won't let me."

"I'm not taking her side but you have to understand where she's coming from. Her daughter was shot, my angel. She almost died. You can't blame her for wanting to protect her child."

He's right, but I don't need to hear that right now.

"She's in the hospital because of me. I have to see her."

"No, she's in the hospital because of the Hard Livings. You're not responsible for that. Stay away from her until she's out of the hospital and can make her own decisions."

I rest my head on his shoulder and look out into the ocean. I want to rant about how unfair it is but he has made it clear which side he's on.

"I've been meaning to talk to you about something," he breaks the silence.

"Yeah?"

"We need to move from this house. Too much has happened here."

I raise my head and face him.

"You want to sell this house? I love this house!"

"Not sell. I'll keep it but we won't live here anymore."

"Where would we move to?"

"Rondebosch maybe? Your choice. We need to move closer to good schools for Ulric."

It makes sense but I'm attached to this house. I used to want to live in the southern suburbs. I remember the first time I saw Elik and Fierce's house. I wanted that life, but this house has grown on me.

"Would we be safer there?" The only reason I would consider moving is if he thinks this house will be raided again.

"We will be. Too much has happened here. I can't have my family living in a stash house. I need to get you and Ricky away from this world."

He has a point. We are practically living in a crime hub.

"Okay." I need to process it some more but I won't argue with him right now. It's not a bad idea. Staying in a big house in Rondebosch doesn't sound too bad. Plus it will be closer to town and everything. It will be good for Ricky too. We are too far out here.

"One more thing."

"There's more?"

He shifts and takes both my hands in his.

"Marry me, my *skat.*"

"What?" He can't have said that so casually, so maybe I misunderstood.

"Be my wife. Let's go all the way."

"Are you joking? Are you serious?"

"I'm serious. Marry me."

If this is a dream, I'll be very pissed when I wake up!

"Donavan?"

"Yes, my angel."

My eyes widen and my mouth hangs open. I can't stop blinking.

"So?" He slightly raises an eyebrow.

"Yes! Oh, my God, yes! Yes, I'll marry you! Yes!"

I pull him up with me and jump on him, my legs closing around his waist.

"I love you so much," I say between the kisses.

"I love you too, my angel."

He walks to the braai area and sits down with me facing him. My legs are around his waist, my arms are draped over his shoulders and my lips keep finding his.

"We have to do the traditional ceremony first. Oh my goodness, what am I going to wear? Are you open to matching outfits? We have to do the *lobola* first before the wedding." My excitement dies as if a switch was flipped and I feel life drain out of my face.

"What's wrong?"

"I have to go home."

I can't get married without mending things with my family. I don't even know what I'll do. I don't have anyone to be with me on my big day. No Chelsea, no Fierce, no grandmother, no mother, no father, no one.

"We don't have to go the long route if it complicates things for you. We can go to court and sign."

"Are you crazy? We're going all the way!"

"But..."

"Don't say it, baby."

"All I'm saying is don't overthink it. Everything will work out as it should."

I know he means well but he's not helping.

"Can I ask you something? Was asking to marry me your idea or did one of your friends put you to it?"

"It was my idea. I love you, Lotus, and I want you to be my wife. I've been thinking about it for a while but the timing was never right. I realised there will never be a perfect moment, so I decided to just ask. It felt right. It was all me, I swear."

Why am I crying?

"I was afraid. I chickened out many times. But today I decided to just go for it. So yeah, it was all me."

"You were afraid of asking me?" That's so sweet.

"Yes. You have this way of making me nervous." He blushes. "But seriously, my *skat*, I haven't been the best to you this year. I didn't know if I was worthy of being your husband. But from now on, I promise to do everything in my power to be the man you deserve and to do right by you and Ulric."

I bury my face on his shoulder and cry. He rubs my back and compliments my hair, which is random, but it makes me cry harder.

His phone rings and I'm happy when he ignores it. He holds me tighter instead. When it rings for the third time, I let go and tell him to answer it.

He goes into the house and I take the chance to make a phone call of my own. It's outside working hours but I'm desperate.

"Hello, Lotus."

"Good evening, Dr. Brown. I'm sorry for calling without an appointment."

"It's alright. How can I help you?"

"My man proposed."

"So what's the problem?"

"In order to marry him, I have to go home and try to make peace with my mother and grandmother."

"Are there any other concerns about this proposal?"

"It also hurts that I won't have any friends with me. Chelsea's mother told me to stay away from her daughter."

"Do you want to get married to your man?"

"Yes, I do. I love him. I never thought he would ask. I want this."

"Then want it for you and you alone. While it may be difficult without your family's support, remember that their acceptance is beyond your control. Your happiness should not depend on their approval. I know how much it would mean to you if your family came on board, but you need to be okay with them not supporting you. You need to be okay with your family being your fiancé and your son. I know it's hard but you have come a long way without them. Don't allow their absence to ruin your special moment."

I could give her a hug.

"Let's unpack everything in detail tomorrow when you come in. Tonight, open your mind to the meaning of his proposal. Embrace it. Your dream came true, so celebrate! Appreciate your man. Dance if you feel like it. Pop champagne. Do everything you want to do. Express yourself. Don't dwell on things you have no control over."

"Yes, Dr. Brown."

"Congratulations, Lotus. I'll see you tomorrow."

"Thank you. See you tomorrow."

You know what? Today, we celebrate! Don deserves the best version of me.

I'm getting married!

# *FORTY SEVEN*

It's been a beautiful week. I've been floating through it all, telling anyone who cares to listen that I'm getting married. Hilton says I'm acting like the first person to ever get proposed to, and Tristan joked about whether it even counts as a proposal without a ring. You know haters gonna hate! But there are still good people in the world. Caleb is happy for me, but he's too worried about Chelsea to care much, and I can't help but feel like he resents me a little, seeing how it was me who was supposed to get shot. Elik is amazing as always. He sent over flowers and champagne. Therapy has been great too. All I talk about is wedding plans. It's been so good, I haven't even been too bothered by being cut off from Chelsea or wondering how my family is going to receive me.

I never thought marriage would happen for me. Even though I wanted it, I had made peace with the idea that maybe it just wasn't in the cards. Ever since I was a little girl, I dreamed of a fairy tale wedding. I imagined wearing a beautiful white gown with intricate lace detailing and a long train. My hair would be styled in elegant curls, a veil draped over my face, and I would carry a bouquet of my favourite flowers. My father would walk me down the aisle of a grand church, the kind with high ceilings and stained-glass windows, like in those old romantic movies. I thought I would have found my father by then. My groom would be waiting at the altar with tears in his eyes because he wouldn't believe he was marrying me. It would be the perfect day and my grandmother would be proud of me.

I'm a bit sad that I might not get the whole white wedding, walk down the aisle, first dance, and all that. I haven't asked Don if he's up for it because I'm afraid of the answer. But even if that part doesn't happen and we end up in a courtroom somewhere, I'll still be happy. It's a miracle that I'm here in the first place, engaged to the love of my life, planning our future together, and having the most beautiful baby in the world.

I'm going home today. I've been ignoring the thought for days, but now that the moment is here, I'm scared. The last time I saw my grandmother, things were different. I was different. My hands were clean, and I hadn't seen or done the things I have. I feel like she will sense the darkness in my spirit and cast me out like a demon. She didn't even know I was pregnant, and now I have a whole baby. I'm scared of her disappointment the most. I had a child out of wedlock with the kind of man she warned me about. I'm terrified of the questions she'll ask, the explanations I'll have to give, and the lies I'll need to tell. Most of all, I'm scared of her rejection. How do we get over the months of silence? What if I'm dead to her like I am to my mother? I desperately want her to understand, to accept me, to forgive me. But what if she can't? What if she doesn't want me back?

Despite all the fear, there's a small part of me that's hopeful that she'll at least accept my son. I don't really care how my mother reacts. It's my grandmother's approval I need.

My nerves are on edge. I check and recheck if I packed everything. The thought of flying with Ricky is making me nervous. Having a restless baby on a flight is something I'm not looking forward to. I've heard enough horror stories of babies who don't stop crying throughout a flight. Ricky is oblivious to the journey ahead. He's drooling all over his toy and making happy noises. This is the first time I'll be with him without any help for a long time. I don't think I'm ready for the challenge but I guess my baby, my problem.

"You ready to go?" Don walks in.

"Yup. Just waiting for Tristan."

"He's in the living room with your stuff. Let's go." He takes Ricky and his bag, and I pull my suitcase behind me.

I stash the dresses Tristan brought into my suitcase. Who cares if they get wrinkled? I'm sure there is an iron where I'm going. I bought two traditional dresses. If my family welcomes me back home and accepts my union with Don, then I'll have dresses for the ceremony. If they don't, well, I'll still have dresses.

"I'll take them to the airport," Don says to Tristan.

I guess he cancelled his meeting because the plan was for Tristan to take us.

Tristan helps me with my suitcase while Don straps Ricky in. Ricky is fighting him. I take out my phone and capture the father-son moment. They are so adorable, I can never get enough of it.

The road is clear, but man, the airport is far! Another good reason to move to Rondebosch. I'm fighting my thoughts as we drive. What if they don't welcome me back home? What if they don't forgive me? What if they say horrible things to me? What if I shouldn't be taking this trip?

"Everything will be fine... You look beautiful by the way."

Does he not get tired of telling me I look beautiful? I appreciate it though because it made me abandon my torturous thoughts and focus on him instead. I hold his free hand in mine and smile at him. He is everything and more. I wouldn't trade him for the world.

He pushes the baggage trolley to the check-in counters while I carry our bundle of joy. I wish we were travelling together. Don is good with

Ricky; he would handle him better on the flight.

We part at the security checkpoint and he waits until we are out of sight. Ricky is behaving so far and I hope it remains that way.

We don't wait too long before boarding begins. I find our seat, and after settling in, I take a selfie, with Ricky's tiny hand on my face. I send it to Don with a *'We love you'* message.

The plane starts moving, and just my luck, Ricky starts crying. Not a little whimper, but loud, piercing screams that fill the whole cabin. I try my best to comfort him but it's like he wants everyone on this plane to know he's upset. I really wish Don was here. He would know what to do. Now everyone is looking at me like I can't handle my own child. It gets worse when the plane takes off. I wish I could hide under the seat.

He calms down for a while when we are in the air and then he starts again. The other passengers are giving me disgruntled looks. I don't know what to do. A flight attendant passes by and gives me a sympathetic look. I'm not sure what I expected her to do. I thought maybe she might help. I try walking up and down the aisle when the seat belt sign goes off but it doesn't help, so I end up in the toilet, drying tears from my eyes and negotiating with Ricky. I can't stay in here forever though so I return to my seat. He's so restless, the short flight feels like two days.

I'm beyond relieved when we touch down. I can't wait to get off and get away from the judging eyes.

I'll never get used to Port Elizabeth being called Gqeberha. The name change hasn't settled in my mind; it will always be PE to me. I collect my suitcase and find my way to the car rental. After completing the paperwork, I take the keys and finally breathe.

I browse through hotel options, letting out deep sighs at intervals. The original plan was to drive straight home but reality hit hard. I don't have the guts to face my grandmother right now. Also, Ricky is very restless, I think his ears are still painful from the flight. I can't take him to people when he's like this. I need to get us a place for the night. I scroll through hotels, looking for something good enough. My heart skips a beat when the hotel Dalu held me hostage in pops up. I quickly swipe up and force myself to remain calm.

I call Don and tell him we had a great flight and everything is going great, so he doesn't stress about us. I also really just needed to hear his voice. Thankfully, he doesn't ask many questions when I tell him about the change of plans.

I book an expensive room in a luxury hotel because the last thing I need is an uncomfortable room and trashy views. I also don't have the mental capacity to deal with bad service common in low-star hotels.

I play *Baby Shark* as I drive, hoping to cheer Ricky up. It doesn't work but at least he's not screaming anymore.

The receptionist welcomes us warmly and makes the check-in process smooth. The lobby is gorgeous, with crystal chandeliers, marble floors and gorgeous decor, but I'm too anxious to care.

I feel better when we make it to our room. This is exactly what I ordered. It's tastefully decorated with a blend of modern and classic furnishings. The plush king-size bed, soft pillows and high-thread-count sheets - exactly what I need.

After getting out of my shoes and sweater, I sit with Ricky by the large window, taking in panoramic views of the city, watching people and cars going about their business. I tell Ricky how scared I am of going home and how I left home in the first place. I tell him how I met his father and how an ex almost unalived me in this very city. But he's more interested in playing with my phone than listening to me. I can't wait for him to start talking so we can have actual conversations, not these monologues.

I order a seafood platter from the room service menu. I'm not very hungry but I could eat. I video call Don while waiting for the food, and I'm cheered up in no time. Ricky keeps trying to get into the phone to reach his daddy, disturbing our chat. I might just be the luckiest girl in the world.

\* \* \* \* \*

I took a long shower, got Ricky ready, and had a hearty breakfast in the room. Anxiety wouldn't let me enjoy the food even though it looked really good. I wish we could stay here another night but I can't delay the inevitable any longer. I make sure Ricky is comfortable in the car before strapping him in. He's laughing a lot this morning, thankfully.

"Alright, my boy. Let's go and see your grandmothers."

He smiles, as if reassuring me that even if my family doesn't take me back, I'll still have him.

I put on some music to distract my thoughts. Nothing much has changed, if anything, the road is worse now. It's shocking how big the potholes have become. Does the government really not care that much? Come election time, they will be begging us for votes yet they can't use taxpayers' money for basic things like roads.

I look in the rear view mirror and Ricky is sleeping peacefully. Being a child is so nice; I wish I was as at peace as he is. My heart is one beat away from a heart attack. I'm so nervous, I'm holding the steering wheel a little too hard to keep the car on the road.

I stop near the *spaza* shop and open the window to breathe. I feel like I'm running out of air and my chest will explode any minute. I want to turn the car around and come back tomorrow. I don't know if I can handle whatever is waiting for me at home.

I see my mother's friend approaching and I quickly roll up the window and start the car. I'm not capable of talking to anyone right now. I drive slowly down the bumpy road until I'm parked in front of my grandmother's house. The gate is locked so I have no option but to hoot.

So much has changed since I was last here. I'm happy my mother used the money I left behind to finish renovating the house. I wasn't sure because she didn't update me. She also disabled blue ticks on WhatsApp so I wasn't sure if she was seeing the designs and everything I was sending her to guide the renovations.

I can't see through the new gate. It's solid unlike our previous one, so I can't say for sure if they did a stellar job. But judging by the tiled roof, new gate, new wall and bigger house, I think it's safe to assume so. It warms my heart because at least I did something for them.

I hoot again and the gate slides open. My mother is standing there, hands on her waist, chewing gum like it's going out of fashion. My heart palpitates out of control as I drive in. She closes the gate and heads back into the house without waiting for me to get out of the car. I pull the handbrake up and hesitate for a moment before turning the engine off. I try to steady myself; I can do this. I look back at Ricky and his innocent eyes meet mine, so blissfully unaware of what I'm going through.

I'm not sure if I'm supposed to knock or just go in. My knees are shaking so badly, I hold on to the wall so they don't buckle and make me drop Ricky. I decide against knocking and step into the kitchen. The aroma of *vetkoeks* fills my senses with bittersweet memories that I quickly shake off.

I slowly make my way into the living room. My grandmother is sitting next to my mother on the couch. She looks at me briefly, then back at the TV as if I'm invisible. My mother is glued to her phone. She does not lift her face or do anything to acknowledge me. The air is so thick, you can almost touch it. I kneel in front of them, holding Ricky in my arms. My heart is racing and I'm breathing through slightly parted lips.

"Mama, Sisi." My teeth rattle as I greet them.

My grandmother slowly turns her gaze to me and I fail to hold the stare.

"I'm sorry." I start whimpering like a puppy in pain. "Please forgive me."

Ricky squirms, trying to reach for my grandmother's *doek*, not caring about the tension. He's never this friendly with strangers so it's a good sign.

"I know I disappointed you. I'm so sorry." My voice is barely audible this time and I stifle my sobs.

Ricky is about to start crying and I'm trying my best to calm him. I wish they would say something, or at least look at me.

"I'm sorry for everything. Please forgive me," I find my voice again.

Silence follows and I whimper, trying not to fall apart. I wish they would acknowledge me at least.

"Is this the child?" my grandmother eventually speaks.

"Yes, it is." I'm not sure what she means by that but I'll go with yes.

I rock back and forth on my knees trying to calm Ricky. He's now screaming at the top of his lungs. He must be absorbing my distress. I hate myself for unravelling like this in front of him.

"You're upsetting the child. Pull yourself together!" my grandmother says sternly before snatching Ricky from me.

I'm not sure what to do or say, so I remain on my knees.

I turn to my mother but she's still glued to her phone and her lips are pursed so tightly, I'm afraid of what might come out of her mouth if I keep begging her to talk. I keep begging anyway.

"Sisi, please talk to me. I'm really sorry. I shouldn't have done what I did to you. I shouldn't have put you through that. Please forgive me. Please, I need you. I need my mother. Ricky needs you. We need you. I was stupid. I wish I could go back in time and do things differently. Please, Sisi, I'm begging you." I hold on to her legs and cry shamelessly.

She gets up, shakes me off and walks away, leaving me on the floor. I want to follow her but I don't think it's a good idea. I crawl to my grandmother's feet and cry on them.

"Get up!"

I slowly stand, struggling to hold back tears that continue to stream down my face.

"Sit down."

I sit where my mother was.

"Why are you here, Lotus? What is this?"

"I'm here to ask for forgiveness. I want to come back home."

She looks at me and shakes her head. "Did I chase you away from home?"

"No, you did not."

"Did I say you should never return home?"

"No."

"So what is this, *mntanam*? You decided to leave home all on your own. You didn't bother to say goodbye. You just packed your bags and left and we didn't see you again. Now you're making it sound like I chased you away."

My tears keep falling. I don't know what to say.

"You hurt me, I'm not going to lie to you. You hurt me deeply. I'll never understand why you did what you did. What did I do to you that was so bad you couldn't say goodbye? You kept your entire pregnancy from me. You hurt me beyond words."

"I was afraid. I didn't think things through."

"And that's the problem, isn't it? You never think things through. You're very selfish. Everything is about you. Everything should be on your schedule. You're always the victim. Do you ever think about other people? Do you ever stop and think how your actions affect other people? I thought I raised you right. Where did I go wrong with you?" Her voice is strangely calm.

I want to throw myself on the floor and apologise, but I remain seated, sniffling and whimpering. "I'm sorry."

"Don't be sorry. You made your choices."

I wish I had done things differently.

"What's his name?" she asks after a long pause.

"Ulric. We call him Ricky."

She runs a finger along his jawline, studying his features and looking into his eyes. He grins at her, trying to claw her face with his little hand.

"His name is Daluxolo, the bringer of forgiveness, the peacemaker." She continues drawing lines on his face. "He's a beautiful boy."

Daluxolo is such an old name. My poor baby.

She looks at me. "I've been waiting for you to bring him home. I wanted you to find your way back on your own."

"I'm really sorry for everything, Mama. I was selfish and stupid."

"The person you hurt is your mother. That's who you should be apologising to. Go and talk to her. Daluxolo and I will be here."

Daluxolo? I shudder when I realise that people might call him Dalu. I slowly get up, not trusting my feet if I rush them. I find my way to the bedroom and push the slightly open door in. My mother is sitting on the bed, staring at the wall. There is no space to kneel in front of her, so I stand and take her hands in mine. I'm about to start talking when I realise she's crying. I take a leap of faith and wrap my arms around her head, resting her face on my stomach. I fall apart when she starts quivering in my arms.

"I'm so sorry," she says, catching me by surprise. I'm the one who came to apologise.

"It's okay, Sisi. It's okay. I'm sorry too. I never should have."

She pulls away, her face wet with tears. "You had every right to. If I'd just told you the truth, you'd never have needed to do what you did. After the funeral, I sunk into depression. I didn't know what to say to you until I just never spoke to you again. I hoped you would come back home, until I accepted that you never would."

That's strange considering how she was very happy with Chelsea, ignored me on WhatsApp and logged me out of her Instagram. Chelsea also made a similar excuse. But you know what, I'm here to make amends not to tally wrongs. I need us to make peace and move on.

"Sisi..."

"I'm your mother. I should have done better by you."

I wipe her tears and the fresh ones that follow. I should have come home sooner. She's broken. Maybe I should have extended her more grace. Anger keeps creeping into my heart but I keep swatting it away. She should have been there for me! She should have been a mother to me! She should have never chosen Chelsea over me! She should have responded to the million messages I sent her!

I hold her tightly, trying to drown out my emotions. After a long time, we dry our faces and try to get it together. There is an ache in my heart that's not going away but I'm determined to ignore it. She failed me.

"Mama hijacked your grandson. She even gave him a new name, Daluxolo. That's such an old person's name!"

We chuckle through our tears, trying to survive the awkwardness.

"What do you expect from an old woman? It's a beautiful name though. Let's go and meet him. You have to tell me all about him. I've missed out on so much."

*And whose fault is that?*

"He's adorable, you'll love him."

She follows me to the living room and my grandmother reluctantly hands Ricky over to her.

"How long are you staying?" My grandmother turns her attention to me.

"A few days, a week maybe. If you let me, that is."

"This is your home. You can stay as long as you want."

I really should have come home sooner.

"Where is his father?"

"He's in Cape Town."

I don't know if now is the right time to give them the letter that Don's people wrote, asking to come and do what's necessary to make me an honourable woman. Don's people being Hilton, Elik, Caleb, Tristan and me. We had so much fun drafting the letter. None of us knew much about serious traditional ceremonies, but as always, Google saved the day.

"Where are your bags? Go and get them. We finished your bedroom last week but you need to dust the furniture and make the bed."

I get up and walk to the car, smiling through tears. The house was neatly renovated and to my taste. They really did everything I wanted. We still need to update some of the furniture, but so far so good.

My mother follows me outside and I know she has lost Ricky to my grandmother.

"So what exactly brings you home? I feel like there's something you're not letting out."

"Am I that obvious?"

"You're my child. I know you!"

*Yet you didn't know me all the times I needed you. I cried myself to sleep for nights on end, thinking of you. I needed you when my father died in front of me. I needed you when I was in labour and scared out of my mind. I needed you after I gave birth and didn't know what to do. I Googled things you should have told me. I had a newborn baby and had no idea where to start taking care of him. Did you know me then?*

"Well, Don asked me to marry him and I told him I couldn't do that without your blessing. So he wants to come on Saturday and ask for my hand."

She lets out a squeal and wraps her arms around me in an uncomfortable hug. I did not expect that excitement from her! Awkwardness creeps in and she lets me go. I can't have that, so I hold on to her and hide my face.

It takes a while before I let her go. I'm battling so many mixed emotions, I wish I could sit alone in a locked room.

"I'm happy for you. You deserve all the love Madonna gives you." She hugs me again.

*Since when do you like him?*

I tell her about the proposal, exaggerating everything to my liking. She is so excited, you would swear she's the one getting married.

She helps me with the bags and with cleaning my room. Resentment keeps creeping into my heart but I'm fighting it with all my might.

"Let's go and see Dalu," she says after we have made the bed.

"Not funny!" That name is such a trigger for me.

My grandmother has completely taken over Ricky; the rest of us have faded into the background.

\* \* \* \* \*

My mother and I are in the kitchen preparing lunch. It's still a bit awkward-ish but we are getting there. She asks more about Don: how he's been doing, what our future plans are and if he has changed since she last saw him. I don't know if it's genuine or if she's pretending to care. She is very interested in Ricky as well. She asks about his habits, his favourite foods and how he sleeps. She even asks about my experience with labour and giving birth, and about my life in Cape Town in general. I find myself opening up more than I expected, only leaving out the details she has no business knowing. For the first time in a long while, it feels like we are connecting. Even her questions about Chelsea don't make me feel replaced for once.

When I'm done chopping the vegetables, I step outside to call Don. He has been such a rock through it all, letting me vent as much as I want and gently grounding me after. Coming home was the right decision. I wish I had come sooner or tried harder to reach out. I was just convinced they had written me off.

Now I hope my grandmother will accept Don. I will give her the letter this evening.

# *FORTY EIGHT*

I've spent the week bonding with my grandmother and my mother. Sometimes it feels like a dream. Ricky really brought peace and a lot of joy into our home. Dinner has become my favourite part of the day. We stay up late into the night, laughing and talking about anything and everything, with the hours slipping by unnoticed.

When my grandmother asked about Don, I told her he was a soldier and had gone through a lot in Mozambique, where he had been deployed. She looked so proud as she praised him for protecting civilians. She can't wait to meet him. I don't know why I said that but it worked and it will explain the scars and tattoos. I just have to keep Hilton hidden from her. His appearance is something I can't begin to explain to anyone. The ink on his face, the shadows in his eyes, the dark tattoos, the blank look - no story about military trauma could ever explain that.

We were up very early. The sun is shining differently today. It's as if it's celebrating this milestone with me. All is set and ready, but we have a little problem - how the negotiations will be carried out. My grandmother said we won't be doing *lobola* in the strict sense but will just be uniting two families. I didn't understand what the difference was. I just need everything to go well. I'm ready to exchange my surname for Don's. Maybe I could double barrel, but maybe not. My surname is already three words, adding a fourth might be stretching it, excuse the pun. Wait, surname change only happens in court, right? So I don't change anything today? Disappointing.

Preparing for today only took a single trip to town, since we're keeping it small and intimate. We bought a few things, a lot of food, ready-made outfits for my grandmother and mother, and gifts for the ceremony. I hope everything will go well.

My mother and grandmother budge into my room without knocking. They look royal in their Xhosa attires. The black and white beads make them look like goddesses. We are all wearing *doeks* that match our black and white dresses. Mine has three buttons beautifully aligned in the front. I know everyone will think it's decoration, but the dressmaker put them there so I would know how to tie the *doek*. He said he was worried I would ruin the look.

"Come and greet your aunts," my grandmother says after complimenting how good I look.

"Just a second. Let's paint our faces first."

Using calamine lotion, my mother carefully dots an S that runs from the side of my left eye, crosses the bridge of my nose and ends on the lower right side of my face.

"Now you look like a queen's daughter."

Did she just call herself a queen?

My aunts got the memo. They are well-clad in Xhosa traditional regalia. They have been family friends for so long, they are practically family. I couldn't get hold of my uncle in Cape Town, the one my mother stayed with before I was born. Her running away damaged the relationship beyond repair. To be honest, I didn't try hard enough. So the women in my life will handle the negotiations.

We take a lot of gorgeous pictures, then I thank my aunts and head back to my room. I wish I could post these pictures on Instagram, so instead, I share them on my WhatsApp status with saucy captions about the beauty of being desired and loved all the way through. I finish with a status about how a man who respects you will meet your family and do right by you.

"Lolo, Mama wants to talk to us." My mother walks in and sits next to me. She takes my phone and I rest my head on her shoulder as she scrolls through the pictures.

"I made you beautiful. You should thank me."

I giggle and scroll to a picture of the two of us. "See how much we look alike in this one?" We are smiling the same way and standing the same way; we look like siblings.

"I know I wasn't the best mother to you but I hope you always knew that I loved you. I love you. You're my only child and there's nothing I wouldn't do for you."

Man, I hate emotions. I hate it when she says things like this because history has proven that it's not true. But nothing will spoil my day, so I hug her. She wasn't a perfect mother at all. She was terrible in fact, but she tried her best. Even when we were not talking, I loved her. I was angry but I loved her and wanted to be with her.

"I love you, Sisi."

"I love you too, *sana lwam.*" She rarely calls me her child, so this is something.

"Let's go before Mama throws a fit and starts praying for us," I say to her as we both dry our tears.

My grandmother has her Bible next to her and a rosary in her hands. I don't wish to know what she was praying for. She once told the Lord that she knew it was too late for me but asked Him to try anyway. I almost sit on her Bible and she slaps my arm and says my big bums should not touch her holy book. Her body structure is similar to mine but she constantly points out how all the food I eat goes to my behind and attracts the wrong men.

"Is it that bum that attracted that man of yours?"

"Among other things, yes. But I think it was either this innocent face or this good Christian heart of mine that drew him to me." I make puppy eyes.

She laughs so heartily, I can't help but laugh as well. She takes my hands in hers and looks at me warmly. "Your mother and I did the best we could to give you everything. We love you and we hope your marriage will be blessed. You're our pride and joy. Marriage is not easy, my child. You have to nurture it, but as long as there's love in the home, you'll be alright."

I fight back tears. I'm so emotional today.

"Pray hard and read the Bible, my girl. When it gets hard, get on your knees!"

I chuckle at the pun and my mother slaps me at the back. I couldn't help it.

"Make him believe he's in charge even when he's not. Men love that. And a happy man is a happy you."

I find myself nodding and holding onto her hand.

"Don't embarrass us, Lotus!" she says sternly. "If things don't work out, remember that I didn't chase you away from home. Come back home. If he beats you up, come back home. Men don't change. The abuse never gets better, so leave when it starts before you accept it as normal. Don't wait until you come back to us in a coffin. Do you hear me?"

"Yes, Mama."

I doubt Don would ever lay a hand on me but I understand what she's saying.

"I'm proud of you. As much as you leaving home broke my heart, I'm proud of you for following your heart. You have my blessing. Don't just make one child like your mother. Don't be that lazy! Make a lot of them so I can see them before I get old. Give me five grandchildren at least."

I burst out laughing. *Yho!* I don't think so. Five?

"Lazy? You also have one child, Mama!" my mother complains.

"Don't start with me. This is not about me." My grandmother gives her the eye we grew up afraid of.

My mother is about to start her own speech when one of my aunts knocks and says, "They are here."

"Can I go and welcome them?" I light up.

"*Uphambene?* (Are you out of your mind?)" they say at the same time.

Mxm. Such kill-sport! I miss my man.

I go to my mother's room to check on my baby. He's having a good time with the babysitter, one of my aunt's daughters. He is such a good boy and she's good with him. I promise to check on him regularly.

I go to the living room to make sure everything is where it should be. I hope they know they will be sitting on the floor while my people will be on the couches. I'm sure King Hintsa will turn in his grave today. Women negotiating *lobola* and being superior to men? The demons of patriarchy will rise from hell!

They asked me how much Don could afford and I told them to ask for a reasonable amount. If they ask him for more than he has on him, he might top up with bricks of cocaine, straws of ice and guns. I can already see the shock on my grandmother's face and the trauma that will follow her all the days of her life.

"Lotus." I hear a familiar voice. I must be dreaming!

I turn around and it's Chelsea in the shortest Ankara dress I have ever seen. It's generously cut out in front; it's a miracle her nipples are not peeping. She's wearing her hair in a ponytail and her face is beaten to perfection. My heart is beating fast and I remain glued to the floor. I don't know what to do or say.

"Are you going to stand there forever or are you going to give your best friend a hug?" She smiles nervously.

I stop thinking and walk into her arms. "What are you doing here?"

"Like I'd miss your big day for anything!"

I hold on to her, afraid she might not be real.

"I'm sorry, babe. My mum had no right to say what she said to you."

"All that matters is that you're here." I'm still in shock so I don't really know how I'm feeling.

"But how did you know? How did you get here?" I let the hug go.

"Caleb, obviously. I hope he takes a hint today."

"Okay! You have to tell me everything. Come, let's go to my room."

I hug her again. I hope her styling gel is dry. If she messes my dress, I'll skin her alive.

"You look good. Very good." I make her turn around. *Yho!* There is barely a dress there. This is an oversized blouse, if anything. It's cute, just not for the occasion.

"And you too. You look stunning. You might not need to go under the knife after all. Where's the fat?"

"Healthy eating, working out, stress and heavy sex sessions."

I put on a gown to cover up because these hugs will stain my dress soon.

"I'm worried about today. What if things don't go well?"

"Don't worry. Donavan loves you, so he made sure everything is sorted. Lumka tagged along to lead the negotiations. He's Xhosa so I'm pretty sure he's well versed in your culture."

"Lumka is here?"

"Yes, he is." She bites her lip in sheer lust and I almost ask if she's ever slept with him.

"Elik is here too. He might not speak Xhosa but at least he has a good head on his shoulders. He'll handle everything in a civilised manner, unlike some people we know."

I will pretend I didn't hear that.

"How many people are here? Did you drive in different cars?"

"No. We all came in a Quantum. Imagine! I had to watch Elik and Fierce sucking face all the way. Yuck! I hate that man."

"Fierce is here too?" I get nervous and she gives me a disapproving eye.

"Yes, probably grinding on Elik as we speak." She rolls her eyes.

"He's her man, Chels. Let it go."

I can't have her ruining my day. I'm not picking any sides today. Today is about me and only me. Don should have given me a heads up. They arrived in Port Elizabeth last night and he didn't mention that Chelsea and Fierce were there. He made it sound like it was just him, Caleb, Hilton and Tristan.

Chelsea looks sad and I feel bad.

"Babe, I know you feel whatever you feel for Elik, but please let it go. You'll mess up what you have with Caleb, and for what? Elik loves Fierce. He's not coming back to you. He's never going to leave her. Please let him go."

I open my arms and she rests her head on my chest. *There, there, little lamb. Your broken heart will heal one day.*

"I know. I love Caleb, I really do. But Elik has this hold on me that I can't explain. It's just, you don't understand. He helped me a lot through my healing. He showed up for me in ways no one else ever did. He cared, babe. He introduced me to a love you only see in movies."

*Love? Don't you mean lust?*

Elik never loved her; it was just sex for him.

We reunited minutes ago and we are already waist-deep in men drama.

"I understand, but remember how it went last time. If you mess up again, I don't think Caleb will forgive you."

I don't understand this new Chelsea. She excels in continuing like nothing ever happened. Shouldn't we be talking about the shooting and what happened between then and now?

"You're right."

"I'm sorry. I truly am." *For everything, and for the way men hurt you.*

I want to ask her about Fierce. I'm not settled with her being here. I'm not exactly her favourite person, but she's a sore topic to Chelsea so let me keep it to myself.

"Let's start over. How have you been?"

"It's been surprisingly good. I moved back to Wellington. My parents are not yet comfortable with me staying alone, which really sucks because I can't spend quality time with Caleb. But maybe we needed that, you know? We have slowed down on the sex and we spend more time talking and doing other things during the day."

"Have you resumed work?"

"Yes, I have but I don't work in Cape Town anymore. I'm working at my uncle's law firm in Wellington for the time being."

I want to ask why she never got in touch with me when she got a new phone but maybe I shouldn't.

"But I'm moving back to Cape Town soon. I have great news!"

"What is it?"

Before she can tell me, my mother shows up and hijacks her. I mentally will myself not to be mad. Yet in a way, I'm relieved. I was getting mixed emotions, so I appreciate the break.

I text Fierce, *'Come through. I'm in my room'.*

*'Who spoiled the surprise?'* she texts back.

*'You were supposed to be a surprise?'*

*'I was... I'm coming through.'*

*'I'll pretend to be surprised when I see you.'*

I'm so edgy. The last time I spoke to Fierce, she threatened to destroy me. She was so mad, she never spoke to me again. And her being here today with Chelsea around is a recipe for disaster.

I hear my mother's loud voice directing someone to where I am. I take off the gown and open the door. I loved Fierce a lot but she always made me feel less than I am, I don't know how to explain it. I think she intimidated me. And then she just hated me for Chelsea's sins and cut me off as if I never meant anything to her.

She looks gorgeous in a Xhosa dress, complete with a *doek*. See people who do their homework! Not the Chelseas.

"Hey, Lotus. Oh my goodness. Look at you!" She stares like she's looking at Beyoncé.

"I tried, right?" I say with a wide grin.

"You didn't try, you did! You killed it. Lemon is going to propose again when he sees you."

"He better! Come in."

She sits with me on the bed and awkward silence follows.

"Can I say something?" She turns to face me.

"Yes?"

"I'm sorry for the way I treated you. It was unfair of me to blame you for Elik's actions. I was wrong and I have no excuse for it. It wasn't your fault and I never should have lashed out at you. I hope you don't mind that I came here today."

I look at her and she looks down.

"It wasn't the first time Elik cheated on me, but it was the first time it was with someone I have to be around. I was angry and I took it out on you. I'm sorry."

"It's alright, I get it. I'm happy that you came."

She looks at me as if thinking *'Just like that?'*

"Tell you what, how about we talk about everything another time? Today, let's celebrate and have fun." I understand her. Roland had me feeling the same once upon a time. I was angry at everyone except him.

She hugs me unexpectedly. "I missed you a lot. I was afraid you wouldn't want to see me."

"I missed you too. Now let's stop with the serious talk! Tell me about you. Where have you been? What have you been up to?"

She tells me all about her adventures in Asian lands I have never heard of. She talks about herself a lot! Borderline self-absorbed if you ask me. I know I asked but wow! I'm a bit jealous until she says, "We're doing the next trip together. How is next month? Are you able to leave your baby behind?"

Say no more, I'm in! Ricky is a big boy and he has a father. My excitement dies down when I remember how she promised me a trip to Thailand just like this and then ghosted me. So I will believe it when it happens.

"Are you ready, for married life I mean?"

"I don't know. Is anyone ever ready?"

"I don't think so, but with the right person, it's always worth it. I guess I mean how do you feel? Is this what you want?"

"Yes, it's what I want. Don is my world."

"Then it will be perfect. He loves you. He couldn't stop talking about you on the way here. Whatever you're doing to that man, keep doing it."

We laugh and then return to awkward silence.

"Fierce, be straight with me. Are you okay with Chelsea?"

She looks at me as if unsure whether to tell me the truth or not. "I'm trying my best. I almost didn't come, not because of you but because of her. Kofi had to practically beg me to come. I'm trying my best to be okay with everything but she's a constant reminder of what Elik did. I really wish I never found out. They say it was years ago, but he still let her into my house and I don't know what exactly happened. I don't know what to do. I just want everything to be okay and for me to not be so angry at her all the time."

"Your feelings are valid, babe. But Chelsea was never your friend. She never owed you any loyalty. That's all on Elik. You decided to stay with him, so you have to let it go. It happened. Nothing you say or do will reverse them sleeping with each other. You still have the man and she has Caleb now. Both of you are happy. Let the past go."

She looks down and plays with her fingers. "It's difficult."

"I can imagine." I can't imagine! I would kill someone if I was in her shoes.

She sniffs again and hangs her head.

"Hey, don't mess up your face now. I'm here for you, okay? You're not alone. Elik loves you. That man worships the ground you walk on. Don't let something that happened years ago destroy that. He resisted Chelsea when she came onto him again. He chose you because he loves you. He doesn't love her. He never did."

"Really?"

"Yes, really. He never felt anything for her beyond the physical. It's you he has always loved. You're his soulmate."

She looks at me and my heart breaks for her. I pull her into my arms and she breaks down. Men won't see heaven *shame*.

"I'm so sorry, Lotus."

"It's okay, love. I'm here now. It's going to be okay for all of us." I coo to her and let her get it all out. The things men put us through!

Chelsea comes back and stands dead in her tracks. "What's going on?"

"Nothing. Fierce and I were just talking, and you know how emotional these ceremonies get. Come, sit."

Fierce rubs her eyes and Chelsea gives her a big hug. I look at them suspiciously.

"We had lunch the other day and we talked," Chelsea says. She must have read my face.

"So you girls are good?"

"We are. With Elik and Caleb being friends, we had to make peace at some point," Chelsea says.

"Whose idea was the lunch?"

They look at each other and I don't know what that means. I just hope they pretend long enough to make it through the day without any drama.

In no time, the three of us are excited and exchanging stories about our men. They don't believe that Don has never cheated on me. They are convinced that he sleeps with other women because that's what the Wolves, and men in general, do. They call me delusional. I know he doesn't. Don has never slept with anyone else since he met me. I asked him and he doesn't lie. Like he said, 'After I had you, I didn't want to have anyone else'. I don't know about Caleb. I doubt he cheats though but who is to say? I could ask Don, although I'm sure he wouldn't tell me.

I realise that dwelling on men cheating will go south quickly if we shine the light on Elik, so I change the topic to Chelsea's dress. I have an extra dress that I wanted to change into later. She should wear that one so that she fits in.

The three of us look royal, if I do say so myself. Sometimes you have to blow your own horn. I know I do that more than the average human, but I'm not average, am I?

They fill me in on the journey and how rowdy the guys were. There were ten people in the Quantum: Chelsea, Fierce, Don, Lumka, Elik, Caleb, Hilton, Tristan, Kofi and the nanny. Bringing the nanny along was a brilliant idea. Apparently, the guys were smoking weed in the car, and when they got to the hotel, they were laughing so loud, they almost got thrown out of the bar. I'm shocked when Fierce says Elik also smokes weed. He doesn't strike me like the type. I wish I had been part of the road trip but this week at home has been good for me. I'm back in my grandmother's good books.

Apparently, Lumka, Elik, Caleb and Hilton will sit in for the negotiations. I love Hilton but he can't be part of the team. He makes people uncomfortable without saying anything. He has a strong presence that makes people want to run away. I know for a fact that my grandmother will be repulsed by him. So I'm sorry but he can't be part of the team.

"Are we turning up tonight? I have the perfect party dress that will have Caleb committing to me." Chelsea says excitedly.

"No, we'll chill right here all night. No small dresses, please."

We laugh at her and she makes a face.

"You two have your men committed to you. How about me? I also want to get married," she sounds hurt so I don't laugh this time.

"If you love Caleb, then be faithful to him. Don't sleep with his friends. If he loves you then one day he might ask for your hand in marriage. If he doesn't, it's also fine. Remember men only marry women they deem worthy to be their wives. Some women are just good for dating, nothing more. Marriage is not for everyone," Fierce says.

Wow! That's a lot of sass.

"Thank you. I needed to hear that," Chelsea says sarcastically.

My mother comes in to check on us. She makes us stand so she can take pictures of us.

"We're going to start now. We forgot to tell them our clan names so I don't know. Let's see how creative they are," she says.

I'm a Janse van Rensburg, but that's a borrowed surname. I have a 'true' surname that comes with clan names and ancestors. I don't know how to explain it. I guess it's a *'if you know, you know'* situation. That's why when I speak to Xhosa people and tell them my surname, they ask for my real surname.

I ask Fierce to text Lumka my clan names. I don't want them saying 'Janse van Rensburg' when addressing my people. Everything has to be perfect today.

"Let's go to the other room. We can see the gate from there. We can watch through the curtain."

We follow each other to the spare room.

"Is Don wearing a suit?" I know I'm pushing it but he could surprise me, you know?

They burst out laughing.

"Does your man have anything else in his wardrobe besides hoodies and sneakers?" Chelsea teases.

Mxm.

Elik and Lumka are having a conversation and I wish I was close enough to hear what they are saying. They are in black suits, white shirts and black ties. I find myself picturing Don in a suit, looking sinfully divine. Too bad it's only wishful thinking. Tristan, Kofi and Caleb crush my dreams and walk into the yard in jeans and sneakers. At least they are wearing blazers. I'm glad that Tristan and Kofi replaced Hilton. I hope Hilton didn't take my message the wrong way. He knows he has a negative effect on people, and he's proud of it. He used to scare me the same way Don scared Fierce. They have those auras that I can only describe as an acquired taste.

I wonder where Don is. I want to see him, and maybe kiss him and thank him for seeing this through. I know a friend of a friend who cheated on her boyfriend and thought he didn't know. As revenge, he asked to pay *lobola*, had the girl inform her family and set up everything. Then on the day, he switched off his phone and checked in on Facebook in some resort having the time of his life. I doubt I would survive the humiliation.

Judging from body language, Lumka is the one talking and the others are listening. I smile like an idiot as he calls out my clan names. There is something about someone calling out to your ancestors. That thing *mann* that the Chelseas and Dons will never understand.

Fierce says in her country they leave the *lobola* crew standing outside for hours, calling out clan names. Then they demand as many as twenty cows on top of many goats, chickens, sheep, groceries, blankets, cash and clothes. That means Zimbabweans have money! I thought us calling them billionaires was a way of mocking their useless money. I didn't even know that the money we see is not in use anymore and they use US dollars, Rands and every other currency they can get their hands on. She tries to explain how their 'new' currency compares to other currencies, but I don't get it. I'm glad she doesn't call me dom. Dalu once tried to explain it as well and I didn't get it then either. In the next life, Don should come back Zimbabwean and bless my grandmother with all that money. In our culture, we don't ask for much. *Lobola* is not a get-rich-quick scheme. We don't sell our children, no offence.

Don doesn't believe in *lobola*. He doesn't understand the concept. He's doing it because it means something to me.

One of my aunts ushers them into the house. With nothing left to watch, we have no choice but to go back to chit-chatting. Fierce does not like Chelsea at all! To be safe, I need us to stop talking about men before Chelsea pushes her over the edge.

"So what are your plans career-wise? Do you want to go back to work?" Fierce asks.

"I don't know. I think I'd love to but you know how hard getting a job is." Tristan got me thinking last time. I would love to go back to work and keep busy.

"I'll be opening my lab soon. I can offer you a position."

I don't know what's more impressive - her starting her own company at her age or offering me a job.

"Are you serious?"

"Of course. I'd love to work with you. You don't have to give me an answer now. Just think about it."

"Are you crazy? There's nothing to think about. I'm in!"

We are so huggy today!

"Great! We'll talk about the details when we get back to Cape Town. Today we're not talking shop. Let's have fun!"

I can't wait to tell Don. This day just keeps getting better and better.

\* \* \* \* \*

My nerves are getting the best of me. What if someone messes up for me? What if my grandmother changes her mind? What if she doesn't like Don?

"What's taking so long?"

"Calm down. Everything will be fine." Chelsea takes my hand.

Easier said than done.

"Everyone in there has your best interests at heart, so don't stress." Fierce takes my other hand.

It hasn't been long at all but from where I'm sitting, it feels like a decade.

*We're done. It wasn't much of a negotiation. We were told what to pay and we paid it.* Fierce shares the text Elik sent her.

"That was quick!" Chelsea says.

It really was if I'm being logical. Is it because my family didn't follow the process, or were Don's people Yes-Men? Either way, I'm relieved it's done.

We are still celebrating when my mother comes to get us. We collect ourselves and follow her to the living room.

The women are comfortable on the couches and the guys are sitting on the floor. We kneel and my grandmother introduces us to the groom's people. I don't get the point of this part. We all know each other, some naked even.

Lumka looks respectful and well put together. I'm sure my grandmother wishes it was him I was marrying. Elik is Elik, all suave and dapper. He looks wrong sitting butt down on the floor in that expensive suit. Caleb looks well-groomed and refined. Chelsea should get her life together and make it work with him. His signature smile forces me to smile back when I shake his hand. Tristan winks at me and I smile back. He's a pretty boy, like his brother. Kofi looks like he's up to no good, as always.

My grandmother talks about how *lobola* was important even in the Bible, and how it's the essence of marriage. That's a bit surprising because she's more Christian than most, so shouldn't the essence of marriage be the church wedding to her? She sounds very happy and in high spirits, you wouldn't believe we were strangers two weeks ago.

"You may go and call our son-in-law. Let us welcome him to the family."

I volunteer and everyone looks at me like I'm crazy. I don't wait to be told to sit down.

I find Don sleeping in the back seat of the Quantum. He must be exhausted. I know he sleeps flat out like this when he has had many sleepless nights. I gently wake him up and he slowly opens his eyes. I'm looking directly into them, drowning as I keep staring, falling in love all over again. Say what you may about soulmates but I found mine. The way our eyes connect is on a spiritual level.

"My angel," he says with the croaky waking-up voice I love.

"Hey, baby."

He sits up and rubs his eyes. "Shouldn't you be calling me husband, or are they not done yet?"

"I'm sorry, baby. I mean, husband."

He smiles and I plant a wet kiss on his lips.

"Are you happy?"

"I'm happy. I'm very very happy. Thank you for this."

"Anything for you. Can I finish sleeping now?" He's too casual for someone who hasn't seen me in a week. He should be lifting me up and telling me how much he missed me.

"Get up. They're waiting for us."

He's so cute when he's sulking, now we know where Ricky got it from.

"Don't you have another hoodie?" Couldn't he have put on a suit?

He shakes his head and I want to cry. How did his friends let him wear a hoodie with skulls, coffins, a tombstone, skeletons and occult symbols? It has the horns of Baphomet, the eye of Horace, an ancient Egyptian god and an upside-down cross. Yeah no, my grandmother will exorcise him at first sight. Although I'm 99% sure he has no idea what these symbols mean and that it's Hilton's hoodie.

"I'm kidding, wife. Let me get my jacket." He laughs at me and I slap him on the arm. He almost gave me a heart attack.

"Hey, Hilly. You're awake." I turn to Hilton.

"Lotus."

"I missed you." I would hug him if we were outside.

"Should I say congratulations or condolences to my little cousin?"

"Why?"

"He's stuck with you for life now. It sounds worse than a life sentence in Pollsmoor." He sounds so serious, I have to laugh.

"Excuse me! Your not-so-little cousin is lucky to have me for the rest of his life. He should be offering a burnt sacrifice to heaven right now."

"*Shame.*"

"You know you love me. Why else would you be here if you didn't love me?"

"I was commanded by my Alpha to show up. I'm only here because my Alpha is a bully like his woman."

"Is that so? So do you hate me?"

"Hate takes time and energy. I have neither to waste. Haven't I told you before?"

"It's okay, Hilly. I have enough time and energy to love you enough for the both of us. Now I would love to sit here and talk to you all day but I have to go back inside."

Don is waiting outside the Quantum. He looks even better than he did on that first dinner he had with my mother. He cleaned up so well, I can't believe it. The tattoo under his eye is perfectly concealed, thanks to Chelsea's make-up skills.

"Hilton, catch." Don tosses the hoodie he was wearing earlier. "Can I have your watch?"

"No one wears my things, you know this."

"But I always take your hoodies and T-shirts when I sleep at your house. Matter of fact, that one belongs to you."

*So he sleeps at Hilton's place often? So all those nights he was AWOL, he was at Hilton's house? What a relief!*

"You said you bought an identical one at Access Park when mine went missing!"

"You're the Access Park, Cuz. Sorry." His face says he's not sorry at all.

I'm still enjoying the show when Hilton turns to me and says, "What are you grinning at? Are you happy you're marrying a thief?"

I quickly apologise and scold Don for being a shameless thief. How dare he steal Hilton's hoodies when he has a closet full of his own!

"On a serious note, Hilton. Thank you for doing this. I appreciate you being here, and thanks for all the support you give us. You're loved by us."

"Both of you irritate the hell out of me. Tell your husband to bring back my things or I swear!"

"I'll personally see to it that he brings all of them back. See you in a bit."

I hook my arm around Don's as we walk towards the house.

"You look beautiful, *skat.* I can't believe you're mine."

"You look really good yourself, husband."

"Thank you." He stops, his expression suddenly serious.

"For what?"

"For everything. For loving me. For all of this. For giving me Ulric. For not giving up on me. I'd be nothing without you. You're my life."

If the intention was to make me mushy, he has succeeded.

# FORTY NINE

We are only leaving now, after lunch. Looking at the time, we will get to Cape Town late at night. My grandmother forced us to stay because she told Don that in our culture, it's rude to leave without eating. She made us cook a feast for the visitors, even though everyone was half asleep and stuffed from breakfast. Elik, Caleb and their brothers left this morning, and they were gone for a long time, another reason why we are only leaving now. I suspect they parked somewhere and slept since they were up all night. They had to take Lumka to the airport. Elik drove my rented car behind the Quantum so he could drop it off for me.

Before I get into the Quantum, my grandmother pulls me aside.

"You're a mother now, Lolo. You're not spending enough time with that little boy. That lady is not his mother, you are! Daluxolo needs you more than he needs anyone else. Being a mother is a huge responsibility!"

I look down, feeling a bit hurt. I hate it when people question my mothering skills.

"You have chosen this man and accepted to be his wife. He loves you; I can see it in his eyes, and I believed him when he said he'll take care of you. Don't take that for granted. That boy and that man are your full responsibility now. Do right by them and carry yourself with respect."

"Yes, Mama."

"Be a good girl, *mntanam*. I don't trust him one bit, but I have to trust that you know what you're doing. Remember, this will always be your home."

I hug her and promise to behave. We had an argument yesterday because she was convinced Don was not a soldier but a gangster and not good for me. As I predicted, she asked why I didn't settle with a good Xhosa man like Lumka. I defended Don with everything and told her that being judgemental and discriminative were not a good look for a Christian. When I was done, she believed that even though his father was a gangster, he isn't and is living a respectable life serving our country.

My mother hugs me and says she will visit soon. I promise to take her to a full-day spa at a wine farm when she comes and she says she's free in two weeks and will text me her dates so I can book her flights.

"I'm sorry for the delay," I apologise to everyone but no one seems to care.

Everyone is in a good mood, except Hilton. He just looks bored.

Chelsea is carrying Ricky and I'm leaning into Don as if I want to live under his skin.

"We should have left earlier. I'm sorry my family kept you all morning."

"I don't mind. They're my family now too, right?" He looks at me as if for reassurance.

"Yes, baby, they are. Prepare yourself for Christmas with them."

He makes a face and I can't stop myself from laughing. He knows I'm not joking, right? We have to come down for Christmas or else my grandmother will flip.

Some distance after Port Elizabeth, we turn off the main road, following signs to a private game reserve.

"Are we stopping for lunch?" We ate so much, I don't understand how anyone could be hungry. Besides, we have enough snacks in the car.

"Not really. I want to do something quickly," Don says.

Oh boy, here we go with unnecessary detours! I know he loves game parks but it's late. If we are to make it to Cape Town today, we have to keep moving. I don't voice my thoughts though.

We park outside the reception. It looks alluring with its stone finishes on the outside and animal statues all around. I'll ask Don to bring me here on our way home for Christmas.

Elik and Don jump out and return with two guys wearing golf shirts with the game park's logo. They get back into the Quantum and the guys from the game park lead the way in their car. They guide us down a bumpy dirt road to a car park.

"We're spending a few days here. I've been bursting to spoil the surprise," Fierce whispers excitedly in my ear.

"For real? Why didn't you tell me?"

"I promised not to tell." She smiles animatedly.

"Wow! Oh my goodness, you guys! This is beautiful!"

"I know, right! We're going to have so much fun."

She's so excitable, it's adorable.

We are divided up, Don and me, Caleb and Chelsea, Elik and Fierce, Tristan and Kofi, the nanny and Ricky, and Hilton.

"Today we can turn up." Fierce throws her hand over Chelsea's shoulder.

"Yay! I have the perfect dress for it," Chelsea says.

They go on about what they will wear.

Turn up where in the bush? And when will they stop pretending to like each other?

Elik says we should all go to our chalets or do whatever we want, then meet in the Boma at supper. I'm the first to agree. I could use some alone time with Don. We haven't had the chance to celebrate on our own.

"Let me help you with the bag," Elik offers.

"I'll take the other one," Caleb says.

"Lotus, I need to talk to you," Hilton says.

He has been so quiet, I had forgotten all about him. I wonder what it is he wants to say to me. It must be serious.

We remain behind after everyone has left.

"Congratulations, you're the reason I'll be sleeping in the bush today."

"You're so dramatic, Hilton! But you're welcome. You'll enjoy it, you'll see."

"I won't. There are mosquitoes."

"Well, I'm sure there's repellent in the rooms. If not, we'll just ask at reception. Don't stress about it."

"I don't like it, but what can I say, we do what we do for family."

"Am I your family?"

"Are you not?"

"I am."

"Then why are you asking?"

"Hilton!" I slap his arm. "You said you want to talk to me about something."

"I already did."

"Huh?" I'm so confused.

"I wanted to talk to you about mosquitoes."

Oh wow! He's a special case. I'll get him some repellent.

"One other thing. Remember when you said you could organise for me to remove the tattoos on my face that I don't want?" He looks down, slightly fidgeting with his hands.

"Yes."

"I'm ready to do it."

"Really? That's great. I'll organise everything when we get back to Cape Town. I'll be there with you at every session, I promise."

This is so exciting! I want to make a big deal of it but I know how quickly he shuts down when uncomfortable topics are stretched, so I let it go. I suggested it after I found out how his father force-tattooed him as punishment. He wasn't open to it then and I'm happy he is now. He doesn't deserve to carry reminders of his father's abuse on his face.

There is no one in sight; I'm sure they are in their chalets now. We walk towards the biggest chalet. I hope it's mine and Don's.

"Have you been here before?"

"Of course not." He looks at me as if the mere thought of him having been here is absurd.

"Oh well, I just hope we got a dreamy honeymoon suite, with gorgeous amenities and all the special perks. I could use a lot of luxury."

"Are you expecting gold-plated toilets too?"

"Well, a girl can dream. Besides, you never know when a golden toilet might come in handy."

He shakes his head.

"I hope there's a bush spa, and a jacuzzi, and an infinity pool."

"I don't know how Alpha survives you."

"He loves me." I nudge him. "And you also love me. Admit it."

He just smirks.

"Whatever! You know you do. I hope they have room service. I don't want to be going up and down for food."

"Or maybe they have a 'Keep Lotus quiet' service. I'd pay extra for that."

"You're just jealous because I know how to have a good time."

He looks at me like I'm a lost cause.

"Oh, come on, Hilly! Loosen up a little. We're here to celebrate, remember?"

He sighs. "Lotus, it's like you run on batteries."

He's so unintentionally funny, I love him.

We are finally at the door of the chalet.

"Now, let's see how fabulous this suite is."

"The Source help us all," he mutters under his breath.

"I heard that!" I look at him over my shoulder.

I open the door and my hands fly to my mouth.

"What!?" I shriek.

The floor is covered in rose petals, and there are candles, balloons, flowers and champagne all around. It's like I walked into a fairytale. For a second, I think I'm imagining things. I stand there, my hands still over my mouth. When it sinks in that it's real, I scream again.

Chelsea and Fierce are grinning from ear to ear, recording the whole thing. I turn around and find Hilton leaning against the door, watching me like I'm a boring movie.

"Thank you," I mouth silently.

He gives me a small nod and I smile, more like grin, fighting back the tears threatening to spill over.

I turn back and almost faint. "What... What's going on, baby?" I stammer, trying to snap myself out of the daze.

Don's on one knee, holding an open ring box. From the corner of my eye, I catch Elik giving him a thumbs-up.

"My *skat*, I know I already asked you, and I asked your family, and I'm not sure but I think we're already married, but let me do this right, in front of everyone. Lotus, my beautiful angel, my *skat*, my ride-or-die, mother of my child, will you accept this ring and make me the luckiest man on earth?"

I push his hoodie back so I can see his face properly. *Is this really happening?* We are already married traditionally, but this, this is my dream. I always wanted this.

"So? Will you marry me? Will you be my wife?"

I nod like a bobblehead on a dashboard. "Yes! Yes, I'll marry you. I'll be your wife. Yes!"

He slides the ring onto my finger, and before I can even process, he's lifting me off the floor and we're kissing so passionately, we are practically making out. It's so sensual, it has me wanting to mount him right here, right now. I can't believe he went all out for me like this.

"Don't cry, my baby." He puts me down and pulls me into his chest.

Congratulations are flying all around and I'm hugging and thanking everyone, all the while trying to stop the tears. I can't believe they pulled this off! When did they even plan this? Is that why Elik, Caleb and their brothers disappeared this morning? Oh my goodness, I'm so stunned. I feel so loved.

"Baby!" I'm still in shock. I'm so happy, I could burst.

"You like it?"

"Like? I love it. Look at my ring. You got me a ring!"

"I'm not the one who bought..."

"Shh!"

He smiles and kisses me on the forehead. "The guys said I had to propose the right way, you know, get you a ring."

"Shh! Don't say another word." I place a finger on his lips and we both laugh.

He knows he could have pretended it was his idea, right? Even though deep down I'll have known the truth. This means the world to me. I wanted a ring with all my heart but I was ready to do things his way. All I know right now is I need him. I'm craving him. I desperately need to be alone with him. I need everyone to get out of our chalet.

When the door closes and it's just us left, he lifts me off the floor and my legs close around his waist. I drink him up and we go at it like wolves. He puts me back on the floor, peels my shirt off and unsnaps my bra. His clothes fly off his body one by one and my jeans join them on the floor. He lays me down on the couch. I'm not sure how to react when I cum on the third stroke. He looks satisfied with himself as I quiver in his arms. I want to keep going but we are squashed. I need freedom.

He carries me to the other room and lays me down on the bed. I pull him down towards me. Feeling his heavy weight on my body and his lips ravishing mine is enough to make my toes curl and my eyes roll. I push myself up to feel more of his skin, rubbing my nipples on his chest. He stops and I open my eyes to find out why. The fresh haircut, the blue of his eyes, the ink on his neck, the bone structure of his jaw - he's perfect.

"You're so beautiful," he says, making me bite my lip.

His lips come down on mine before I can return the compliment. He traces down my neckline with his tongue, awakening every nerve as he goes. A deep moan escapes my mouth when his lips find my right nipple. Then he moves down and spreads my thighs. I let out a scream when his tongue caresses my folds. He's sucking and licking with precision. My legs start shaking uncontrollably and he holds me in place until I come undone. He comes up with a satisfied look and a wet mouth.

All my senses desert me when I feel the first deep thrust. He lowers his face to kiss my forehead, then he starts moving. I grab a handful of sheets and moan his name over and over. It's so deep, so hard, so intense. He takes his time reminding me who's the Alpha. When he's done fucking me, he intertwines our fingers and makes love to me, kissing me, cupping my breast in one hand, breathing on my skin, gently stroking me out. I wish I could freeze time right at this moment so I can feel this for all eternity.

"Keep it open for me... that's a good girl... just like that."

Another wave of ecstasy starts building up and he talks me through it, the sound of his voice making it more intense. When I calm down, he holds me closer and whispers, "I love you" in my ear as he goes deeper. I hold on to him, feeling my soul merging with his and my body fragmenting into a million pieces as another wave flows from my head to my toes, spreading through every cell. I surrender my body to him, letting him all in with no inhibitions. His hand gripping my ass, his breath on my neck, his body crashing on mine - I have found my heaven right here with my husband.

# FIFTY

I slept like a baby after our intense lovemaking. Now I need to get up and get ready for supper. I wish we could stay in bed, but everyone will be waiting for us, so we have to go. Don joins me in the shower, and just looking at him makes me wet. Like the good old days, I go down on my knees, water falling on my back, and take him in my mouth. He grabs my hair, and when his grip tightens and he gets harder, I know I'm doing something right. When my mouth can't contain him anymore, he helps me up and turns me around. I push my ass back and receive him, standing on my tippy toes and balancing on the wall for support. I wish we could do this every hour.

When we are done, I stand in his arms, listening to the water falling on our bodies. When I finally can stand on my own, I gently lather soap on his back. I pause when I reach the tattoo of his ex's name. I wish I could erase *'Candice'* and replace it with *'Lotus'.* Jealousy threatens to spoil the mood, so I push my feelings aside and focus on his upper back. He returns the favour, and the way he is lingering on my breasts is going to make us late.

I'm very chatty as I go through my clothes. I'm excited about everything and I keep referencing my ring every third sentence. Don is half on his phone and half chipping in with his own stories that have nothing to do with what I'm talking about. I finally find the perfect outfit - something effortlessly chic that brings out my femininity. Its soft lines and subtle floral pattern capture my mood perfectly. When I ask for his opinion, Don nods his approval with a smile. I take my time dressing up, chatting away and laughing, maybe too loud.

We make our way to the Boma hand in hand. I have an extra spring in my step today. It's as if nothing else in the entire world matters. I can't contain the smile that spreads across my face every time I look at Don.

"What?"

"You."

"Me? What did I do?"

"I'm just so lucky to have you as mine. You're amazing, husband."

He blushes and presses a kiss on my head.

"Love birds, finally you join us!" Chelsea says when we approach.

I bite my lip and look down, feeling like everyone knows what we were up to before we came here. Tristan and Kofi have beers in their hands and are laughing hard. Fierce and Chelsea have champagne glasses.

On the other side, Caleb, Elik and Hilton seem to be engaged in a deep conversation. Don sits next to Elik and I join the girls.

"Champagne or a ginger sparkler like me?" Chelsea offers.

"A ginger sparkler, please." I will have the non-alcoholic option for a start, in solidarity with her journey of sobriety.

I look around and my heart swells with gratitude. Everything is perfect, right down to the atmosphere. The sun has dipped below the horizon and is painting warm hues of orange and purple, casting a soft glow on the rugged landscape. The sky is stained with a few streaks of wispy clouds and is carrying the promise of a starry night. I'm surrounded by laughter, love and the beauty of nature. I can't help but smile at the magical way my life is unfolding.

A waitress asks us to move inside for dinner. We leave our drinks outside and find our way through the doors. There are all sorts of dishes, hot and cold, each more tempting than the last. *Yho*, sensory overload! There are cheese platters, charcuterie boards, fruits, bruschetta, lamb on the spit, pork roast, chicken, beef, seafood, salads and desserts - I'm overwhelmed.

I finally settle down next to Elik with a full plate.

"Will other people be joining us?" I ask Elik.

"You mean strangers?"

"Yes, other guests."

"No. I booked the whole place. We needed time out without sharing spaces."

"Really? You're amazing, you know that?"

"Fierce tells me that sometimes."

"You really are. Thank you for this and for all the lessons you give Don. That proposal was more than I ever dreamed of." I look at my ring and smile. "And I know the flowers and little romantic gifts he gives me sometimes are things he learnt from you, so thank you."

"That's what family does."

"I thought you were out of the family." At least that's what Tristan said.

"I am, but Lemon will always be my brother, so you'll always be family."

I love the sound of that.

Kofi sits next to me and starts talking, disturbing my conversation with Elik. He's something else. I understand why he's friends with Tristan.

I excuse myself after dessert. I need to go and check on my son before I can dive back into the festivities. I take the tray with the food that was dished out for the nanny. Fierce offers to come with me. I'm glad she did because it's quite dark outside. Although there are lights on the ground guiding the path, they are not bright enough.

"How is it going?" What I mean to ask is how it's going between her and Chelsea.

"Great actually. Elik and I sexed out our differences this afternoon. Everything is dandy now."

"You go, girl! I know the feeling very well. Don had me speaking in tongues this afternoon." I'm not even exaggerating.

We bond over our sexcapades and I feel safe enough to ask her what I really want to ask. "So you and Chelsea?"

"I don't know about her but I'm good. We won't ever be friends but I'm now at peace with her existence. No hard feelings towards her whatsoever."

"You mean that?" I find that hard to believe.

"I do. You were right."

"I'm happy to hear that."

We go back to talking about our men and our adventures between the sheets. These men will drive us crazy one day.

Ricky is all smiles as usual. It's past his bedtime so we can't stay long. Fierce is so taken by him, she can't stop exclaiming how cute he is, as if it's her first time seeing him. He has that effect on people.

"Goodnight, my darling. Mummy loves you." I place a gentle kiss on his forehead.

"If you need anything, just give me a shout," I say to the nanny.

"Of course, madam. Have fun."

We find the group back outside and the party in full swing. The fire is crackling, drinks are flowing and stories keep getting juicier by the minute. I hold on to Don the way Chelsea is clinging on to Caleb, and Fierce to Elik. Everyone is having a good time, even Hilton. He's cracking up with Tristan and Kofi. They got through to him, and whatever they are telling him must be hilarious. Everything worked out in the end and I couldn't be more grateful.

Tristan and Kofi are leaving for Europe next week. Tristan got his MBA and he will be getting laser treatment to get rid of his wolf tattoo. Chelsea will be moving back to Cape Town soon; her career will kick off better there. She got a condo in Clifton. Her parents finally decided life is too short for their daughter to live below their means. With Tristan gone and Caleb left all alone at their house, he agreed to move in with Chelsea. Chelsea says convincing him was difficult because his pride was making it hard for him to accept living in his woman's house. It took Hilton telling him that he could handle the bills and make sure Chelsea's car always had fuel for him to agree. It's a big step but I'm excited for them. Fierce and Elik are no longer moving to Joburg. She's opening her lab in Cape Town so I'll officially start work soon. As for Hilton, well, besides getting rid of his tattoos when we get to Cape Town, there is nothing new there.

We will be turning the Gordon's Bay house into a centre for children from the Cape Flats. All the contraband that was stored there has been moved to the stash house in Manenberg. Merishka is handling the move and I'll be more involved with the children from now on. I'll take care of the tutors and career guidance workshops, and make sure they go on more educational trips.

It's late in the night but I don't feel sleepy at all, and judging by how loud everyone is, it's safe to say no one does. A shooting star crosses the sky and I make a wish before turning around to seal it with a kiss. Don holds me close as I savour his lips. I pull back and look into his eyes, their blue glowing brightly, and the shadows of the flames dancing on his face.

"I love you, my *skat*," he whispers against my cheek, sending a familiar warmth through my body.

"I love you too." I snuggle up to him.

He keeps his arm around me and kisses my head. I don't think I have ever been happier. Even with everyone laughing and talking too loudly, it feels like it's just the two of us.

"My *skat*."

"Yes, baby."

"Thank you for choosing me, even though I wasn't the logical choice."

I tense and wait for him to continue. He doesn't, so I silently breathe out and hold on to his arm. For a moment there the past crossed my mind.

"It couldn't have been easy choosing between me and Viper's son."

My eyes pop open and I pull away from him. I open my mouth but my voice dries in my throat. He looks at me calmly and that further throws me over the edge. I stand up meaning to run away, but my legs betray me. I stumble and barely manage to catch myself on the low wall. I'm gasping for air, my heart is threatening to beat out of my chest and my knees are buckling. I stagger away, desperate to get as far away as possible. I'm clutching my throat as if I can hold in the pressure building inside me. It feels like someone is suffocating me from the inside.

"Lotus, are you alright?" someone calls out, their voice sounding distant.

"Don't worry, I'll take care of her," Don says.

He catches up to me as I round the corner. I want to push him away and run as fast as I can, but I remain rooted in front of him.

"Breathe, my angel. It's alright. Just breathe."

My body is shaking with sobs even though no tears are falling, and my head is spinning so fast, I'm getting dizzy. How long has he known? Why didn't he say anything sooner? Was everything that happened today a joke? I try to push him away but he holds me tight until I stop fighting.

"Sit down." He helps me to the ground and sits next to me, our backs against the wall, not caring about whatever creepy crawlies are lurking in the dark.

"Who told you?" I manage to choke out.

"It doesn't matter who told me. I've known all along, come on. It just took me some time to decide what to do. I won't lie, I wanted to do the worst, and sometimes I had to stay away from you for days just so I wouldn't look at your face. I couldn't afford to hurt you. You were pregnant and you were trying your best to make amends."

He's strangely calm. I open my mouth to say something but my teeth chatter so violently, I fail to get a single coherent sentence out.

"Hilton talked me out of doing something stupid countless times. He made me realise that I wasn't completely innocent in the matter. It took me a while to accept it."

I'm clutching my hands tightly and breathing through my mouth.

"Did you want to kill me?"

"I won't say I didn't think of it... I gave you my heart and you betrayed me in the worst of ways. You made a fool out of me."

I try to speak but my lips tremble and no words form. I hold my arms to try and control the shivering.

"Some days were better than others. Some days I loved you more than anything, and others I needed to stay far away from you. Then I held my son in my arms in that hospital and I forgave you in full. He was mine. You gave me the most beautiful thing in the world. I grew up without a mother and it messed me up badly. You grew up without a father and it messed you up badly. I didn't want that for our son. I wanted him to grow up in a happy home, with both parents... with his mother."

"I never meant to hurt you, Don. I was lost and confused. I didn't know what I wanted. It had been months of silence. I just..."

"I know."

"But why now? Why bring it up now after all this time?"

"Because I need you to know that I forgave you. That despite everything, I love you. I can't imagine my life without you, *skat*. You don't have to live in fear of me finding out anymore."

*You knew about that too?*

"I'm really sorry."

"It's okay. Come here."

He pulls me into his arms and holds me tight as if afraid I'll escape if he lets go. We sit there for what feels like an eternity. My mind is spinning out of control. I don't know what to think right now.

"I love you, *skat.*"

I hang on to those words like a lifeline.

# EPILOGUE

We have been waiting in the car for a long time and my nerves are starting to get the better of me. Ricky's small hand is clutching my finger, and he's making happy noises, lost in his own innocent world. Don is unusually quiet. He's on edge; the anxiety in his eyes is mirroring my own. I know he is thinking what I'm thinking. *What if something else went wrong?*

The metal gates swing open and Pops walks out carrying the bag I left with him that time. What a relief! They kept postponing his release. It was one complication after another; he almost didn't make it out.

We get out of the car and I cradle Ricky in my arms.

"Pops." Don opens his arms. They embrace each other tightly and stay glued for a long time.

Pops eventually breaks the hug and looks up to the sky with open arms. "Freedom at last!"

I can't imagine what it feels like for him to be free after so many years. It must be surreal. Don hugs his father again, burying his face in his shoulder. He eventually brings his face up and dries his eyes.

Pops shoots me a smile, finally acknowledging my presence. "You promised to bring my grandson to see me." He shakes my hand and looks down at Ricky.

"Here he is. Better late than never."

It's as if we cease to exist as he holds Ricky in his arms for the first time. He smiles down at him, and Ricky grins back, reaching for him with his tiny hands. A tear falls out of Pops' eye and splashes on Ricky's hand.

"Please wait in the car, *skat*," Don says.

They stand in a two-man circle, looking at Ricky, three generations bonding. I close myself in the car and focus on my phone so they can have the privacy they deserve.

I sit in the back with Ricky, while Don drives and shares the front with his father. They speak in Afrikaans slang all the way; I'm as good as non-existent. I don't mind, although a small part of me is curious to know what they are talking about.

We turn into Rondebosch and drive past the gym I go to, then turn further down into a street with fancy houses and neat lawns. The driveways lead to grand entrances, and you can spot luxury cars if you look closely. A woman in biker shorts and a bralette is jogging down the road with her dog, reminding me that I need to go for the Park Run on Saturday.

"The people here are living large! This is what success looks like!" Pops exclaims in English.

I agree with him. Moving here was an excellent idea. This is exactly the kind of life I deserve.

We drive past the church Ricky and I come to on Sundays, before turning into our street. We pull into the driveway and wait as the gate slides open.

"Are we visiting someone?"

"No, Pops. This is our house. We moved here," Don says, with a hint of pride in his voice.

"I'll be damned! This is all yours?" Pops says in wide-eyed awe.

"Yes, Pops. It is."

"The Source be praised! This is something else, Donny. Well done, son. I'm proud of you."

We drive into our long driveway and Don parks my car behind his Raptor. Elik really is a strong influence on my husband. I'm not complaining though. Don looks good behind the wheel of that Raptor.

Pops steps out and marvels at the house. "I can't believe this! I'm proud of you." He pats Don on the back.

This house stole my heart the moment I laid my eyes on it. It's a perfect blend of charm and luxury, and has the perfect balance of style and safety. The swimming pool is so stunning, it's already a regular on my WhatsApp status. There is a nice braai area near the pool house and plenty of space all around. The garden is my favourite. It's blooming in vibrant colours, and the fountain in the middle adds the perfect touch to the overall aesthetics. Inside, there is a fireplace, perfect for game night on chilly evenings, and many rooms. The nursery is so gorgeous, when Don asked me for a second child last night, I agreed. I know I said my baby making factory is closed but he asked so nicely, I couldn't say no. Besides, one more baby won't hurt.

Pops will be staying in the cottage at the back until he decides what he wants to do with his life.

\* \* \* \* \*

"Don't forget about Tuesday," Chelsea says as she hugs me goodbye.

"We'll be there, babe. Thank you for today."

"Anytime."

She jumps into her car and I promise to call her in the evening. She came to help me cook and prepare everything. We set a table in the garden, complete with flowers for the ambience. She and Caleb are hosting us - me, Don and Hilton - for dinner in their condo in Clifton on Tuesday.

I find Don in the living room with Pops. He's anxious but he's putting up a brave front. I know my man, so I take his hand and lead him to the kitchen.

"It's going to be okay, trust me."

"I hope so."

"It will, my love. It's going to go so much better than you expect."

He doesn't look convinced, but before I can reassure him some more, the intercom buzzes.

"They are here. Go change out of that hoodie. Put on something plain."

"Yes, ma'am." He kisses me on the forehead.

They park in front of the garage and I welcome them cheerfully. I hope I'm not smiling too much. I usher them inside, and as I walk in, I bump into Don. One look in his eyes and I wish I could hug him and reassure him. He looks helpless. I know how much he hates being at the mercy of anyone. Pops also seems anxious, probably not sure how to behave in front of people that have shunned him for so long.

"Please come in," I try to dispel the tension. "Make yourselves at home. Baby, Pops, we have visitors."

Don extends a hesitant hand towards his grandfather. "Good to meet you, sir."

His grandfather shakes his hand with a warm smile. "Call me Oupa. This is your Ouma."

His grandmother looks at them both with a sharp eye and keeps her hands glued to her bag as if she is afraid they will snatch it and run away.

"This has gone on for far too long. We need to make amends. We're willing to give this a chance," Oupa says.

"Thank you. That's all we're asking for." Pop's eyes light up with hope.

"Family is about forgiveness and second chances. We've missed out on too much already. I know we've had our differences, but I've always regretted not being there for you, my grandson. And now you have a child; I don't want to miss out on that too," Oupa says.

Don nods, looking down.

A collective decision seems to be in the air, so I figure now would be a good time to get everyone to the garden and serve drinks and let them get acquainted.

Ouma is not very nice, but her husband compensates with warmth enough for both of them. I guide them to the table in the garden. Chelsea and I should seriously consider doing decor as a side hustle because this is beautiful.

Everyone picks a seat and mine remains vacant next to Don.

I serve drinks and starters before joining them at the table. I missed some of the conversation but I'm happy to see everyone loosening up.

"Our daughter loved you, Evan. She chose you. We disgraced her memory by not respecting that. It has been many years, and from my family and me, we're very sorry for how we treated you," Oupa says.

"Thank you, sir. I appreciate that," Pops says.

I go back into the house for ice. I quickly text Hilton that things are going in the right direction and then return to the table.

"So, Donavan, what have you been up to?" Oupa asks.

Don glances at Pops before answering. "Working. Trying to build a life for my wife and child."

"Through crime, or have you left that behind?" Ouma interjects with a snarky edge in her voice.

Don's jaw tightens and he exchanges a quick glance with Pops. The air thickens and the silence that follows is so tense, it's as if the entire backyard is holding its breath. She just had to take it there!

"He's been making some changes, trying to go straight," Pops says.

Ouma looks unconvinced. "Changes? Going straight? Donavan, we know your story. You can't just wipe away your past. And you, Evan," she points at Pops, "You did this to him! You raised him to be a career criminal!"

"We've all made mistakes, but he's genuinely trying to make things right. He has a wife and a child now," Pops tries to extinguish the fire.

"That never stopped you!" she says.

I find myself folding my fist.

"I'm still in that life and I'm not ashamed of it. It's who I am," Don says.

"Stop interrogating the child. We're here to make peace not to start a war," Oupa tries to blow out the flames.

Ouma looks at him briefly then directs her gaze back at Don. "We want to be a part of your life, but you need to leave crime behind!"

Don smirks, his defiance now on full display. "You never cared about me before, so why are you bothered now? I've survived without your approval all my life. I don't need it now."

Ouma glares at Don as if she wants to slap him. "Why are you so uncouth? Who raised you? Your stinking attitude won't change the fact that you need to make a choice, Donavan! Family or crime?"

Oh no! She should not have said that.

"I choose both. My family is Lotus, Ulric, Hilton and Pops. That's my family. You people never cared. You turned your backs on us when mummy needed you the most. You judged Pops and you judged me without understanding what we had to go through. I grew up with no one. My cousin Hilton took me in and he was a child himself! Where were you when Pops went to prison for me? When I had nothing to eat, where were you? When I was arrested, where were you? When I was in a coma, where were you? Now you think you can waltz into my life and demand change? Who do you think you are? If you think so little of me, then why are you here? I don't have time for this. Please feel free to leave." He pushes his chair back, the legs scraping against the stone tiles, and storms off toward the house.

What a mess! They promised me they would be civil. I hoped everything would go smoothly. I exchange a worried look with Pops before I follow Don.

I find him pacing in the living room.

"Baby, please." I place a hand on his shoulder. "This is your chance for a fresh start with them. Your mother wanted this, my love. Please, for her sake, take it easy on them."

"Why do I have to change for them? What kind of questions are those? They never cared about me!"

I take a deep breath and choose my words carefully. "It's not about changing for them. It's about making peace and moving forward. Let's go back out there, talk to them, and find a way to make this work. Please, my love."

"No!"

"Don't let her ruin everything."

"It's too late for that. She doesn't understand."

"I know, baby. But you can't let anger ruin everything."

"It's not just anger, Lotus. It's a lifetime of neglect and judgement. It's a reminder of how they treated mummy and me. How they disrespected Pops. I needed them. If it wasn't for Hilton, I would have died. I had no one, Lotus, no one!" His voice breaks and he blinks away tears.

"Come here." I take him in my arms and I'm glad when he clings on to me.

"It will be alright. If this doesn't work out, you still have me and Ricky. You have Pops. You have Hilton. We'll all be right here."

He holds me tighter.

After a moment, he lets me go and looks away. When he has pulled himself together, we return to the table.

Oupa nudges his wife and she clears her throat.

"I know I wasn't there for you and your mother as I should have. I regret the distance that grew between us. It's not an easy admission, but I acknowledge my mistakes, and I'm willing to try and mend what's broken." She sounds so formal, you would swear she is reading from a book.

Don keeps his eyes cast down.

With a hint of remorse, she adds, "When your mother married your father, it was a difficult pill for me to swallow. We gave her everything. We sent her to the best schools and raised her right. I had high hopes for her, so seeing her choose a path I couldn't approve of hurt me deeply. I let my disappointment blind me, and for that, I apologise." She takes a deep breath and her eyes soften. "I failed as a mother and as a grandmother. I was blinded by my own expectations. Your choices hurt me because I saw them as a reflection of my daughter's choices. I realise now that I was wrong. Seeing the man you've become, the father you are, it makes me realise that I might have missed out on a lot. I may not agree with your choices, but I can see the love you have for your family. You are my family. I hope you can find it in your heart to forgive me."

*That's more like it!*

"Yeah, well, apologies don't change the past, but I appreciate the sentiment," Don says.

I elbow him. He can't say that! He can think it but he shouldn't say it out loud. We are making progress, he shouldn't ruin it.

"Look, Ouma, I appreciate the words. We all have our baggage and it's been a rough road for me. I'm just trying to make things right for my family. Every step I take is all in an effort to make things right for my woman and my son. It's not easy for me, and I get that it's hard for you to understand. If you stick around, maybe in time you'll see the changes I'm trying to make."

I hope they know the *changes* he's talking about have nothing to do with turning away from his life. He means he's running the Wolves in a more organised manner, is working closely with the Peacemakers, and has called a truce with the Hard Livings. For now, everyone is staying on their turfs. There is a semblance of peace, but like Hilton said, there can never be peace among gangs. It's like keeping wild animals in a confined space; sooner or later, tensions rise and they start fighting. Every gang wants to expand their territory, push more products and gain more control. So this calm we're seeing is just temporary.

Ouma pushes her chair back and slowly stands. I'm thinking *'what now?'*

She walks around and stops next to Don.

389

"Look at me, Donavan."

Don looks up, and only now do I see how glassy his eyes are.

"I may not fully understand your path, but I'm willing to be a part of your life. I'm asking you to let me be a part of your life. I owe you an apology for neglecting you and for the pain I caused you. I want to make things right and be there for you. You are all I have left of my daughter and I'd love to let go of this anger I've bottled for years." She takes his hands. "You have your mother's eyes. It's like seeing her again. I see her strength in you, and her stubbornness too. I may not have understood her choices back then, but seeing you now, I can appreciate the love and courage she carried. I'm sorry for not being there for both of you when it mattered. Can you forgive me?"

He blinks and a tear rolls down his face. She wraps her arms around him, holding him close as her own tears start to fall. For the first time in a long time, Don lets his guard down and allows his emotions to flow. His shoulders shake a little, and she holds on tighter, rubbing his back and apologising over and over again. I can feel a knot in my throat, and before I know it, I'm crying too. Pops reaches for my hand and squeezes it.

"Thank you, Lotus," he says, his voice thick with emotion.

We stay in the moment for a while, each of us slowly picking ourselves up. The air is heavy and raw, and even Pops and Oupa are dabbing at their eyes. Ouma eventually lets Don go. My tears fall harder as I watch her dry his face and cup it like he's a little boy. She kisses him on the forehead and says something I don't quite catch. When she takes her seat, I reach for Don's hand and hold on tightly.

The conversation gradually shifts as we all settle back into our places. This time we are laughing and having light-hearted conversations. I keep wiping away the occasional tear and Don squeezes my hand every time I do.

I excuse myself and go to the house to get Ricky. Bad idea because he immediately steals the show. His great-grandmother practically snatches him from my arms and coos over him like he's the most precious thing she's ever seen. She is hoarding him, talking to him more than she's talking to the rest of us.

I serve the main meal, and compliments come pouring in. I feel all mushy when Ouma asks for the recipe and says we must cook together sometime. Don says I must cook every day, and Pops and Oupa agree. That makes me laugh. But you know what? I'll gladly cook every day if it means our family staying together.

"My grandson is very lucky to have you. You're a wonderful woman, Lotus," Ouma says warmly.

"That she is!" Don and Pops say at the same time, making me blush.

It feels good to see everyone enjoying themselves like this. The laughter, the jokes, the stories - it's more than I imagined. Everything feels right. All the pieces are finally falling into place. It's overwhelming in the best way, and I blink away a tear before anyone notices.

Even though everyone is complaining about how full they are, I still bring out the dessert.

"Just have a little," I say to Pops when he teases that I'm trying to burst his stomach.

When I finally sit down, Don takes my hand and kisses it. I look at him with a soft smile, knowing exactly what he's thanking me for. I'm more than pleased with myself for making today happen.

Oupa is in the middle of a hilarious story. His animated gestures and the way he delivers each punchline have us all in stitches. We are laughing so hard, we are in tears.

Despite all the noise, Ricky somehow falls asleep in Ouma's arms. It's like he completely tuned out the chaos and decided to take a nap.

After I have taken Ricky to the nursery and cleared the table, we invite Oupa and Ouma to tour the house. They are impressed by how big and beautiful it is. It's heartwarming to see their exaggerated reactions. It makes me so happy to hear them saying how proud they are of Don.

"Fill it up with many children!" Ouma says.

"That's the plan," I reply.

Don looks at me curiously. "How many?" he asks.

"Three or four," I say, still smiling.

"Are you serious?" Don holds my hand and looks into my eyes.

I nod.

I know I initially said one, then two, but I don't see why we can't make more beautiful humans. Don has always wanted more kids. He asked me for a second child and I agreed, but I think I'm ready to give him more. My body will be fine. After all, there's nothing a good surgeon can't fix.

Don's eyes widen and he lifts me up and twirls me around. We both laugh as he puts me down, and he quickly apologises to the elders for getting too excited.

"*Skat,* are you serious?"

"I am!" I playfully cross my fingers in front of his face.

He beams and pulls me into a hug. "Thank you," he says, his voice a bit choked up.

Pops, Oupa and Ouma just look at each other, probably wondering what's going on.

Before they leave, I hand them the gift baskets I put together and thank them for coming.

"Take good care of her, Donavan. Treat her well," Ouma says as we walk them out.

"I always will. I'm lucky to have her."

Ouma's face softens and she hugs all of us. She starts with Pops, then she wraps her arms around me. I close my eyes and savour the comfort of her embrace. Finally, she moves to Don and gives him the same affectionate hug.

"Please join us for lunch next Saturday. We'd love to show you our estate."

"We'd be honoured," Don says for all of us.

"Goodbye now. See you on Saturday," Ouma says before getting into the car.

We wait until the car turns onto the road and the gate closes.

"Well, that went better than expected."

"All thanks to you, my *skat*. Thanks for making it happen."

Pops nods in agreement. "Thank you, Lotus. I'm sure Donna is smiling down from heaven."

Don takes Pops' hand in one of his and mine in the other, and we walk together towards the house.

\* \* \* \* \*

As the sun gracefully bows out, Don and I sit on our porch, wrapped in the quiet of the evening. We watch the sky turn into a mosaic of warm colours, like a canvas painted with sunset. We don't say much; we don't need to. His hand finds mine and our fingers intertwine in a familiar comfort. I rest against his shoulder, his arm around me, my eyes on the sky. At this very moment, everything feels just right.

"I love you, Lotus."

"I love you, Donavan."

# *The End*

*Every ending is a new beginning.*

## To My Dear Reader

As you reach the end of this journey, I want to take a moment to express how much you mean to me. You hold a special place in my heart, and your support means more than words can ever express. As you journeyed through the pages of this book, I hope you found moments that made you feel something; that made you smile, reflect, laugh, curse, or perhaps even shed a tear. I hope you heard my voice through the pages.

I wish you the very best life can offer. But more than anything, I want you to remember to live life fully. Laugh freely, love fiercely and do more things that bring you joy. Please take care of yourself. Chase your dreams. Treat yourself with kindness. Define your own happiness. And never forget how amazing you are. There's no one like you. I appreciate you deeply.

Thank you, from the bottom of my heart.

With love,

**Yvonne Maphosa** ♥ □

## ABOUT THE AUTHOR

**Dr. Yvonne Maphosa** is a multi-award winning, bestselling author from Plumtree, Zimbabwe. She is the author of the *The y in your man is silent, Grasping at Straws and Heart in Two.* She also contributed to *Vagina Monologues Africa* and published *Luvone: An Anthology of Short Stories,* a collection of works selected from a writing competition she sponsored to showcase emerging writers.

Yvonne holds a PhD in Food Science & Technology and is a lecturer, researcher, philanthropist, globe trotter, blogger and mountaineer. She is passionate about charity work, and loves family, nature and coffee. You are most likely to find her on Twitter at 3 am sharing Bible verses or hilarious tales from her everyday life.

### Social Media Handles:
Twitter (X): @Yvonne_Maphosa
Instagram: @Yvonne_Jacquie
Facebook: Tales by Yvonne Maphosa
TikTok: @Yvonne_Maphosa

Other books by **Yvonne Maphosa**

### The y in yOUR Man is Silent

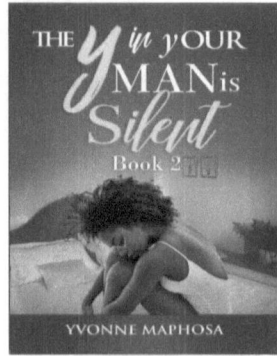

### Grasping at Straws

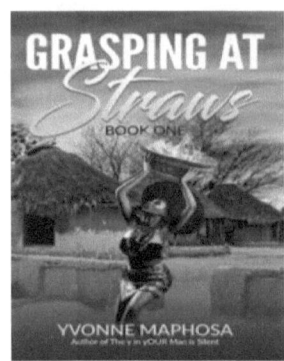

### Heart in Two

www.ingramcontent.com/pod-product-compliance
Lightning Source LLC
Chambersburg PA
CBHW051316250626
47155CB00007B/2340